Dare to Derek: A Football Manager 2017 Story.

By Daniel Tacon.

For myself, to prove that I could, but also for my family and friends

for all their love and support in everything that I do.

INTRODUCTION.

The game of football has always been a massive part of my life, for as long as I can remember. Whether that is watching, playing, discussing, debating, just anything to get me my fix. For well over a decade now Football Manager has been a large part of my football intake. I play more than I should, for much longer than I should and it definitely matters a whole lot more than it should. I love the games, there is nothing like unearthing the next superstar, signing him for peanuts and taking him to the top of world football. I love the narrative a save creates; it sucks you in and takes on a life of its own.

I have always loved the Football Manager games; the first instalment that really had me hooked was Championship Manager 01/02, the one with the iconic red cover. I was thirteen years old and played it at the house of a family friend. I doubt he remembers it, but I will always go back to that moment as the spark that ignited over a decade of football management journeys and a love for a computer game that has only intensified as I've gotten older.

As a young man the Championship Manager games satisfied my insatiable thirst for all things football. I loved knowing about players before my mates, I knew players nationalities and where they had been signed from thanks to the hours I was racking up as a virtual manager. That hasn't changed as I now enter my thirtieth year; I still have an almost unhealthy obsession with the game.

I love the game primarily because it allows me to become a football manager and take control of my favourite team or manage the greatest players, but what I really enjoy is the narrative of a save. How you can develop a deep affinity to a player you have never heard of, or in many cases, one that doesn't even exist in the real world.

You can play the game how you want to play it. There is no right or wrong way with Football Manager and that is part of the charm. I have always played with a preference for developing younger players and searching for the next big wonderkid to bring into my squad. Although I have had the odd save as manager of Barcelona or Real Madrid the majority of my Football Manager careers have been spent in England, more often than not, the Premier League and usually staying with one club rejecting any job offers that may come my way.

As I played through the various FM's and countless saves I started using an alias and developed an FM alter ego of sorts. FM saw the birth of Derek Cooper, a part of me that only surfaces during my visits to whatever save I am playing through. I realise how insane I sound, my girlfriend thinks I'm mental and I doubt she will ever understand. My friends are aware of Derek and I think it vaguely amuses them; I have even tried to persuade other FM playing friends to adopt their own managerial alias.

In recent years I found myself working in jobs which afforded me time to play more FM than I had been used to and I began to take more of an interest in the Football Manager community as a result. I began to watch some videos on YouTube from content creators such as Work The Space and Doctor Benjy. From there I found other creators like Loki Doki, Fox In The Box and Lollujo which helped to further scratch the Football Manager itch.

Soon I found myself reading Football Manager Blogs online and following numerous members of the community on Twitter. Podcasts and Twitch came next with the always excellent 5 Star Potential podcast and the We Stream FM guys. Through listening and watching how others play the game I began to tweak my playing style, investing a little more time on developing tactics, tweaking how I look for players and I found myself becoming braver with my save plans. I was thinking of trying something a little different to my usual Premier League saves and I wanted it to be a test.

I have played hundreds of hours on Championship Manager and every Football Manager since its debut in 2004. Derek has taken Lowestoft up the leagues on FM 2016 and managed teams from Aldershot to Barcelona;

he has even tried his luck at winning England a World Cup. We have played many saves together across all of the FM games, but FM17 saw me play through my most enjoyable save to date. Some past saves have stuck in the memory of course, but every avid FM player has that one save that will always be their favourite, one that they have emotionally invested in and will always have fond memories of.

I had played through my usual Beta save as manager of Liverpool and when the full FM17 game was released I was ready to put my new found confidence and enthusiasm to the test and chuck Derek Cooper in at the deep end. I had decided to start at the very bottom with a lower league management save in a league that was outside those that were included in the vanilla game.

I chose a club I knew well having played for them over 200 times in real life. Derek Cooper would be managing my local semi-professional club Kirkley and Pakefield. I wanted the save to be as realistic as possible so Derek was given the same playing and coaching experience as myself, which is not a lot. He would be twenty-nine years old having played as a semi-pro at the regional level with no coaching qualifications.

The grand plan was to move Kirkley through the leagues and hopefully taking them into Europe, upgrading facilities and the stadium as we went. A real road to glory type save that would be a slog, but ultimately very rewarding.

I would like to tell you the story of Derek Coopers FM17 save in the style of a football manager's biography. I have read many biographies and autobiographies over the years and I want to share the story of my FM17 save with you in a way that I haven't seen done before.

What had started life as one type of save quickly turned into a whole other journey entirely. It was full of great moments, great players and a great narrative throughout the years. It became the sort of story that could only be thrown together by a Football Manager game.

Hopefully you will enjoy reading about the career of Derek Cooper as much as I enjoyed playing through it. I have tried my best to remember and recreate all the best moments and the most influential players from the very beginning of the save way back in 2016 at Kirkley and Pakefield.

Originally I had intended for this book to contain screen snips of various transfers, results and other visual aids to compliment the telling of Derek Cooper's story. Unfortunately due to the cost of printing in colour it simply wasn't viable. I wanted to make the book to the best of my ability and include as much information as possible, but I also wanted it to be affordable for all who would like to read it. Hopefully I have managed to do that by omitting the pictures and it hasn't taken away from the narrative.

CHAPTER ONE.

Kirkley and Pakefield are a very modest club playing in the Eastern Counties Premier League. Located in East Anglia in a town called Lowestoft, their home Walmer Road has only the most basic of facilities. Two small stands occupy spaces behind the right hand goal and on the far touchline with seating for no more than fifty supporters and a maximum capacity of just 3,000.

Upon taking the job Derek Cooper was introduced to the club by the chairman and taken through the clubs history before meeting with a solitary journalist from the local paper. Cooper used the chat to outline his intentions for the club, developing the facilities and moving through the leagues. Making the football league was the ultimate goal and then from there who knew. Derek wanted to regenerate the club from top to bottom. That meant new facilities, new staff, new recruitment, and eventually a new home befitting of a club who planned on an upwards trajectory.

On his first day in charge Derek Cooper arrived at a club that was predicted a season of mid table mediocrity and a squad that looked incredibly light on numbers. His first summer in charge was to be a busy one. He would need to utilise the free transfer market and look to bring in solid free agents on affordable wages. Staffing was also an issue with recruitment, a key area for Cooper and his football philosophy, in dire need of more bodies. It was vital that Derek add some scouts to his backroom staff and start scouring the market for available players.

It was a busy window and one that saw Derek add players in key areas, most notably Chico Ramos, a goalkeeper with plenty of experience in the lower leagues. He signed striker Alando Lewis to add some pace and hopefully goals to his frontline, playing alongside local lad and club captain Ross King. Danny Phillips was brought in to be a ball winning midfielder and bring some steel to the middle of the park, but he also possessed the quality to get the ball down and play too. Matt Cunnington was brought in to bolster numbers with him being capable of playing across the backline, his versatility being one of his main strengths.

Pre-season was a time for Cooper to impose his tactical philosophy, a simple 4-4-2 that would be based on hard work and a structured style of play. Defensively the back four would be relatively bog standard consisting of full backs and two central defenders. The midfield would utilise Danny Phillips as a ball winning midfielder alongside another central midfielder. Out wide Cooper would instruct them to play as wide midfielders, trying to squeeze as much out of them as possible. Ross King would act as a target man with the pace of Lewis being utilised as an advanced forward.

When it came to training Cooper decided to work on team cohesion hoping this would further solidify the hard work he was putting into his tactical set up. He also asked his players to all work individually on their assigned roles ensuring each individual was working towards maximising their efficiency in the team's tactical plan.

Coopers first pre-season at the club was slightly disappointing, which was not entirely unexpected, players and staff were settling into their new surroundings and the new managers' ways of working. Cooper arranged a fixture programme that would see them take on a range of opposition, from Charlton and Nottingham Forrest to local sides Stalham Town and Cromer. The mix of very tough fixtures with games against teams of lesser opposition would give Cooper the chance to fully evaluate his squad ahead of the season's opening competitive fixture away to Newmarket in the FA Cup Extra Preliminary Round.

Kirkley and Pakefield travelled to Newmarket hoping to gain an away victory and set themselves up perfectly for the curtain raiser in the league at home to local rivals Gorleston. The game started well with Alando Lewis opening his account for the club after just seven minutes. Newmarket were never out of the game and replied just before half time to level the tie. An early second half red card saw the home side reduced to ten men and allowed Coopers side to press for a winner. A winner which duly came in the form of a well struck shot from man of the moment Alando Lewis. A brace for his new front man was enough to secure Cooper's men passage into the next round and allow them to head into a derby match on the back of a hard fought victory.

Tuesday the 9th August 2016 would see a twenty-nine year old, inexperienced Derek Cooper lead his side out for a league fixture for the first time in his fledgling career. A crowd of just fifty-six had come through the gates at Walmer Road hoping to see their side triumph in the first local derby, a game under the floodlights against Gorleston.

It was a tough start for Cooper who saw Kirkley and Pakefield fall behind early in the game and go into the interval trailing by one goal. He used the break to tell the team that he was disappointed in their first half performance, but that he had faith that they could turn it around. With his half time team talk now behind him he would need to turn his attention to his squad and how best to use his substitutions in the second half. Ross King and Alando Lewis up top were struggling having played ninety minutes just three days before. Kyle Baker was fresh and would come on to replace King with ten minutes gone in the second half in a change that would eventually pay dividends as Lewis and Baker both hit the back of the net without reply to win the game 2-1. Cooper had his first three points as a manager and he was determined that it was to be the first of many.

Wins followed for Cooper and Kirkley and Pakefield, in fact they wouldn't lose for just over a month, a terrific start to life in the Walmer Road hot seat. In his opening ten fixtures as a football manager Derek won seven, drew twice and lost in that tenth match away to Mildenhall (3-0).

Along the way there had been league victories against Godmanchester (1-0), Wivenhoe (1-0) and Brantham (3-0) with draws against Ipswich Wanderers (0-0) and Felixstowe (1-1). The 3-0 defeat against Mildenhall was an abrupt way to end the impressive start, but they were amongst the favourites to win the league and they proved to be a very good side on their visit to Walmer Road.

There were two FA Cup victories included in the opening run of form, a win away against Atherton Colls (2-0) in the preliminary round before a win at home against Chalfont St. Peter (3-0) in the first qualifying round. The F.A cup saw a big boost in attendance with local fans flocking to watch one of the historic cups matches. Walmer Road had been used to crowds of less than 100 for league matches, but a crowd of 547 turned out to see the FA Cup first qualifying round with the increased gate revenue a welcome addition to the club coffers. Cooper had hoped for a small run in the FA Cup knowing that the extra money and exposure progress in that competition would mean for the club. It was considered an important part of his long term development plan for Kirkley and Pakefield.

It was then a mixed bag for Cooper and Kirkley and Pakefild as they ended 2016 and entered into 2017. They recorded wins, but couldn't manage anymore than three consecutively. The wins were more often than not punctuated by a frustrating loss that seemed to curtail any chance of getting a lengthy run of form going.

Disappointment in the FA Cup followed the Mildenhall defeat as Kirkley and Pakefield were eliminated in the second qualifying rounds away to Poole. A decent crowd of 618 had come through the turnstiles, so at least there was a decent gate for them to take a share of home to Lowestoft.

A league win against Thetford (2-0) preceded another cup exit, this time in the FA Vase at the same second qualification round. With a tiny crowd of just sixteen present Warminster won 2-0. It was then back to the Eastern Counties Premier and their only remaining cup competition, the Eastern Counties League Cup for Kirkley and Pakefield which duly saw results pick up again. A draw against Hadleigh (1-1) was followed by wins against Walsham-le-Willows (1-0) and Newmarket (5-2) in the league as well as a 2-0 away win to Haverhill courtesy of two own goals from the home side in the second round of the Eastern Counties League Cup.

A run of bad form plagued the side in their next three matches drawing with Ely (2-2) before losing to both Safron Walden in the league (1-0) and Haverhill Borough in the next round of the cup (3-1). All three games had been played away from Walmer Road and it proved to be a tough ten days for Kirkley and Pakefield. They responded well when they did return to action at home beating Swafham (3-0) in front of the largest league crowd to date with 100 spectators in attendance.

The Bloaters, Great Yarmouth Town were up next in another local derby which saw Cooper and his side make the ten mile trip up the A47 to The Wellesley Recreation Ground. Kirkley turned in an impressive performance with Alando Lewis on fire in front of goal. Lewis grabbed a hat-trick, the first of his career, as Great Yarmouth were hit for six in a 6-0 derby victory for Derek Cooper. It was a very happy ten miles back to Walmer Road on the mini bus following that victory.

Inconsistency began to creep in again and Kirkley were unable to build on the impressive wins losing at home to Clacton (2-1) who managed to hold onto their lead despite going a man down with twenty-five minutes still to play. Another run of wins came off the back of that loss as Kirkley beat Long Melford (2-0), Fakenham (2-1) and Haverhill (3-1). A strong crown of 115 were in Walmer Road for the Fakenham game, another improvement on the attendances from earlier in the season. Word was spreading that the team were doing well in the league and it was beginning to attract some interest from the locals.

Kirkley closed out December with a New Years Eve defeat at home to Stanway (2-1) before embarking on their patchiest form to date with every win being followed by an immediate loss. January and the second half of the season started with another win against Godmanchester (3-0), but that was quickly followed by defeat to Ipswich Wanderers (3-0). And so the pattern repeated as a win at Wivenhoe (2-0) was followed by defeat to Hadleigh (1-0).

Derek Cooper and Kirkley and Pakefield were performing above expectations in the league that much was true, but Cooper also felt that there was a lot more in the tank. His side had played well, but were capable of better and Derek genuinely believed that if he could iron out the inconsistent form he could have a real shot at promotion either automatically through winning the league or via the playoff system.

Kirkley and Pakefield responded to their managers' beliefs that they were in with a shot and stated their credentials with a six game unbeaten run which included a win on Derek Coopers twenty-ninth birthday away to Mildenhall (3-2). Other wins came against Brantham (3-1) which included Alando Lewis' second hat-trick of the season, Felixstowe (5-1), Gorleston (1-0), Thetford (2-1) and a draw against Walsham-le-Willows (2-2).

Kirkley had dragged themselves back into contention and couldn't be ignored as potential champions. Beating league favourites Mildenhall on his birthday was a great feeling for Cooper and doing that off the back of a big victory at home to Felixstowe, another of the stronger sides in the league, made everyone stand up and take note.

Including the Walsham-le-Willows draw Kirkley and Pakefield failed to win for three games as February became March and Cooper was worried the inconsistent form that had dogged their first half of the season was about to make an unwelcome return. A loss away to Newmarket (1-0) and a draw with another league rival in the form of Ely (0-0) meant momentum had been lost going into the final month and a half of the season.

All was not lost, Kirkley were still very much in the mix and barring a return to that earlier poor form Cooper could see his Kirkley and Pakefield side challenge to be named Champions. Ely and Mildenhall were the other teams at the top and Derek felt that they were likely to drop points in an intense run in having taken points off both sides himself. He just needed to make sure he kept his side focussed and capitalised on other team's mistakes.

Derek Cooper and Kirkley and Pakefield kept up their end of the bargain winning their next six fixtures. They took on all comers home and away and emerged with the three points in each game. They beat Saffron

Walden (2-0), Great Yarmouth (2-1), Swaffham (3-0), Long Melford (3-2) and Haverhill (3-0) to set up their final two fixtures perfectly. Kirkley would play Fakenham and Stanway knowing that if they avoided defeat in both games it would be enough to see them crowned champions should Ely win both their remaining games. Three points in the first of their two remaining games away to Fakenham would secure the title for Derek Cooper.

Fakenham away were up first and in a nervy display a ninth minute goal from midfielder Rob Horton was cancelled out by the home sides Simon Frater. Kirkley and Pakefield's cause wasn't helped by the dismissal of their other central midfielder just after the hour mark. They returned home from Clipbush Lane having managed to hold onto a point, taking the race for the title down to the final game.

It was onto Hawthorns the home of Essex club Stanway and a draw would be enough to secure the title, but Cooper was determined get his side over the line with all three points. The game started badly for Cooper and Kirkley found themselves on the wrong end of end of a 2-0 score line. Stanway scored midway through the first half and then added a second after fifty-eight minutes. Cooper was unaware of the score in the Ely match, but he had to assume they were beating Haverhill. As if sparked into life by the second goal Coopers men began to respond and immediately pulled one back through substitute Kyle Baker. Game on. Danny Phillips was missing the game through suspension and his replacement in the team Jack Ryan pulled off an unlikely comeback with twenty minutes left on the clock. Kirkley were back in control of the title and would finish the ninety minutes with the score at 2-2 meaning they had done enough to be crowned Eastern Counties Premier champions 2016/17.

Cooper had his first piece of silverware in his very first year in the job and it was a fantastic feeling. He wanted to take Kirkley up through the leagues and to do that he hoped for a fast start on the pitch that would drag the development of the club along with it. Becoming a professional side and playing in the football league was the goal and with promotion to the Isthmian Division One North they were now one step closer to that dream.

There was no official presentation of the trophy at their final league match and Derek had to wait until the clubs presentation evening at the end of the month to get his hands on the first trophy of his career. He was proud of his team and reflected on a season that had seen many more highs than lows. Wins like the 6-0 away to Great Yarmouth and the 5-1 dismantling of Felixstowe were particular highlights. It hadn't all been plain sailing though and Cooper was frustrated that his side had lost five times at home that season; it was a record he hoped to improve upon in the future.

In the forty league fixtures of the 2016/17 Eastern Counties Premier League Cooper would claim twenty-four victories, eight draws and lose just seven games. Kirkley and Pakefield would finish as league champions ahead of Ely in second and Mildenhall in third. Alando Lewis finished as the sides top scorer with twenty-six goals from his forty-five appearances as his strike partner and local lad Connor Doddington, who had joined on a free having been released by town rivals Lowestoft, claimed the player of the season award with an average rating of 7.22 scoring nineteen goals in his thirty-two appearances.

It had been a long and hard season with seven members of the squad having made forty plus appearances throughout the campaign. Cooper had been delighted with the commitment of the players and was happy with the job they had done for their rookie manager

One season down and one league title in the bag Derek Cooper turned his attention to preparations for the upcoming 2017/18 season and Kirkley and Pakefield's first venture into the Isthmian Division One North. It was another busy off season which saw Cooper add numerous new faces whilst taking some tough decisions in letting current players leave the club. Derek planned on sticking with his preferred formation of 4-4-2, but he had also used the summer window to strengthen the squad with the addition of wingers able to play high up the pitch in an attempt to broaden his team's tactical capacity.

With the step up Cooper needed to look at and assess the players in the squad that would be staying on with the club and those that would need to find pastures new. Local boys Scott Manning and Kyle Baker were two players that would not be joining Cooper on the next part of the journey leaving the club at the end of their deals.

David Segura was one of the players recruited by Cooper in the summer having left Colchester at the end of his contract. Segura was 20 years old, Spanish and capable playing off the left wing or through the middle as a striker. He was the type of player Cooper had looked to sign; young, versatile, room to improve and had experience in the Isthmian leagues having spent last season on loan at Maldon and Tiptree. Dereece Gardener was another striker signed; Gardener had bounced about in the lower leagues for a few seasons having started his career at Aston Villa and latterly Watford.

Kirkley and Pakefield played through a relatively poor pre-season winning only three of their nine friendly matches. It wasn't too much of a concern for Cooper as all preparation was geared towards the clubs Isthmian debut at home to Thurrock on the 12th of August 2017. The new faces were settling in well and Dereece Gardener in particular impressed with four goals in his pre-season appearances.

Derek Cooper needn't have worried about his sides pre-season performances as his side really turned up when it mattered on the opening day of the league campaign. Kirkley and Pakefield blew Thurrock out of the water and were 4-0 up without reply before they away side managed an eighty-fifth minute consolation. Doddington picked up where he had left off last season and helped himself to a brace to kick off the new season.

The Eastern Counties Premier season of 2016/17 had seen Kirkley and Pakefield fly out of the blocks and 2017/18 was no different. Cooper was making a habit of starting seasons with an unbeaten run, this time they started the campaign with three victories and one draw, scoring eight and conceding only two. Kirkley seemed to have settled into life in the Isthmian League with a draw at Enfield (1-1), a win against Corinthian-Casuals (2-1) in the F.A. Cup preliminary round and two more league victories against Waltham Abbey (2-0) and Norwich United (1-0). During that run of fixtures Alando Lewis, David Segura, Connor Doddington and Dereece Gardener all found the net which was hugely pleasing for Derek Cooper.

A packed September schedule saw Kirkley and Pakefield contest eight fixtures from the 30th of August through to the same date in September. It was a gruelling run of games that would really take its toll on the squad and their results. Defeat at home to Soham (4-2) was followed by an FA Cup match against weaker opposition in Evesham. A 2-2 draw meant the sides would contest a replay just three days later, a replay that Evesham would comfortably win (3-1) with Cooper's men beginning to suffer. A slightly longer four day break wasn't sufficient and Chatham proved too much for Kirkley and Pakefield in their next match inflicting another league defeat (1-0) on Cooper's men.

It was now the halfway point of the congested fixture schedule and Kirkley finally managed to record a win managing two consecutive victories in the league. Kirkley travelled away to Witham (2-0) and Brightlingsea (1-0) and recorded maximum points on both occasions. There were then two more fixtures to be played before the end of September and Kirkley failed to win at home against Aveley (2-1) before managing a draw away to Romford (1-1) the hometown club of ex-Arsenal man Ray Parlour.

October wouldn't see Kirkley fair much better and results continued to be poor throughout the month. There was a draw away to Bowers and Pitsea (1-1) before elimination in both the F.A Trophy at the hands of Histon (1-0) and the Ishtmian League Cup courtesy of Aylesbury United (3-1). A rare win at home to Pheonix Sports (3-2) was then followed by back to back defeats against Thamesmead (4-1) and Tilbury (3-2).

Derek entered November hoping that he would be able to turn fortunes around. They had picked up wins, but they were few and far between. On the plus side many of the defeats had come in the knockout cup competitions and Derek hoped this would allow him some time to concentrate on the league with his players benefitting from a more manageable fixture schedule.

Kirkley and Pakefield kicked the month off with back to back wins against Great Wakering (3-2) and Cheshunt (3-0) before Needham Market ended the return to form with a 1-0 win at Walmer Road. Last month that defeat at the hands of Needham would have seen Cooper's men follow it up with another defeat or two, but it seemed they had turned the corner and came out of the defeat fighting. They won their next three games against Brentwood (4-0), Ware (3-1) and Heybridge (2-0) to take them into mid December.

There was another example of this new never say die attitude when Kirkley fell to another defeat, this time away to Bury (3-0) on the 12th of December. Again Kirkley returned to action and racked up three consecutive victories taking nine points from the matches against VCD (3-2), Grays (5-2) and Thurrock (2-0). The third match against Thurrock represented the first match in the second half of the season and thus far Kirkley and Pakefield had played twenty-four matches winning fourteen, drawing three and losing the other seven. All things considered it wasn't a bad first half of the season and left Cooper harbouring hopes of a playoff spot should they be able to maintain their form and dare he say and automatic promotion spot if they could improve their consistency and eliminate the losses.

If form had been good closing out 2017 then the start of 2018 couldn't have been any more different. Derek Cooper was to face the first real crisis of confidence in his managerial career to date as his side failed to win in six games only picking up two points from a possible eighteen. Any thoughts of a title challenge quickly faded to nothing and the poor form seriously threatened to derail any promotion hopes.

Following the win against Thurrock Kirkley drew with Enfield (2-2) and Norwich United (3-3) as well as suffering defeats against Waltham Abbey (1-0), Soham (1-0), Bowers and Pitsea (2-0) and Chatham (1-0) which would see Kirkley fail to find the back of the net in all four defeats. Cooper was obviously worried; if you weren't scoring then you had little to no hope of winning a football match.

Derek and his boys would need to dig really deep and stop the rot; they were dropping points as they approached a vital point of the season. They managed to claim all three points in their next match at home to Witham (2-0) hoping it would be the catalyst needed to kick-start their faltering season. Unfortunately, it was to be a false dawn and defeat soon followed against Brightlingsea (2-1) in the following fixture. Now came the real test, would they cave under the pressure and return to the poor form that had dogged the second half of their season so far? Or could they turn it around and begin to string a few much needed victories together?

The answer came in the form of four successive wins that saw them score fifteen goals and set them on their way to a run of matches that kept them unbeaten for the remainder of the season. Cooper was pleased with the change in fortunes, tightening up a leaky defence and giving the attacking players the confidence they needed to hit the back of the net again.

Morale played a huge part in the turnaround, the drop off in form coincided with a noticeable decline in morale. Talking to players individually to praise their conduct had been vital in raising the morale of the squad to somewhere near where it had been previously.

The four wins that came immediately after the watershed loss to Brightlingsea came at the expense of Aveley (2-0), Romford (3-0), Pheonix Sports (6-3) and Tilbury (4-1). There was then a break in the victories with a draw away to Great Wakering (3-3) before Kirkley returned to grabbing all three points away to Thamesmead (3-2).

Unfortunately the consecutive victories couldn't be maintained, but Kirkley showed a previously unseen resilience in their next four matches ensuring that whilst missing out on the win, they would not be beaten. Although not ideal when chasing an unlikely title or a playoff spot draws are most certainly better than defeats with one point being better than none at all. Cheshunt (2-2), Needham Market (1-1), Brentwood (2-2) and

Ware (2-2) were all matches that Kirkley and Pakefield may well have lost earlier in the campaign, but here they meant Cooper's side remained unbeaten taking that run into double figures and ten matches.

Just four remaining fixtures stood between Cooper and a potential playoff spot. There was now no chance of them winning the title with Needham Market looking to have that tied up ahead of Bowers and Pitsea, but it was all to play for behind the two leading teams. Cooper needed a top five finish to qualify for a shot at the playoffs and it was more than doable.

Kirkley remained unbeaten in those final fixtures beating Bury Town (2-1), Heybridge (2-1) and Grays (3-1) with a draw coming against VCD (1-1) in the penultimate league fixture. Kirkley and Pakefield would finish in third place as a result and in do so qualify for one of the four playoff spots. In their forty-six matches Kirkley would win twenty-three, draw eleven and lose twelve amassing a points total of eighty and setting up a playoff semi final against Cheshunt with whom they had beaten and drawn with during the season.

Coopers managerial career to date had seen very little progression in the one off match cup competitions. He had prioritised league form over the various cups and now found himself in a playoff semi final where a one off match could make or break his season. Would a lack of experience in such matches prove a stumbling block for Kirkley & Pakefield or could Cooper conquer Cheshunt and progress into a playoff final?

The playoff semi final against Cheshunt was to be played at The Weston Homes Community Stadium, home of Colchester United and was to be the biggest game of Derek Cooper's career to date. The match started at a frantic pace and saw Danny Phillips put Kirkley & Pakefield ahead after only six minutes of play. Cheshunt recovered well and a quick fire double from them meant that Cooper's men were trailing 2-1 after fifteen minutes. A goal from Kirkley and Pakefield's Spaniard David Segura five minutes before half time levelled the tie only for Cheshunt to recover well again, attacking straight from kick off to win a penalty that was duly converted. Kirkley were now 3-2 down and Derek Cooper was trying all he could to stay in the match. He threw all he had at Cheshunt and was rewarded in the eighty-third minute when striker Connor Doddington poked home from close range.

Extra time was to follow, Cooper had done all he could, he was out of subs and he had carried out his final team talk sending his men out telling them passionately that he had faith in them. Cheshunt came out equally fired up and struck first blood in the ninety-fourth minute to make it 4-3. Kirkley and Pakefield went for it, they had to and Cooper pushed his wide men higher up the pitch trying in vain to create an overload on the opposition, but it wasn't to be. Cheshunt stubbornly held on to their lead and progressed to face off against Chatham in the playoff final leaving Cooper and Kirkley & Pakefield facing a second season in the Isthmian Division One North.

Alando Lewis had once again had a fine season in front of goal as he finished the clubs top scorer for the second season running, earning him the player of the season award at the end of season bash as well. With thirty-one goals from forty-nine appearances and an average rating of 7.22 he edged out his strike partner and new boy David Segura who notched up seventeen goals in his fifty-two appearances with an average rating of 7.04. They were the two standout performers of 2017/18 and had it not been for their goals Coopers side may well have found themselves at the other end of the table.

Ultimately the 2017/18 season had ended in frustration for Derek Cooper, he was disappointed to have missed out on the chance of back to back promotions, but it was with off the pitch matters where he was beginning to become increasingly frustrated. Several attempts to progress his coaching qualifications and gain his National C Licence had been rebuffed by the board and the club was lacking the necessary funds for investment in their very basic facilities and youth recruitment. On top of that several prominent members of the squad were pricing themselves out of new deals with the club leaving Cooper staring at the possibility of losing many of his starting eleven.

Derek had reached a potential crossroads in his career. He was left wondering whether his plans to take Kirkley & Pakefield up the football league were just a pipe dream. Did he stay at the club and try to change the mentality of the club as a whole or would the grass be greener elsewhere? Was there a club out there with the structure and facilities already in place that would allow him to fulfil his coaching potential and eventually manage in the English football league system? These were questions that Cooper had no idea he would be asking himself in the summer of 2018, just two seasons in to his job as Kirkley and Pakefield manager.

As the football season of 2017/18 came to an end managers up and down the country were handed their P45's and thanked for their efforts with their respective clubs. Cooper was a manager who was in a secure job, the fans had already proclaimed him one of the clubs icons and he had a squad that had only just missed out on promotion, but there was no guarantee he could keep that squad together or find better players with sufficient interest to replace those he may lose. He was a manager who was willing to hedge his bets and he took the decision to keep an eye on the job centre and apply for any interesting vacancies that came up.

After several applications had been cruelly laughed off by fans and chairmen alike in the press it became clear that Derek had limited options. It was looking more and more likely that his next club would be playing in either the Vanrama North or South with clubs from higher divisions failing to respond to his calls and emails.

Cooper attended a couple of interviews over the summer of 2018 with no job offers forthcoming. He was diligently preparing his Kirkley & Pakefield side for the upcoming season ensuring he was maintaining his high personal standards when he received simultaneous offers of interviews from both Torquay and Maidenhead. Both vacancies would see him step up a couple of leagues and compete in the Vanarama South, but he would only leave Walmer Road for the right opportunity. He stayed true to his footballing beliefs in both interviews and stated his preference for signing and developing young players and an attacking style of play. He was unwilling to compromise on his ethos and ideas for the club as a whole and informed both he would be unwilling to sign high profile players or rely on set plays as a style of play.

It was an exciting, but nervous time for Cooper as the new season edged closer. Was it the right time to make a move? Had he found the right club? Would he even be offered one of the jobs? Derek also had to consider that he would now have very little left of pre-season in which to work with any new club was he to be offered one of the roles.

The call he had been waiting for eventually came on the afternoon of the 24th of July 2018 and after two years and twenty three days as Kirkley and Pakefield manager Derek Cooper was to leave the club to take on a new challenge. He informed the board of his intention immediately, called a squad meeting and began clearing his desk at Walmer Road. He thanked everyone at the club for giving him the opportunity to kick off his managerial career with a side that meant so much to him. They had shared some great times and he left the club in a better position than when he arrived, which was important to him. The board and Derek drafted a joint statement and the news would break in the Lowestoft Journal the following morning.

CHAPTER TWO.

A sunny morning on the 25th of July 2018 saw a buoyant Derek Cooper unveiled to the press as the new manager of semi-professional Vanarama South club Maidenhead United. Torquay had decided against offering Cooper the vacant managers' job opting for a man by the name of Simon Mensing instead, but this was an exciting opportunity for Cooper and he couldn't wait to get started. Derek had promised the board an attacking style of play using young players from both within and outside the club and that was exactly what he aimed to deliver.

The 2017/18 season had seen Maidenhead finish a disappointing fourteenth winning sixteen of their forty-two games, which was two less than the eighteen that they lost. Cooper was determined for that not to be the case in 2018/19 and his preliminary look through the squad suggested that there was plenty within the ranks for him to work with. He was keen to impress his favoured training methods and instantly swapped training so it was based around team cohesion and began working on his preferred formation of a no nonsense 4-4-2. He moved quickly behind the scenes to rearrange some of the senior squads pre-season fixtures, arranging a potential money spinner at home to Manchester City's U23 side which he hoped would see the fans flock to York Road.

Derek had to work fast with his first transfer dealings at the club and was reluctant to make snap judgements on any of the current Maidenhead players. There were minimal funds available with Cooper preferring to put what little money there was into his wage budget. That way he was able to work on adding some promising players who were available on free transfers, with another couple coming in on season long loan deals.

Derek Cooper was particularly excited by Leon Okubuyejo, a young English striker who had been released from Championship club Reading and Cooper hoped to bring to Maidenhead on a permanent contract. Billy Reeves was another player on Cooper's radar and he had been following for a while whilst in charge at Kikrley and Pakefield, but had never had the opportunity to bring in. The speed with which Cooper was being forced to work meant that whilst he was happy with some of his potential additions there would be question marks over some of the lads signed in the window and it would be up to them to prove that he had been right to take a punt on them.

Derek Cooper managed to fit four pre-season fixtures in before the season opener away to Margate on the 11th of August. Maidenhead won three of the four games with their only defeat coming against that Manchester City U23 side in front of a 2,700 strong crowd, Derek Coopers biggest to date.

Cooper and Maidenhead kicked off their Vanarama South campaign with Derek still very much in the market for a host of players and staff as he continued to tweak the club set ups of the playing and non-playing staff. Derek had been used to fast starts with Kirkley and Pakefield and the 2018/19 season would be no different as he guided Maidenhead through a seven match unbeaten run.

An opening day draw away at Margate (1-1) was followed by a very enjoyable victory over Torquay United and Simon Mensing (3-1) when they came to town with Derek Cooper delighted to have shown them what he was capable of in front of a 456 strong home crowd at York Road. Another win against Burgess Hill (3-1) followed before another draw, this time with Welling (2-2). Two draws and two wins took Maidenhead to four games unbeaten and they would extend that further taking maximum points off Hampton and Richmond (2-1), Eastbourne Boro (2-0) and Wealdstone (3-2). Seven matches, five wins and two draws was an ideal start to life in the Vanarama national for Derek Cooper and he was pleased with how things were going.

By now Cooper had wrapped up the bulk of his transfer dealings and backroom re-shuffle although he would continue to keep an eye on the transfer market should a suitable player become available. Leon Okubuyejo signed a permanent deal with the club on the 30th of July and joined ex-West Ham trainee Alfie Lewis and Billy Reeves at Maidenhead United football club.

Staffing wise the main addition saw Daniel Brown fill the vacant assistant manager's post with Derek Cooper impressed by his man management skills and his ability to judge potential. Brown had played his entire career in the lower reaches of English football with the likes of AFC Sudbury and Bowers and Pitsea and the job here at Maidenhead would be his first non-playing role. It was a bold move for Cooper to appoint a thirty-three year old with no backroom experience as his right hand man, but it was a decision he felt oddly comfortable taking. Rob Myers, Nic Jones and Barry Hogan came in to the club as scouts and would work closely with the manager to identify any transfer targets and hopefully a few potential stars.

The start Brendan Pooni had made to life under Derek Cooper had been particularly pleasing. Pooni was a player that was already at the club when Derek had arrived, but had been part of the U23 side rather than the first team set up. Derek and his coaching staff had seen his potential and had given him the opportunity to make that step up, an opportunity he was taking with five league goals in the seven matches played so far this season.

The other strikers at the club, new signing Leon Okubuyejo and the experienced Sean Marks, were also doing their bit and chipped in with a further five goals between them. Central midfielder Kyran Wiltshere was another Maidenhead player, who had already been on the books at the club that was turning in impressive performances in the opening sequence of results, bossing the midfield and contributing with assists and the odd goal of his own.

After the customary good start form dropped off slightly. Staines rolled into town and knocked Maidnehead out of the FA Cup second qualifying round (1-0) to continue Cooper's poor record in the cup competitions. That defeat would have a knock on effect to the good start in the Vanarama South and Maidenhead went three games with only one point to show for their efforts losing to Hungerford (3-0), Bath (3-2) whilst managing a draw with Staines (1-1).

Wins finally returned through what was left of October and Maidenhead got their season back on track with victories against Woking (1-0), Chelmsford (2-0) and Bishops Stortford (2-1). Three consecutive wins raised the team morale and there was understandable disappointment from manager and players alike when they then went down 2-1 to Hemel Hempstead in the next fixture.

There was however a slight improvement next time out and Maidenhead picked up a point at home to St. Albans (1-1) before bursting back into life with another three match winning streak taking all three points in games against Oxford City (1-0), Chippenham (1-0) and Greenwich (3-1). Brendan Pooni grabbed a hat-trick at home to Greenwich and took his total to the season so far to fourteen, an impressive tally for a player who hadn't been in the first team picture when Cooper arrived at the club.

There was then a break from Vanarama South action and the opportunity for Cooper to make an impression on one of the cup competitions with a game against Northern Premier League First Division North outfit Shildon in the FA Trophy third qualifying round. To date Cooper had largely failed in cup competitions and he was determined to change his poor record. The game started well with Brendan Pooni finding the back of the net seven minutes in, but it wasn't to last and the underdogs recovered well with two goals of their own in the first half. Try as they might Maidenhead couldn't find a way past Shildon and they would hold on for a surprise 2-1 win.

Consistency would then be very hard to come by for Cooper and his Maidenhead side. A pattern developed that saw them seemingly unable to get back to back wins or put together any sort of run of form. A win at home to Dulwich Hamlet (1-0) would be followed by defeat away to Dartford (1-0). A win at home to Gosport (2-0) was followed by a home defeat against Margate (3-1). It took until early January 2019 for Maidenhead to break the pattern when a win away to Burgess Hill (4-0) followed a pleasing New Year Day victory down in Torquay, with Cooper adding further insult to injury in a 4-2 win.

The break from the win one lose one pattern proved only temporary and Maidenhead slipped back into old ways again with defeats against Welling (2-0) and Eastbourne Boro (2-0) coming either side of a victory away to Hampton and Richmond (3-1). Maidenhead had now entered early February and were somehow hanging on to a spot in the upper echelon of the Vanarama South table.

Coopers first season at Maidenhead was going well despite the immense frustration he felt at his inability to string together a succession of wins as he had done in the first few weeks. It looked as though Cooper had been working to a win or bust philosophy. Draws had been hard to come by and the attacking mentality of Maidenhead may have contributed to the loss of some valuable points. Thanks to their excellent start they were still very much in the race for the title with it all to play for coming into the closing months of the season.

Results seemed to improve once again and Maidenhead went unbeaten in five matches, their longest run since the opening months of the season, but it was actually far from convincing and of those five matches only two would end in victory. The five matches started and ended with wins against Wealdstone (3-1) and Woking (3-0). There was exactly a month between the two victories and in the intervening period Maidenhead played out draws against Hungerford (2-2), Staines (1-1) and Bath (2-2). The draw against Staines was particularly important for Maidenhead as dropping points to the London side would have meant losing ground to one of their closest title rivals.

With just ten league fixtures remaining Maidenhead United were still very much in contention alongside sides like Staines, St.Albans and Bishops Stortford, it would be a tight title race, but Cooper was determined that they would give it a good go. Of those final ten fixtures Maidenhead would slip into old habits and would win five and lose the other five as they continued their distaste for draws, sticking to Coopers attacking style.

Title rivals Bishop Stortford would inflict a painful 1-0 defeat at York Road in front of the home faithful, but Maidenhead recovered well to win against both Hemel Hempstead (4-2) and Chelmsford (2-1). Having recovered from a rival defeat Maidenhead once again conspired to damage their title hopes once more. Back to back defeats at such a vital time of the season could be disastrous, but that is exactly what Derek Cooper got against Oxford City (1-0) and another title rival in St. Albans (4-0).

Losing to both St.Albans and Bishop Stortford was far from ideal and although still in front of both sides the gap had been closed and momentum had most definitely been lost. Reclaiming that momentum was important with time running out and just five games left to be played. Wins against Chippenham (2-1), Greenwich (3-1) and Dulwich Hamlet (2-1) were just what Maidenhead needed to rekindle their title hopes and cement a place at the top of the table with the title now theirs to throw away.

Just two games remained, a visit from Dartford before the final game of the season away to Gosport. Dartford came to York Road in the mood to spoil the party and they did just that beating Coopers men 1-0 with a goal in the seventy-fifth minute. A draw would have been enough to secure the title ensuring Staines would be unable to catch them. Luckily for Cooper and Maidenhead their loss at the hands of Dartford proved to be irrelevant as Staines had been beaten by Maldon and Tiptree 3-0 away from home effectively handing the Vanarama South title to Derek Cooper and his Maidenhead side.

A final day loss in their fixture against Gosport (2-0) had no impact on the title and it saw Maidenhead's Captain get his hands on the Vanarama South trophy, the first in the clubs history. Fortunately Maidenheads patchy wins had been enough to see them over the line and crowned champions with seventy-six points from their forty-two matches, just one more than Staines who finished second with seventy-five points and three more than St. Albans who finished third on seventy-three points.

Not only had Cooper won the league, but in doing so had fulfilled his promise to improve on the points total of the season prior to his arrival at the club. He had comfortably done that, exceeding his own expectations by taking Maidenhead from the fifty-six points of 2017/18 to seventy-six and the title in 2018/19, a twenty point improvement.

Derek Cooper and Maidenhead fans owed a lot to the performances of front men Brendan Pooni and Sean Marks who had both been terrific in front of goal. Young Pooni finished the season with twenty-two goals from his forty-one appearances and achieved an average rating of 7.00. Whereas veteran Sean Marks managed a slightly better average rating of 7.16 contributing sixteen goals from his forty appearances. Both players were at very different stages of their careers, but both had been the driving force behind Maidenheads title winning campaign.

Personal awards were to follow for Cooper as he was named the Vanarama National League South manager of the year for 2018/19. Being recognised as a young and up and coming manager was an important step in his career and would further strengthen his resolve when it came to gaining his coaching qualifications. Unfortunately, as with Kirkley and Pakefield, the Maidenhead board had yet to stump up the funds to cover the cost of Coopers National C Licence course. One thing the board had been willing to agree to was an extension to his contract with improved terms for the Vanarama South manager of the year.

One season under his belt at Maidenhead and one title in the bag, next season would see Cooper and the club make their debuts in the Vanarama National League just one step away from the promised land of the football league. It would undoubtedly be another big step up in terms of quality coming up against teams like Cheltenham, Eastleigh and Barrow. Cooper was already relishing the prospect of testing himself once again in a new division as he worked his way towards the football league.

As with every summer of his management career thus far Derek Cooper faced an uphill battle to find players of the required and desired quality to improve his squad using the budgets available to him. The purse strings at Maidenhead were just as tight as they had been whilst at Kirkley and Pakefield, working at bringing players in on free transfers or loan deals was likely to be the only course of action. Working at improving club finances was very much a priority for Cooper as the benefits of a more positive cash flow could not only help the club progress, but see him finally get the chance to grab his first coaching licence.

The summer of 2019/20 was tough for Derek Cooper there can be no doubt about that. With very limited resources and only a small pool of players interested in joining him and his project he was forced into taking more risks with player signings than he would have liked. Cooper was very much targeting young players who had recently been released from clubs in higher divisions hoping they had slipped through the net and would be able to adapt quickly to life in the VanaramaNational. Cooper was trailing several lads who fitted the bill hoping to secure them a deal with the club including; Louis Nutt and Keith Slater who had been released from Wolverhampton Wanderers, Phil Day from Fulham as well as Adam Lake from Stoke and John L'Estrange from Southampton.

Behind the scenes Cooper was still continuously looking to improve his backroom staff, the way he saw it his staff were as important to him as his playing squad, just for entirely different reasons. He already had an assistant he could trust in Daniel Brown who he leaned on to offer advice on opposition instructions as well as team talks. He needed a team of scouts whose judgement he could trust and coaching set ups for both the senior and youth sections that would maximise the potential of his playing staff. As with attracting players it was difficult for Cooper to get the staff he really wanted, but he was happy with those he had managed to bring in at Maidenhead and he was satisfied that he had the best possible set up available to him at this time.

With players and staff being monitored it was onto pre-season and preparations for the upcoming campaign. With such a large playing squad Cooper organised an extensive programme looking to maximise squad performance. Money spinning games at home to larger reputation opposition such as Crystal Palace, Bolton and Aston Villa were important to the club financially as well as on a footballing level. These bigger fixtures were mixed in nicely with games against lesser opposition, important for the retention of team morale. There was even an opportunity for Cooper to return to Walmer Road as a gesture of goodwill to his former employers, taking a full strength side down for a friendly that saw Kirkley and Pakefield hang on for a 1-1 draw.

Pre-season served up a mixed bag of results and performances which included wins against the likes of Windsor (4-1) and Billericay (2-0) with defeats against the better opponents in Aston Villa (6-3) and Crystal Palace (1-0). Cooper still had some question marks over his summer dealings and negotiations with several players would continue in the following weeks. He was also unsure of his best option going forward; stick with the 4-4-2 that had served him so well or evolve the teams playing style to a more fluid 4-3-1-2 with a man in behind the strikers. Neither tactic had performed consistently well and so Derek decided it was best to stick with what he knew best for now, which was the 4-4-2.

By the time the first game of the Vanarama National season was looming Derek had conducted the majority of his transfer dealings, although it was looking like the deals to bring some of the younger players identified by Cooper were taking a little longer than he had originally hoped for. One of the main stumbling blocks for Cooper had been the players themselves holding out on signing for him in the hope that a better offer would come along. It wasn't ideal to be kept waiting around, but Derek had little choice with his recruitment options limited.

Saturday the 10th of August 2019 saw Maidenhead and Cooper make their long awaited Vanarama National League debuts. They had been given a tough opening fixture away to Aldershot, one of the more established teams in the division and it was a tough game. Cooper managed to come through the season opener with a clean sheet and a 1-0 away victory. Attacking midfielder and new signing Kevin Douch with the goal. The former QPR trainee had started his Maidenhead career in the best possible way with a debut goal to secure the win. It had been their first test at this level and both players and manager had come through to claim all three points, Coopers customary unbeaten start was surely to follow.

What did follow the opening day victory was the toughest run of form a Derek Cooper side had ever experienced, one defeat rolled into another, then another with the losses only briefly punctuated by the odd draw. A win was nowhere to be seen and by late October the opening day victory at Aldershot was a distant memory. Nobody knew where the next three points were coming from; morale was at an all time low, Cooper was chopping and changing formations and mentalities desperately trying to find a win and the media had started to raise concerns about the sides' poor form.

Cooper was a manager in a tailspin; nothing he tried came off. His sides lack of experience was hurting them and he had no way to change that, he had to make big decisions; choose a tactic and a style of play and stick at it or continue tweaking and taking stabs in the dark in the hope that something found the mark and got them that elusive win. Desperation was setting in, the team were rock bottom and winless in the league for over two months. His only saving grace was that no-one had managed to pull away from them and leave his Maidenhead side adrift at the foot of the table.

Those fifteen Vanarama National games without a win saw Maidenhead lose eleven and draw four. Narrow losses like a 3-2 home defeat to AFC Fylde saw the away side score the winner in the ninetieth minute which was tough to take, but there were also results like the defeats to Eastleigh (5-2), Boreham Wood (3-1) and Wrexham (3-1) where Maidenhead were simply not up to the standard of their opposition. Wrexham were 3-0 up within eighteen minutes in the match at The Racecourse Ground.

Even when Maidenhead showed some fighting spirit and managed to stay in the game it proved time and time again that it wasn't enough for them to get the three points. Fixtures against Forest Green (1-1) and Morecambe (1-1) saw Derek Cooper's side score late goals to grab a point, with his side showing at least some of the character they would need if they were to save their 2019/20 season.

The only positive result Maidenhead managed during that truly diabolical run came in the form of a win in the FA Cup 4th qualifying round replay against AFC Fylde. Cooper had a very poor record in the cup competitions and the unexpected victory was a nice change from the league defeats. The first match between the two sides had ended 1-1 at York Road and Maidenhead travelled away from home for the replay fully expecting to be eliminated, but they emerged victorious against the odds winning on penalties after the match finished in another draw (2-2).

After locking himself in his office and spending hours poring over reruns of old matches and checking all the stats of his various tactics compared to one another Cooper had decided to revert to 4-4-2 and take his side back to basics. There was a recall for Brendan Pooni who had so far failed to recapture his form of last season, but was due a chance in the team with the current strikers L'Estrange and Lake failing to pull up any trees or put any balls in opposition nets.

These managerial decisions eventually paid dividends in early November when his side, led by the goals of Pooni, would record three straight league victories and go unbeaten in the Vanarama National for seven matches, winning six and drawing one. Maidenhead were almost unrecognisable from the side that had been so consistently poor. Wins came against Kiddeminster (2-1), Newport (2-1), Chester (3-1) and St. Albans (3-1) who had joined Maidenhead in promotion from the Vanarama South last season. Instead of the FA Cup providing a respite from the losses this time it proved to be a break from the wins and Cooper wouldn't be able to take his side any further than the first round with defeat away to Barrow (2-1). Overall the feeling of relief around the club was palpable and Cooper began to recover some of the swagger that had deserted him in his darkest hours.

There had been a bounce around the club throughout November, Derek Cooper had been named manager of the month and there was now a real belief that the club was back on track and moving in the right direction - up the league. The run of good form had lifted Maidenhead off the bottom and seen them rise to a relatively safe distance above the relegation zone. Cooper could begin to relax and enjoy the football again, the stress and pressure of propping up the rest of the league seemed to dissipate having previously weighed so heavily on him. The return to basics had eventually turned their form around and had proved a steady foundation for the sides improved performances as they approached the halfway point of the season.

Derek Cooper went into the Christmas period and second half of the season optimistic that his side had turned the corner and were beginning to make an impression in the Vanarama National. Unfortunately the purple patch failed to last and the side slipped into the patchy form that had dogged them during their title winning campaign of last season. Back to back wins were followed by two or three game periods with no points, or at the very best draws. Wins were sporadic and it was beginning to affect the morale of both the players and the manager once again. Cooper was working night and day to stop the side sliding back into a relegation battle having played so well to pull themselves out of danger.

In amongst the inconsistent league form Cooper managed another cup victory as Thetford, a side close to his hometown of Lowestoft, visited York Road in the FA Trophy 1st round. Maidenhead easily dispatched the Eastern Counties Premier side 4-0 in front of a modest home crowd of 464. The next round of the Trophy saw another match up with AFC Fylde which once again went to a replay and resulted in another win for Cooper and Maidenhead, this time managing to do it in the ninety minutes (3-1).

Impressive wins like the one achieved away to Forest Green (3-1) were followed up by back to back defeats at the hands of AFC Fylde (1-0) and Wrexham (2-0) with this type of inconsistency the norm for the second half of Maidenheads league campaign. The wins in the F.A Trophy wouldn't last either and Maidenhead were eliminated in the third round by Vanarama North side Stockport (2-0).

Februay and March were not good months for Cooper and Maidenhead. His side were sliding down the league and were once again flirting with the possibility of relegation. A win at home to Whitehawk (1-0) was followed by defeat away to Morcambe (2-1) to close out February. March started with a victory against another relegation candidate in Newport Co (3-2), but once again Maidenhead failed to build on that by losing the next game away to Kidderminster (1-0). March continued to see Maidenhead struggle with a further defeat against Cheltenham (1-0) and a draw at home with Maidstone (1-1).

Four wins from thirteen matches was relegation form and Cooper knew it. He was holding team talks and individual talks in an attempt to raise morale and inject a performance in to his players. Cooper had a run in which included more fixtures to play at home than away and he would need to make the most of the home advantage against fellow strugglers St. Albans and Sutton United. He needed to see something from his players as slowly but surely Maidenhead were being sucked down the league and faced the possibility of a swift return to the Vanarama South.

Crunch time arrived for Cooper and the last month of matches started with a hugely disappointing draw away to Chester (2-2), Maidenhead took a late lead with just seven minutes left to play believing they had done enough to secure a much needed victory when disaster struck and Chester were awarded a ninety-third minute penalty. It was gutting for Cooper and the Maidenhead fans who were all hoping the lads could hold out for the vital three points.

There were now just four games left with St. Albans at home up first. They were also struggling down near the bottom of the table and a win here would see Maidenhead move above their opponents and away from the relegation zone. Once again it was a tough result to take for Maidenhead and their manager as Derek watched on helplessly as St. Albans scored in the eighty-fifth minute to win 2-1. It was the sort of result that could well break the squads resolve, just three games remained now and they desperately needed wins.

Sutton at home on the 13th of April 2020 was being billed as a huge six pointer for both clubs by media and pundits alike. Sutton sat in the relegation zone and were on a dismal run of form themselves having only won twice in their last eight Vanarama National matches. It was a horrible match, tough to watch for Cooper from start to finish. It was a match that was ruined by the possible ramifications for both sides. Fortunately for Cooper Adam Lake managed to find the back of the net midway through the first half and there would be no late goal for their opponents this time as Maidenhead held on for the most important 1-0 of Derek Coopers managerial career.

Sutton United were still the main threat to Cooper and his side going into the final two fixtures. Maidenhead were in twentieth on fifty points and Sutton were twenty-first on forty-eight points. With just a two point cushion Maidenhead would need one win in their next two matches to ensure they survived relegation. Failure to win either would mean they were reliant on Sutton continuing their poor form and losing at least one of their final two fixtures.

Sutton were at home to Ebbsfleet whilst Maidenhead travelled to Barrow. On paper Sutton had the easier fixture, Barrow were sixth with Ebbsfleet down in fourteenth, but anything could happen on the day. Maidenhead fell behind early and would never recover going on to lose 4-2 to a good Barrow side. Luckily for Cooper and Maidenhead Sutton had also failed to win their match losing 1-0 to a goal in first half injury time. One game remained. Maidenhead still needed that win to guarantee safety; a draw might not be enough with their goal differences being so close.

The final game of the 2019/20 season was like a cup final for Maidenhead. They needed to win; they needed to get the three points that would eliminate any possibility of a return to the Vanarama South. They faced 16th placed Southport who had nothing left to play for away from home whilst Sutton hosted 5th placed Harrogate who were very much in playoff contention. Form had been so bad for both clubs heading into this final day that it was almost impossible to call. Fifteen minutes into both matches and the news was good for Derek Cooper. Sutton had conceded two early goals and were already well behind in their match whilst it remained level at 0-0 in the Maidenhead Vs Southport fixture.

The clocks ticked down at both matches and neither Sutton nor Maidenhead managed to find the back of the net. As the 90th minute arrived Harrogate put it beyond all doubt with a third goal that would see Sutton lose 3-0 and get relegated from the Vanarama National. Maidenhead would have been safe regardless of their score line, but they held on for a credible 0-0 that saw them live to fight another day.

Maidenhead and Derek Cooper had survived by the skin of their teeth. Four of the twenty-four sides in the Vanarama National league had to be relegated and somehow Cooper's side had not been one of them, finishing just three points above the drop zone. The purple patch of November proved to have been just enough to see them over the line. Without that upturn in form Cooper's men would surely have been relegated back to the Vanarama South.

The summer break was a welcome reprieve for Derek Cooper after what had been a stressful campaign. He was left to ponder what had gone wrong and what he could do better next time around. The standout player for the season had been Tunji Akinola, a central defender who had joined the club in October and was considered the catalyst for the upturn in form around that time. Akinola was a graduate of the West Ham academy and he won the player of the season award for 2019/20 having made twenty-nine appearances, scoring once, with an average rating of 7.23.

Goals had been a major issue for Maidenhead throughout the season and this was evident in the fact only one player made it into double figures for goals scored. Brendan Pooni made it to ten goals in eighteen appearances, but the other strikers within the squad posted lower totals. Adam Lake scored six, Leon Okubuyejo scored seven, John L'Estrange and Keith Slater also only managed six goals each. It was a problem that Cooper would need to look at. Would those players come back stronger next year? Was there room for them to develop? They were all inexperienced players and there was possibly a case for Derek Cooper bringing in an experienced and recognised goal scorer at Vanarama National level, but how was he meant to do that with no funds available to him?

The summer of 2020 would see Derek Cooper do some soul searching as he watched the European Championships. The 2019/20 season had seen him really struggle for the first time; was he able to learn from the experience and motivate himself to go again at a club that was struggling financially that proved a stumbling block moving forward? Were the players he felt he needed to survive another season available and willing to sign for Maienhead? The break was a welcome one and provided Derek the chance to evaluate all options available to him. He had once again failed in his attempts to convince the board to send him on a coaching course or invest in the clubs youth recruitment and the club finances were beginning to become a real problem, stopping investment in both the playing staff as well as the clubs facilities.

Derek Cooper took the decision to keep one eye on potential vacancies whilst he did all he could to prepare the club for another difficult campaign. Whilst organising a potentially profitable tournament to be held at York Road Derek was alerted to a managerial vacancy north of the border at Scottish Championship club Livingstone. He made tentative contact with the club and declared a public interest in the role through the local media, something that was risky, but could give him the edge over other candidates. Cooper waited by the phone, but the only calls he received were from Birmingham, Cardiff and Aston Villa confirming their attendance at the pre-season cup.

Derek eventually heard back from Livingstone and attended an interview with the club in a side room of their Tony Macaroni Arena stadium. Once again Cooper stayed true to himself and promised attacking football with a preference to develop young players. The Livingston board quizzed him on his recent struggles and asked why he had been unable to guide Maidenhead to a much safer league finish. Derek headed back down to Maidenhead satisfied that he had come across well in the interview and hopeful that they would be in touch soon with positive news.

Two days later, on the 22nd of June Livingston got in touch to inform Cooper that although he had interviewed well he was not the man for them at this moment in time. They had decided to go with a more experienced candidate in Craig Harrison who was to be announced the following day. They asked for his discretion with the impending appointment and wished him well for the season ahead.

Down, but undeterred following the news of Harrisons appointment Derek Cooper had a brainwave and quickly fired up the laptop in his office and headed to his email. Craig Harrison had been manager at The New Saints over in Wales, a side that had dominated the Welsh Premier league for a few years now and regularly qualified to play in the very early rounds of the UEFA Champions League. As he typed out an email enquiring as the status of the now vacant post he could hear that iconic Champions League theme playing over and over again in his head.

The next two weeks would see a productive channel of communication opened as TNS interviewed their selected candidates. Derek Cooper had been amongst those shortlisted for interview as the TNS board decided who they wanted to take them forward into the 2020/21 season. On the 11th of July 2020 whilst his side hosted Cardiff City in their pre-season cup competition the TNS chairman left a voicemail on Derek Coopers phone asking him to call them back at his earliest possible convenience.

CHAPTER THREE.

Derek Cooper was presented to the Welsh media on the morning of 12th of July 2020 as the new manager of Dafabet Welsh Premier League champions The New Saints, or TNS, as they were commonly known. He was asked several questions by the gathered journalists who wanted to know more about the newest manager in the league. Was he excited to get started in Wales? Did he feel he was the right man to take TNS forward despite his lack of experience? The answer to all these questions was a resounding "Yes" from the man of the moment. This was Derek Cooper's first managerial post at a full-time professional club and he intended to work hard behind the scenes as well as on the pitch to make sure he made the most of this fantastic opportunity.

Cooper arrived in Wales as a man with a plan, a plan that involved self development as much as progress with the side on the pitch. Gaining those elusive coaching qualifications was still a priority and ensuring his side remained as the dominant domestic force whilst looking to progress in a European competition would surely aid his cause. Sadly he would not get the opportunity to manage in the Champions League of 2020/21 with the club having already been knocked out on penalties in the first qualifying round by Glenavon prior to his arrival.

In a strange twist the first game of Derek Cooper's tenure was a testimonial match organised against Blackburn Rovers to be held in honour of former manager Craig Harrison who had recently left the club to take the Livingston job. Cooper took the decision to let his recently appointed assistant manager, Louis Wells, take charge of the fixture rather than take the limelight for himself and away from someone who had been a fantastic servant to the club. It would allow Cooper to watch on from the stands and evaluate the players he now had at his disposal. It was a worthwhile exercise and it afforded Derek the chance to meet the fans, sample the stadium and its atmosphere and pick out some of his potential key players.

Striker Wes Fletcher, attacking midfielder Mark Harrison and Omar Sowunmi who was able to operate as both a central defender and striker, similar to Dion Dublin of years gone by, looked to be some of the standout players. Young central midfielder Cameron Berry also impressed the watching Cooper with a decent performance. For the most part Derek Cooper came away from Park Hall Stadium that night happy with the players at his disposal, they had had a good season the year before and minimal additions would be needed to a squad that was reigning champions and looked more than capable of retaining that honour.

As with every other club he had worked at Cooper was quick to establish his backroom setup, adding staff as required and replacing those he deemed as not up to the task. It was a busy first few days in the job with multiple additions joining his team across all departments ready for the new season. Louis Wells joined as his new assistant manager, Mike Waters and Geraint Frowen would work as scouts under the newly appointed chief scout Luija who was to head up Cooper's new recruitment team. Cooper was sure there would be further additions as the season went on, but he was pleased with the speed at which he had been able to get new bodies on board.

Cooper had until the 22nd of August 2020 to get his squad ready for their opening Welsh Premier League fixture and he still had transfer targets he was chasing whilst some players had already joined the club. The new look squad was settling in and adapting well to life with their new manager. Pre-season had been a success and although it was early days Cooper was convinced that he had made the right decision in coming to the Welsh league. He was confident it would give him the chance to add silverware, play European football and maximise his coaching potential. The only negative he had come across in his early dealings with the club was the reluctance of some of his transfer targets to commit to the move over to Wales despite TNS being the country's top club with the potential for European football.

There were limited arrivals ahead of the season opener, but Sean Willis had made the move over from QPR on a season long loan and players such as Tom Fry, Rollin Menayese and Jamie Williams had arrived on free transfers to add depth to an already strong first team squad.

The Welsh Premier League kicked off and Derek Cooper was back to his unbeaten best with TNS. An opening day win at home to Prestatyn (4-0) was followed by an away win at Haverfordwest (2-1) before they managed another two four goal hauls at home to Airbus UK (4-0) and away to Aberystwyth (4-2). Derek Cooper also progressed through the first round of a cup competition for what felt like the first time in ages beating Rhyl (3-0) in the Nathaniel MG cup second round, a competition Cooper was hopeful of winning this season. A shock home defeat came next, the first of his time at TNS against Carmarthen (2-0), causing an abrupt end to the early season unbeaten run that had kicked the 2020/21 season off.

The wins soon returned and Cooper guided TNS through the 3rd round of the Nathanial MG cup with an away victory against Bangor City (4-2). Further victories followed in the league as TNS won six of their next seven matches, with one draw coming against Connah's Quay (1-1). There was a solitary defeat nestled amongst the league victories and that defeat came in the Challenge Cup fourth round away to Scottish opponents Partick Thistle (4-2). Although TNS had been picking up wins some had come courtesy of very late goals with Cooper's side taking their time to break through the defensive set ups of their domestic opponents. Wins against Haverfordwest (1-0), Prestatyn (2-1) and Port Talbot (2-1) all came courtesy of goals within the last ten minutes of matches.

It was now early November and TNS were to make their entrance into the JD Welsh Cup at the third round stage. They had been drawn at home to Carmarthen who had been the only Welsh side to have beaten Cooper's men in the league. Once again Carmarthen proved to have the better of TNS and were 2-0 up before half time. TNS rallied in the second half through a Sowunmi goal, but ultimately it wasn't enough and Carmarthen would gain another victory, winning 2-1 this time out.

There would be nearly a month of football played before Cooper's next defeat and that month saw a Nathaniel MG Cup semi final victory at a neutral venue against Prestatyn (4-2) with two goals each for Omar Sowunmi and Mark Harrison. There were also two disappointing draws in that period as TNS failed to capitalise on their dominance against both Aberystwyth (1-1) and Connah's Quay (0-0). When the defeat arrived it came six days shy of Christmas away to Llandudno who inflicted a heavy 4-1defeat which saw the home side take a four goal lead.

In a fixture quirk TNS would face off against Newtown twice in the league in a matter of days. The first saw a Boxing Day win (4-2) at Mid Wales Leisure, Latham Park - home of the Welsh part timers. Then the unbelievable happened and in the first fixture of 2021 on the 2nd of January Newtown exacted revenge at Park Hall Stadium in a shock 1-0 victory. TNS had foruteen shots to Newtowns four, but their case wasn't helped by central defender Jamie Williams who got himself sent off with two yellow cards coming just five minutes apart in the sixty-third and sixty-eighth minutes.

TNS recovered with a couple of routine league victories against Bangor (4-1) and Port Talbot (3-0) ahead of the Nathaniel MG cup final on Sunday the 24th of January. The cup final was the final game before the Welsh league split into the championship and relegation conferences. Just 706 people turned out at Parc y Scarlets to watch the final with Cooper left disappointed at the turn out for the first cup final of his career, hopefully there would be more to come with larger crowds there to witness his success. The game was a close one despite TNS being the overwhelming favourites to take the trophy home. Second half goals from Sowunmi and Wes Fletcher came either side of an Andrew Jones strike for plucky opponents Caernarfon.

Derek Cooper had the first cup victory of his career and TNS had the first silverware under their new manager with the league hopefully to follow. Cooper was delighted to have a cup victory under his belt and he was confident it would be the first of many during his time here. The league was entering its final stages and TNS were more than capable of winning it within the coming weeks.

There were ten league games left for Cooper and TNS were comfortably in the driving seat heading into the championship conference. The run in began with another comfortable victory, this time against Llandudno (2-0), but next up was Coopers bogey team in Wales - Carmarthen. Cooper had faced off against Andy Furnell and his side three times already this campaign and Furnell had come out on top on two of those occasions winning 2-0 and 2-1. This time Carmarthen would really pile on the misery and dismantle TNS on their way to a 4-1 win, to match the biggest defeat of Cooper's season. New signing Kyle De Silva, formerly of Exeter and Eindhoven in Holland scored a late consolation for TNS to save a little face.

February through to the seasons end in May saw TNS play out their final eight fixtures. Cooper and his side had already built up a commanding lead in the league having lost only four times so far. The league title would be wrapped up well ahead of time provided they didn't completely chuck the towel in and fail to pick up another point. The eight remaining fixtures saw form drop off slightly, but at no point was there any risk of them not claiming the 202/21 league title. TNS won just three of their final games, but they didn't suffer another defeat, drawing the other five. The results in the run in were tinged by an element of complacency as the title was already in the bag with TNS finishing well ahead of bogey team Carmarthen in second spot with an eighteen point cushion.

2020/2021 Had been a successful first season in Wales for Derek Cooper. He had one league title and one domestic cup to his name, three Manager of the Month awards as well as having gained his National C Licence along the way. Wes Fletcher had been crowned the top scorer in the Welsh Premier Division with his total of eighteen goals whilst Omar Sowunmi actually outscored him across all competitions with a tally of twenty five. It had been a good season for many of his first team squad and right back Joseph Jones had stood out with an average rating of 7.35, which was only bettered by that man Sowunmi again and his average rating of 7.46.

Attention now turned to the upcoming 2021/22 season and competing in the early rounds of the UEFA Champions League, a competition Cooper had only dreamed of coaching in when he started his career back in 2016. At the age of just thirty-three he was only months away from fulfilling that dream and managing the Welsh champions in the premier European competition of club football. It was a genuine pinch yourself moment for Derek Cooper.

Cooper and his squad had cruised to the double last season and he was confident that more domestic honours would follow, but he wasn't the type to rest on his laurels. New players would be joining the club and it had been a busy summer for Cooper and his scouts, casting their eye over several young players and one or two lads with a bit more experience who were available on free transfers.

Derek Cooper wanted to make a decent fist of competing in Europe hoping that the financial rewards for progressing through at least some of the qualifying rounds would benefit the club long term. Chris McCain came in as the new number one, Albanian centre back Valentin Gjokaj added some experience and former Newcastle United striker Adam Campbell joined the club in somewhat of a marquee signing with Cooper hoping he could get the best out of him. By the end of July Cooper had added a total of seven players to his squad, one on loan with six joining on permanent free transfers.

There was also a number of departures from the reserve and U19 squads over the summer, but no regular first team players left as Cooper kept hold of his first team regulars. Not losing any of his regulars had been important, Players like Kyle De Silva, Jose Gabriel Cortes and Ashley Carter had joined the club very late into the previous season as Cooper finally convinced them to join him in Wales and he was keen to see what they could bring to this season alongside the latest new additions.

The seasons start would be upon TNS and Cooper so quickly that they would only have time for a hastily arranged inter club friendly against the reserves before they were thrust into the Champions League action and a first qualifying match away to Andorran outfit Sant Julia. The in house friendly on the 26th of June allowed Derek to get minutes into as many of his squad as possible, not ideal preparation obviously, but it would have to do. The side travelled to Andorra ahead of the first leg which was to be played on the Wednesday night with the return leg seven days later. The excitement was palpable around the club and Cooper couldn't wait to get stuck in to his first European adventure.

Derek Cooper would contest his first European fixture in front of 3,305 people at the Estadi Nacional and it would be a debut to remember for the boss as his boys ran out easy victors in a 3-0 win. Leaving Andorra with three away goals was a nice buffer heading into their home match which was to be played at the unfamiliar Greenhous Meadow, home of Shrewsbury Town, to ensure the pitch and stadium facilities complied with UEFA regulations. Cooper needn't have worried about the setting of the match as TNS easily outclassed Sant Julia to win 4-0 on the night and 7-0 on aggregate. Striker Adam Campbell claimed a brace away from home and would go one better to complete his hat-trick at home, scoring five of the seven goals across the tie. Not a bad return for Coopers new signing in his first competitive fixtures in the green and white of TNS.

The second qualifying round was drawn and saw TNS put up against Sheriff, the Moldovan top flight champions. It was another step into the unknown for Cooper who had minimal information on his opposition and a very quick turnaround between the two rounds. There was just enough time for a heavily rotated side to play in a friendly defeat at home to Oxford (1-0) and keeping players fresh was important with such a busy schedule so early in a season. The first of the two legs saw TNS travel away from home hoping for a repeat of their first round away victory and Cooper set his side up to attack from the off. It was a decision that worked out brilliantly as TNS returned home on the right end of a 4-0 victory in a one sided match that could have seen more goals scored. Adam Campbell continued his fine form in front of goal and added a further two goals to his Champions League tally which was now up to seven.

The second leg should now be a formality with all the hard work having been done in Moldova. Cooper continued to set his side up to play the attractive attacking football that had won them three out of three so far. Sheriff obviously never got the memo and rolled into town like a team possessed. Two minutes in and 4-0 became 4-1 with them getting an away goal of their own. Sheriff continued to push forward and Cooper quickly adjusted his sides' mentality switching to a counter attack style in the hope he could keep men behind the ball, protect their lead and make the most of any breakaways.

The change of style worked and dulled the regular Sheriff attacks, with half time approaching TNS looked comfortable despite being 1-0 down on the night. TNS couldn't make it to half time unscathed and although they didn't concede again, a poor tackle from right back Joseph Jones saw him receive a straight red card. The break allowed a reshuffle and reassurances to the team that they were doing OK, they were ahead on aggregate and although a man down had a comfortable three goal cushion on aggregate. Cooper told them to go out and keep it tight, frustrate the opposition and the result would surely come. What he did not suggest was going out and conceding a sloppy goal within five minutes of the restart.

Two goals down on the night and a man light Cooper began to panic and switched the style once again opting for a defensive approach looking to shut the game down and keep all ten men behind the ball. It didn't work and Sheriff found another goal just after the hour mark. With little over twenty minutes of the tie left Cooper was facing the very real possibility of throwing away the first leg victory. Derek could feel the game and his qualification hopes slipping away from him. His side were on the ropes and Sheriff were looking to finish them off. Cue Derek Coopers saviour, a man named Nikolay Scherbakov who completely lost his head and needlessly got himself sent off at a time when Sheriff were very much a team in the ascendancy. It was a blow they would never recover from and TNS limped over the line with a very lucky 4-3 aggregate win, their away win being just enough to see them through to the third round, a round of the Champions League that TNS had never made before.

TNS were still alive in their quest to qualify for the Champions League, and they were now in uncharted waters. The potential opponents included some very good European sides with history in the competition and Cooper couldn't wait. This was what it was all about, big European nights for his relative minnows. The third qualifying round would see TNS take on European football regulars Dinamo, former club of Luka Modric and ex-Arsenal man Eduardo. It was an exciting draw for Cooper who couldn't wait for his next Champions League fixture, but first it was back to pre-season duty and an easy, morale building friendly win over local side Llanfair (3-0).

Wednesday 28th of July 2021 saw another night of European football arrive for Derek Cooper, the biggest game of his season and undoubtedly his career to date, as he pitted his side against champions of Croatia Dinamo. Nobody could have predicted such a young manager to be the man to take TNS the furthest they had ever been in the Champions League, but Cooper wasn't fazed and he was enjoying every second of the experience. No-one had expected TNS to get this far and he told his players as much in their pre-match team talk telling them that they were the underdogs and that they should relax and enjoy the occasion.

It was a record home attendance that turned out to support TNS with 9,529 spectators making the journey to the teams temporary European home. Fans responded to Coopers rallying cry in the local media for every woman, man and child to get behind the side and cheer them into the Champions League playoffs.

TNS couldn't have wished for a better start and with just ten minutes on the clock they were 2-0 to the good with goals from that man Campbell and his strike partner Jose Gabriel Cortes. Derek was in dreamland, this was going better than he ever thought possible. His side were blowing Dinamo away, a decent side that had recently nurtured the talent of Croatian Wonderkid Ante Coric .

Half time came and went with the Croatian side barely laying a glove on Cooper's men, they were in cruise control and a good performance only got better on seventy-nine minutes when wide man Rees Greenwood put TNS 3-0 up. The crowd were going wild, 3-0 up against a genuinely good European side, not one from Andorra or Moldova. Ironic chants of "We're going to win the cup, we're going to win the cup" were now ringing around the terraces. It proved to be a bit premature and Dinamo spoiled the party just two minutes later when striker Dino Klaric nicked an away goal for Dinamo, putting a dampener on the mood and sewing a small seed of doubt in the mind of Derek Cooper with his sides' recent second leg collapse still fresh in his memory.

With a week between the two legs of the Dinamo tie Cooper cancelled the friendly that had been arranged for that Saturday. His side were in good form, good condition and high morale; he didn't want to risk any of those factors on a fixture that meant next to nothing in the grand scheme of things. Successfully navigating his way through this Dinamo tie would see European minnows TNS only a playoff round win away from the actual Champions League group stage, it was unbelievable.

Training in the week leading up to the second leg had been good, players were putting in the work and the coaches were pleased with how the team were shaping up. Travelling to Croatia with a two goal lead was obviously fantastic, but TNS were still very much the underdogs in the tie with pundits and fans alike still writing off their chances of progressing despite their first leg victory. Derek Cooper was quietly confident although he was also all too aware of what had happened in the previous round against Sheriff, a team who were nowhere near the standard of his current opposition. Tactically Derek debated sending his team out to try and win the game as he normally would, but he had to consider playing it a little more cautious and look to hit Dinamo on the break, they were the side who needed to attack after all.

Game day arrived and Cooper had put his faith in an unchanged eleven who would go out and play the exact same way that had seen them get the result in the first leg. If it isn't broken then don't fix it was very much the philosophy for Derek Cooper. The teams lined up in the tunnel with Cooper having recycled his team talk from the week before telling his side nobody expected them to get a result and to go out and enjoy themselves. His lads looked focussed and relaxed, ready for their date with destiny.

Cooper took his place in the dugout and the potentially historic game kicked off, he barely had a chance to take in the surroundings of Dinamos historic stadium before his side found themselves a goal down. Domagoj Pavicic broke through the TNS backline with only a minute on the clock to make it 1-0 on the night and 3-2 on aggregate.

Derek Cooper couldn't have envisaged a worse start and it now became a case of his side finding the right response to not fold under the pressure and concede another goal. TNS responded magnificently; collecting themselves to not only stave off the Dinamo attacks, but to mount some of their own. They were to be rewarded just over ten minutes later when Adam Campbell continued his European heroics grabbing his eighth Champions League goal to level the tie and get that vital away goal.

TNS were now 4-2 up on aggregate, had cancelled out the away goal of Dinamo with one of their own and had settled into a match that had shown the potential to spiral out of their control. On thirty-fourminutes a new spanner in the works began to wrench the tie away from TNS as deputy right back Mael Davies, in for the previously suspended Joseph Jones, lost his head and was shown a straight red card. Derek needed to get his side in for half time and regroup, but for now it was damage control. Cooper opted for a defensive approach and prayed that his side could make it to the interval unscathed. Mirko Maric had other ideas and as the fourth official withdrew the board showing two minutes of added time he crashed one in from the edge of the box, TNS were now 2-1 behind and a man down to boot.

As his players trudged into the dressing room with their heads down and looking defeated Cooper knew he needed to bring them back to life. He stood up tall, puffed out his chest and told his players that despite the score they were doing ok and he knew there was more to come from them. Individually he told each unit that he had faith in their ability, all bar Mael Davies that is, he was aggressively told that he had let the side down by being sent off so early. Derek changed from the defensive approach they had been using to a counter attacking mentality; he wanted to sit back and keep men behind the ball, but he didn't want to offer too much encouragement to Dinamo, it was still his game to lose after all.

The start of the second half would see an early goal much like the first half had only this time it would be TNS midfielder Kyle De Silva scoring within a minute of the kick off. Derek Cooper couldn't believe it; the first half had started so badly that part of him assumed it would happen again, but this was just what he needed, another away goal and his side back on level terms at 2-2. Cooper punched the air, but his celebrations were mooted as there was still so much of this tie left to play, the roller coaster of emotions would surely continue?

For the next twenty minutes his side coped with whatever Dinamo could throw at them, but Mirko Maric finally managed to find a way through TNS' resolve and in the sixty-eighth minute he cut the aggregate deficit to just one goal at 5-4. That second away goal for TNS was now proving to be crucial, without that already in the bag they would need to push for it with a man less. As it stood another goal for Dinamo would not be the end of the world with it meaning TNS would still progress via the much debated away goals rule.

TNS continued to defend stubbornly and rebuffed attack after attack, but it was coming at a cost; his side were tiring as the game went on and were posing less and less of an attacking threat with Campbell working hard up top on his own chasing into the channels and harassing defenders. Cooper was debating a bold change when his mind was made up by Dinamo's Maric completing his hat-trick. Another goal now would be disastrous and it forced Cooper to make his proposed change. Striker Campbell would come off to be replaced by a central defender rather than another striking option. TNS went to 5-4-0 for the remaining 8minutes plus stoppages and played to contain the opposition, to slow the game down and waste time wherever possible.

There was not a single highlight to speak of between Maric's third goal in the eighty-second minute and the final whistle. TNS had been able to shut the game down and put the tie to bed. It finished 5-5 and meant it was a memorable away goals victory for Derek Cooper. The tie was much tighter than he had hoped for pre-match, but then he never expected to be in Croatia on a Wednesday night in early August anyway, he was already far past what he had thought his side capable of.

The draw for the playoff round would take place the following morning and Derek Cooper went to bed that night wondering who would be up next on their European adventure. So far it had seen them play matches in Andorra, Moldova and Croatia. Cooper and his coaching staff all huddled around Sky Sports at the hotel the next morning eagerly awaiting The New Saints to be read out from one of those little balls used in the European draws. It didn't take long; they were drawn in the first fixture out of the hat going away from home in the first leg to face AEK Athens of the Greek Superleague. Cooper knew very little of AEK and their playing staff, but he did know that they had troublesome striker Mario Balotelli amongst their ranks. In two weeks time Derek would be in Greece facing off against Super Mario and his AEK side with a place in the Champions League group stage at stake.

The two week break from Europe meant a return to friendly fixtures and wins against Prestatyn (3-0) and AFC Liverpool (3-1) to keep his squad ticking over. The threat of injuries meant that for the most part Cooper played heavily rotated sides aiming to keep his strongest eleven as fresh and injury free as possible. There was a lot on the line not just for Cooper and his personal glory, but for the players and the club too. The club finances were already benefitting from the influx of prize money and the money to date had been peanuts when compared to what would be available should they pull off another upset against AEK.

Going away from home for the first leg was a return to the norm for Cooper having previously started away to both Sant Julia and Sheriff in earlier rounds. AEK Athens presented another real test for TNS and would undoubtedly prove very tough opposition. They had Mario Balotelli, formerly of Manchester City, Liverpool, INTER, AC Milan and Nice fame, whereas TNS lined up with Adam Campbell formerly of Newcastle United, Carlisle, St. Mirren and Exeter alongside Jose Gabriel Cortes who had been plucked from obscurity on a free transfer.

It was going to be a night to remember for Cooper regardless of the result as he managed in front of his biggest crowd to date, a whopping 24,944 were in attendance on the evening he would try to conquer Greece. The game kicked off and thankfully it didn't see his side fall behind in the opening minutes, instead it was a cagey affair with not much in the way of highlights to open the tie. As expected Mario Balotelli looked to be the main threat of the opposition and that was proved to be the case in the twenty-third minute as he put AEK 1-0 up, much to the delight of the home crowd. TNS were still very much in the game and never looked out of their depth or overwhelmed by the quality of Athens and they continued to plug away with measured attacks. Coopers side were rewarded for their endeavours on the stroke of halftime with free transfer Cortes levelling the score.

A quarter of the tie gone and it was level pegging with another important away goal in the bag for TNS. Cooper wasn't too concerned and would have definitely taken this score-line had he been offered it before the match. The performance so far had given him confidence and the away goal would ensure they went into the home leg with that added security.

TNS kicked off for the second half and instantly went about their business hassling AEK, looking to get ahead in the match. The fast start would bear fruit when wide man Rees Greenwood added another important

Champions League goal to his one from the Dinamo tie. 2-1 up with an hour gone and TNS were in cruise control never looking in any real danger.

It was then the turn of centre back Ashley Carver to have a moment of madness and make it three red cards in as many rounds for Coopers team. Now came a real dilemma for Derek. The game was finely balanced and although AEK hadn't looked much of a threat TNS were beginning to tire and had become less and less likely to score themselves. Adding another centre back had worked previously for Cooper and with a bit of a reshuffle he withdrew both strikers to revert to the 5-4-0 that had worked so well in closing down the Dinamo game. It was more of a risk this time given that there was much longer to go in the match this time out, but he felt like this was the best of his limited options. TNS just needed to hang on to their slender advantage and claim another truly impressive victory.

For the most part the tactical change worked and the game began to ebb away with no real highlights to speak of, but in the very last minute AEK and that man Balotelli managed to work an opportunity that Cooper assumed meant an undeserved equaliser was coming. Luckily for Derek and TNS it wasn't to be and the chance was squandered. The full time whistle sounded soon after and TNS could celebrate their most unlikely victory of this European journey, but Cooper was acutely aware that the job was only half done and second legs had a habit of biting him in the bum.

Before the return leg there was the matter of Welsh Premier League action starting with the 2021/22 season opener away at Cooper's bogey side and last year's runners up Carmarthen. The crowds of European nights gone by were a distant memory as TNS laboured to a 1-1 draw in front of 349 fans at Richmond Park. A late goal from Campbell, on off the bench, was enough to earn a point in a game that should have seen them take all three and put an end to the Carmarthen hoodoo. In truth Derek Coopers head was far from where it needed to be for a domestic curtain raiser, he was away with the Champions League fairies distracted by what he could do to take that momentous final step into the UCL group stage.

Tuesday the 24th of August 2021, the Champions League theme was playing over the Greenhous Meadow PA system with Derek Cooper facing the biggest game of his time as a manager with TNS on the verge of making history. AEK Athens were the visitors looking to overturn their 2-1 first leg defeat. Cooper went with just one change, replacing the suspended Ashley Carter after his red card in the previous match. He was so close he could almost taste the excitement that qualification for the next round would bring, competing alongside European luminaries such as Real Madrid, Juventus, Bayern Munich to name but a few.

The clock soon hit 19:45 and the referee got the game underway. AEK were the side who needed to come from behind and Cooper was cautiously optimistic he would be able to out manoeuvre them and catch them on the break. He started the game with a standard mentality planning to change that as and when the game required him to do so with a counter attacking style being his most likely plan of action.

As expected AEK started brightly looking to take the game to TNS and it wasn't long before Cooper went to Plan B hoping to weather the storm and catch them with an incisive break away. The first half was slowly passing by for Cooper who prowled his technical area full of nervous energy, heading or kicking every ball for his players. With only five minutes left of the first half it was TNS who broke the deadlock when Jose Gabriel Cortes tucked home and sent the home fans into raptures. 1-0 Up on the night and 3-1 up on aggregate Cooper went into the half time break a very happy manager asking for more of the same from his men; a steady start to keep it tight before nicking another goal to seal the tie.

The second half got underway and Derek Cooper had barely got himself comfortable in the dugout before Mario Balotelli clawed one back for AEK and got them an away goal of their own. It was now 3-2 on aggregate, one more goal for AEK and the away goal rule that had been on Cooper's side in the previous round would not go in his favour this time. TNS would need to respond well and keep their heads in such a crucial match, a quick second goal now could be disastrous. As the minutes slowly ticked by TNS settled back into the game and although under pressure from Athens, looked to be coping with their attacks. Slowly the Welsh side grew in confidence again, beginning to assert themselves on the AEK defence and causing them problems of their own. It was that man Cortes again who managed to get Cooper, his coaching team and the home fans back on their feet again with a second goal for TNS in the sixty-fourth minute. 4-2 with twenty-five minutes remaining, they were all so close to making history, but another away goal, although not a winning goal, would really put the pressure on TNS.

For the next fifteen minutes TNS worked hard to maintain their lead, rebuffing AEK and looking to be positive in possession themselves. At 2-1up on the night they didn't look to be in any danger, but that all changed on seventy-nine minutes with attacking midfielder Marko Jankovic netting a second away goal for AEK Athens. The second goal meant that they were still behind over the two legs, but a third goal would see them through on the frustrating away goals rule.

TNS needed to keep their heads now more than ever, they had done so well after conceding early in the second half, and a similar reaction was just what Cooper needed. He resisted the urge to make radical changes to shape and mentality using the rationale that his side had responded magnificently earlier in the game, but he was quickly left to rue the decision as barely a minute later the ball was back in the TNS net again after a goal from Moroccan Adnane Tighadouini.

In those mad two minutes all of the hard work was being undone and instead of shutting up shop late on in a European fixture Cooper was forced to push his wingers and full backs on in a desperate bid to rescue their qualification hopes. The remaining minutes flew by in an agonizing whizz of frustration and regret with his side unable to play their way back into the tie. AEK Athens had hit them with a late one, two combination that had derailed all their hard work.

The European adventure was over and Cooper couldn't have been more disappointed and proud. A real conflict of emotions were washing over him as he attended to his post match commitments, praising his lads for their efforts and lamenting what was so nearly his greatest night in football management.

For Derek Cooper the morning after the European night before was like experiencing all the pains of the worst hangover imaginable, but instead of the headaches or sickness, it was just the regret and the realisation that he was coming down from a massive high. The Welsh Premier League and three domestic cup competitions were to be his pick me ups, encouraging his mind to focus on the chances of more silverware and recognition amongst his peers, but that nagging feeling that they had been so close was tough to ignore.

Derek's wallowing and self loathing was interrupted by the office phone and a conversation with his personal assistant that would brighten his mood considerably. Derek Cooper had been so caught up in what might have been that he had failed to pay attention to the fact that those sides knocked out of the Champions League qualification at the final hurdle automatically qualified for a place in the Europa League group stages. The European adventure was back on and that went some way towards healing the immense disappointment he had felt after their away goals defeat the night before. On the 30th of August Cooper would be in Monaco to learn who his side would be facing in the 2021/22 UEFA Europa League which was a nice consolation prize.

It was a swift return to domestic action and just four days later TNS played their first home game in the league which saw them breeze past Bangor City (3-0) with a hat-trick for Adam Campbell. Their next fixture was a MG Cup second round victory that was watched by just forty-nine spectators away at Prestatyn. Cooper had arrived for the cup match on the 31st of August off the back of a night in Monaco to witness the draw for the Europa League group stage. TNS would join SK Rapid Wien, Sparta Prague and Lyon in a very competitive group I.

Two more league fixtures were to follow ahead of the clubs Europa League debut and they saw back to back victories for TNS away to Airbus UK (3-0) and a hammering of Llangefni (6-0) on home soil. Four games in and TNS were undefeated at the top of the league, through to the next round of their MG Cup defence and a return to European action was on the horizon.

SK Rapid Wien were first on the agenda for Cooper in a group that he felt cautiously optimistic about his sides chances of qualifying from given their performances thus far this season. A good start at home could prove to be vital for his hopes of causing a shock in Group I. Sadly it wasn't to the start Cooper had wanted and a resilient Rapid Wien would silence a new record home crowd of 9,827 to win 2-1 on the night. The Europa League debut hadn't gone as well as Cooper had hoped, but he was still optimistic that his side could bounce back and qualify and he intimated as much in his post match press conference.

Airbus UK were the visitors to Park Hall Stadium just three days later and a heavily rotated side were unable to break them down in a frustrating MG Nathaniel cup match that saw a drab 0-0 go all the way to penalties with the Airbus UK spot kick takers holding their nerve and knocking the holders out of the competition much earlier than expected. Not what Cooper had planned for their defence of the cup. Back to back defeats was not ideal and not something Cooper was used to as manager of TNS so it was important to get that winning feeling back the following Saturday against Barry, a side that shouldn't pose too much of a problem. TNS won 3-0 and were back to winning ways keeping their unbeaten start to the league going.

It was then time to return to European action with a tough fixture away to Sparta Prague. Cooper knew that TNS realistically needed three points to keep any hopes of qualification alive. Another defeat would leave them needing to take at least three points off Lyon, the standout team in the group, and win both return fixtures at Wien and Prague which would be an improbable task.

Cooper travelled to the Czech Republic promising TNS fans he would take the game to their opponents and go down fighting with an attacking brand of football. In a narrow game Mark Harrison came off the bench to score a late winner in a narrow 2-1 victory for TNS and Cooper. It would be nearly a month before their next Europa League match and beating Sparta Prague was vital to keeping their optimism alive whilst they returned to domestic duties.

That month of Welsh league and Challenge Cup action saw TNS draw with Llandudno (1-1) and beat Rangers U20's away (3-0) in the Challenge Cup thanks to another Adam Campbell hat-trick. Back to back league victories followed against Connah's Quay (2-0) and Port Talbot (3-1) with TNS leaving it particularly late against Connah's Quay with goals in the eighty-sixth and ninetieth minutes.

Away from the pitch Derek Cooper was keen to continue his personal development and went to the boardroom asking them to consider sending him on his National B coaching licence. Cooper felt that with the on pitch successes combined with the boost in club finances it was only fair he was put forward by the club to gain the qualification. Initially the board were hesitant stating their fears that he would be developed at their expense before looking for a bigger job. Whilst Cooper was confident his long term future would see him go on to bigger and better things he emphasised the benefits that a more qualified manager would bring to the club and they duly reconsidered their decision telling Cooper that he would be sent on the next available course with the club covering the costs.

Back to on field matters and arguably the toughest European fixture the club had faced to date. Cooper would face off against Bruno Genesio and his Olympique Lyonnais side which still boasted players such as Nabil Fekir and Alexandre Lacazette. The club had sold a record amount of tickets for the match, breaking the attendance record for at least the third time this season alone. 9,875 spectators were in the crowd for the game and Derek Cooper was relishing testing himself against one of Europe's big hitters. Cooper decided to go for it and chanced his usual attacking style of play, he was the home side and he wanted to show that TNS could be a threat to anyone.

It proved to be a naive tactical ploy for Cooper who was made to quickly regret the decision after just fifteen minutes of play with his side already 3-0 down. Lyon had been lethal in front of goal and seemingly scored every chance they had. Vladmir Puskinov opened the scoring after only six minutes, Bastos added another a minute later and DeAndre Yedelin piled on the misery after fourteen minutes.

Cooper immediately swapped to a more cautious, counter attacking style and managed to temporarily staunch the flow of Lyon goals. It was a resistance that wouldn't last long and further embarrassment for Cooper and TNS came in the twenty-third and twenty-eighth minutes when Karol Linetty got in on the act and Puskinov added his second goal. At this point there was nothing Cooper could do, his side were being outclassed all over the pitch and were 5-0 down at home in front of a club record crowd. On the stroke of half time a rare foray into the opposition half resulted in a Jose Gabriel Cortes goal for TNS and a whole host of sarcastic cheers from the crowd.

Derek Cooper was furious, his side had really let themselves down, he called for a much better performance from his side in the second half, knowing it was unlikely that things could get much worse. However TNS started the second half in almost exactly the same way they had the terrible first half. On fifty-one minutes five became six for Lyon with Myziane Maolida scoring his first of the game before adding his second just five minutes later to make the score 7-1.

TNS and Cooper were getting a real hiding and there was still well over half an hour left to play. Mercilessly the remainder of play saw Lyon take their foot off the pedal as substitutions from both sides stopped the flow and momentum of their performance, but by that point the damage had already been done. Cooper was embarrassed and frustrated because he genuinely believed that his side would have enough character to put in a performance that would at least test the Lyon side. That definitely was not the case and Cooper had to face the media having suffered the heaviest defeat of his career.

It was very much a welcome return to domestic fixtures for Cooper and TNS after their 7-1 mauling. A chance to get some more league victories under their belt and rebuild the confidence of his side before the return fixture against the rampant Lyon side. Aberystwyth, Bala and Carmarthen were the sides Cooper would come up against and he expected to pick up the maximum nine points on offer. A routine victory at home to Aberystwyth (2-0) got them off to a comfortable start, but Bala proved to be a more stubborn opponent than Cooper had bargained for and managed to keep TNS out before nicking what would prove to be the winner in the eighty-fourth minute. Six points from the possible nine was now a must and Cooper expected his side to overcome Carmarthen despite their recent poor performances against them. TNS really struggled against Cooper's bogey side and only just managed to scrape a 3-2 victory against a side that had ten men for more than half the match. It was hardly the barnstorming return to form Cooper imagined and he was now staring down the barrel of a side that had smashed seven past his just two weeks ago.

TNS and Cooper travelled to France and the Parc Olympique Lyonnais desperate to restore some pride, but would settle for saving a little face. Lesson learned from two weeks ago Cooper set his side out to be tougher to beat rather than trying to match the firepower of an obviously superior side. However, TNS managed to hold out for just five minutes longer than they had at home before conceding in the eleventh minute as Paolo Lazzaroni broke the deadlock. With over 41,000 people in the crowd it was a big stage for TNS, a much bigger stage than they were used to and it would have been easy to fold under the pressure again. Despite Maolida making it 2-0 just before the half an hour mark Coopers side showed the resilience that had been lacking at home to limit Lyon to just a 2-0 win, which was markedly better than the showing of a fortnight ago.

Qualification from their Europa League group, whilst not impossible, was looking increasingly unlikely and it would take wins in their remaining two fixtures to even be in with a shot of making into the knockout stages. Aside from the humbling defeat to Lyon his side had performed admirably thus far and he was hoping that the remaining fixtures against Rapid Wien and Sparta Prague would give them the platform to kick on and really stake a claim for progression.

Domestically TNS overcame Carmarthen again (4-0) in the JD Welsh Cup 3rd round, before going on to record a three further victories, two in the league and another in the Challenge Cup with a quarter final win against Bala (2-0). It was now late November 2021 and at this stage of the season Coopers side were through to a Challenge Cup semi final, the 4th round of the JD Welsh Cup, top of the Welsh Premier League and still in Europe, albeit unlikely that they would progress. The sides only real disappointing competition performance to date was their poor defence of the MG Nathaniel Cup which saw them knocked out in the 3rd round earlier in the campaign.

Qualification from Group I was now reliant on TNS winning their remaining fixtures and hoping other results went their way. They arrived in Austria looking to avenge the 2-1 defeat earlier in the campaign against a Rapid Wien side that looked beatable. Without a win here there would be no chance of progressing further in this year's Europa League. A draw wouldn't be enough to keep TNS qualification hopes alive either, it had to be all three points.

Cooper was fully aware of the requirements and looked to play with a controlled, but attacking, approach. He would stick to his favoured 4-4-2 and hope that his men were up for the occasion, putting in the performance that they needed. Unfortunately things did not go to plan and a now familiar early goal was scored by Wien in the seventh minute to really dampen spirits and kill any momentum Cooper had hoped for. Although TNS battled bravely and were always in the match a penalty just before half time made it 2-0 and effectively ended their European adventure. It would remain 2-0 and despite a number of positive moments in the match TNS were unable to capitalise and Wien looked comfortable in victory.

Europe was all but over for Cooper and TNS, but there were still three domestic titles up for grabs by way of consolation prizes. Cooper was particularly keen to add the Challenge Cup to his list of honours. It is primarily a competition for the Scottish clubs, including some of their under 20's sides as well as guest teams from the Irish leagues and the Welsh Premier Division.

Cooper was keen to make an impression outside of Wales and this was a perfect opportunity to do so whilst upsetting the apple cart and having a "guest" side take home the trophy. The league was considered a formality for TNS and Cooper had them well on the way to back to back league titles, but a cup or two to compliment the titles would be more than welcome for Derek Cooper.

Three more Welsh Premier League fixtures would follow to end November and start December. Two wins and one draw would see them remain at the top of the league and go into their final Europa League fixture hoping to give the home crowd something to cheer about and grab the home win that had eluded them so far.

Sparta Prague were the visitors and the only side that TNS had managed to beat in the group. Another win was to follow courtesy of an own goal from Ondrej Mazuch with pretty much the last kick of the game in the ninety-fourth minute of a match with very little of note. The win not only restored some faith within the home supporters, but also ensured TNS had not finished bottom of Group I. Not bad for a team's first venture in a European competitions group stages. Cooper was happy to have had a go and not been the whipping boys in every match, as many had predicted.

With European football now off the agenda the full attention swung back to their Welsh Premier League campaign. The 12th of December saw TNS lose away to Connah's Quay (3-2) in a disappointing performance, but it was one of only two league games they would lose in just less than five months.

Cooper didn't have it all his own way though and although they were unbeaten in thirteen of fourteen fixtures six were draws, many of them with TNS failing to score and they only took maximum points in seven games. Oddly Connah's Quay had become Coopers new bogey team beating them again in the penultimate game of the 2021/22 season 2-0 at home. The amount of draws were less than ideal and the lack of goals was very concerning.

TNS failed to score in matches against Aberystwyth in two consecutive 0-0 draws, Bala in another 0-0 and 2021/22 bogey side Connah's Quay. TNS did manage to find the net against Newtown, but it would only be enough to earn a 1-1 draw. In a month of stalemates there was a solitary victory for Cooper's side which came in the JD Welsh Cup 4th round away to Buckley (2-0) with two goals for Adam Campbell.

The drop off in winning form from TNS got worse as the season ended and Bala were given a glimmer of hope that they may catch and overhaul Cooper's men. TNS approached the final three league games picking up a draw against Newtown (0-0) before a defeat at home to Connah's Quay (2-0). Thankfully these two disappointing results came off the back of a vital win away to title challengers Bala (1-0). Bala had been really ramping up the pressure in the final weeks of the season and this defeat essentially killed off their title charge. Adam Campbell scored in the thirty-third minute of the 1-0 victory to secure the title for TNS and the first back to back title for Derek Cooper.

The Bala title charge combined with Coopers men trying their best to fluff their lines meant that the league campaign was looking like ending up a lot tighter than many expected. Maybe it was a European hangover, or maybe his side took their eye of the ball during the run in. Either way Cooper was delighted to have his first back to back title in the bag, but was also disappointed with the sides form during the run in.

The 2021/22 JD Welsh cup campaign had seen TNS progress 2-0 in the fourth round against Buckley before a much tougher quarter final tie against Caernarfon - last season's MG Nathaniel Cup final opponents. With the match tied at 2-2 it went to penalties and Coopers TNS penalty takers held their nerve and saw the side home and through to a semi final tie at the Queensway International Stadium against title challengers Bala.

Not only were Bala aiming to usurp TNS in the league they were also determined to end Coopers hopes of a domestic league and cup double for the second season running. The semi final was a tight affair with Bala very much the in-form side coming into the fixture. After ninety minutes the sides couldn't be separated and extra time followed the poor 0-0 in normal time. Things got interesting for the neutral on one hundred and six minutes when Valentin Gjokaj was shown a straight red card to reduce TNS to ten men. It didn't seem to matter though and the game remained 0-0 for the full one hundred and twenty minutes. Penalties would be needed to see who would progress to the final of the competition.

Omar Sowunmi and Joseph Jones would miss their spot kicks for TNS as Bala's players kept cool heads to score all four of the penalties required to see them through and eliminate the favourites, ending Cooper's hopes of winning the JD Welsh Cup.

In the Challenge Cup, having already come through previous ties against Rangers Under 20's and their JD Welsh Cup semi final opponents Bala, Scottish Ladbrokes League 1 side Stranraer would be their semi final opponents. It was a close game away at Stair Park with Stranraer going ahead in the nineteenth minute and holding on to that lead well into the second half before their luck ran out and the game turned in TNS' favour. Firstly Kyle De Silva levelled the scores in theseventy-seventh minute before Wallace Duffy was then shown a straight red card for the home side. Finally Adam Campbell piled on the misery with a late winner for Coopers men and against the odds TNS had made it to the Challenge Cup Final against Dunfirmline Athletic who were riding high in the Scottish Championship.

Saturday the 26th of March 2022 was Challenge Cup final day and Derek Cooper was suited and booted for the occasion. He had been to the boardroom and ensured that his TNS side would be kitted out nicely for the day in bespoke suits for their cup final appearance.

Broadwood in Scotland was to be the venue with a crowd of 5,521 packing the terraces for the spectacle. The game was tense and extremely tight with neither side able to assert themselves enough to make an impact and with ninety minutes on the clock the game would go into extra time.

In a game this tight Cooper knew that it could take just one goal to win them the tie. He said as much in his final team talk at the end of normal time. "One goal will win us this game, go out and get it". The goal he had asked for would arrive just three minutes into extra time with substitute and loanee Sean Willis on the score sheet. Sadly that goal would not be enough to win the match and with only three minutes left of extra time Gary Jeffrey pegged TNS back and took the match to a penalty shootout.

Cooper had suffered mixed fortunes in previous shootouts and sadly this would be another occasion that would go against him with Dunfermline being clinical from the spot scoring all five of theirs to claim the trophy Cooper had coveted all season. On a positive note Derek Cooper the manager had garnered some positive media attention in Scotland during his run to the final, with any exposure outside of Wales considered good for his career prospects.

The last few weeks with TNS had become very frustrating for Cooper. His side had noticeably dropped off when it mattered in the league and had lost out on penalties in two season defining shootouts. Derek felt he had no choice but to re-evaluate his career plans and objectives.

When he had arrived in Wales he set himself three primary objectives; to achieve domestic success, to play European football and to further his coaching development by attaining the coaching qualifications he lacked. His time in Wales had since seen him win back to back league titles as well as the Nathaniel MG Cup, he had taken the club further in Europe than they had ever been before and he had gained both the National C and National B coaching licences. To his mind he had achieved the three objectives he had set himself when taking the job nearly two years ago now. Maybe it was time for him to look for the next challenge of his managerial career and Derek Cooper began to take a look at some of the potential summer vacancies.

Derek Coopers stock had slowly been on the rise over the course of his career with four league titles behind him and those now being complimented by his new coaching qualifications. He was on the lookout for a club with potential, TNS were already consistent champions of their league when Cooper arrived and he was hoping to find a club that he could manage on an upwards trajectory.

Derek Cooper had taken a cursory look at available jobs before TNS had headed into the final fixtures of the season. He had already wrapped up the league title and wanted to browse early to potentially get ahead of the curve should any interesting vacancies become available. His attention was instantly grabbed by a job that was already being advertised with a caretaker manager currently in the job. It would pose a really interesting challenge for Cooper at a club with plenty of potential and playing in a league with a vastly improved reputation. Cooper instructed his recently hired agent to make the necessary calls and set the wheels in motion for the next potential job of his managerial career.

Ahead of the final game of the season away to Carmarthen on the 4th of May 2022 Cooper had been decisive and his agent had made the necessary calls. Derek Cooper had been shortlisted for an interview, interviewed and had agreed a contract with the new club which he was happy to commit to.

TNS had been desperate to keep Derek Cooper and had made an improved contract offer in an attempt to dissuade him, but unfortunately his head had already been turned and before the clubs final game of the 2021/22 season, after 648 days in charge, six manager of the month awards, two league titles, one cup win and a cup final loss Derek Cooper would say his goodbyes to his players and staff at the training ground wishing them well for the future. Derek would be heading north to begin life with his new employers and he hoped more success would be on the cards.

CHAPTER FOUR.

Derek Cooper was in Scotland, more specifically the press room of Ross County's training ground to meet the local and national media for the first time as manager of the club, outlining his grand plans. Plans that had persuaded the board to give him the keys to their kingdom. The gathered journalists were intrigued by Cooper's choice to leave the safety and security of TNS, who could offer him Champions League football, for a side who last season finished fifth in the Scottish Ladbrokes Premiership. The answer he gave was simple, it was a chance to test himself in a more competitive and reputable league with the opportunity to build a young and tenacious squad that would have to potential to take the club forward. That was exactly the vision he had sold to the board and was the foundation of his appointment.

Derek Cooper left the press room and headed straight for his office, he was a man with work to do. He had taken the job just before the end of the 2021/22 season and Ross County still had two league fixtures remaining of their season. As things stood Cooper had no real idea of who was capable of what within his squad, he had only really been able to watch playbacks of their previous matches on his laptop. It was also vitally important for Cooper to proactively sort his backroom staffing, as always they would be an extra pair of eyes and ears for him, he always prioritised bringing in the best possible staff and it was never more vital than now, at the biggest club of his career to date.

Derek Cooper got straight on the phone and squeezed in an impromptu friendly against a local side for the Sunday afternoon, whilst not an ideal time for a friendly fixture, it would allow Cooper to have a look at the players at his disposal and begin to implement his tactical plans. Coopers now standard 4-4-2 was an option, but he was toying with the idea of playing a holding midfielder in a variation of a 4-3-3 formation that would use wingers and a lone striker. Training would be geared to Coopers preferred focus of team cohesion in an attempt to improve the inconsistency that had dogged their performances under the previous manager

For the next three days Derek Cooper barely left the training ground, if he wasn't out on the pitches taking training sessions he was in his office on the phone recruiting bodies to bolster his backroom team. Cooper needed to fill the voids that had been left when the previous manager, Allan Johnston had taken some of his staff with him when he left for league rivals Rangers.

By the Sunday of their hastily arranged friendly the bulk of the work had been done and Cooper was happy with those he had been able to bring in. Cooper had been back to former club Maidenhead to appoint his old assistant manager Daniel Brown, a man he knew he could rely on, and to TNS for his former chief scout Luija, a man whose judgement had always served him well in the past. The majority of his appointments were of staff members who were out of work, but entirely capable in their respective fields. By doing this it allowed Cooper to keep costs to a minimum and save any money available for his summer recruitment drive.

Sunday the 24th of April saw Cooper take charge of Ross County for the first time, albeit in a friendly fixture, and whilst it looked a pointless exercise on paper Derek hoped it would offer a much needed insight into the players and personalities currently at the club.

Clachnacuddin, a lower league semi-professional outfit, would be the opposition in an easy 3-0 victory for Ross County at their Global Energy Stadium. Cooper had his first game and his first win under his belt, had been in the dugout and sampled his new home. He had given a run out to a full complement of twenty-two players giving most a full forty-five minutes to make an impression on their new gaffer.

Striker Stevie May and winger Duane Holmes had been on target for Ross County, but there were impressive performances from all areas of the pitch. All things considered it had been a productive few days and the remaining games against Hearts and Rangers were on the horizon with players and fans especially keen to get one over Rangers and ex-Ross County boss Johnston.

Training had been good in the week leading up to Cooper's first outing in a competitive fixture. He had played against some Scottish clubs earlier in the season whilst at TNS and felt he had a good grasp of the leagues pace and style. Derek was relishing the chance to get his team out on the Tynecastle pitch for the game against Hearts.

Ross County were impressive in spells and whilst always in the game would succumb to a solitary goal from Adama Diomande just before the hour mark. There was no shame in losing narrowly away to Hearts; they sat in fourth place, one place ahead of Ross County's fifth. Cooper was impressed with his sides' reaction to going one behind and actually felt his side had done enough to earn a share of the points. It was a disappointing result in the end and one that effectively ended their season leaving them unable to catch Hearts with just one game to go and four points clear of Aberdeen behind County in sixth. The final game against Rangers would be all about pride and spoiling Allan Johnston's start.

Coopers first home game was the last game of the campaign for Ross County and it saw a slightly disappointing turn out of only 6,541 for the visit of Rangers. Derek had been hoping that the off the pitch narrative of new and old managers facing off would have been more of a draw for the County fans.

Nevertheless Derek Cooper was determined to make an impression on the new home faithful. He would look to take the game to Rangers, playing a free flowing attacking style whilst trying to keep things tight at the back. Stepping out on to the Global Energy Stadium touchline for the first time competitively was a real moment for the now thirty-four year old Cooper; he was the youngest manager in the league and determined to prove the doubters wrong.

The Rangers game kicked off and instantly the teams began pushing forward in waves of pulsating football. It was the away side who drew first blood on eight minutes when Jules Mbia found the back of the Ross County net. Coopers side responded well, but were to go 2-0 down when striker Lys Mousset added another for Johnston's men. A goal was just what County needed and it was exactly what they got. Almost straight from the kick off Scottish striker Lewis Vaughan pulled one back, dragging his side back into the tie. Ross County went into the break 2-1 down, but their tails were up with the players chomping at the bit to get back out for the second half.

Cooper sent his lads out fired up, eager to show their ex-gaffer just what they were capable of under the new man in town. Just four minutes in and midfielder Ian McShane slotted home. It was now 2-2 and Ross County continued to look for the next goal really trying to take all three points. For twenty minutes they probed without joy until American winger Duane Holmes put them ahead for the first time in the match.

County were on the front foot now and continued to take the game to a faltering Rangers. An incisive breakaway from the visitors would halt the County momentum as Jack Carter scored Rangers' third goal to level the game at 3-3. Yet again the onus was on the Ross County lads to respond in the right way and they did just that as striker Stevie May, on off the bench, had the desired impact to put the home side back in front.

Cooper was trying to get a message across to his side to concentrate to try and kill the game off, but Rangers had other ideas. County were caught napping direct from the kick off as Rangers launched forward at pace with Jules Mbia adding another to his earlier strike. Fuming with his sides' lapse in concentration again having worked so hard to get themselves in front on more than one occasion Cooper threw caution to the wind and really went for the victory that he felt his players deserved.

It was a tense final ten minutes with Rangers seemingly happy to have got themselves back on level terms and settling for the draw. It looked for all the world like they would be able to hang on to take a share of the points back to Ibrox, but diminutive Winger Duane Holmes had other ideas and as the clock ticked over into the ninetieth minute he beat his man and shot across the keeper to win the game for Cooper.

It had been a real blood and thunder type of match that had the perfect ending for those of the Ross County persuasion. Players and fans alike were delighted to be sending Johnston home with his tail between his legs and the fact it was a last minute winner in a nine goal thriller made it all the sweeter. Not a bad way to sign off a season and excite the fans for what could be in store for the seasons to come.

Those final few fixtures provided a brief introduction to life in Scottish football for Derek Cooper and it left him with a summer to plan how he could improve on consecutive fifth place finishes for Ross County. With the loss in his opening game in charge against Hearts Cooper had been unable to move the club from the position they had been sat in when he took charge. Motherwell had won the league, claiming their third consecutive title and staking their claim to be viewed as the dominant team in Scottish football ahead of Celtic.

Ross County finished well off the pace of the leaders with fifty-four points to Motherwell's seventy-nine, a big gap and something Cooper would look to drastically reduce with a full season in charge. Finishing fifth did however mean Cooper would once again get to compete in Europe with the club entering the Europa League at the 2nd qualifying round and aiming to make the group stage.

The three games played at the end of the 2021/22 season had also allowed Cooper to assess his squad ahead of the summer and whilst there was some quality he was acutely aware that he would need to add some new blood as well as move on some of the deadwood. Overall Derek Cooper was excited at what lay ahead for him and was fully behind his decision to leave Wales in favour of a new challenge.

There was to be no summer holiday for Cooper, who as well as studying for his National A licence, was holed up at the training ground working his way through a mountain of scout reports and training plans ahead of the upcoming season. The scout reports seemed to be endless having sent his scouts far and wide working them as hard as he could. Every day saw his email inbox clogged with assessments of players from across the world. Cooper was a man looking to make the most of limited resources and capitalise on the oversight of other clubs hoping to discover a real diamond in the rough - someone with potential to be special.

Some reports looked promising with Cooper instructing whichever scout was in the area to take a second look, whilst some were instantly discarded. Once several targets had been established his attention would turn to striking a deal with the player, club or agent to bolster the squad numbers. There were also several outgoing player deals to be negotiated to ensure he boosted the clubs modest transfer and wage budgets helping them to attain his primary targets.

Cooper looked extensively at the free transfer market, having planned to put the majority of the money available into the wage budget, but he was also active in the loan market looking to capitalise there too. There was only one paid transfer that Cooper would complete in the summer window and it was one that he was particularly excited about. Scouting globally and doing due diligence of all countries had paid off and for just £475 and a bag of balls Cooper had secured the signing of a twenty-one year old Costa Rican international named Carlos Salas. The work permit was now being processed and he was hopeful that Salas would be able to join up with his new team mates soon.

Other standout deals that had been completed for the club saw Portugese central midfielder Raffael Guyer join on loan, young centre back Alain Maillard also joined the club on loan, Iuri Nunes and Jose Bessa agreed deals which saw them leave their native Portugal on free transfers with promising Dutchman Rutger Schmidt swapping Celtic for Ross County once his contract with them had expired.

In terms of player departures Cooper was delighted with his dealings brining a much needed £1.6m into the club. Central midfielder Ian McShane left the club in the biggest deal of the summer joining Ipswich Town for £1.4m. Other players to leave the club were all fringe players and included Tim Chow, Jamie Robson and Ross Munro for a combined £234k.

Pre-season was well underway and although Cooper was putting the hours in on the phone to various clubs and agents he made sure he was on top of club affairs, having gained his latest coaching qualification and ensuring his players were working hard in training and friendlies. With Europa League qualifying fixtures coming up very early in their fixture list Cooper was keen to maximise playing time for as many of his lads as possible, the best way to do this was to arrange an in house friendly between the first team and the Under 20's with all first team players being given a run out for either side.

Following the in-house friendly there were two domestic friendly matches against Alloa and Clyde. With just three games under their belts it was onto the first competitive fixtures of the season with Europa League qualifiers against Slovenian side Domzale. A tight 2-1 away win with a Lewis Vaughan brace was followed by a 4-1 dismantling of them at home with Vaughan once again on the score sheet, securing a hat-trick alongside an unfortunate Domzale own goal.

The first Europa League qualifier successfully navigated there was no rest for Cooper and the Ross County squad as they were drawn against Stromsgodset of Norway in a fixture to be played just seven days after the last round. Drawn away from home again for the first leg Ross County comfortably won 4-0 with goals from Vaughan, Holmes, Hodorogea and new boy Schmidt. Cooper was very pleased with an impressive away performance which should now see his side through to the playoff round. The second leg was a formality that Ross County won 1-0, Schmidt impressing again to get his name on the score sheet. Cooper and Ross County were into the playoff and one game away from the group stage.

There was a range of potential opposition in the draw and Derek was hoping the balls would be kind to him. As he watched the draw unfold he was disappointed to see Swansea pulled out of the hat against his side. Any Premier League opposition was bound to be tough with the riches available to the English top flight clubs. Although the draw could have been kinder Derek Cooper still felt his side were more than capable of making it over the final hurdle.

Before that final and all important Europa League qualifier attention would turn to domestic fixtures and a league and cup double against Inverness CT. In a strange twist of fate Ross County would face off against Inverness twice in four days, firstly in the league and then again in the Betfred Cup second round.

In the league fixture away from home Ross County would win 2-0 as holding midfielder Connor McGrandles and central defender Alain Maillard did the work of the attackers to bring home the opening three points. The cup game at home saw a rotated side win by the same score line as Schmidt and right back Paul McNeil found the back of the net to send the Inverness fans home unhappy for the second time within a week.

The final fixture before Europa League action saw Allan Johnston and Rangers roll back into town looking to avenge the 5-4 defeat from last season. Unsurprisingly after last season's goal glut the game had been picked up for television coverage and Cooper wanted to set his stall out and make an impression. It was to be a different game this time out and it took until the thirty-seventh minute for the ball to find the back of either net. Sadly it came from Rangers and their striker Lys Mousset who struck first blood. Ross County came out for the second half and responded magnificently; three goals without reply would see them blow Rangers away in the second half for a comfortable 3-1 victory. Vaughan bagged himself another brace in the match, continuing his fine scoring start to the season with the third an own goal.

An unbeaten start to the season so far was just the sort of form Cooper would have wanted travelling to the Liberty Stadium to take on a Swansea side who had qualified for the Europa League through an impressive EFL Cup win the previous season. Cooper had received a further boost in the lead up to the fixture as his exciting summer signing Carlos Salas had been granted a conditional work permit and was finally able to play a part in his plans for the match. Over 18,000 people were inside the Liberty Stadium for the 19:45 kick off and Derek was relishing being back amongst the European nights.

Derek Coopers new £475 man Carlos Salas had been named in the starting eleven and he would have an instant impact putting Ross County ahead on his debut for the club with just over half an hour on the clock. It was a lead that would last less than ten minutes as Swansea battled back impressively to equalise through their French striker Odsonne Edouard. The half time whistle sounded with both clubs still more than capable of winning the match.

Cooper used the break to encourage his side and tell them that there was more to come, adding that he had faith in each member of the team. Ross County were sent out by a manager who had seen enough to believe that they had a real chance of getting a decent result to take back for the home leg. Sadly the second half performance would fade away as Swansea sensed the fatigue showing in the legs of the Ross County players. Cooper and County made it to the final ten minutes of the match, but couldn't hold out any longer conceding two late goals in the eighty-fourth and eighty-eighth minute, Odsonne Edouard with his second and former Spurs player Joshua Onomah scoring the other. Half time optimism had turned sour for Cooper and he was left wondering what could have been. The away goal was the only consolation for the travelling fans on what had turned into an incredibly frustrating evening. A 2-0 home win would see them qualify and whilst not impossible it would be a very tough ask given the quality of the opposition.

Fixtures would continue to come thick and fast with a league fixture away to Dundee sandwiched between the two Swansea matches. With their European aspirations hanging in the balance Derek Cooper and his staff took the decision to rotate and make the most of the squad in the league, hoping to save some tired legs for Swansea. The game started well for County with Stevie May taking his chance and opening the scoring. Again it was to be a lead that wouldn't last longer than ten minutes with Dundee midfielder Tom Adeyemi getting them back on level terms. It was Groundhog Day for Cooper as he watched his side lose concentration late on and give away a ninety-fourth minute penalty that Brad McKay duly converted to steal all three points. Incredibly frustrated and more than a little angry Cooper was left to lament his side conceding three goals in the final ten minutes of their last two fixtures, both of which ended in defeats. He hoped it was a minor blip rather than the emergence of a self destructive pattern.

Derek Cooper had another four days between fixtures to prepare his men to save their European season. A 2-0 win would see them through on the away goal rule, a 3-1 win would see the tie go to extra time and another set of late goals would see them watching the remainder on the competition on Thursday nights on Channel Five. Swansea were seen as superior opposition and their 3-1 advantage from the first leg only served to strengthen those opinions.

Cooper wasn't intimidated and felt that there was enough quality within his team to get the victory they required. The game kicked off with Cooper and his boys desperate to prove the doubting pundits wrong and make amends for the defensive lapses of the last week.

The match saw Ross County start positively, playing with a real determination to strike first and apply pressure to Swansea. That early pressure would force Swansea centre half Jordi Amat into a mistake that saw him put the ball past his own goalkeeper. Buoyed by the early breakthrough Ross County continued to press Swansea hoping to catch them out again as they recovered from the first goal. But as they often say "you are most vulnerable just after scoring" and the old adage would prove to be correct as Swansea got an away goal of their own just six minutes later to halt the home sides momentum.

Cooper used half time to try and rally his troops again, they were not out of the tie yet, but the next goal was crucial, if Swansea scored a second it would mean Ross County needed to score five. Fortunately the next goal would go the way of the home team with talismanic striker Lewis Vaughan netting to put them 2-1 up on the night, one goal away from extra time and two goals away from an aggregate victory. Cooper would do everything bar throw the kitchen sink at Swansea, pushing forward with reckless abandon, but Swansea's resolve could not be broken and there would be no late goal scored or conceded by Ross County in this match.

They had fallen at the final hurdle and sadly there would be no more European nights for Cooper and County this campaign, but it had collectively strengthened the resolve of everyone at the club to ensure they would qualify automatically through their league position in 2022/23.

Without the European distraction the focus shifted solely to domestic competitions for Derek Cooper. He aimed to reduce the point deficit of last season and guide the club to European qualification through their league finish. Progressing up the league and qualifying consistently for Europe were seen as vital parts of his development plan for the club. It was important to show they were capable of challenging domestically and to continue to do that they would need the finances and reputation that came with competing in European competitions. As the club grew in stature so would their manager, essential for Cooper as he continued his path of personal development in the world of football management.

Following the Swansea result Cooper and Ross County would be faced by a demanding fixture list that would see them take on last year's Champions Motherwell at home and Celtic away within a month. There was also a Betfred Cup quarter final against Aberdeen to be played at the iconic Pittodrie.

From the first game on the 28th of July Ross County would go on a fantastic run of form that would see them go unbeaten in the league for thirteen matches beating Motherwell (2-1) home and (3-0) away and taking all three points in a win at Celtic Park (2-0) along the way. Of those thirteen matches they would notch up nine wins and four draws. A home win to Dundee (5-0) was another highlight as County exacted revenge for the defeat suffered earlier in the season.

This run of good form had catapulted Ross County to the upper echelons of the league table seeing the club competing with the likes of Motherwell and Cetlic. Sadly the only blot on the Cooper copybook during this unbeaten run of league football came in the a disappointing Betfred Cup quarter final defeat. In a tight match that went past the normal ninety minutes Lewis Vaughan put Ross County ahead after one hundred and four minutes of play, but it was not enough as Aberdeen found a way back in and equalised with just 5minutes left to take the game to the lottery of a penalty shootout. It was a lottery Cooper was to lose as Aberdeen progressed to the semi final. The unbeaten league run would then abruptly come to an end in mid December with back to back defeats, away to St. Johnstone (2-1) and home to Celtic (2-0) in a poor team performance. Impressive Scottish full back Alex Kerr, on loan from Motherwell, had been sent off in the St. Johnstone game hampering Ross County as they poured forward in an effort to find an elusive equaliser.

Reacting to back to back defeats was important for Cooper as he looked to maintain the clubs excellent league position. It would be a real pivotal moment for the club as a crisis of confidence could begin to unravel all the good work that the side had been doing on the pitch. Ross County travelled to Pittodre again to face Aberdeen, the scene of their recent penalty defeat in the cup. Cooper was confident his side would get the win and turn their form back around. The training in the week leading up to the game had been excellent and the players knew exactly what was required of them.

Aberdeen had already shown they were no mugs and they did so again scoring the opening goal of the game after eight minutes, the perfect start for the Dandies. Luckily for Cooper and County Portuguese attacker Iuri Nunes had some fire in his belly and really turned up for the occasion. He levelled the tie almost immediately and would go on to get himself a brace with the winner coming on sixty-eight minutes. Nunes was a class above for Derek and put in an exceptional player of the match performance. Aberdeen had been a test of the sides' character and Ross County had passed, but they now needed to put together another run of results to solidify their title intentions. That was what Cooper had his eyes on now; not just improving the clubs fifth placed finish of last season, but seriously challenging Motherwell at the very top of the league. The run from late July to December had shown Cooper that they were more than capable of a shot at the title.

What came after the Aberdeen fixture was another unbeaten run that saw the club go one better than last time winning twelve and drawing two in a fourteen match league sequence that once again sent them to the summit of the Ladbrokes Premiership.

Six straight league wins against Hibernian (3-0), Dunfirmline (3-2), Inverness CT (2-0), Motherwell (2-0) and Rangers both home (2-1) and away (3-0) would come off the back of that victory at Aberdeen. Ross County then suffered a minor blip against Dundee who briefly put the brakes on the winning streak with a 1-1 draw in which Romanian defender Robert Hodorogea was sent off with thirty-six minutes to go and Ross County 1-0 up.

That draw with Dundee on the 4th of February 2023 marked the start of the second half of the fourteen match run with wins against Partick Thistle (4-2), Hearts (1-0), St. Johnstone (1-0), Aberdeen (2-1) and Dunfermline (3-0) with another draw, this time against Celtic (1-1). There was also the obligatory cup defeat amongst the league wins with the club being knocked out of the Scottish Cup in the 4th round by Celtic (1-0).

The second stint of excellent form would come to an end on the 8th of April 2023 as Hibernian would notch up a 1-0 victory at County's Global Energy Stadium. The Hibs defeat came with Ross County amongst the top teams and being touted as potential league winners. It was also the final fixture before the Scottish Ladbrokes Premiership was split into the Championship and Relegation Groups for the final five matches of the season; much like the Welsh league had done in Cooper's time there.

Cooper led Ross County into the Ladbrokes Premiership Championship Group as the surprise league leaders. He now needed his men to replicate the bouncebackability they showed in December and not be effected long term by the Hibernian defeat. Motherwell, Celtic, Rangers, St. Johnstone and Hibernian were the five other clubs making it to the Championship Group with Motherwell and Celtic the only two teams that looked likely to be serious competitors for the league title. A drop off in form now could have disastrous consequences as Ross County would be in direct competition with the teams around them in the table. This was obviously the most crucial part of their league campaign and Cooper was once again hopeful that he had the players within his squad to continue their excellent domestic season.

Derek Cooper's optimism quickly turned to frustration as Ross County went on an unwanted and unlikely run of four straight score draws. There were 2-2 draws against St. Johnstone and Hibernian with 1-1 draws at home to both Celtic and Motherwell. The loss of form couldn't have come at a worse stage of the season and the Motherwell result effectively put the title out of Derek Coopers hands. Ross County would go into the last game of the season against Rangers knowing that they needed to win and hope that Motherwell would drop points in their final league game away to St. Johnstone.

Rangers had already sacked the ex-Ross County manager Allan Johnston early in the New Year so there was to be no repeat of the grudge match that had ended last season. The game would take place the Global Energy Stadium on Sunday the 21st of May 2023 and title rivals Motherwell would be in action simultaneously away to St. Johnstone. Cooper would be in regular contact with one of his coaching staff who would have up to date news on all the action at McDiarmid Park.

The run of form was less than ideal coming into the game, but Cooper knew his side were more than capable of beating anyone in this league on their day. The match kicked off and was a nervy affair given what was at stake for the home side, but just after the thirty minute mark midfielder Rutger Schmidt broke the deadlock to ease the heart rate of the boss. With the news that the Motherwell game was still goalless Coopers men were sitting pretty atop the Ladbrokes Premiership and everything was going to plan.

That changed just five minutes later as previous goal hero Iuri Nunes turned into the pantomime villain and got himself sent off for a ridiculous bad tackle. This really put the cat amongst the pigeons as far as the title race was concerned, but the news from McDiarmid Park was still good and just before half time it got even better as Ewan Gallacher put St. Johnstone one goal ahead. Half time came and went with Cooper encouraging his side to do all they could, whilst singling Nunes out for a dressing down telling him aggressively that he had really let his teammates down.

Ross County appeared for the second half facing forty-five minutes with ten men against a decent Rangers side. Ross County defended valiantly until the seventy-third minute when Lys Mousset found a way to level the game and potentially dash Coopers title hopes. Whilst Rangers were now level, all was not lost as Motherwell were still trailing to St. Johnstone. Derek instructed his men to be a little more adventurous as they needed to take all three points, a draw would just not be enough. This left County susceptible to the Rangers attack and the eighty-third minute saw a double blow that would curtail their title chances.

That man Lys Mousset found his second of the game at Global Energy Stadium whilst veteran Scottish striker and ex-Celtic man Leigh Griffiths pulled Motherwell level at McDiarmid Park. This now meant that even if Cooper could get Ross County back ahead their inferior goal difference would see them lose out to Motherwell. It looked like the title had gotten away from them in the final weeks of the season and the final whistle signalled not just the end of the match, but the end of County's title challenge. Ross County had been in the driving seat going into the final games of the season, but their good run of form couldn't extend to the Championship Group and see them over the line. As Cooper stood to face his side post match he felt a bittersweet mixture of disappointment and pride, but he was grateful for all that they had given him throughout the season.

It was the third season of Cooper's managerial career that saw him fail to win any of the trophies available to him, but he knew he had this squad moving in the right direction and the new season would represent a chance for him to right the wrongs of this campaign. He was right to highlight the positives of such a season, after all he had been manager of the month three times throughout the season. His view was then further vindicated when he was named as the Ladbrokes Scottish Premier League Manager of the Year for 2022/23 as voted for by his fellow league managers.

The class of 2022/23 had played their part in Cooper's success on the pitch with the majority of the squad achieving an average rating of above seven. Lewis Vaughan contributed thirty-six goals in forty-two appearances with his twenty-eight league goals securing him the runner up spot in the race for the golden boot behind Ezequiel Ponce of Motherwell. Wingers Iluri Nunes and on loan Nicolas Fernandez chipped in with eleven goals apiece whilst Derek Cooper got his money's worth out of Carlos Salas who made forty-one appearances in his debut season at the club.

Derek Cooper looked back on the campaign as a missed opportunity of course, but he also realised that he had managed to get some special performances out of his players. Lewis Vaughan had been clinical in front of goal and that, coupled with impressive average ratings across the board, had elevated Ross County to previously unthinkable heights. Their fifth place finish from the season before was a distant memory and Derek Cooper had fulfilled his promise to reduce the points gap by almost eliminating it entirely. That twenty-five point gap had become just three and there really should have been no deficit to mention at all, but it was now time to Derek to go away and reflect. There were big decisions to be made, he needed to ensure that the club continued on the upwards trajectory in the 2023/24 season.

The summer of 2023 would prove to be as full on as the ones that had gone before with Cooper once again holed up at his training ground office laying the groundwork for various new arrivals of both players and staff. He was also concentrating on pressing ahead with attaining the coaching badges that were available to him. Over the summer he had already obtained the Continental C Licence and was now working towards the Continental B Licence the next badge on the coaching ladder.

As the season ended Derek Cooper took the decision to release a few members of his backroom staff, it was not a decision he had taken lightly as he never liked to see anyone lose their jobs, unfortunately it was just the nature of the beast. The head of youth development, first team goalkeeping coach, chief scout and an under 20's coach were all told that their contracts would not be renewed and they were handed their P45's.

Cooper didn't want the club to standstill so he went out to actively recruit new members of staff that would push the boundaries and bring some fresh ideas to the table. Sergi Domenech was someone who fitted that ideal; he had been chief scout at Racing Santander over in Spain for the last couple of years and had a good backroom pedigree having worked at Barcelona previously. He would come in to spearhead Derek Cooper's recruitment team, a team he worked very closely with.

Derek had also been beavering away securing deals for players both arriving and leaving Ross County. Despite finishing as league runners up the Ross County board were only offering another modest transfer and wage budget structure for the summer activity. The club would need to qualify for the UEFA Champions League group stage to really benefit financially from their second place finish. Without that Cooper would be in much the same position as last summer, trying to cash in where possible and work his magic with loans and free transfers.

Cooper had already signed Raffael Guyer who had been on loan at the club last season on a pre-contract deal that would see him join permanently on the 1st of July. Talks with Alex Kerr, another player who had been on loan last season, were ongoing as his Motherwell contract was due to expire at the end of June and Cooper had been impressed by the young Scottish full back. Alan Maillard was yet another loanee to impress at the club last season and Derek had been in touch with his parent club, Lorient, to try and extend that loan, but it was looking like a lost cause with them keen to integrate him into their own first team setup. All of this work was running alongside the hectic pre-season schedule Derek Cooper had lined up in an effort to get new signings to adapt to their new teammates and the sides' way of playing.

Over a period of a month from the end of June to the end of July Cooper arranged ten pre-season fixtures against a range of opponents. Ross County started their run of friendlies with an in house match against the Under 20's before taking on a broad spectrum of teams that included Liverpool, Dinamo, Sampdoria, Alloa, Dumbarton and Northampton. Over the ten fixtures Ross County would win eight, draw one and lose one, with the only defeat coming against the boyhood club of Derek Cooper and arguably their toughest opponents, Liverpool. It had been a busy yet productive month as his squad got plenty of minutes out on the pitch learning and adapting to one another which was the perfect way to introduce several new players to the squad dynamic.

Sadly Cooper and Ross County were dealt a blow pre-season when Alex Kerr opted to sign for Arsenal instead, despite Cooper offering a very handsome long term contract at the club. Alan Maillard would also not be returning to the Global Energy Stadium for another loan spell as Lorient stubbornly refused to let him rejoin for another season.

Despite those two deals not coming to fruition it was still a window that saw Cooper bring in reinforcements that would not only improve the quality of the squad for the here and now, but would also put them in good stead for the years to come with some decent young Northern Irish players arriving later in the window signed to lengthy deals with the club. Raffael Guyer had now joined up with the squad as well as another two fellow Portuguese players on free transfers. Luis Santos was a promising defensive midfielder and Armande Certoux was a young striker who joined the club from Nacional de Madeira.

The loan market had also been productive once again and saw an exciting arrival in the form of Belgian central midfielder Phelippe Petit from Standard and a Romanian right back by the name of Marian Patrascu, both of whom would play an active role in the first team squad. All in all Cooper would bring fifteen new players into the club spending less than £30k in the process, quite unbelievable business for the club all things considered.

To ensure the club was able to cover the cost of the new arrivals and their contracts Cooper would look to offload players where possible, which was tough as he didn't want to make a habit of selling off his best assets. After an impressive showing in their league campaign there was no shortage of suitors for some of his best players with Connor McGrandles and Lewis Vaughan attracting the attention of both Rangers and Celtic.

It was American winger Duane Holmes who Cooper would decide to cash in on amid interest from Spanish side Alaves. Holmes had been a good player for Ross County, but he was a player unlikely to improve any further and with players coming through to challenge him regularly the decision was made to accept the £1.8m offer that was on the table. It was well above his £600k valuation and Ross County were unlikely to get a better offer anytime soon. The money would be a welcome boost to club finances and would only see them lose someone who was now a squad player at best.

Stevie May and Andrea De Vito were players who were the wrong side of thirty, on sizable wages for their diminished roles and were both released at the end of their contract. Back up central midfielder George Byers was allowed to join Partick Thistle for £250k as he searched for regular first team football. It was another summer that saw Cooper bring in much more money than he had spent, but he was happy with all additions made whilst hanging onto the core of his squad from last season.

With pre-season out of the way it was down to the serious business of trying to make it through the qualifying rounds of the Champions League. Ross County had been handed a very tough best placed qualifier round three tie against Sporting Lisbon - a side that traditionally made it through to the group stage. If Ross County could make it past the Portuguese side there would be a playoff round before ensuring they were in the pot for the group stage - it was going to be a tough ask. Derek and his side had been drawn away for the first leg and travelled to Lisbon as the overwhelming underdogs according to the bookmakers.

Early season form had been good, Cooper felt he had a better squad than last season and he was more determined than ever to secure Champions League football for Ross County Football Club. Derek would go with his now preferred formation using a holding midfielder and wingers behind a lone striker, it was a system that suited his players and had worked well in the league last season. Ross County would be looking to keep it tight at the back and hope to nick a Vaughan goal, steal the victory and gain an advantageous away goal.

The game kicked off starting as the cautious, cagey affair that Cooper had expected. Lisbon proved tough to break down and posed a real threat going forward, but Ross County were showing themselves to be just as stubborn at the back . Half time came and went without anything of note and Cooper could sense the away victory slowly ebbing away from them as Sporting continued to defend resolutely. The full time whistle would sound at Estadio Jose Alvalade Seculo XXI with neither team able to break the deadlock in a rather dull 0-0. Cooper saw it as a reasonable result, it was certainly better than a defeat, but the lack of an away goal was frustrating and meant that it was advantage Sporting as a score draw would now be all they needed to progress.

It was back to Scotland and the Global Energy Stadium for their league opener against Rangers, which strangely was a repeat of the final fixture of last season. Whilst Cooper and County would avoid a repeat of the 2-1 home defeat suffered that time out they once again failed to find the net in another 0-0 bore draw which saw County fail to score in back to back games for the first time since Cooper took charge in 2022. It was a poor start to their league campaign and less than ideal preparation for an important second leg in the Champions League. A comfortable home win would have been preferable, but sadly it wasn't to be and Derek Cooper needed to rally the troops for the visit of Sporting Lisbon in three days time.

Those three days passed without any injuries and Cooper was pleased to have a full complement of players available for such an important game. Lisbon rolled into town looking to spoil the party, but could only manage twenty-six minutes of play before Lewis Vaughan was able to rediscover his goal scoring touch and settle the nerves of the home crowd. The game was finely balanced and Cooper was acutely aware that a one goal advantage would not be enough with the away goal threat looming over his Ross County side.

During half time Cooper ensured his side that they were doing well and passionately told them that there was much more to come from them, this game was theirs to win if they wanted it. Sporting needed to take the game to Ross County, but every time they tried they were rebuffed by a defence that had kept consecutive clean sheets. Cooper needed that resolve to last and make it three clean sheets from as many matches, but it wasn't to be and with sixty-seven minutes gone a former Celtic loanee, Robim Schaufelberger, equalised. Advantage Sporting.

Cooper needed to act and he tried pushing more men forward, asking his full backs to attack more in an attempt to overwhelm an opposition who had the result they needed. Sporting were reluctant to commit too many men forward knowing that the away goal would be enough to see them through. They soaked up the Ross County pressure for the remainder of the match as Cooper paced his technical area willing his side to grab that late goal that would see them over the line. It wasn't to be and Lisbon held on for the 1-1 draw and an away goal victory that saw them progress into the next round. Ross County were out of the competition before it had even really begun.

This time Cooper was aware that failure to progress in the Champions League would mean a second crack at European qualification through the Europa League, although unlike his playoff defeat with TNS, the loss to Sporting would require one last qualification match before the group stage. Ross County had been drawn against Serbian side Partizan and Cooper would face them away from home first in just under two weeks time.

Before venturing back into Europe Derek needed to get a win under their belts in the league if they were to assert themselves as serious title contenders. St. Johnstone away were up next and shocked County with a humbling 3-0 defeat that yet again saw Ross County fail to score. A win away to Alloa (2-0) followed in a break from league football with a Betfred Cup 2nd round match. Young Portuguese striker Armand Certoux took his chance in the rotated team to score a brace that would put him in contention for a starting spot in the following league fixture at home to Partick Thistle. Derek Cooper made the bold decision to stick with several of the players who had taken their opportunity in the cup match and he was duly rewarded by wingers Nicolas Fernandez and Nemanja Tomasevic who scored the goals in a 3-0 home win to record the first three points of the season.

The match in Belgrade was up next and Cooper rotated some of his usual starting eleven back into his side to face Partizan. Lewis Vaughan returned up top replacing Certoux, but Tomasevic had found some form out on the left wing and he would retain his place having scored in the Partick Thistle game. Both players would repay the faith shown in them with goals in a comprehensive 3-0 away win for Ross County. Lewis Vaughan opened the scoring just before the half hour mark before Tomasevic netted twice in two minutes of the second half to kill the game off and secure the away win. Cooper was content that Europa League qualification should now be a formality with a three goal advantage to take into the home leg.

Before the visit of Partizan there was a trip to title rivals Motherwell who had just about hung onto their crown last season. It was to be a bad afternoon for Cooper as his sides stuttering league form continued. Alistair Thorpe-Read put Motherwell ahead and they secured a second goal late on when Ezequiel Ponce scored in the eighty-fifth minute. In truth Ross County had been poor, but 2-0 did slightly flatter Motherwell who scored with their only real chances in the match. League form was now a real concern for Cooper and although he was keen to extend their stay in Europe he didn't want it to come at the detriment of their league results. The league was their bread and butter and everyone had worked so hard to cut the points deficit and move the team up the table to their impressive second place finish last campaign. Ross County would need to turn their fortunes around quickly in order to save their domestic season.

The second leg of the Europa League playoff was soon upon Cooper and he was grateful that they had managed to get most of the job done in Belgrade. A Lewis Vaughan penalty was enough to win the home leg and finish the job off for Cooper and his team. Partizan had proved to be a little easier than many expected, failing to score and conceding four goals against a County side that had hardly been at their best so far this season. The 4-0 aggregate win put Ross County through to the Europa League group stage and Cooper would make the journey to be present for the draw. He was in the audience to see Ross County drawn in Group F alongside FC Kobenhavn of Denmark, Basaksehir of Turkey and Russia's Spartak Moscow. It was a group that looked winnable in the eyes of Cooper and he returned to Scotland pleased with the outcome.

League form thus far had been patchy at best and Cooper wanted to rediscover those winning streaks that had served them so well last year, a thirteen or fouteen match unbeaten run now would force the other clubs with title ambitions to keep pace with them. Hearts at home and Celtic away were the league games awaiting Cooper as they looked to bounce back from the disappointing defeat against Motherwell in their last league fixture. An Iuri Nunes brace with goals in the fiftieth and fifty-eighth minutes would be enough to see of a brave Hearts side who grabbed one back through Ryan Hardie. Celtic were up next and a tough trip to Celtic Park would bring a third goal in two games for Nunes and take maximum points (1-0) in front of a 58,000 strong home crowd. Six points from those two league matches was just what Cooper had wanted and he hoped to carry that form into the opening Europa League Group F fixture at home to Basaksehir.

The Turkish side arrived at Global Energy Stadium having been largely written off by many fans and pundits with Ross County expected to pick up the win and start well in the group. Coopers side started strongly and looked too much for Basaksehir from the off. Lewis Vaughan would put County ahead early doors, but Coopers men failed to capitalise on their early dominance. That fifth minute goal seemed like a distant memory by the time Ghanaian John Owusu-Ansah levelled ten minutes before half time.

Cooper wasn't too troubled by the first half performance, his side were by far the better team and he used the break to assure them they were doing well and the result would come if they continued to work hard. Coopers half time words had missed the mark and his side looked complacent in the early stages of the second half. Their complacency was duly punished in the fifty-sixth minute as Yusuf Yazici scored the second goal for the visitors as they proved to be much stiffer opposition than many had given them credit for. Ross County struggled to find their first half rhythm despite playing the last twenty minutes against ten men with Ilie dismissed for Basaksehir. What had looked like a potential dream start in the group for Ross County had turned into a nightmare. Winning home fixtures was vital if you wanted to progress in European competitions and their most recent defeat had left Cooper immensely frustrated.

Attention turned back to the Ladborkes Premiership and three domestic fixtures before returning to European action. First up was the visit of Falkirk, another winnable home match for Cooper's side. They proved to be more resilient than expected and only a late Tomasevic goal spared Ross County blushes in a 1-1 draw . The draw wasn't disastrous as at this stage with no side having made an obvious claim for the title, but it was important for Ross County to get that winning mentality back.

Rangers were in town for the next league fixture which was always a difficult match. An impressive display from on loan Phelippe Petit was capped off by an eighty-fourth minute winner, nicking the points for County in a 2-1 victory. The third and final league fixture in this break from European football saw Cooper and Ross County travel to take on Aberdeen at Pittodrie. George Hirst put Aberdeen ahead before the break and it was Tomasevic to the rescue again scoring the leveller early in the second half. Ross County were unable to continue their momentum in the match and find the winner they had been pushing for as the game finished 1-1.

Denmark and FC Kobenhavn were next on the agenda for Derek Cooper and his side arrived in the Danish capital hoping to show what they were really capable of on the European stage. The Basaksehir defeat was very much on the players minds and they wanted to give a better account of themselves in this match. There was a crowd of 30,000 in Telia Parken with a strong away contingent present to witness Ross County fail to get going in a game that was never out of Kobenhavn's control. Goals from Benjamin Verbic and Andreas Cornelius either side of half time were enough to seal a 2-0 victory and condemn Ross County to bottom spot after gameweek two.

The defeat hurt Cooper as he remained desperate to make his mark in a European competition, proving that he was becoming a manager capable of competing on the bigger stages. Having recently acquired the Continental B licence he felt his off field development was progressing well and he wanted to translate that success in a way that would see potential suitors sit up and take note.

Putting European disappointment behind him was becoming something of a habit for Cooper and early October saw Ross County travel to Dundee looking to do just that. Striker James Vincent came up big for Dundee and treated the home fans to a brace at Den Park in yet another poor Ross County performance. A 2-0 loss was far from the result Cooper had hoped for and felt he needed to ensure his side stayed in contention at the top. The result was tougher to take as his side now faced nearly a fortnight to stew on the result over the international break.

Derek Cooper wasn't a fan of these international breaks when in good form, but when playing badly it allows that negativity to linger and fester, not good when you want to be challenging at the top end of the table. Cooper decided that it was an opportune time to arrange a friendly against weaker opposition as a way to boost confidence. With several players away on international duty the game against East Fife also allowed Derek to have a look at some of the fringe players and get some minutes under their belts. Nemanja Tomasevic and striker Armand Certoux notched in a routine 2-0 victory that delivered the win Cooper required.

Lewis Vaughan returned from the break a fully fledged Scotland international and celebrated by bagging an impressive hat-trick in a win over Dunfermline (4-0) with on loan winger Nicolas Fernandez adding the other. The unusually timed friendly seemed to have been just what the side had needed and Cooper hoped the boost in morale and confidence would last long enough to see them bag a European victory against Spartak Moscow midweek.

Cooper went with an unchanged side despite the quick turnaround and his decision paid dividends as both Vaughan and Fernandez rewarded him by finding the net again in a 3-0 victory. Vaughan added two more goals to his hat-trick at the weekend as Spartak Moscow failed to cope with the in-form front man. Cooper now had that European victory he had been craving and it kept Ross County's qualification hopes alive.

Three games in ten days would have been too much for the same starting eleven players to cope with so the Betfred Cup semi final match against Aberdeen saw Cooper test the depth of his squad. Hampden Park was the venue for the game which could see Cooper potentially make the first cup final of his tenure at the club. Aberdeen had knocked Ross County out of this competition at an earlier stage last season and it provided the opportunity for Cooper to make amends and exact his revenge. Dutch midfielder Mohammed Mallahi made the most of a rare start for Ross County and got his name on the score sheet after twenty-four minutes with Cooper's side firmly in control. Lewis Vaughan would make an appearance off the bench and continue his hot streak in front of goal adding a second in the eightieth minute. As the full time whistle sounded Cooper was mobbed by his backroom staff and players as they celebrated making the final and a chance of winning some silverware come the 3rd of December.

European and domestic cup fixtures out of the way it was time for a win in the league. It came against Rangers (2-0) at Ibrox, a tough fixture, but one that had seen Cooper win more times than he had lost. Lewis Vaughan bagged another brace with one goal either side of half time to win the game for Ross County and send them to the top of the league for the first time that season.

It had been a brief, but fruitful return to league action ahead of the long trip to Moscow for gameweek four of the Europa League. Moscow would be an arduous trip at a time that had seen Ross County competing with a congested fixture list. The weather in early November saw Derek Cooper wrap up warm in an attempt to beat the cold and ignite a performance from his side. A tired looking County never managed to get going in a poor game that saw an early Spartak penalty converted to put them ahead before Vaughan scored again to make it 1-1 and nine goals in five matches to secure a point in what had been a tough match.

Returning from Moscow in the early hours of Friday morning was far from ideal preparation for a Sunday afternoon fixture against Partick Thistle and it showed in a game that petered out to a very dull and uninspiring 0-0. Another international break was just what Cooper needed this time around as it afforded him the chance to rest his flagging squad and recharge the batteries for the fixtures to come.

Fully rested and recharged Ross County faced St. Johnstone at home in late November looking to stay amongst it at the top of the league table. Lewis Vaughan and Iuri Nunes were both at the double for Cooper again in a comfortable and convincing 4-0 win. Cooper and Ross County once again had little to no time to rest before jetting off to Turkey. Everyone at the club was keen to avenge the home defeat back in gameweek one.

The Turkey trip couldn't have come at a worse time for Cooper with the Betfred Cup final against Celtic scheduled for just three days after the Basaksehir fixture. Cooper was desperate to progress in Europe as well as win his first trophy with the club and to do both would require careful and delicate balancing of his squad to ensure he got the most out of them for both matches. Basaksehir were up first and Cooper went with a strong eleven in the hope they would get the win. Goals from Hodorogea and Connor McGrandles either side of the interval were enough to secure the 2-0 win and get the revenge the fans wanted.

It was a mad dash back to Scotland for the Betfred Cup final at Hampden Park against a Celtic side that were slightly off the pace set by Ross County in the league. Derek was suited and booted for the occasion and hoping that his side could get the second win he wanted despite working against a tough schedule and player fatigue.

A crowd of nearly 52,000 turned out for the occasion and Celtic put on a first half performance worthy of a cup final. Ryan Christie fired them ahead in the opening five minutes before on loan Spaniard Jose Vicente bagged himself two goals before half time. 3-0 Down Ross County had been completely blown away by a Celtic side that had benefitted from a more forgiving fixture schedule.

Cooper tried to lift his players off the dressing room floor and he sent them back out to try and get themselves back in the game as a matter of pride if nothing else. Lewis Vaughan managed to pull one back in the sixty-ninth minute, but Ross County simply didn't have enough left in the tank and Celtic never looked in any real danger of losing their lead. It finished 3-1 and Derek Cooper would collect his runner up medal questioning whether he made the right decision by playing such a strong side in the midweek fixture in Turkey.

Derek Cooper wouldn't have long to ponder his regrets as it was straight back to league action on the Wednesday night away to Hibernian. With the extra couple of days to get the travelling out of their legs Ross County, and Lewis Vaughan in particular, were back on it at Easter Road. A 3-0 win and another hat-trick for Vaughan was the best way to banish the cup final demons. Hearts at Tynecastle followed the Hibs game and a mad twelve minutes saw three goals scored in favour of the home side with Ross County losing 2-1. Another European night was just around the corner and it would be a decisive fixture with qualification hanging in the balance.

FC Kobenhavn were to be the next and potential final visitors of this seasons Europa League campaign. They arrived in town unable to progress from the group themselves and were playing purely for pride. Ross County could still qualify, but they would need all three points to do so. Cooper was hopeful he would be able to get the result, they had been beaten in Copenhagen, but at home and with qualification at stake Cooper felt victory was not beyond his side. Unfortunately for Derek Cooper and Ross County they were unable to break the resistance of Kobenhavn and the game slipped away from them in a poor 0-0.

The draw was not enough for Ross County and their Europa League campaign was now over having finished third in the group, two points behind both Spartak Moscow and Basaksekir. Cooper and County had not disgraced themselves although reaching the knockout rounds had been his personal goal the board had been happy to see the club compete in the group stage and were happy with the clubs overall performance.

Out of Europe Ross County would have a lengthy run of League fixtures before a Scottish Cup match at the end of January. The six weeks of league action was being targeted by Derek as the time to really straighten out their league form and cement their place at the top of the table. It was possible that Europe had become a distraction that had been hampering their Ladbrokes Premiership form. The run of eight games leading into the Scottish Cup fourth round tie saw them take on Motherwell, Celtic, Rangers and Aberdeen in what could be a season defining run of fixtures.

Of those eight games Cooper and County won five, drew two and lost just the once. They started with another draw against Falkirk (1-1) before back to back home wins against Motherwell (1-0) and Celtic (2-1). A ninety-third minute own goal in the Motherwell game and an Armande Certoux brace against Celtic had seen Cooper beat his closest title competitors to solidify their position at the top. A Boxing Day trip to Aberdeen ended in a 3-0 defeat that put the dampeners on the festive spirit, but the side bounced back and saw in the New Year with four matches unbeaten drawing to Dundee (0-0) and beating Dunfermline (2-1), Hibernian (4-0) and Rangers (1-0).

Derek Cooper was back in his office celebrating taking all three points at home to Rangers with members of his backroom staff when he received an unexpected phone call from his agent. A member of the board from a historic European club had been in touch to sound out Cooper's interest in moving on from Ross County. The club in question had just sacked their manager and were looking to take the club back to its footballing roots with a young manager who would look to play football the right way. Derek Coopers name had been mentioned and he was rumoured to be on the shortlist of managers that they were hoping to speak with regarding the vacancy. Cooper listened intently and told his representative he would sleep on the idea and call him in the morning.

Derek Cooper didn't leave the office until the sun was almost up and he was unable to sleep when he did finally make it to bed. His mind was going a million miles an hour with question after question. Did he want to leave Ross County when he could potentially win them their first league title? Would his tenure be seen as a failure if he left without winning a single trophy? Was he ready to move abroad and start over again? Could he afford to pass up on the opportunity to manage at such a reputable club? Would he get another chance at such an illustrious club? These were all questions that needed answering and come midday he had made up his mind. Cooper called his agent back, instructing him that he would like to speak with the club in question and see what they had to say, there was no harm in that.

Cooper attended a meeting the very next day at a neutral location and he put forward his ideas for the club with a heavy emphasis on his attacking brand of football and preference for younger players. These were two philosophies that sat well with the board and they were keen to see their club return to that way of working. It had been a productive meeting for both parties and Cooper seemed to have been received in a positive manner. Derek was pleased with how it had gone from his point of view, satisfied that he had stuck to his footballing beliefs and given a good account of Derek Cooper the person.

The outcome of the meeting was shelved upon his return to Scotland and he navigated his side through an easy Scottish Cup 4th round tie away to minnows Stirling Uni. Armande Certoux helped himself to four goals with an own goal and a Philippe Petit strike completing the 6-0 rout.

The phone call came on the 30th of January. Cooper was sat at home when his agent delivered the news. It had been decided that Derek Cooper was the manager they wanted. Derek accepted the job offer on the spot, told his agent to sort the necessary paperwork and called the chairman of Ross County immediately. They were sad to hear he would be leaving, but they were also hugely thankful for all his hard work and understood the pull of his new employers, Ross County would not stand in his way or make it difficult for him. Cooper had agonised over the decision, but ultimately decided that it would be a mistake to pass and hope that another opportunity came along further down the line.

A solid contract offer was with him by six in the morning the next day and Cooper was already in his office clearing his desk down ready for the next man in charge at Ross County. The move saw Cooper pocket a significant pay rise and travel across the North Sea to take up his first coaching role outside of the British Isles. He said his goodbyes to both players and staff feeling sadder than he had expected to be at leaving them behind. He felt confident he would be remembered for doing a good job at Ross County and he left the club in with a real chance of winning their first Scottish Premier League title.

It had been decided that Fitness Coach Xavier Bernain would be stepping in to take over from Derek Cooper in a caretaker manager role until at least the end of the season, they would decide from there who they wanted to succeed the thirty-five year old Englishman. It was time now for Cooper to head off for pastures new, but he would always look back fondly on his time in Scotland and considered himself a Ross County fan, he would always keep an eye out for their results as he bedded into the next chapter of his career.

CHAPTER FIVE.

Derek Cooper was the man Ajax had chosen to replace the outgoing Thomas Letsch who had only managed one league title in just over three years with the club. Cooper had been tasked with ushering in a new generation of young footballing talent with Ajax looking to revert to the ethos that had seen them become an iconic club in European and world football. The history of the club and all that it symbolised was the main attraction for Cooper who hoped to emulate the managers of yesteryear and develop a side full of technically gifted players who would go on to play at the very highest level. Looking to recruit talented youngsters and promote from within was how Cooper liked to work and it was a methodology that struck a chord with the chairman during his interview leaving an excellent impression and landing him the job.

Ajax had been a side in decline in recent years and had won just one Eredivisie title in their last five seasons. A record deemed not good enough for arguably the biggest club in Dutch football. They needed a return to the top and Cooper was confident he could be the man to do just that.

Derek Cooper had arrived in Amsterdam at an awkward time with the transfer window about to slam shut. It was deadline day across Europe and Cooper had his work cut out for the remainder of January 31st 2024. There was a small budget available to him, but the clock was working against him and his recruitment team as they would struggle to garner enough information on any potential signings. He was working with unfamiliar scouts against the clock which would force him to lean heavily on them for any information on the players available to them. Cooper asked for a detailed squad report from his coaching staff and locked himself in his new office to work out what areas needed improvement before time ran out.

Having quickly looked at and analysed his playing staff across the senior, reserve and U19 squads Cooper noticed a lack of depth in wide areas as well as in the middle of the park. With time running out Derek was forced to make snap judgements based on the opinions of others, which wasn't ideal for your first few hours in a new job.

There were countless scouting reports emailed over to him, but there were very few that seemed like real possibilities. There was one standout player, a young Brazilian winger who could operate off either flank and although a risk, the £2m compensation he would cost could well be worth it.

Derek pulled the trigger and Quissama signed from Fluimenese with only minutes left in the transfer window. The only other deal finalised saw Cooper agree a loan deal for right back Zoran Lukic of Borussia Dortmund to come and gain some first team experience at the club. Only time would tell if Coopers £2million gamble would pay off for the club.

Derek Cooper's first game in charge was against Heracles Almelo five days into his tenure and he got to soak up the Amsterdeam ArenA atmosphere for the first time in a 2-0 debut win. Six foot five Argentinean striker Matias Crosa particularly impressed and got himself on the scoresheet alongside Brazilian winger Yan.

Matters on the pitch were off to a good start and Cooper was still working hard behind the scenes getting his usual support network up to the standard he required. By the time the Heracles match had kicked off Cooper had added no fewer than thirteen members of staff across a variety of positions. Derek had revisited Ross County to pluck four of his trusted former scouts as well as adding international experience with former elite players Zlatan Ibrahimovic and Giorgio Chiellini in coaching roles with the U19's.

The next month saw the games come thick and fast as Cooper found himself thrown in at the deep end looking to gain as many points as possible and climb up the league. The five match run would start with a draw at FC Utrecht (2-2) before back to back wins at home to Willem II (3-0) and away to Cambuur (2-0), but the good results would not last and Ajax would suffer a drop off that would bring two defeats against teams they really should have beaten. PEC Zwolle would inflict a home defeat (2-1) and FC Twente would record a win (2-0) against Cooper's side to take the shine off what had been an excellent start to life in Holland.

The real shining light in that opening month of fixtures had been the outstanding performances of front man Matias Crosa who made a real impression and scored eight of the clubs nine goals in the six matches since Cooper arrived including a hat-trick in the Willem II victory.

Ajax and Cooper wanted to bounce back in the three matches before the international break at the end of March. PSV were up first and represented another club who found themselves in a league position unfamiliar for a club of their stature. Derek Cooper added to their misery with a 3-1 home victory which was particularly pleasing as standout players from the U19's Tim de Lange and Michael Roodenburg joined Crosa on the score sheet.

Two very disappointing draws would follow away to league rivals N.E.C (1-1) and at home to VVV Venlo (0-0).Those two draws had introduced a small amount of negativity into the team dynamic and Cooper felt the international break would provide him with the chance to host two confidence building friendlies that would hopefully serve the players well going into the final five league fixtures.

Lower league Dutch outfits Aalsmeer and DESK were both hit for seven by Ajax in the friendly fixtures that served their purpose. Player's young and old got lots of minutes to boost morale and confidence. Veteran midfielder Jon Obi Mikel managed a goal and the young Brazilian Quissama got a brace for himself in the first fixture.

When interviewed for the Ajax job Derek Cooper had promised the board he could achieve Champions League qualification, but in truth that was always going to be a very big ask and going into the final fixtures of the 2023/24 season qualification was looking unlikely.

Only the top side would be guaranteed qualification with the runners up being entered into the best placed third qualifying round. Cooper took the job hoping he would be able to grab enough results to break the top two, but sadly the number of dropped points meant all his hopes were likely resting on now qualifying for the Europa League. To manage that and avoid a European playoff match against another Eredivisie side Cooper would need to ensure a third place finish. If Derek failed to secure European football of any sort going into the 2024/25 season he may well find himself out of work with the sack a real concern.

Determined to avoid his Ajax tenure being deemed a total failure Cooper focused on the final five matches and set his side the task of taking maximum points. The run in was relatively kind on paper with Herenveen their only opponents in the top half of the table. Vitesse, De Graafschap, ADO Den Haag and FC Groningen were all sides that were marooned in the mid to lower half of the table and were more than beatable.

De Graafschap were up first and Ajax rolled into town to blow away the opposition in a 4-1 victory that got them off to the best possible start. Vitesse at home was up next and another solid performance saw Ajax pick up all three points with a 3-1 win. Two victories and six points from a possible six was exactly the form Cooper was after.

Game three was away at Groningen and all of Derek Coopers strikers got themselves on the score sheet leading Ajax to a 3-0 victory. Ajax went into the Herenveen match, the fourth game of the run in knowing that only a win would leave them with any faint hopes of Champions League qualification. Unfortunately the Herenveen match signalled the end of the winning streak with a 2-1 defeat for Cooper's men. The win for Herenveen cemented their place as runners up and secured them a chance to play in the Champions League. Derek Cooper went into the final game of 2023/24 needing a win to beat off the challenge from NEC Nimjen who were mounting a surprise challenge for third spot.

ADO Den Haag were the side standing between Cooper and potential Europa League qualification. Ajax put in an excellent performance with a home win (4-0) that saw both Crosa and fellow striker Filip Zuberski bag a brace each. Whilst Ajax had seemed to thrive under the pressure it was not the same for league rivals NEC who succumbed to a 2-1 defeat at Willem II. Cooper and Ajax had secured third spot in the Eredivisie and whilst they didn't manage the full five wins from their final games four victories had ultimately been enough.

Feyenoord finished the season as Eredivisie champions on eighty-five points ahead of Herenveen, their closest challengers, on seventy-three points before Coopers Ajax in third on sixty-four points. Coopers priority for his first full season in charge was to change the league dynamic and make sure that he was the manager of the side coming out on top. Ajax were simply too big a club to be playing catch up and he wanted to put them back where they belonged as the number one side in Holland.

Cooper had some players at the club that were more than capable, but the squad faced a massive overhaul in the summer with Derek keen to bring in reinforcements where required whilst moving on some of the older players on larger contracts. Twenty-one points was a big gap to bridge, but Cooper had achieved a similar feat with just one transfer windows work whilst at Ross County and he had confidence in his ability to do so again.

Cooper trusted in his recruitment team and their judgement identifying potential signings and he was working hard on an exciting new tactic that would seem him really take the game to the opposition. 2024/25 was shaping up to be a big season for both Derek Cooper and Ajax Football Club.

Away from Ajax Derek Cooper had been keeping a close eye on his old side Ross County who he had left top of the Ladbrokes Premiership in January. He had kept in contact with his former fitness coach Xavier Bernain who had been given the job permanently following a brief stint as caretaker manager. Bernain had justified the board's decision as he lost just four times in nineteen matches leading Ross County to a momentous league and cup double.

Cooper was over the moon to see Ross County building on the foundations that he had laid and he took great satisfaction in their league and cup victories knowing that he had played a vital part in them both, despite there being no official recognition of his contribution recorded.

Derek Cooper had big plans for Ajax in the upcoming 2024/25 season. He had planned the busiest pre-season to date and would be working his players hard to ensure the best possible start when competitive football came around. As always he would be working tirelessly behind the scenes throughout the summer to make the most of the resources at his disposal with both the playing and non-playing staff.

Scouts had been deployed worldwide with an intense focus on the South American market in particular. The work permit regulations in Holland were a lot less stringent than he had been used to in the UK and Cooper felt he could find better value for money down in that part of the world. Colombia in particular was a nation that interested Derek and his recruitment team and they were exploring several possibilities there. That was not to say Derek Cooper would neglect the markets that had served him so well previously and he would still look throughout Europe having already agreed several promising pre-contract agreements since his tenure had begun in January.

The big backroom changes of the summer would include a new right hand man for Derek Cooper, whilst he had shared a good working relationship with the outgoing Joop van der Lei Derek felt it was best for all parties if his contract was not renewed with the club. After careful consideration Derek Cooper decided that Jon Andoni Goikoetxea of Spanish side Levante was the man he wanted to work with and struck the deal to bring him on board. Other staff members recruited that summer included a new head physio, goalkeeping coach, head of sports science and a chief data analyst to bolster an already impressive set up.

Players would be arriving at the club throughout a rigorous pre-season fixture list that saw eleven games played in total. Ajax U19's were the first up in a behind closed doors match that afforded minutes to as many players as possible before competing in a testing friendly competition named the Amsterdam Cup against Arsenal, PSG and Man City.

Following the Amsterdam Cup were fixtures against three of Derek Coopers former clubs; TNS, Maidenhead and Ross County as well as matches against a variety of other opponents. Red Bull Leipzig and Borussia Dortmund of Germany would provide the tougher matches with games against Carlisle and Blackburn designed to boost confidence and tactical familiarity. By now Cooper was playing his new attacking 4-2-4 style formation making the most of the attacking options available to him both through the middle and in the wide areas.

Pre-season proved to be an immensely successful period for Ajax and Cooper as his side went unbeaten in all eleven matches with numerous new signings settling in very well. Colombian Striker Yamilson Ramos had signed for an initial £9m (America (MEX)) and was immediately amongst the goals. Young German central midfielder Tim Erwig-Druppel (Bayern Munich) was technically sound, slotting into the middle of the park and justifying his £9.5m price tag. Portuguese goalkeeper Hernani Goncalves was looking like a real gem having joined the club on a free transfer from Maritimo in Portugal. Brazilian centre back Wesley had signed for £7.5m (PON) and Turkish full back Gokhan Oz signed from Borussia Dortmund for £8.5m.

Cooper had also moved to secure the signatures of some of world footballs hottest young stars and he was particularly excited by Colombian Michael Perez who he signed from Millonarios in a £1.1m deal and a bargain £575k deal for Luka Kozina, a pacey Polish winger with bags of potential that he had spotted playing for Hadjuk.

With so many players joining the club Derek Cooper was a busy man balancing the books and offsetting the expenditure with big sales. Some transfers he was happy to get over the line, but one deal in particular was very hard for him to take. The star man of his early days in Amsterdam had been the Argentinian striker Matias Crosa and Cooper had been keen to reward his star man with a bumper new deal, removing a £12.75m release clause in the process. Sadly Crosa had been unhappy that the club weren't able to offer him Champions League football and was stalling on signing any sort of new deal. The news went public and Villareal swooped in offering to pay the required amount to trigger his release clause. Cooper continued to try and offer Crosa improved terms, but the players mind had been made up and Derek was powerless to stop him leaving the club.

Other players to leave the club during pre-season included Jon Obi Mikel who retired and ex-Arsenal man Joel Campbell, who was very much in the twilight of his career, released on a free transfer.

Before the start of the Eredivisie season Cooper had offloaded a number of players for decent money including defensive midfielder Aschraf El Mahdioui to Watford for £8.75m, central midfielder van den Boomen to Everton for £12.5m and centre back Ramy Bensabaini to Burnely for £6.5m. Cooper was able to utilise the wealth of the English clubs to balance the books and cover some of the cost of his summer investments.

By the time Ajax played their final pre-season match away to Maidenhead a brave move by Cooper had seen Brazilian left winger and prominent first teamer Yan sold to German club Mainz for a decent fee of £18.75m. Selling Yan was a risk, he was probably entering the best years of his career, but Derek had young players coming through and Yan remaining at the club could block their development. The money Mainz were offering was too good to turn down with an offer that high unlikely to be made again. It left Cooper satisfied that he had been able to trim the fat of the squad, reduce the average age and also cut some of the higher earning players from his wage budget.

The 2024/25 Eredivisie campaign started at home to FC Utrecht and Cooper was confident that his summer dealings had the squad in a much better place than when he had taken charge. Ajax now had a much younger squad with a lot more competition for places.

In Yamilson Ramos, Fillip Zuberski and Cetin Baskir he had three very good strikers coming into their peak competing for the two starting spots. Winger Michael Roodenburg was being pushed by Quissama and young academy prospect Andre Alblas who at sixteen years old was already looking to break into the first team squad. Tim Erwig-Druppel was running the show in midfield alongside young South American stars Michael Perez and Julio Peralta who were in direct competition for a starting berth. All things considered Cooper was hopeful of a successful season with a squad he felt was capable of competing in multiple competitions.

Ajax won their season opener at Utrecht (2-1) and went on to beat FC Groningen away (3-0) and PSV at home (3-2) before a tight draw away to last season's runners up Herenveen (1-1). Cooper was pleased with the start and the mix of the new and old players were gelling together nicely with Erwig-Druppel and Wesley joining Baskir and Roodenburg amongst the goals across the four matches.

Four league fixtures played it was on to deadline day to close out the summer's business for Cooper. It had been an immensely busy window, but deadline day came and went without any deals being done. The last player to join had been another Colombian midfielder, Michael Sandoval for £500k, who had arrived a couple of days prior to the deadline.

Once the deadline had passed Cooper was able to fully admire the fruits of a laborious yet rewarding summer. In total he had signed twenty-seven new players for the club costing £49m, which was a considerable outlay for a club of Ajax's stature. It was only thanks to Coopers bravery and hard work in the outgoing deals that he had such funds at his disposal.

Twenty-seven new players at a cost of £49m had been possible because of the departures of twenty-five players brining in £65m for the club. Not only had Cooper improved the first team squad, but he had also invested in the future of the club with a number of promising young players who he hoped would cut their teeth in the U19's before making the step up to the senior squad.

With the summer transfer window now shut it was full steam ahead for Cooper as he looked to add more trophies to both the clubs and his personal honours list. Winning the Eredivisie was his primary objective and they had made a strong start on that front with their opening four results.

A return to league action ahead of European and domestic cup duties saw Ajax continue their strong start to the campaign with wins at home to De Graafschap (1-0) and away to Heracles Almelo (3-1). The home win came courtesy of a 92nd minute winner from impressive young striker Zoran Rudan who had joined the club in the summer at the age of eighteen. The win away from home was more comfortable and Cooper was impressed with the resilience his side were showing with their early season form.

Ajax had qualified for the Europa League with their league finish of last season and had been drawn in Group H with Hamburg, Hadjuk and Zorya. A relatively kind group with Hamburg looking like their strongest opponents.

Hamburg were up first in gameweek one and Cooper was keen to lay down a marker of his intentions to make it into the knockout rounds for the first time in his managerial career. The board were expecting qualification too and he didn't want to let them or the fans down. League form had been good and the new 4-2-4 was getting results so Cooper was brave with his team selection for an away fixture in Europe.

The game was a real end to end affair with both sides doing everything possible to win the game. Ajax would never fall behind in the back and forth of the match and would find a late winner from Paraguayan midfielder Julio Peralta in the eighty-eighth minute. The game ended 4-3 to Ajax and Cooper was pleased that his attacking intent had seen them outscore potentially their closest rivals within the group. Conceding three was not ideal, but he was happy that his side had been able to outgun their opponents.

The break from league football continued into the weekend as Ajax competed in the Dutch Cup 2nd round at home to RKC Waalwijk. Cooper rotated the starting eleven and Ajax looked comfortable at 3-0 up going into the final ten minutes, but RKC rallied late on to scare the home fans and management with goals in the eighty-sixth and ninety-first minutes to make the game a lot tighter than it needed to be. Cooper was pleased with the character shown in hanging on when things weren't going as planned, that was a vital quality of all sides looking to compete for trophies and Ajax were now through to the third round of the Dutch Cup.

October brought four Eredivisie fixtures punctuated by returns to action in both the Europa League and the Dutch Cup with Cooper guiding Ajax through a seven match unbeaten run to continue their excellent form. There was an away draw at PEC Zwolle (1-1) to start which was followed by an emphatic Europa League victory against Hadjuk (6-1) and a very impressive hat-trick from Bulgarian front man Fillip Zuberski.

Matches three and four in the unbeaten sequence would yield two more wins with nine goals scored. N.E.C were hit for four in a 4-0 away win before a home victory against ADO Den Haag (5-1). Zuberski was in fantastic form during this time adding a single and a brace to his earlier hat-trick taking his tally to eleven goals in twelve games in all competitions.

Zorya away in Ukraine came next in a busy fixture schedule and it was a night to remember for Zuberski who scored goals number twelve and thirteen either side of a Zorya goal to win the game (2-1) and make sure Ajax had maximum points in Group H at the halfway point.

Reigning Eredivisie champions Feyenoord were the visitors to the Amsterdam ArenA in the next league match. Quissama struck early on to get Coopers side off to the best start, but ultimately they would have to settle for a share of the points as Feyenoord equalised through Uros Djudjevic mid way through the second half to grab a draw (1-1).

The seventh and final match in a packed month of football was the Dutch Cup 3rd round tie against lesser opposition in SC Joure. A rotated side easily dispatched the underdogs 6-0 with Chelsea's on loan striker Alen Blaic banging in a hat-trick and sixteen year old academy graduate Andre Alblas scoring to become the clubs youngest ever goal scorer at 16 years and 234 days old.

It was now approaching the end of October and you would have to go back to the 5th May and a match against Herenveen at the end of the previous season to find Ajax's last defeat. That run was even more impressive when you added the eleven non-competitive matches in pre-season to the competitive matches. It was a run Cooper hoped to extend approaching his first winter break in football management.

There were eleven fixtures to be played before the winter break, seven in the Eredivisie, three in the Europa League and one Dutch Cup match. FC Twente and a 1-0 away win in the league courtesy of Brazilian centre back Wesley was the ideal start to another gruelling run of fixtures. Confidence was high as Ukrainian side Zorya arrived for gameweek four of the Europa League. It was to be another victory (2-0) that all but saw Ajax through to the knockout stage of the competition.

Yamilson Ramos and Fillip Zuberski were proving to be a handful for opposition defences and having both scored in the 2-0 win over Zorya they both found the net again in a league victory over Roda JC (3-2). Zuberski with two whilst Ramos grabbed the other. It was another show of character from an Ajax side that were all pulling in the right direction.

The goals continued to flow in an Eredivisie win against VVV Venlo (5-2) with club captain and South Korean international centre back Sang-Hwan Kim getting amongst the goals. Four games and four wins, Hamburg at home were up next in the Europa League and there would be no repeat of the swashbuckling 4-3 of gameweek one as Ajax easily won this tie (3-1) to make it five wins from five in Group H. The only downside to the Hamburg victory was the needless dismissal of German central midfielder Erwig-Druppel.

Three Eredivisie fixtures were up before the final group match and Cooper led Ajax to wins in all three scoring seven and conceding none along the way. Victories at home to AZ (4-0), home to Willem II (2-0) and away to Cambuur (1-0) saw Yamilson Ramos continue to find the back of the net scoring in all three matches whilst fellow striker Cetin Baskir made the most of his opportunity against AZ scoring three of the teams four goals in that match.

Hadjuk were the final European opponents of Ajax's Group H campaign and although qualification as group winners was a certainty Cooper wanted the clean sweep and the statement that would make. A Zuberski double and a late Roodenburg goal sealed the final win Ajax were after (3-1).

The final two games before the winter break saw Ajax win at home to VVV Venlo (4-2) in the Dutch Cup fourth round in a match that was nearly a repeat of an earlier 5-2 league victory. The final game was to be another win, this time at home to Vitesse (3-0) in the Eredivisie with Ramos cementing his place at the top of the leagues scoring charts adding another two to his tally.

The eleven games leading into the leagues winter break had been a complete success and Derek was enjoying the best run of form in his career to date. Ajax had comfortably qualified for the knockout stage of the Europa League as group winners and were sitting top of the Eredivisie at the halfway mark with seventeen games played having accumulated fourteen wins and three draws.

Derek Cooper was a very happy man, delighted with form and the performances of his young side. The Ajax squad had the youngest average age of any in team in the Eredivisie, but his players were turning in performances that belied their ages. The performances in the Europa League had been particularly pleasing as it was a competition Derek had managed in twice, but had been unable to progress past the group albeit managing at much lesser clubs than Ajax. To qualify from the group without dropping a point had done wonders for the squads' morale and Cooper felt they maybe now believed that they had a real chance of progressing further than just the first knockout round.

Derek Cooper was not used to a winter break; the leagues in England, Scotland and Wales were yet to implement a break of any sort so it was uncharted territory for him. As such he decided it would be smart to delegate the arranging of friendly fixtures during the break to his very able assistant manager. Jon Andoni Goikoetxea organised four fixtures against a range of opposition including Brazilian side Corinthians and Germans Hertha Berlin. Ultimately the break allowed Cooper to evaluate the condition of his squad and rest players accordingly. Fringe players and U19's regulars were given some minutes alongside sparse appearances from the first team regulars.

As January arrived the transfer window was once again opened and Cooper was able to welcome an exciting new player to the club. Mohamed Zogbo was an Ivorian right back who had impressed a couple of the Ajax scouts with his performances for his club side - ASEC. Zogbo was nineteen years old and already a member of the senior Ivory Coast set up, so a £1.1m deal was considered a no brainer by Derek. He arrived to offer cover for Gokhan Oz at right back and was definitely one to look out for in the future.

There were plenty of other irons in the fire with Derek looking at some possible pre-contract deals for players to join in the summer as well as some deals for this window with Dutch striker Rocky Homoet and Swedish midfielder Jacob Lindvall both high on his January shopping list.

Ajax played Corinthians at home on January 4th 2025 and it was their first defeat in any match since the 5th of May, just one day shy of eight months. It was a disappointment, but in the grand scheme of things it didn't really matter. Competitively their unbeaten record remained intact and Cooper was intent on keeping it that way.

The four winter break friendlies threw up two wins and two defeats, not ideal, but then also not important either. Cooper just wanted to keep all the players ticking over going into the business half of the season. During the break Cooper had also been able to attend the draw for the Europa League knockout stage which were to be played in late February. Ajax were drawn against Turkish side Besiktas and avoided tricky draws against the likes of Juventus, AC Milan and Tottenham who were still in the competition.

Wednesday the 22nd of January signalled the end of the break and a return to Eredivisie action for Ajax in a repeat of the opening fixtures. FC Utrecht, FC Groningen, PSV and Herenveen were all to come before the Dutch Cup quarter final away to N.E.C.

Cooper had his Ajax side starting the second half of the season in the same form they finished the first half. A win away to FC Utrecht (4-1) would get them started and a home win against FC Groningen (4-0) would sustain the winning run. PSV were up next ahead of the match against Herenveen and a nervy 1-0 win for Ajax extended that winning run to ten straight Eredivisie matches.

Last season's Runners up Herenveen were off the pace in 2024/25 and hadn't posed the threat Cooper had expected, but he was still out to put them in their place. Another nervy 1-0 would be enough to do just that and Yamilson Ramos found the net yet again in the Eredivisie to take the three points.

N.E.C and a Dutch Cup quarter final was up next for Cooper and he was fully expecting his side to be in the hat for the semi finals. Unfortunately he discovered your excellent league form means nothing in the cup and N.E.C clearly didn't get the memo running out 3-1 winners in a game that had seen Baskir put Ajax ahead. Out of the cup after suffering their first competitive defeat in thirty-one matches it was back to league action against De Graafschap who they had only just beat at home earlier in the season with a ninety-second minute winner. It was to be another narrow win for the home side, which sadly in this case was not Ajax.

January had been and gone now and that meant the transfer window was once again shut until the summer. As well as Mohamed Zogbo Cooper had managed to get deals over the line for both Rocky Homoet and Jacob Lindvall. Central midfielder Lindvall joined from Malmo FF for £2.2m and striker Homoet joined from Eindhoven of the Jupiler League for an initial £700k which could eventually rise to £1.2m after clauses. All three were likely to play a small part in this season, but had been signed very much with the future of the side in mind.

Ajax had gone unbeaten in the Eredivisie for twenty-two matches from the 12th of May 2024 through to the 2nd of February 2025, but the De Graafschap defeat had ended that run and it was important for the team to bounce straight back with Europa League knockout football just one league game away.

That league match was against surprise package Heracles Almelo who were defying relegation predictions under the guidance of one of Coopers favourite ex-Liverpool players, Dirk Kuyt. Derek would get the better of one of his former heroes with Ajax beating Kuyt's Heracles at home (3-0). It was a comfortable win heading into a tough European fixture away in Turkey, a notoriously tough place to go and get anything from a football match.

Ajax travelled to Besiktas with most pundits struggling to split the two teams. Besiktas had come through a tough group which had contained Marseille, Braga and Sparta Prague so they were not to be taken lightly. Cooper had faith in his lads and he trusted the 4-2-4 system that had gotten them this far.

40,000 People turned out to see Ajax take a 2-0 lead through Wesley and Cetin Baskir, who scored against his old club, before Besiktas staged an impressive three minute comeback. Firstly impressive Swiss attacking midfielder Jurgen Hoxha, on loan from AS Monaco, scored on sixty-two minutes before Nahuel Quinteros levelled from the spot on sixty-five minutes. It remained locked at 2-2 and Cooper returned to Holland with a credible draw and two important away goals. There was a week and one league match before the next leg with a real chance of progression into the 2nd knockout round for Ajax.

PEC Zwolle rolled into town in between the two Besiktas ties and were beaten 2-1 with a late consolation making the game look a little tighter than it actually was. It was a routine victory that continued to keep Ajax well out of reach at the top of the Eredivisie.

Besiktas visited the Amsterdam ArenA just four days later and Cooper cleverly rotated his starting eleven to a 3-1 victory against the Turkish side. Cetin Baskir would once again come back to haunt his old side having been rested for the league match against Zwolle passing goalscoring duties in that match to Ramos and Zuberski whilst Dutch right winger Michael Roodenburg scored the other goal in the tie against Besiktas which would finish 5-3 on aggregate in Ajax's favour.

The draw for the second knockout round was made the following evening with Ajax being paired against fellow Dutch side PSV. PSV were struggling domestically, languishing outside the top four, but were clearly playing well in Europe having seen off Basel in the first knockout round.

Games against Vitesse and ADO Den Haag came before the PSV tie with Vitesse representing Cooper's closest rivals in the league, although they were still well off the pace set by his Ajax side. It was still a game Cooper didn't want to lose and that was exactly what happened. Ajax lost 2-1 with former front man Mateo Casierra grabbing both the Vitesse goals, one of which was a ninetieth minute winner.

ADO Den Haag proved to be no pushovers in the next fixture as they very nearly held on to a claim all three points too. At 3-2 down and with just ten minutes to go Julio Peralta saw red for Ajax throwing a real spanner in the works, but Colombian midfield star Michael Perez would come to the rescue with ninety-five minutes on the clock to steal a draw for Ajax (3-3). Not ideal preparation for a big European fixture, but Cooper remained confident his side could beat PSV over the two legs; he was yet to lose to them during his time in Holland.

The away leg was up first and it was a 51,000 sell out at Philips Stadion for the all Dutch second knockout round match. Ajax were considered the superior side and would look to assert their dominance here, hopefully by winning comfortably and scoring those vital away goals.

The game was a tight affair and both goals came within a couple of minutes of each other. PSV took the lead in the sixty-third minute, but were unable to protect that one goal advantage and Fillip Zuberski equalised just two minutes later to ensure Ajax left with an away goal. The game finished 1-1 and it would be back to the Amsterdam ArenA in a weeks' time to settle the tie.

Before that second leg there was an Eredivisie game at home to N.E.C to be played and Ajax owed them one for knocking them out of the cup early in the New Year. Revenge was well and truly served as goals from Quissama, Baskir and two from Ramos put them to the sword with a 4-1 defeat.

Thursday the 20th of March 2025 was the return leg of the PSV tie and Ajax were one win away from the Europa League quarter finals. The N.E.C match had ignited the confidence of the side and they were simply too good for PSV running out easy winners 4-0 on the night and 5-1 on aggregate. Yamilson Ramos bagged another double with Baskir and Wesley completing the scoring. Ajax had asserted themselves as the dominant Dutch side in Europe as well as domestically now and Cooper was thrilled his side were still in the competition for the next round.

There were some very good sides left in the competition and Derek Cooper faced the prospect of a very tough quarter final draw. Juventus, AC Milan, Lyon and Porto were all possibilities, but it was to be German club Bayer Leverkusen that Ajax were drawn against with the first leg to be played away from home.

There were three domestic matches before the next European night and Ajax would score eleven goals across those three games, winning two and drawing one. The draw would come in an exciting match with Feyenoord (3-3) before a win at Roda JC   (5-1) and another win on home soil against FC Twente (4-1).

Ajax confidence was high going into the Leverkusen game with form away from home in Europe having been pivotal in getting them this far in the competition. Cooper had great belief in his sides scoring capabilities with them having found the back of the net at least once in every Europa League fixture so far this campaign.

Leverkusen proved to be a defensively sound side and they defended stubbornly as Ajax drew their first blank of theEuropean run. They came away from Germany and the BayArena on the wrong end of a 1-0 score line. Not the end of the world, but it left them with it all to do in the home leg against a side that had proved to be very tough to break down.

The weekend's domestic action saw another 1-0 result, but this time Cooper was on the winning side as striker Zuberski scored the only goal against VVV Venlo in the match that secured Ajax and Derek Cooper the Eredivisie title they both wanted. With fixtures still to be played Coopers side had run away with the league title, they had flown out of the blocks and never looked back. Celebrations were put on hold however as it was back to Europa League action midweek and a must win game if they were to stay in the competition.

Were they to go out at the quarter final stage Cooper couldn't complain, he had surpassed the expectations of the board and fans, but he was hungrier than ever to continue the journey. Leverkusen were the side standing in his way and he would need to win by two clear goals to get past them which although tough, was not impossible.

By the time the half time whistle sounded in the second leg match Cooper had the two goals he required with Yamilson Ramos and Wesley having beaten the Leverkusen keeper. Cooper made sure to calm his side down during the interval telling them it was only half the job, adding that he had faith in them and that there was more to come.

The tie looked done and dusted come the eightieth minute when Leverkusen's Marco Barros put the ball in his own net to make it three for Ajax, but just a minute later the German side had rallied and grabbed an away goal. It was all hands on deck defensively as Cooper desperately tried to stop them finding another away goal that would all but end the tie. The relief when the full time whistle went was palpable and Cooper could finally relax having kicked and headed every ball for the last ten minutes. Ajax were into the Europa League semi finals and Derek Cooper was beginning to believe.

It was back to the Eredivisie action, but all minds were on the Europa League and the semi final draw. Ajax would be joined in the semi finals by Juventus, Gelsenkirchen and AC Milan, all very good sides who were more than capable of winning the competition. The draw was made with AC Milan versus Gelsenkirchen the first match to out of the hat. That tie was followed by the now inevitable Juventus versus Ajax tie with the first leg to take place at the Amsterdam ArenA on the 8th of May 2025.

There was just one domestic fixture to be played before that crucial semi final first leg and it was back to the 1-0's as Quissama scored the only goal for a rotated Ajax side away to AZ. Ajax already had the title in the bag, but it was important to keep their league momentum going if they were to sustain their impressive European performances.

Thursday night's Europa League semi final was upon Derek Cooper and he was nervous. He never really expected to make it this far into the competition and he was up against football royalty in Juventus who had won the competition three times previously. There was a sell-out crowd inside the ground and Ajax wanted to put on a show for their fans, but ultimately Cooper would settle for a narrow win and not conceding an away goal.

His Ajax side stuck to their task well and came through a tight game with their clean sheet intact. Sadly their Italian counterparts had also managed to keep opposition strikers out and Ajax had been unable to find a goal to secure a narrow win. Cooper would now travel to Turin in seven days time with a Europa League final spot still up for grabs.

Domestically Cooper chose to field a heavily rotated side for the Willem II fixture which fell between both the Juventus games. The fringe players did not let him down and as always proved their worth with an easy away win (4-0). Academy product Tim de Lange scored a penalty late on to add to goals from young striker Martin Vesely, Cetin Baskir and on loan centre back Jose Luis Camarasa. Baskir had particularly impressed in his player of the match performance against Willem II and Cooper felt he had seen enough from the front man to retain his place for the second leg of the semi final.

Juventus Stadium on a European night was an impressive sight and it was vital that Derek and his side weren't overawed by the occasion. His side were young and relatively inexperienced, but what they lacked in age and wisdom they more than made up for with their work rate and endeavour. At 0-0 it was anyone's game to win and Cooper was praying his side would see them through to a European final.

Cetin Baskir did indeed retain his place up front alongside strike partner for the evening Yamilson Ramos who had been particularly good in front of goal throughout the season. Juventus were a team with immense quality, but Baskir and Ajax put them to the sword on their own patch with goals either side of half time to secure a Europa League final spot after a 2-0 away win.

Cooper congratulated every single one of his men in the changing room, praising their courage and resilience in making the final on the 28th of May. Gelsenkirchen had emerged as 3-2 winners in their semi final against Milan and would be the side waiting for Ajax in Lisbon to compete for the Europa League trophy.

After the high of Turin it was on to Amsterdam and a home match against Cambuur that had a party atmosphere right from the off. Ajax were to be presented with their Eredivisie trophy on the pitch in front of the home fans at the end of the match and Cambuur succumbed to the wills of the 50,000 strong home crowd by rolling over in a routine win for Ajax (3-1).

Cooper lifted the trophy with club captain Sang-Hwan Kim and led his players in a lap of honour to celebrate not only making up the twenty-one point deficit of the previous season, but opening up a nineteen point gap of their own. It had been a fantastic first full league campaign in charge, but there was also the chance of a historic league and European cup double that would really announce Derek Cooper the football manager.

There was a ten day break between the final Eredivisie fixture and the upcoming Europa League final and Cooper made the decision to travel earlier than scheduled to Lisbon to allow his players time to rest and recover in a warmer climate. Training was still a priority, but he also wanted his players to be well rested mentally before taking on Gelsenkirchen. In the lead up to the game there were no new injuries sustained and Cooper was able to select from virtually a full complement of players.

Ajax lined up with their usual 4-2-4 formation with Yamilson Ramos and Cetin Baskir paired up front as they had been against Juventus. Cooper had managed at the Estadio Jose Alvalade Seculo XXI once before, whilst in charge of Ross County, and had only managed a 0-0 draw on that occasion. He hoped for a different result against the German opponents that would see Ajax crowned as Europa League champions for only the second time in their history and their first since 1992.

Ajax started as the much brighter side with Cooper having used his pre-match team talk to praise his players and tell them again that he had faith in them. Yamilson Ramos in particular was looking very lively and he managed to break the deadlock after just ten minutes. The Colombian would continue to be a thorn in the side of the Gelsenkirchen backline and added his second of the evening after a further ten minutes.

Twenty minutes into the final and Ajax were 2-0 up, Cooper couldn't have wished for a better start and by the time Baskir added a third just before half time Coopers pre-match jitters had all but disappeared and he was actually beginning to enjoy himself. He reassured his side at half time, telling them that he was pleased with their performance so far, but quick to avoid complacency, added that he felt there was yet more still to come.

Derek had been right and it was to be that man Ramos again as he completed his hat-trick and a night to remember with fifty-one minutes on the clock. Four goals up and with the contest effectively over Cooper told his team to take the sting out of the game, slowing it right down and retaining possession.

The remainder of the game flew by as Cooper let himself get swept up in the sense of the occasion. As the full time whistle blew he shook hands with the opposition manager Dieter Hecking before he was hoisted up into the air by his players and backroom staff to be paraded around the pitch as a double winning manager of Ajax football club.

As the curtain came down on a fantastic season for Derek Cooper and Ajax there were a couple of personal honours to add to the double won by the side. Derek was named as the Eredivisie Manager of the Year and his Colombian striker Yamilson Ramos, who he had bought to the club less than a year ago, was named as the division's top scorer with twenty-four league goals. Cooper's sense of pride at having his own achievements recognised was eclipsed by the fact that a young player he had signed for the club had gone on to win personal honours.

There had been impressive goal tallies across all three of the senior strikers at the club. Ramos had scored thirty-five in forty-one appearances, Cetin Baskir had managed nineteen in thirty-four and Filip Zuberski had twenty-nine goals in forty-one appearances to his name. Between them they had scored a mighty eighty-three goals across all competitions for Ajax in 2024/25.

The new signings had settled in well and many had been in contention for the player of the season award which was ultimately won by Yamilson Ramos who boasted an average rating of 7.60 for the season. Gokhan Oz (7.26), Wesley (7.47), Erwig-Druppel (7.14) Hernani Goncalves (7.10) and Jose Luis Camarasa (7.30) were all new arrivals at the club and had been in contention for the award.

Derek could not have dreamt a first full year in charge like the one he had just had. A huge squad overhaul with investment in young promising players, a twenty-two match unbeaten run, his first Dutch league title, one European trophy and personal accolades too. Cooper felt at home in Amsterdam and he had his side playing some of the best football he had seen as a manager. He couldn't wait to continue the Ajax tradition of winning trophies and developing promising footballing talent.

There was no risk of Cooper taking his foot off the pedal now and he threw himself into preparations for another long and arduous season that would include a return to the Champions League for Ajax. Although Cooper had been pleased with his squad he was working hard to recruit the next batch of potential superstars as well as evaluating which players he was able to move on and cash in on.

Pre-season proved to be just as busy as last season and Cooper arranged nine friendlies ahead of the Dutch Super Cup which would open the competitive season against AZ on the 3rd of August 2025. Cooper and Ajax also had another early season cup final as they would be competing in the European Super Cup against Paris Saint-Germain, the 2024/25 UEFA Champions League winners ten days later in Germany.

Throughout the gruelling pre-season schedule Cooper would add players to the club. Many of those signed in this time were brought in to begin life with the U19 side as part of the long term plan to develop players from abroad as well as from within the club. In fact by the time Ajax had played the majority of their friendly fixtures; which included the usual in house match as well as matches against Manchester United, Dortmund, Porto and Benfica , Cooper hadn't added any players over the age of twenty-one.

Edwin Gutierrez, a young Colombian left back joined the club in a deal worth £500k and Cooper was delighted with the signing believing that the eighteen year old had the potential to go right to the top in world football. Jefferson Cordoba was another member of the Colombian U20's national team who would be joining the club at the tender age of eighteen to develop and hopefully force his way into the Ajax first team. At just £350k Cordoba represented excellent value for money and Cooper viewed it as speculating to accumulate as he was certain that he would be able to make a substantial profit on the player should he not make the grade at Ajax.

Derek and his recruitment team were working hard to scout and hoover up as many promising and affordable youngsters as was possible, boosting the pool of talent coming through from beneath the senior squad. Cooper saw this type of recruitment as essential to his way of working and part of his long term project for the club.

A defeat to Manchester United (2-1) was to be the only loss for Ajax as they embarked on another impressive pre-season. A win against Porto (5-0) and another against Benfica (3-0) were both impressive wins in a schedule that saw them win eight of the nine fixtures arranged. It had been another very good preparation period and Cooper was confident his side were ready for competitive action.

AZ in the Dutch Super Cup were up first and the chance of another trophy for Cooper to add to his honours list. The cup saw the Eredivisie winners take on the winners of the Dutch Cup in a one off game similar to the Community Shield of England. Ajax were at a slight advantage going into the match as it was to be played at the Amsterdam ArenA.

Ajax wasted no time in putting that advantage to good use and in the familiar surroundings they raced in to a 2-0 lead with twenty minutes on the clock in a similar fashion to their Europa League final just over two months ago. Cetin Baskir and Yamilson Ramos both picked up where they had left off in Lisbon with a goal each before Ramos added his second and a third for Ajax before half time.

Once again the cup was all but won for Ajax as they started the second half, but it was pleasing to see them finish the game off in style as Baskir grabbed himself a second not wanting to be outdone by his strike partner. It finished 4-0 and Cooper had his third trophy as manager of Ajax and the eighth trophy of his career to date.

The Super Cup win was a good way to kick off the 2025/26 season and Cooper hoped to continue the winning mentality as there was a league opener at home to PSV and a European Super Cup tie over in Nurnberg against the Champions League winners Paris Saint-Germain on the horizon.

The League opener against PSV was a good game for Ajax as they looked to set an early marker for their Eredivisie title defence. Coopers men recorded a fairly comfortable win (2-0) with goals from Baskir and Quissama.

It was then off to Germany and the European showpiece which saw Champions League and Europa League winners face off to be crowned winners of the European Super Cup. PSG were formidable opponents having beaten Manchester City 4-0 in the Champions League final of last season and having spent over £500m on players in the last three years.

Paris Saint-Germain were one of the super clubs of European football and Cooper was relishing the chance to test himself against them and their manager Yohan Pele. The 4-2-4 Cooper had developed at Ajax was untested against the most elite clubs, although it had managed to see off Juventus and Leverkusen in last season's Europa League run.

The game kicked off in front of 50,000 fans and Ajax went toe to toe with PSG for the opening ten minutes before Croatian winger Marcko Pjaca opened the scoring in the eleventh minute. Ajax were on the back foot now and scrambling to keep in the game with a strong PSG side looking to capitalise on their dominance. Pjaca added his second of the game on twenty minutes and then PSG would grab a third before half time with Colombian winger Gustavo Rodriguez scoring in the thirty-fifth minute.

Cooper used the break to regroup and demand more of his players. He knew they were better than they were showing and he was keen to save face and avoid an embarrassing score line. He sent his side out for the second half hoping to stage a comeback, but realistically he would have settled for keeping PSG out for forty-five minutes.

Ajax managed to get back in the game and even threatened a late comeback when Cetin Baskir took advantage of PSG taking their foot off the pedal to score two late goals in the seventy-first and eighty-eighth minutes. Sadly, despite pushing hard, Ajax couldn't find that third goal to take the game in to extra time.

Cooper was proud of the second half performance and the spirit shown by his team to not let a disappointing first half get to them. Losing 3-2 in a final to PSG was nothing to be ashamed of. They had players such as Kevin de Bruyne, Alessio Romagnoli, Saul and Geronimo Rulli amongst their ranks, if anything playing against such strong opposition had only whetted Cooper's appetite for the upcoming Champions League campaign.

European Super Cup over and done with it was back to Eredivisie action for four matches before Ajax began their Champions League campaign and Cooper's first venture into the group stage of Europe's elite club competition. He had come a long way in the nine years since his days at Walmer Road with Kirkley and Pakefield.

Ajax started their four game domestic run against ADO Den Haag and laboured to a very poor 0-0. It was then on to NAC, Willem II and their first real test against title rivals Feyenoord. Coopers men put the dour 0-0 behind them and recorded three wins from the fixtures with victories against NAC (1-0), Willem II (1-0) and against Feyenoord (2-0). Five Eredivisie games down and Ajax sat top of the table unbeaten with four wins and one draw. A good start and likely title winning form if Cooper could maintain it.

Going into the Feyenoord game Cooper had been busy closing out all of the summer business for the football club. It had been a window in which Cooper had decided against signing expensive and well known players and instead opted to recruit a vast number of talented youngsters from across the globe in a further push to enhance the quality of player coming through at the club.

This decision was a brave one for Derek given that he had sold some of his more established players, including club captain Sang-Hwan Kim in an £17m deal with Red Bull Leipzig. Tim Erwig-Druppel was bought back by Bayern for the previously agreed buy back clause of £15.5m and experienced Brazilian left back Jorge rejoined Porto for £5m.

There were also some deals which saw Cooper part ways with some of his young talents, but only for the right money and with a hefty 50% of next transfer fee clause included in any deal. Cooper was reluctant to lose some promising players, but he was making a substantial profit as well as the potential for further income down the line should the players develop as he expected and be sold on again. Luka Kozina joined the club in 2024 for £525k and he went to PSG for £4.5m, , a decent profit for a left winger signed just a year earlier.

Chilean defender Raul Mendez was another who left the club for £4.5m joining Juventus and netting Cooper a cool £3.5m profit in the process. Midfielder Wim Esser, striker Ryan Profjit and attacking midfielder Daniel Chalmers all left the club with sell on clauses inserted in the deals.

Of the players joining the club Derek Cooper had high hopes for the previously mentioned Colombians Gutierrez and Cordoba as well as Mexican central defender Enrique Meza (£1.5m initial fee from Pumas) and Jozef Bjaza a Slovakian right winger who was arriving for an initial £650k from Trencin.

During Ajax's run of fixtures and Cooper finalising the clubs transfer business the Champions League groups had been drawn and Ajax had been placed in Group B alongside beaten finalists Manchester City, Panathanikos and Leverkusen. It was a good group for Cooper who was looking forward to taking on City and reacquainting himself with Leverkusen from last season's Europa League quarter final.

Leverkusen were up first in gameweek one and on the 16th of August 2025 Derek Cooper made his Champions League debut in the group stage. It would be a successful debut with goals from strike partners Ramos and Baskir enough to secure a home win (2-1).

Ramos and Baskir struck again in another win in the next match away to Herenveen (2-1) as Ajax returned to league action. A huge win followed in the Dutch Cup second round (9-0) with Cooper giving chances to many of his young stars. Swedish midfielder Jacob Lindvall and Colombian striker Cesar Montoya took that chance with impressive performances and goals in the game.

Lindvall grabbed himself one whilst there was a hat-trick for Montoya on a full debut to remember. Not to be outdone by his understudy fellow Colombian striker Yamilson Ramos would notch a hat-trick on his return to the side as he scored all three in the win over De Graafschap (3-0), Ajax's final Eredivisie match before a return to European action.

It was off to Greece for Cooper and Ajax as they faced off against Greek side Panathanikos in gameweek two of the Champions League. There was to be a familiar score line with two familiar faces amongst the goals as Ajax won (2-1) with the goals coming courtesy of Ramos and Baskir for the third time in recent fixtures. They were forming a very reliable partnership which provided a steady stream of goals for the side.

Two wins from two was a very pleasing start to life in the group stages, but Cooper was all too aware their toughest test was yet to come with Manchester City home and away up in gameweeks three and four. These types of games were the exact reason Cooper wanted to be in the Champions League, playing against elite opposition and competing at the very top of club football.

Cetin Baskir carried his fine goal scoring form into the domestic action as he netted an impressive four times, including a thirteen minute hat-trick, in a win against Heracles Almelo (5-1) with winger Roodenburg scoring the sides other goal. He scored his fifth in just two games a week later, but it would not be enough to prevent Ajax suffering a defeat away to Groningen (2-1). Centre back Wesley received his marching orders just before half time with Ajax already a goal down in the match, so Coopers men were always up against it at the Noordlease Stadium. It was the sides' first defeat of the league campaign and it was important that the side recovered to maintain that title momentum, even so early in the season.

Before trying to bounce back in the league Ajax would host Manchester City in gameweek three of the Champions League. It was a capacity crowd to welcome the side who were beaten in last season's final. It was a tight game that was to be decided by a goal from Brazilian striker Gabriel Barbosa who lived up to his 'Gabigol' nickname.

Ajax had been the underdogs and Cooper wasn't too disheartened by the result. The games against Manchester City were not going to be the games that decided their qualification so as long as they picked up points against Leverkusen and Panathanikos any points at home or away against City would be a bonus.

Go Ahead Eagles were the opponents Ajax would need to overcome to put back to back defeats behind them. Baskir and Ramos were on target again as Cooper led his side to a routine away win (3-0). A Dutch Cup third round tie followed and Ajax survived a late rally from Eindhoven to win (3-2) with another rotated side given the run out to rest the majority of Coopers first team regulars. Cesar Montoya took his opportunity again and added a solitary goal to his hat-trick in the previous round.

It was then back to league action and a fixture against N.E.C which saw Baskir do what he does best and find the back of the net twice in a win for Cooper's men (2-0). It was only the first of November and Baskir already had eighteen goals to his name across all competitions in 2025/26, just one off his final tally of the season before.

Just like that it was time for Champions League action and a trip to the City of Manchester Stadium for gameweek four and the reverse fixture of the home defeat suffered just a couple of weeks ago. It was always nice for Cooper to return to England and try to build his reputation there. He had only ever coached in the lower leagues of English football and hoped one day to return to England to manage in the Premier League. He was very much in the minority of English coaches plying their trade outside of the United Kingdom.

Ajax gave a good account of themselves and started superbly in Manchester trading blows with Pep Guardiola's men in an exciting 4-3 match that had it all including seven goals and a red card. Baskir and Ramos were on the scoresheet again, Baskir grabbing himself a brace as Ajax raced into a 3-0 lead. Midfielder Michael Perez got himself a thirty-ninth minute red card and the ten men of Ajax battled right to the final whistle, but were ultimately on the wrong end of the 4-3 scoreline. Manchester City scored three goals from the seventy-sixth minute onwards to win the game as Cooper's attempts to close the game down failed and the numerical disadvantage proved to be too much.

After the pulsating game in Manchester Ajax returned to Eredivisie action with a home win against Excelsior (3-0). Baskir, Zuberski and Quissama were all on target for Ajax. Vitesse were up next away from home and ex-Ajax front man Mateo Casierra came back to haunt his old club with a goal either side of half time in a 2-1 win for Vitesse. Although not sold by Cooper and having never played for him Casierra looked delighted to have gotten one over his former employers again and celebrated taking all three points for his current side.

Leverkusen were the opponents for gameweek five in the Champions League and the trip to Germany saw Ajax play out a tight draw (1-1). For the second European game in a row a lack of discipline would see an Ajax player receive their marching orders. Brazilian centre back Wesley was sent off just before the hour mark, but Ajax held onto the draw that a fifth minute goal from Baskir had earned them. The group was finely poised and Ajax were still in with a decent chance of joining Manchester City in the knockout stage. It would be in their hands going into the final game against Panathanikos and a win would secure qualification.

Before the Greek side made the trip to Amsterdam in early December Ajax faced three Eredivisie fixtures with Cooper and Ajax keen to put the Vitesse defeat behind them. In those games Ajax notched up eight goals, conceded one and picked up seven points from a possible nine.

There were wins against VVV Venlo (3-0) and AZ (5-1), with another Baskir hat-trick, and a tame draw away to FC Utrecht (0-0) which saw Ajax play nearly 70minutes with ten men after German left back Tobias Moser was sent off. The win against AZ was particularly impressive as they were emerging as the team most likely to pose any sort of threat to Ajax's hopes of retaining the Eredivisie title.

The final gameweek of the Champions League group stage rolled around with Cooper and Ajax in control of their own destiny. It was simple, win and they would join Manchester City in progressing from Group B. Once again it was Baskir and Ramos who put the opposition to the sword with it being the turn of Yamilson Ramos to notch a brace in the win (3-0).

A Baskir penalty set Ajax on their way and Ramos added his two goals late in the game to finish Panathanikos off. Ajax also continued the recent tradition of finishing fixtures with a man less as academy product and central defender Ezra Kok was shown a needless red card with ninety minutes already on the clock and the game won.

That red card was a blemish on an otherwise perfect night that would see Ajax compete in the knockout stage of Europe's premier football competition. It was also the seventh time an Ajax player had seen red this season, which was something Cooper would need to look at and address going forward.

The winter break was now looming for Cooper and Ajax with just three fixtures left pre-break. PSV were up first and although Yamilson Ramos scored early on it was only be enough for a draw (1-1) and a share of the points. It was then on to Feyenoord and a tough fourth round tie in the Dutch Cup. Yamilson Ramos would again strike early, grabbing goals in the third and eleventh minutes to continue his rich vein of form, but again it wasn't enough as Ajax conspired to throw away a two goal lead in the second half to lose (3-2) meaning the Dutch Cup would continue to elude Derek Cooper. Just four days later a rotated side faced off against NAC in the final league game of the campaigns opening half. Goals from Quissama, Cesar Montoya and a double from Zuberski saw Ajax run out as easy winners (4-0). It was now time for Cooper and Ajax to recharge heading into the business end of their 2025/26 campaign.

The transfer window would be reopening within the week too and Cooper had again been working hard behind the scenes to secure several promising players from across the world. He was looking forward to the arrivals of Martin Almlov from Norwegian side Molde for £325k, Ivan Matic for a slightly larger fee of £2m from Hadjuk and Colombian Carlos Arboleda from Millonarios for £625k.

Cooper was also in lengthy negotiations with Boca Juniors of Argentina and the agent of their player IgnacioVarennes in a deal which could cost around£11.25m, a big outlay for Cooper and his current recruitment model. Varennes was an impressive Argentinian ball playing centreback who had been on Coopers radar for some time now. It would represent a considerable outlay given Coopers transfer policy to date, but he was confident it would also be an excellent long term investment with the players' peak years still ahead of him.

Cooper was also negotiating several deals that would see some more fringe players leave the club. Milan Jevtic was likely to join Saint Etienne in France for £4.5m and the now obligatory 50% sell on clause. The deal for Jevtic meant Cooper had secured Ajax £4m in profit from their £500k spend on the left back. Igor Vucinic and Niels Bogers also left the club in cut price deals to join Ross County - the former club of Derek Cooper. Milan Toman was allowed to leave Ajax and join league rivals PSV, but Toman was a player who Cooper had seen enough of to know that he would never make an impact at this level and he was happy to take £500k off the PSV manager.

The winter break came and went with Ajax having played a number of friendlies, including a testimonial match at Dutch lower league outfit De Treffers. Coopers men returned to competitive action on the 21st of January 2026 away to PEC Zwolle and their line up included recent signing Varennes who had completed his £11.25m transfer from Boca Juniors a week into the transfer window.

Ajax picked up where they had left off and scored four goals on their way to a 4-1 win; Roodenburg, Ramos and Baskir (2) on target for Coopers men against Zwolle. It was then on to ADO Den Haag and yet again Ramos would find the back of the net and see his side not win the match. His fifty-fourth minute goal wasn't enough to overcome their plucky hosts who would hold on to earn a surprise 2-1 victory.

Ajax were now into a lengthy spell of domestic fixtures before returning to European action having been drawn against English heavyweights Chelsea in the first knockout round of the UEFA Champions League.

In the five games following their unlikely Den Haag defeat Ajax went unbeaten winning four and drawing the other game in a fantastic return to form ahead of the home leg against Chelsea. Willem II (4-0) were hit for four with a hat-trick from Zuberski before a tight away win at Feyenoord (2-1) with the ever reliable Ramos and Baskir on the score sheet.

PEC Zwolle were up next and proved stubborn opposition in a poor draw (1-1) for Ajax before a win against De Graafschap (3-0) and a home win against Herenveen (3-1) which included another goal for the now seventeen year old academy player Andre Alblas. Chelsea at home was now up next and Cooper was determined to make an impact in the competition with his impressive young side.

In front of a packed Amsterdam ArenA Ajax faced off against their Premier League opponents in a match that went better than Cooper could ever have imagined. Everything Ajax tried in the first half came off and they blew away the opposition racing to a 4-0 lead by half time.

New boy Carlos Arboleda had a fantastic evening in front of goal and grabbed his first competitive goals for Ajax alongside the always reliable Fillip Zuberski and an unfortunate Chelsea own goal. The damage had been done and the second half passed without incident leaving Ajax with a commanding 4-0 home leg victory to take to Stamford Bridge in just under a months' time.

Before the return leg against Chelsea Derek Cooper and his Ajax side faced three Eredivisie fixtures. Groningen at home before Heracles Almelo and N.E.C away. It was a run of games in which Ajax claimed maximum points, scored nine goals and kept three clean sheets.

Fillip Zuberski really came to the fore during this period scoring seven of those nine goals with an impressive hat-trick coming in the win away to Almelo (4-0). It also meant Ajax had recorded six straight victories across all competitions with the added bonus of four consecutive clean sheets. Varennes had slotted into the defence perfectly and was already more than repaying the £11.25m Cooper had invested in him.

Tuesday 17th of March 2026 saw Cooper return to his native England as eager as ever to prove himself on home soil. Stamford Bridge was hosting the Champions League first knockout round second Leg match between Chelsea and Ajax and it was a packed house as the hosts looked to beat the odds and overcome the big 4-0 win back in Holland.

Cooper set Ajax up to be a little more reserved than usual with the impotence very much on their opponents to come out and try win the game. Coopers plan to kill the tie worked perfectly and his team defended brilliantly to record yet another clean sheet, their fifth in a row. The game ended 0-0 and in truth was a fairly dull affair with few highlights, but that suited Cooper down to the ground and he returned to Holland job done with a 4-0 aggregate victory.

Coopers reward for beating Chelsea would be a Quarter Final tie against Italian side Napoli who were establishing themselves as one of the dominant forces in Serie A and there was just one domestic fixture ahead of that European tie as Ajax hosted Go Ahead Eagles. An early Fillip Zuberski penalty, converted in the third minute, would set them on their way to an easy win (4-0) and their sixth consecutive clean sheet. Both Wesley and Varennes, the two starting centre backs for the game managed to get themselves on the scoresheet as well as keeping the opposition out at the other end.

Ajax had again been drawn at home in the first leg of their quarter final tie and Napoli arrived in town having beaten German side Wolfsburg in the previous round of fixtures. Napoli were a good side without doubt, but Cooper and his players had made light work of an arguably tougher opponent in the form of Chelsea last time out.

Ajax were excellent in that Chelsea win, but there was to be no repeat as Napoli really took the game to Ajax scoring their first of the game in just the second minute. Peruvian striker Moises Otero then added his second goal of the game just before half time to put Napoli firmly in the driving seat. Cooper gave his side a stern talking to in the break, aggressively telling them to show some passion and that they looked like a side that didn't want to win.

Cooper needed his side to score the next goal to keep them in the tie. That next goal would come in the fifty-eighth minute, but it would be for Napoli as Manolo Gabbiadini scored in his second stint with the Naples club. Ajax were now 3-0 down at home and all looked lost for Derek Cooper, they had been well and truly outplayed and couldn't grumble at the humbling score line.

Cooper made immediate changes and uncharacteristically threw on all of his allocated substitutes before the hour mark. It was a desperate move and fortunately it was one that paid off. Fillip Zuberski, one of the players to have started the match, scored goals in the seventy-sixth, eighty-fifth and ninety-second minutes to grab a hat-trick that would keep Ajax hopes alive going to Naples. Given the 3-0 deficit it was an unbelievable comeback and Cooper was delighted with the character shown.

The Wednesday night match at home to Napoli had been a real rollercoaster for Derek and he hoped for an easy domestic fixture before the return leg in six days time. Vitesse were the visiting side and they did all they could to ensure Ajax would have to work hard for the 3-2 victory. The visitors took the lead with another early goal at the Amsterdam ArenA. Saku Ylatupa put Vitesse 1-0 up with just two minutes on the clock. Ajax battled back to a 3-1 lead with Roodenburg grabbing a leveller and Zuberski adding another two goals to his hat-trick midweek. Vitesse rallied late on and former Ajax player Mateo Casierra scored against his former club again to ensure a nervous last five minutes for Cooper.

Vitesse dispatched it was time to travel to Italy and the impressive San Paolo to try and progress into the Champions League semi final. It was very much advantage Napoli as they had managed to get three important away goals in Amsterdam.

Moises Otero once again opened the scoring as he put Napoli 1-0 up on the night with twelve minutes played, but Ajax would respond better than in the previous match remaining competitive in the game until they finally levelled through Baskir in the fifty-ninth minute. The game was now 1-1 on the night and 4-4 on aggregate, but Napoli would be through on away goals.

Ajax continued to press looking for more goals and were punished by Napoli as they took a 2-1 lead on sixty-two minutes through club stalwart and Italian midfielder Jorginho. Zuberski levelled the match again in the eighty-sixth minute making it 2-2 and offering a small glimmer of hope for Cooper.

The game was finely poised and just one more goal would see Ajax progress 6-5 on aggregate and win 3-2 on the night. There was to be another goal, but it came for Napoli through striker Andrea Belotti in the eighty-ninth minute to win the game for the Italian side (3-2). Cooper was pleased with the spirit shown, but left Naples feeling that it had been a missed opportunity to really go deep in the Champions League.

European disappointment behind them it was time for Cooper to win his second Eredivisie title with Ajax. It was almost a certainty going into the last four fixtures and a slip up by their closest rivals AZ meant that the win against Excelsior (2-0) was enough for Ajax to be crowned as league champions.

Back to back titles for Ajax and Derek Cooper meant that he had restored the club to the very top of Dutch football and he was delighted at that particular achievement. The season ended with comprehensive victories against AZ (4-1), and Utrecht (3-1), but would include a surprise defeat at home to VVV Venlo (1-0) in the first home fixture since being crowned Champions.

Ajax finished the 2025/26 league season with eighty-two points winning twenty-six, drawing four and losing four of their thirty-four Eredivisie fixtures. It had been another impressive domestic season which had seen them win the title by a margin of thirteen points between themselves and runners up AZ on sixty-nine points. Both PSV and Feyenoord who had been tipped as potential title challengers failed to make the top four finishing eighth and fifth respectively.

Yet again the three senior strikers of Ajax had done the business and they all posted impressive figures for the season. Yamilson Ramos scored twenty-seven from forty-three appearances, Fillip Zuberski also netted twenty-seven times, but from fewer matches with thirty-one appearances for the Bulgarian hitman.

The standout performer of the trio was twenty-four year old Cetin Baskir who won the clubs player of the year award as well as the award for most assists in the Eredivisie (15) having missed out on the top scorer award by three goals. Baskir scored thirty-two goals in his thirty-nine appearances and attained an average rating of 7.64 across all competitions in 2025/26.

New signing Ingnacio Varennes may well have beaten Baskir to the player of the season award had he played the entire season. Since his arrival in January the Argentinean central defender managed an impressive average rating of 7.67 from his seventeen appearances. It was looking like it would be money well spent by the club.

To further emphasise just how good the three strikers Cooper had at the club were, the next highest goal scorer was right winger Michael Roodenburg, who managed just five goals from his forty-one appearances. That amounted to a drop off of twenty-two goals from the lowest scoring members of the front three.

During the Eredivisie run in and with the second title already in the bag Cooper had held very tentative talks with Premier League side Liverpool about becoming their new manager. Cooper was a boyhood Liverpool fan and dreamed of one day getting the chance to manage the club he grew up supporting. Liverpool were a side that had struggled in recent years and only narrowly avoided relegation in the 2024/25 Premier League season finishing in 17th place under then manager Zinedine Zidane.

Since then Mike Garrity had been given the manager's job and they looked set to finish well outside the top ten for the second season running. They were now looking for a new manager and Derek Cooper interviewed for the role stating that he wanted to continue to develop young talent whilst playing attacking football. His ideas seemed fairly well received by the board and he was hopeful as he returned to Holland.

It was around a week before Cooper heard back from Liverpool as they informed him that he was not the man for them at this time. They had decided to hire forty-one year old William Kvist who had been manager of West Ham United to take them forward into 2026/27.

Cooper felt it was a mistake on their part as he was confident in his abilities as a manager and felt his recent record backed that up. Ultimately it wasn't to be and Cooper was now fully focused on another pre-season with Ajax. There were transfers to be carried out and trophies to be won; he was a man who never rested on his laurels.

The summer of 2026 was a big one for Ajax off the pitch as the board agreed to Coopers request to expand the clubs stadium. The Amsterdam ArenA's capacity was set to be increased to 65,000 with the works looking to be completed by the end of September. Cooper was adamant that this was the right decision for a club that was both cash and asset rich and looking to make their mark among the big boys of European football. They had a big fan base and were the biggest and best known Dutch club so it was a positive move for the club.

Cooper was very active in the transfer market although the summer saw more outs than ins as many young players went out on loan in search of first team football. The club also cashed in on players that didn't look like they would develop sufficiently to break into a very competitive first team squad. Cooper vastly reduced the size of the B and U19's squads bringing in around £19.3m for the club and spending a fraction of that with just £7.8m on new additions.

The biggest deal for a player joining the club was for another Argentinean centre back as Cooper paid £5.5m for the services of San Lorenzo's Fabian Lillo. The deal for Lillo was the only one to break the £1m mark during the summer window. Ajax had made a lot of signings in previous windows and there simply weren't any players available that were better than those already registered for the club and its various teams.

Leaving the club was veteran midfielder Daley Sinkgraven who had expressed a desire to move for more regular first team football. He joined Betis in a £2.5m deal whilst other notable deals saw Lukas Hykel join Spurs (£4.9m) and Aldo Castro leave for Italian side Cagliari (£5m), the biggest fee received by the club that summer.

Both the deals for Hykel and Castro included the 50% of next sale clauses that Cooper was keen to insert into the transfers involving any player with sell on potential. Francisco Javier Corrales, Fausto Cremonini and Jose Diaz were other players to leave the club bringing in a combined £4.4m having cost the club a total of around £500k to originally bring them to Ajax. These types of deal in which Cooper developed players before selling them on for a profit were seen as vital to boosting the clubs finances and ensuring they had the necessary funds to continue to improve both on and off the pitch.

Footballing wise it was another very productive pre-season for Ajax and Derek Cooper. Working largely with an unchanged first team squad he was able to carry on the fabulous form of the last campaign. Between the 30th of June and the 29th of July Ajax played nine friendlies winning all nine.

The highlights of which were without doubt the wins at home against Real Madrid (4-2) and Barcelona (7-4). The two games against the giants of Spanish football were real crowd pleasers, but also proved to Derek that he was taking his Ajax side in the right direction and they were now more than capable of mixing it with the big boys of European football. Pre-season finished with a routine victory away to Croatian lower league opposition Sesvete (2-0). It was a rotated side that had played in the win with the Dutch Super Cup curtain raiser just around the corner for Ajax.

The Dutch Super Cup was contested against NAC on Sunday the 2nd of August 2026 and Cooper wanted to make it back to back victories for Ajax for the first time since 2019 and 2020. NAC proved to be no match for Coopers Ajax on the day and they easily won the tie (3-0) with goals from Roodenburg, Baskir and Zoran Rudan who was beginning to make an impression in the first team during an impressive pre-season.

Attention quickly turned to the start of the 2026/27 Eredivisie campaign and the season opener at home to Groningen. Ajax once again proved to be too good for the opposition easily winning 4-1 having been forced to play the last fifteen minutes of the match with ten men following the dismissal of midfield maestro Michael Perez.

It was a routine start to the season for Derek Cooper and his Ajax side as they won their opening five games scoring eighteen and conceding just a solitary goal which came in that opening day victory. Ajax beat Volendam (2-0), ADO Den Haag (4-0), PEC Zwolle (4-0) and N.E.C (4-0) to kick off their second title defence in the best possible way.

NAC were Ajax's next league opponents and they were keen to exact revenge for the Super Cup defeat in front of their own fans. They turned in a much better showing than that of just over a month ago and held onto a solitary goal scored in the 10th minute by Maritn Claes to inflict a 1-0 defeat on the Dutch Super Cup winners. It was an abrupt and disappointing end to what had been a fantastic start to the season by Ajax, but it was far from disastrous and they had been the better side for the majority of the game having failed to capitalise on their dominance.

The 2026/27 Champions League groups had been drawn and meant Cooper would be facing off against a couple of familiar opponents. Rangers he had played against during his time in Scotland and Leverkusen were a side he had faced in European fixtures more than once in his time as Ajax boss. The third and final team in Group F was to be Manchester United, the giants of English football who were still being managed by Jose Mourinho, now in his eleventh season with the club. It was a competitive group, but a group Derek still expected to qualify from, he knew he could beat both Leverkusen and Rangers and he saw it as both himself and Mourinho as the main challengers to qualify as group winners.

Rangers away would be the first European test for Cooper with the team arriving at Ibrox off the back of that shock league defeat to NAC. Ajax bounced back brilliantly winning 4-0 in front of nearly 60,000 spectators in Glasgow. Braces from both Zuberski and Baskir were more than enough to see Ajax return home with the first three points of the 2026/27 Champions League.

That Rangers game was to kick-start something quite special for Ajax and Derek Cooper as they went eighteen games unbeaten across all competitions winning sixteen and drawing twice in games in the Eredivisie, Dutch Cup and Champions League. It was a quite unbelievable run that included a special home win against Manchester United (2-1), an Eredivisie win against Feyenoord (4-1) and a Dutch Cup victory against NIVO (10-0) in which Yamilson Ramos scored a double hat-trick, a first for Derek Coopers managerial career. The draws both came in the Champions league as Ajax dropped points away in Leverkusen (2-2) and frustratingly failed to break down the Rangers defence at the Amsterdam ArenA (0-0).

Derek Cooper was delighted with the run of form and the performances his side had been turning in. By the 6th of December and the home win against Heracles Almelo Ajax had won all but one of their Eredivisie matches so far and they sat comfortably at the top of the league. Ajax very rarely failed to find the net and more often than not managed to score over a goal a game, in fact, in the eighteen game run they scored an average of three goals a game, only failing to score once.

Heerenveen and Feyenoord were the two sides who looked like they were at least trying to keep up with the impressive form of Ajax, but even they were at risk of being blown away. On the 20th of August Feyenoord visited the Amsterdam ArenA but were unable to live with the home sides attacking football and they returned to Rotterdam on the wrong end of the 4-1 score line. When Ajax travelled to Heerenveen in late November it was rather less comfortable, but Cooper's men still emerged with the win (3-2).

The Dutch Cup was a competition that Derek Cooper was yet to make his mark on and he was hoping the 2026/27 campaign would be the one to see his side lift the cup. They had come through the early rounds with a second round win against Excelsior (2-0) and the massive third round victory against minnows NIVO (10-0). Yamilson Ramos was on fire in front of goal as he helped himself to six of the teams ten goals that day. Younger players Jozef Bajza, Zoran Rudan and academy product Tim de Lange also managed to find the back of the net in the big win and make the most of a rare run out in the first team.

There were now just four competitive fixtures before the Eredivisie winter break. Manchester United in the Champions League, Feyenoord in the Dutch Cup and Groningen and Voldendam in the League. A second win against Mourinho would see Ajax top the group, but it would be a tough ask away in Manchester. Feyenoord were tough opponents in the Dutch Cup, certainly the sternest test to date, but Ajax had beaten them comfortably earlier in the season and Cooper was hoping for a similar outcome this time out. The Groningen fixture represented the halfway point of the season and Derek was confident that his side would continue their remarkable form into the second half of league fixtures, beginning with another win here.

Manchester United away was up first and yet again Cooper was in England hoping to raise his profile by claiming a Premier League scalp. Mourinho had other ideas this time out, and there would be no repeat of the Ajax victory in gameweek two at the end of September. Paul Pogba opened the scoring for the Red Devils before the half hour mark and second half goals from Fernando Compagnucci and David Grimes abruptly ended the Ajax unbeaten run and completed the victory for Manchester United (3-0). The defeat meant that Ajax would qualify as runners up in the group and Cooper was left to rue the draws and dropped points against both Rangers and Leverkusen.

Up next was the game against Groningen in the reverse of the opening day fixture. Ajax had triumphed in that match at home and travelled to Noordlease Stadion hoping to grab another three points. Ajax didn't start the game well and failed to find their rhythm, Groningen took their opportunity and Carlos Fernandez put the hosts ahead in the thirty-third minute. Cooper and Ajax continued to falter and their chances deteriorated further when midfielder Moha was sent off for a crazy two footed lunge in the middle of the park. Cooper had no choice but to continue to push for a goal and his boldness was rewarded just five minutes after the dismissal when Carlos Arboleda scrambled home an equaliser. The game ended 1-1, which Cooper was reasonably happy with given the poor performance and going a man down whilst trailing in the match.

The 15th of December 2026 saw Ajax travel to Rotterdam to play Feyenoord in the Dutch Cup fourth round with their opponents keen to avenge the humbling defeat from earlier in the season. Whilst his opponents were keen for revenge Derek Cooper had his sights firmly set on progressing to the next round of the competition and seeing a return to form for his Ajax side.

Once again Ajax started slowly and failed to make an impression in the opening exchanges. In fact, by the time the match hit the fifty-eight minute mark Ajax were three goals down and looked like a side bereft of confidence. Cooper was frustrated by yet another poor performance when all of a sudden his side sparked into life, scoring almost immediately after conceding the third to make the game 3-1. Ajax remained on the front foot, their confidence slowly returning, but they were unable to get the goals needed to get anything from the game. Front man Baskir managed to grab his and Ajax's second in injury time, but it was too little too late and yet again Cooper was eliminated from the domestic cup competition he was desperate to win.

The 26/27 winter break was now just days away and Cooper was keen to end the first half of the season on a high and mark it with a win. The game against Voldendam represented the perfect opportunity to do just that. They were a recently promoted side who were performing well in the league, but would not be accustomed to playing at a stadium like the Amsterdam ArenA. Ajax toiled and struggled through the first forty-five minutes before they clicked through the gears in the second half and signed off for the winter break with a home win (4-0) reminiscent of their form leading into mid December.

January brought with it some frustrations for Derek Cooper as his best midfielder was being openly coveted by some of the biggest European clubs. The player in question was now refusing to sign a new deal with the club as Cooper was looking to remove a release clause that although fairly large was obviously not enough of a deterrent. Michael Perez had joined the club in June 2024 for a fee of £750k and Cooper had shown faith in the young Colombian player developing him into a first team regular as well as a full international. AS Monaco contacted Ajax in early January to inform them that they would be offering the required amount to trigger the release clause in the contract of Michael Perez.

Cooper spoke to Michael on the phone and tried to persuade him that big offers would come again in the summer, but he knew there was no stopping the ambitious midfielder now his head had been turned. On

January the 8th 2027 Michael Perez said his goodbyes at the training ground and left Ajax in a £28.5m deal, the biggest of Cooper's career and the biggest sale at Ajax since 2020.

Preparations for the second half of the season were going well and Derek Cooper arranged four friendlies to be contested throughout January ahead of their return to league action. All four matches were played against weaker opposition to keep morale high and allow his players to continue finding the back of the net.

The plan worked and Ajax won all of the arranged games, scoring twenty-two and conceding none along the way. The team were well prepared heading into the second half of the Eredivisie and it showed as they smashed ADO Den Haag (6-1) on their return to action in late January. Yamilson Ramos nearly repeated his double hat-trick from earlier in the season, but would fall one goal short as he scored five of Ajax's six that day.

Shortly after the return to league action the transfer window closed with Cooper disappointed to have lost one of his star players. There were no standout transfers joining the club although promising right backs Luis Romero and Rodrigo Diaz joined the club for £800k and £100k respectively and South African left winger Abram Memela joined from affiliate club Ajax CT for a fee of £500k.

Striker Zoran Rudan who had begun to make some first team appearances for the club was making noises about wanting to leave for more first team football and subsequently joined Novara for £2.5m with the now standard 50% of any future transfer clause. Another to leave the club was Norwegian right sided utility man Martin Almlov who had attracted the attention of big spending PSG. They paid £5.25m up front with the 50% clause included in the deal for a player who had joined Ajax from Molde for a fee of just £325k. The Almlov and Rudan transfers were indicative of the way Cooper conducted his business, buying young, developing as much as possible before selling them on for a profit.

Several other players would be departing the club, but only on a temporary basis as Cooper utilised the loan market to further develop those players who had outgrown the B and U19's sides, but weren't quite at the standard required to break into the first team squad just yet.

Those players would only be leaving Ajax on loan if a suitable offer came in. Take Johan Veenboer as an example, he was very highly thought of by Derek, but at the moment was unable to make an impact in his preferred position as a number ten. Coopers current formation was a 4-2-4 with high attacking wingers and two busy central midfielders leaving Veenboer as a bit of a square peg in a round hole.

Cooper didn't want to lose Veenboer permanently; he was an academy graduate who had obvious ability and potential to develop further. He left Ajax in January to join Marseille, a club who would use Veenboer as a key player and provide him with the chance to further develop due to their high standard of training facilities. Other players to join Veenboer on a similar career path were defender Ezra Kok, who joined Hoffenheim, and Jefferson Cordoba who joined Betis in La Liga.

After the enthralling return to competitive action and the previously mentioned win against ADO Den Haag there were three more Eredivisie fixtures ahead of an interesting Champions League first knockout round match against Chelsea. Chelsea and Ajax had faced off at exactly the same stage last season with Ajax emerging victorious over the two legs. The home tie saw Cooper mastermind an impressive win that all but sealed their progress into the quarter finals that season.

Ajax continued their excellent start winning all three league matches against PEC Zwolle (3-0), N.E.C (2-1) and NAC (2-0). Perfect preparation for their European encounter and the visit of Chelsea.

A capacity crowd of 65,000 were in attendance hoping to see a repeat of the drubbing from last season. The game started as a cagey affair and Ajax were nowhere near as effective as they had been twleve months ago. The game was turned on its head just before half time as Swedish midfielder Jacob Lindvall, who had staked a claim for Perez's vacant midfield spot, got himself sent off. Lindvall was shown a straight red card for violent conduct and would leave Ajax down to ten men with the game at 0-0.

The second half kicked off with Cooper predominantly looking to utilise the counter attack and limit Chelsea's chances of grabbing any away goals. Surprisingly Ajax would fly out of the blocks taking Chelsea by surprise and taking the lead through Tim de Lange who was having a very good season and making the most of his first team chances. Chelsea as if stunned into action replied immediately with a goal of their own from Norwegian striker and £51m man Aksel Halvorsen.

A draw wasn't a disaster given the early red card and Cooper would have taken had he been offered it, but that man de Lange had other ideas and he added his second of the game in the seventy-seventh minute to put Ajax back in the lead. Cooper immediately changed his tactic, operating much more defensively and desperately trying to hold onto the unlikely victory. Despite late pressure from Chelsea and a barrage of shots on the Ajax goal Cooper's men stood firm for victory against the odds.

Between Champions League matches there were four Eredivsie fixtures played including the trip to league rivals Feyenoord. VVV Venlo were up first and it was a crazy game which saw Ajax on the winning end of the 7-3 score line. The following game was the trip to Rotterdam and Feyenoord continued their recent upturn in results against Ajax inflicting another defeat (1-0), this time a penalty from Spaniard Juan Bernat was enough to see off Cooper's side. The Ajax cause was not helped in the match as another red card was shown with left back Edwin Gutierrez seeing red in the fifty-fifth minute.

Dutch right winger Michael Roodenburg scored an injury time winner in the next fixture away to De Graafschap as Ajax won (2-1) before a solitary Cetin Baskir goal was enough to see off a spirited FC Utrecht (1-0) in the next game.

After three wins and one loss it was over to Champions League duties and the return leg against Chelsea. Ajax came into the game with a narrow lead, but there was no way Cooper was going to sit back and try to defend. His team and his tactics were built on an attacking philosophy and he knew that on their day Ajax were capable of blowing away very good opponents.

The first half had very little worth mentioning and Cooper had Chelsea where he wanted them, goalless at home and still trailing on aggregate. The second half it seemed would not go as the first half had before it. Julian Brandt scored the opening goal of the game in the forty-seventh minute before helping himself to another and turning the tie on its head just three minutes later.

Ajax were now trailing 2-0 on the night and 3-2 on aggregate with Chelsea having the added bonus of their away goal. Things then went from bad to worse for Cooper as Turkish right back Gokhan Oz brought down an opponent in the area in a clumsy last man tackle that saw him sent off and afforded Brandt the chance to complete his hat-trick from the spot, a chance he duly took. The misery was then complete in the eighty-third minute when Aksel Halvorsen added their fourth in a reverse of the score line from last season's competition. It had been a night to forget for Cooper, but Ajax were almost certain to secure a third consecutive Eredivisie title when they returned to domestic action and he took some solace from that.

Following their Champions League elimination there were two months left of the season with Ajax firmly in the driving seat when it came to the league table. Heerenveen and Feyenoord were still trying to keep pace, but it was becoming obvious it was Ajax's title to throw away.

The league run in would comprise of seven matches including the visit of Heerenveen in mid April. The three matches before that visit saw Ajax beat PSV (3-0), draw with Vitesse (2-2) and beat Dordecht (3-2) in a game that saw Lindvall dismissed once more and a goal for each side in injury time.

Herenveen rolled into town hoping to delay the inevitable and sustain their challenge for the runner up spot. Ajax were in no mood to be beaten and steamrolled the likely runners up 4-0 with an impressive hat-trick for Cetin Baskir. It was a mathematical impossibility that they would be caught now and Ajax were presented with their third consecutive Eredivisie trophy on the pitch post match in front of the home support.

The three remaining fixtures were all but a formality and Ajax scored four goals in each of those fixtures beating AZ (4-1), FC Twente (4-2) and Heracles Almelo (4-2). Striker Baskir really closed out the season in style following up his Heerenveen hat-trick with two goals in each of the final three games to take his league tally to twenty-five and secure him the Eredivisie Golden Boot which he had been so close to winning the season before.

It had been a fantastic season for Ajax and probably Derek Cooper's best as a manager, despite disappointing exits earlier than he would have liked in both the Champions League and that elusive Dutch Cup. He had lost a marquee player in the form of Michael Perez, but was comforted by the amazing strength in depth he had built up during his time at the club.

Jacob Lindvall had come in to replace the departed Perez and had done well, red cards aside. Tim de Lange was making a claim for the left wing spot chipping in with some crucial goals across all competitions in a breakout season for the player.

Cetin Baskir performed fantastically in front of goal yet again to seal his place in Eredivisie history as a top scorer winner with twenty-five league goals. In total he managed thirty-one in thirty-eight appearances during 2026/27. Baskir also retained his player of the season and most assists trophies from last season winning them again with nineteen league goals laid on for his teammates and an average rating of 7.72 this campaign.

Central defenders Ignacio Varennes and Enrique Meza both posted impressive average ratings of 7.56 and 7.64 whilst Tim de Lange and Yamilson Ramos helped out with their ratings of 7.41 and 7.46. Fillip Zuberski had a season that was cut short by a damaged cruciate injury he picked up in November, but he still managed twelve goals in his twelve appearances for the season.

It was a season which saw Ajax win thirty of their thirty-four league matches, losing two and drawing two, scoring one hundred and one goals in the process and only conceding twenty-three. The goals scored tally was by far and away the best total in the clubs history as was the league total of ninety-two points. Both were club records and achievements that Cooper was immensely proud of.

The impressive work Cooper was doing not just for the first team, but for the club as a whole was evident not only with the results of the first team but also with the Under 19's who in 2026/27 beat Manchester United in the Final of the Under 19s Champions League by an impressive 6-2 score line. The extensive recruitment of young talent from not just Holland or Europe, but from around the world was really paying dividends for the club. They still had the youngest average age of any club in the Eredivisie as well as an U19's side that had been crowned as the best in Europe.

Players such as Jesper Gudde, Lukas Mares, Jozef Bajza, Rocky Homoet and Marek Janda were all players that Cooper thought very highly of and believed would go on to have very successful careers either with Ajax or with other top European clubs. Their experience with the U19's and especially in the age groups Champions League competition was a vital part of the development process and success in the competition was all part of Derek Coopers grand plans for the club. Beating teams such as Manchester United in the final of the competition showed Cooper that he had the club on the right track and vindicated many of the signings he had chosen to make in his time with Ajax to strengthen the club as a whole rather than focusing solely on the senior first team squad.

2026/27 Had been a very special season and Cooper hoped that with the same level of hard work and dedication it was just the beginning of a dynasty that would continue to cement Ajax as the dominant Dutch club and elevate them to a previously unthinkable level amongst the elite clubs of Europe.

Such was Cooper's belief that he was on to something special at Ajax he had declined two very interesting job offers from La Liga sides Sevilla and Valencia, both of whom had been very keen for Cooper to bring his brand of football down to Spain. Various other clubs had been tenuously linked with Cooper and made tentative enquiries as to his availability, but as of yet just the two clubs had made concrete offers to the talented Englishman.

There were plenty of vacancies at clubs across Europe, including a couple back in England, but Derek Cooper was Ajax manager heading into the 2027/28 season and his fourth full season at the helm. As always Derek rigorously planned for the upcoming campaign with additions and outgoings across the clubs playing and backroom staff. Cooper was continuously looking at ways to freshen things up and ensure improvement both on and off the pitch.

The opening of the transfer window on the first of July saw talented Tunisian goalkeeper Selahattin Otyildiz arrive having signed a pre-contract agreement with Ajax in January. He was spotted playing for Bursaspor and Cooper liked what he had heard from a couple of his most trusted scouts. He would provide competition for number one Hernani Goncalves and replace long term back up Oscar Tevez who looked likely to join Sheffield Wednesday for £8m in a quest to attain regular playing time. Tevez wanted to remain as the Dutch number one, his adopted country, having deferred from his native Argentina and felt he needed to be playing more regularly to do so.

Frank de Boer who had been back at the club working under Derek Cooper left to take up the vacant manager role at Lazio and Ajax moved swiftly to replace him with OGC Nice's talented Portuguese coach Joao Tralhao who was very highly rated throughout Europe.

On the pitch Cooper kicked off pre-season as he always did with a game against the U19's to give as many players an early chance of game time as was possible. He then launched into an intense period which included seven more games and a training camp in Turkey ahead of the Dutch Super Cup season opener against Heerenveen on the 1st of August.

Those eight pre-season fixtures saw six wins, including a victory against Arsenal (3-1), a draw in the U19's fixture and a solitary loss in the first proper friendly against Manchester United (2-1). Cooper was once again pleased with the performance and application of his players, he was ready to make an assault on the Eredivisie once again and win his fourth consecutive league title.

Heading into the opening fixture of the season Cooper had managed to get all his incoming business concluded and along with the usual recruitment of promising youngsters to supplement the clubs prolific academy. Cooper had secured deals for two talented Portuguese players; winger Federico Atunes for an initial £3.5m with the potential to hit £7m from Vit. Setubal and central defender Manuel Santos from Estoril for £3.2m. There was also a deal for a Czech U21 international by the name of Tomas Silny who was making very promising progress for an eighteen year old. Centre back Silny would join from Czech club Pribram for a modest fee of just £2.5m although that could rise as high as £4m dependant on appearances.

Sunday the 1st of July 2027 and the competitive fixtures once again got underway with the Dutch Super Cup. Ajaxs' home ground would again play host to the occasion as Heerenveen were in town to try and stop Cooper and Ajax winning their third consecutive Super Cup. A capacity crowd of 65,000 packed into the Amsterdam ArenA to see Ajax pick up from where they left off last season. Although not as convincing as they had been at times last campaign Ajax had more than enough chances to put the game to bed and win by a greater margin than the eventual score line. Michael Roodenburg scored the winner as Ajax won (1-0) to make it three in a row for the first time since 2005 through to 2008.

Again it would be a blistering start for Ajax as they really flew out of the blocks in 2027/28. They went unbeaten for the whole of August and into early September winning five and drawing one of their opening fixtures. They scored five goals for three games on the bounce during that run and scored a total of twenty-three across the six games. Ajax also managed to keep it tight at the back conceding just four goals and never more than one in a game. The early run saw them beat Cambuur (4-0), draw with Heerenveen (1-1) before getting back to winning ways against FC Twente (3-1), NAC (5-1), away to Heracles Almelo (5-0) and finally in the match against Sparta Rotterdam (5-1).

Cetin Baskir was still in lethal form, looking determined to hold onto his Golden Boot from the previous campaign and he netted four goal hauls twice, in the matches against NAC and Sparta Rotterdam whilst Tim de Lange continued his impressive form scoring in three consecutive matches.

Deadline day came and went and Cooper had been a busy manager concluding several permanent deals for the club. Oscar Tevez got his move to Wednesday and there were several other considerable transfers of note in the window. Quissama, the Brazilian winger who was Coopers very first signing at Ajax became the latest R.Madrid "Galactico" as they agreed to pay his £32m release clause. Cooper had paid just £2m for the then eighteen year old winger and he had nurtured him into a full international and first team regular who made the club a profit of nearly £30m.

Other players to leave were Tobias Moser who went back to Leverkusen for £7m up front and 50% of any future transfer after losing his starting spot to Edwin Gutierrez. Michel Schmidt, a product of the Ajax youth system, left for Braga after a fee of £10m with the usual sell on clause agreed. Colombian midfielder Michael Sandoval who joined the club for £500k back in 2024/25 was sold onto Borussia Dortmund for £8.5m plus the sell on clause and the final player to leave was someone who had been on the fringes of the first team squad for a while. Czech midfielder Lukas Mares left to join Leicester who paid £3.2m up front for him. It was seen as reasonably cheap given that there was still some development left in the player so the sell on clause was yet again added in for security.

For the 2027/28 Champions League campaign Ajax had been drawn against familiar opponents in Leverkusen where they would be up against Tobias Moser who had just rejoined his former club. The other teams that made up Group G were Barcelona and Polish side Legia. Again it was a group that Cooper fancied his chances qualifying from with the only real threat seeming to be Spanish footballing royalty in Barcelona.

After a six game unbeaten domestic run it was Leverkusen at home up first in Europe. Ajax came into the fixture having scored five goals in consecutive games and they hoped to carry on with that free scoring form. Leverkusen were familiar foes with Ajax having faced them in European competition for the past three seasons. Leverkusen had only got the better of Ajax once, back in 2024/25 in the Europa League, but Cooper had ultimately been victorious over the two legs on that occasion.

Tobias Moser was returning to the Amsterdam ArenA less than two months after his £7m sale. It was to be a very unhappy return for the full back as Ajax once again turned on the style and battered an opponent with another five goal haul. The match ended 5-0 to Ajax and young striker Rocky Homoet had a breakout performance scoring an impressive hat-trick alongside goals from winger Roodenburg and fellow striker Zuberski.

After the Leverkusen demolition it was Eredivisie action ahead of the tantalising trip to the Camp Nou in gameweek two of the Champions League. Ajax scraped a narrow home win against PSV (1-0) with a late Roodenburg goal having played nearly an hour with ten men following the dismissal of Johan Veenboer. VVV Venlo then visited and it was another narrow win (2-1) as Roodenburg scored again and Jacob Lindvall added a second from the spot. The performances hadn't been ideal heading into their toughest game of the season, but they had emerged with the three points despite not playing well and that was something Cooper always took great confidence from.

The Camp Nou on a European night and a crowd of 98,000 was the sort of stage Derek Cooper had only dreamed of whilst starting out at Walmer Road with Kirkley and Pakefield eleven years ago. He had been blessed to have travelled across Europe to many of the elite footballing venues, but as he stood on the touchline watching his side warm up he was beholden to the spectacle before him.

Cooper approached the game tentatively and adjusted his game plan to operate a little smarter against such illustrious opposition. It was a mistake that was evident from the very start of the match as his side also looked in awe of their surroundings. Barcelona were in complete control of the game and a goal at the very beginning and very end of the game did not flatter the hosts at all.

French striker Willy Charpentier opened the scoring inside a minute for the Catalan club and La Masia graduate Joan Moreno finished Ajax off in the eighty-eighth minute. They had been a class above Ajax on the night and Cooper felt entirely responsible. Cooper would lament his tactical choices as the side flew back to Amsterdam that evening to prepare for FC Groningen in a few days time.

It was back to league action and a chance to get back to the form that saw them sitting atop the Eredivisie. Ajax travelled to Groningen hoping to shake off the European disappointment. The game started poorly and Ajax fell behind on the 17th minute and a Derek Darkwa goal. Cooper was confident his boys would be able to get themselves back in the game and Filip Zuberski duly obliged within ten minutes of Ajax falling behind, equalising in the twenty-fourth minute. Unfortunately Ajax were unable to build on that and remained unimpressive before Dutch winger Darkwa added his second of the game mid way through the second half. It was to remain that way as the game finished 2-1 and Ajax faced their first real test of the campaign. Bouncing back against RKC in their next fixture was now important to ensure their European hangover was curtailed before it turned into a real loss of confidence and form.

There were two weeks between the Groningen and RKC fixtures with the international break coming at a good time for the squad. Although many players were on international duty it allowed Cooper and the players a chance to recuperate mentally and physically having faced a fairly heavy fixture schedule recently with six games in the month and a bit leading up to this fixture.

Saturday the 16th of October Ajax travelled to the newly promoted RKC Waalwijk looking to get the three points and end their mini blip. Ajax once again started slowly and were behind in the early exchanges, Marius Hoibraten firing the home side ahead in the eighth minute. This time Ajax would take a little longer to respond, but when it came it was sustained and built upon.

Cetin Baskir, back in the side after a break from action against Groningen, would lead the charge levelling in the tenty-first minute before adding two more in the last twenty minutes to complete his hat-trick. It was a 3-1 win that alleviated Coopers fears that his sides poor form would continue and damage his hopes of another decent season and their chances of more silverware.

Just like that it was back to Champions League action and the first of the back to back group fixtures against Polish side Legia. The first encounter was in Amsterdam and it gave Cooper the chance to play some of the younger squad members and introduce them to European competition. It was a risk for Cooper, but a calculated one as Legia were seen as the weakest team within the group.

It would take nearly twenty-five minutes but Ajax opened the scoring for the first time in four games. Young and exciting right back Mo Zogbo who had been understudy to regular full back Gokhan Oz made the most of his opportunity and got himself amongst the goals. It was the first of another five goal haul for Ajax, their fifth of the season so far. Baskir added two more to his seasons tally and Rocky Homoet also made the most of his chance before an own goal compiled more misery on the Polish side to complete the rout.

Cooper and Ajax were now at gameweek three and the halfway point of the group stages and post match he reflected on what had been an impressive showing in the Champions League thus far. He was of course disappointed by the defeat to Barcelona, but there was no shame in that. Although Barca hadn't made the final since winning it in 2016/17 they were virtual ever presents in the latter stages and consistently competitive at the highest club level.

Cooper was however delighted that his side had managed to score five not once, but twice in a competition of that stature. Scoring five in any match was no easy feat and Cooper was buoyed by the fact the side he had assembled were more than capable of doing just that. He was confident that Ajax could carry this form into gameweek's four, five and six to make it out of the group stage for the third season running.

There were two Eredivise fixtures sandwiched between the Legia fixtures and Ajax continued their return to form recording two victories. Cooper made the most of the excellent depth of his squad and Brazilian central midfielder Junior would join Yamilson Ramos on the score sheet in a win agaisnt N.E.C (2-0). There was then another win against AZ (4-0) as a rotated Ajax side looked fresh. An own goal, Julio Peralta, Cetin Baskir and Rocky Homoet handed Ajax the victory. The squad rotation would be continued into the Legia fixture as Cooper had great trust in the squad as a whole and he wanted to keep legs fresh and competition for places fierce.

Ajax travelled to Poland certain that the three points were there to be taken after the emphatic home victory. The game started well and Ajax were once again the much better side really taking the game to a Legia side who looked scared to be taking on their Dutch counterparts. It took twenty-one minutes for Ajax to break the deadlock, but what followed was a barrage of goals that buried Legia and secured a club record victory in the Champions League. It was also to be the biggest win in the competition in its current form, Dinamo Bucharest were the only side to better the win when they beat Crusaders 11-0 in 1973 in what was then the European Cup.

Ajax comfortably won the game by an almost unbelievable 10-0 score line. There were a couple of own goals including one from the unlucky Daniel Wojciechowski who had also found the back of his own net back in Amsterdam. A hat-trick for Tim de Lange alongside two goals each for Rocky Homoet Carlos Arboleda with a solitary goal for Yamilson Ramos. Cooper was over the moon and it was one of his most memorable results to date despite the lacklustre opposition.

After the hysteria of a once in a lifetime result it was inevitable that Ajax would struggle on their return to domestic duties. Throughout Coopers time in Holland former Ajax striker Mateo Casierra had consistently come back to haunt his previous employers. Ajax's visit to Vitesse on their return from Poland was no different and that man Casierra scored the first of the home sides two goals within a five minute window. Casierra opened the scoring on the forty-third minute and Argentinean attacking midfielder Giovanni Lo Celso added the second on forty-seven minutes. The goals either side of half time were blows that Ajax were unable to recover from and despite a Yamilson Ramos consolation late on it wouldn't be enough to prevent a 2-1 defeat. It was a real come down from the emphatic result just days before, Feyenoord were up next and they always represented tough opposition.

The Feyenoord match saw the Ajax squad respond perfectly with a very good display against a side that the pundits rated as their most likely challengers for the league title. The game was effectively over by half time with goals from Yamilson Ramos (2) and Cetin Baskir to see Ajax into a comfortable lead. Swedish midfielder Jacob Lindvall added a fourth before the end to cap a decent home victory (4-0). The victory against Feyenoord was the first of four in a row in the Eredivisie including wins against PEC Zwolle (6-0), a match against

Volendam (3-2) which included the drama of an Ajax red card and two very late goals before a drubbing of Cambuur (4-0).

The run of Eredivisie fixtures was supplemented by a fixture in the Champions League with Ajax returning to face familiar foe Leverkusen. It was a game that Leverkusen really needed to win to have any hope of catching either Ajax or Barcelona and the 2-2 draw all but ended the Germans hope of qualification.

Gameweek six, the final round of the group stage and the return fixture against Barcelona saw Derek Cooper determined to make amends for the defeat back in late September. Cooper used his tried and tested attacking approach rather than cowing to the presence of Barcelona. Counter attacking had not worked in the Camp Nou and was unlikely to pay off at home, so it was to be an all or nothing, full throttle display from Ajax.

A capacity crowd of 65,000 were in place to witness Barcelona take the lead via Willy Charpentier again, although it was on the twenty-second minute and not in the opening minute as it had been last time out. Ajax responded beautifully, they hadn't looked overawed by the occasion as they had done under the Camp Nou lights and they really performed in the second half. Fillip Zuberski in particular turned it on to score a memorable hat-trick and secure a 3-1 win for Ajax. Cooper had redeemed himself and once again proved that he had a squad capable of mixing it with the big boys.

Following the Barcelona win there were just two fixtures remaining as Ajax headed towards the winter break. ADO Den Haag and Heerenveen stood between the Ajax squad and a well earned break from competitive action. Coopers menhad not been good following Champions League fixtures recently losing their last two games immediately after European fixtures.

ADO Den Haag represented a game that Ajax should be winning, but they would never get going and a Junior own goal was enough to compound them to another post Europe defeat (1-0). Heerenveen on paper looked a much tougher challenge for Ajax and for a good portion of the game they were able to frustrate Cooper and his players. It took until the last twenty minutes for Ajax to break through their resolve with Julio Peralta and Cetin Baskir netting in the win (2-0).

The winter break not only afforded a month long break but it also coincided with the opening of the January transfer window. January the 1st 2028 saw a huge influx of players to the club who had agreed deals prior to the window opening. Cooper and his recruitment team had been busy tying down a host of promising players to deals with the club and many of them were now able to join from South America having turned eighteen, the required age for moving clubs in that region.

There were a couple of players joining the club who Cooper hoped would immediately step into the first team fold. Rodrigo Godoy was an impressive eighteen year old central midfielder that Cooper hoped would eventually step up to fill the void left by Michael Perez and his transfer to AS Monaco. Godoy joined for a relatively small fee of £6m form Argentinean side Newells and Ajax were excited by what he could bring to the side.

Another addition was that of twenty year old Portuguese winger Rui Ferreira who would provide cover and competition in the left wing position. He was joining from Boavista and again would hopefully represent value for money with just £2.2m put down to secure his services.

The January break was a busy one for Cooper as he looked to integrate the new additions whilst also fending off the clubs that were circling some of his top talents. There were non-competitive fixtures to be arranged and training sessions to be planned and scheduled. It was during this period that Cooper received word from his agent that a couple of big European clubs were seriously considering him as a candidate to replace their previous managers. Derek Cooper's agent had been in contact with the clubs in question and had been informed that they would both welcome an application from the Ajax manager having been impressed with his work.

Cooper faced a real dilemma, he was happy at Ajax and was working with a group of players that he was extremely confident in, it was the best squad he had ever worked with. The club were in a very strong financial position with money in the bank, plenty of assets and a transfer budget that was comparable to that of most Premier League clubs, but within all those positives lay the root cause of his suddenly itchy feet. Derek Cooper had become comfortable in his surroundings.

After much soul searching and several meetings with his agent Cooper decided that he had nothing to lose by submitting an application and seeing what another club had to say. Derek could walk away at any point and there was no pressure to take a job that he didn't feel would allow him to continue with his footballing philosophies.

Over the early days of January 2028 Cooper not only set his Ajax side up for the second half of their season, but also flew to Turin for an interview with the board of Juventus as well as to Spain and La Liga club Valencia. The interviews went well with all parties seemingly happy with what the others had to contribute. Cooper was impressed with both clubs as well as their facilities and desire to play attacking football. Juventus in particular impressed and similarly liked Derek's vision of a young and attacking side that would restore them to the top of Serie A having not won the league since the 2020/21 season.

Cooper returned to Amsterdam feeling that he had given a good account of himself in both interviews, but felt that he would only consider taking the Juventus job and would reject Valencia in favour of staying with Ajax. Valencia were struggling financially and had a lesser reputation than that of current club Ajax.

On the other hand Derek Cooper had felt happy that Juventus represented an interesting proposition for him should the offer of a job materialise. For now however, it was back to Ajax and ensuring the off field distractions didn't crossover and effect his working environment.

Cooper returned to a major decision for the club as an £8m deal for right back Gokhan Oz had been agreed with Liverpool. The player had agreed personal terms and all that was left was for Cooper to sign off on the deal and Oz to put pen to paper in England. Six months ago Gokhan Oz had been the undisputed starting right back for Ajax, but the emergence of twenty-one year old Ivorian full back Mohamed Zogbo had threatened and then usurped the Turkish player and he now found himself unable to break back into the side. This fact, combined with the promising youngsters Luis Romero and Rodrigo Diaz also at the club meant that Oz had become a player Cooper was willing to let go and he sanctioned the transfer.

On the same day that Gokhan Oz was unveiled as a Liverpool player Ajax hosted FK Austria Wien in the second of their winter break friendlies. Following the victory (1-0) Cooper worked late into the evening planning training for the upcoming week and it was whilst he was in his office that he received a call from his agent to inform him that there were contract offers on the table from both Juventus and Valencia. Both clubs wanted Derek Cooper to be their new manager and usher in his attractive brand of football.

It was Saturday evening on the 8th of January and he asked for the Sunday to think over the offers before informing them of his decision. He all but discounted Valencia feeling that it was a sideways step at the very best whilst there was only two jobs in La Liga that really interested him at this point and Valencia was not one of them. It was Juventus or Ajax that was now the question for Derek Cooper.

By Monday the 10th of January 2028 Derek Cooper had made his decision and he informed his agent as such. Save the Dutch Cup he had won all there was to win in Holland. He had won consecutive Dutch Super Cups and Eredivisie titles and was likely to add a fourth of each should he decide to stay at Ajax. He had built an impressive squad, the strongest he had had the pleasure of working with, but it was time for a new challenge and the chance to test himself in Italy with a club such as Juventus was simply too good to pass up.

Having already told his agent of the decision he went directly to the board of Ajax and informed them of his resignation with immediate effect. There was then time for a quick goodbye to the players and staff he had so enjoyed working with before he found himself on a plane bound for Turin and the next exciting chapter of his managerial career.

CHAPTER SIX.

Amsterdam to Turin was a short flight, especially when you were flying on the private jet of your new employers as Derek Cooper was. It was a flight chartered solely to cater for the new man in charge at Juventus. It landed in Turin around midday and he was quickly whisked off to a waiting car and driven to the Juventus Stadium to formally sign his contract, receive an introduction to the club from the chairman and meet the national and local press that were gathered for the impending press conference.

Derek Cooper had done his homework and he knew exactly what he would be walking into with his new club. Few managers in world football were as dedicated to their craft. Cooper had worked tirelessly at every club he had been fortunate enough to manage and it would be no different with Juventus.

As a club Juve had been falling short of expectations in recent seasons and they had not won a Serie A title for seven years. The clubs last Scudetto was won in 2020/21 by then manager Jorge Jesus. The drop off in league victories was unacceptable for a club as illustrious as the Old Lady.

Juventus had elected for Derek Cooper primarily because of his excellent track record, he had won seven leagues titles across three countries as well as a Europa League and various domestic honours and he had done all that by starting from the very bottom and working his way up.

Even at Ajax, who were a well known European club, Cooper had to formulate and implement a plan to restore the club. He had chosen to develop players from within as well as investing smartly in promising youngsters to return Ajax to the top of Dutch football. It was a plan that was built on a foundation of the clubs historic football identity. Ajax and Cooper had been a match made in heaven and there was no doubt the fans were saddened by his departure.

Cooper was now back to square one again. A new club with new challenges, many of which he had faced before. Juventus had a high wage bill with an aging squad. It was packed full of talent, but it was talent that were reaching the twilight of their careers. Cooper was very much a manager who liked to work with players at the other end of the career spectrum, raw, fresh and hungry to prove themselves. Players like Anthony Martial, Julian Weigl, Domenico Berardi, Dani Ceballos and Sergi Samper were all quality players with distinguished careers, but collectively they had failed to mount a title challenge for the club.

The star studded squad was taking a toll on club finances too and in leaving Ajax Cooper was swapping a cash rich club for one that was struggling financially. Cooper would be looking to drastically reduce the wage bill and invest smartly in what was always a competitive transfer market. His strategy at Ajax had worked superbly and he hoped to implement a similar recruitment plan with Juventus, Recruiting young players with bags of potential that he could develop before selling on for as bigger profit as possible. With that money then reinvested in the club facilities and its recruitment policy to continue the cycle.

Ideally Cooper would be able to sell the big earners for an initial leg up financially, but that may prove difficult given their age and the wages they would be looking to receive elsewhere. There were also the Serie A registration rules to consider which would restrict the number of non-European players Cooper would be able to name in his squad.

The foreign player ruling would limit Cooper's plans to some extent given that he had worked so intensely in the South American market in the past four years. Working in Italy was going to be a challenge, but it was a challenge that he was greatly excited by, he wouldn't have been sat in Turin in front of a room full of journalists had that not been the case.

Derek Cooper greeted the room in basic Italian before reverting to English as he outlined his plans for the club. Juventus sat fifth in Serie A and were well off the pace of the seemingly dominant forces of AC Milan and Napoli who had held the top two spots in the league for the last few years.

Winning the league was the primary objective, but Cooper had his sights set on much more than that. He had grown up watching Del Piero, Zidane and Gigi Buffon; icons of the club who played a part in Juventus being regarded as one of the biggest clubs not just in Italy, but throughout Europe. Derek hoped that under his tutelage he would be able to bring those glory days back to the club and its devoted fans.

With the meetings and greetings out of the way it was time for Cooper to dive straight into business in his new office at Centro Sportivo di Vinovo, or the Juventus Centre as it was also known, which was where the clubs state of the art training facilities were located. Cooper would needed to add to the backroom staff across not just the first team but the U20's and the U18's as well. The various backroom departments were looking a little light on numbers following the sacking of former manager Luca Rigoni. Training was tailored to his requirements, working on team cohesion extensively as they looked to adopt Coopers now preferred tactic of 4-2-4.

Derek was planning to implement his version of 4-2-4 which had served him so well during his time in Holland. It was a formation that suited his attacking style. Wingers pushed forward to join the two forwards, effectively creating a four man attacking unit flooding the opposition defence. The two central midfielders were there not only to win the ball back, but were used as the creative base from which the attacks were built.

Defensively Cooper was aware that his attacking outlook left them vulnerable at times, especially when asking full backs to push forward and take their line from the central midfield duo. Strong and quick centre backs were preferred by Cooper as they would be heavily relied upon with this tactic.

Juventus had been in rotten form before the arrival of their new manager having not won in the league since the 1st of December against Atalanta. It was a run of five games that Derek Cooper was hoping to stop in its tracks with his first game in charge at home to Bologna on Wednesday the 12th of January.

It had been an intense couple of days for Derek as he was working against the clock to implement his tactics in an effort to turn the clubs season around. He had been pleased with the response from the players and he had enjoyed catching up with a familiar face in Paraguayan central defender Raul Mendez who had played under Cooper at Ajax before being sold to Juventus for £4.5m in 2025.

There was a disappointing turn out for Cooper's home debut as just 37,736 were in attendance to see Juventus take on Bologna. It was yet another sign of how the club had fallen, unable to sell out the modest 51,843 capacity. Derek was slightly nervous pre-match and he had every right to be, he had left the safety of what he had known and opened himself up to a totally new challenge. Nervous he may have been, but he was also quietly confident that his team had the class required to do what was asked of them.

The Bologna game kicked off and straight away Juventus went for the jugular plunging forward desperate to take the lead. Derek and the fans didn't have to wait long and just six minutes in to his reign Norwegian striker Kevin Didriksen scored the clubs first Derek Cooper goal.

It was then two just four minutes later as Belgian international midfielder Orel Mangala slotted home. Cooper couldn't have wished for a better start, two goals up inside the opening ten minutes, it was the type of start new managers dreamed of. There was then another first of Derek Coopers Juventus career as full back Felix Passlack was given a straight red card just before the half hour mark.

It was a needless tackle and one that left Bologna with a potential lifeline and route back into the match. It was an opportunity that they jumped at as Angelo Fulgini found the back of the net almost immediately. Cooper was forced into a tactical reshuffle aiming to frustrate the opposition and stop them getting up any momentum.

The tactical tweaks saw them through to half time and allowed Cooper to encourage his side, telling them they were doing well and to keep going out there. Juventus managed to hold firm and continued to deny the Bologna players the chance to get their tails up. There were a couple of scares, but Cooper was delighted to come away from his first game in charge with the maximum three points.

A victory in his first game in charge was the type of start Cooper and Juventus needed. It was an early vindication of his decision to join the club and strengthened his resolve to reinvigorate Juventus Football Club whilst it began to show why the board had put faith in the Englishman.

Unlike his arrival at Ajax, Derek had arrived in Turin in the middle of the January transfer window allowing him some time to scout any potential reinforcements. Unfortunately the board weren't able to provide much in the way of transfer funds despite the club having sold their star man, Amadou Mane, to Borussia Dortmund for £19.25m rising to £28m in the days prior to his arrival. That meant he was keen to exploit the pre-contract market, targeting those players who had less than six months to run on their current deals. Within just a couple of days Cooper had established a handful of potential targets and he was working hard to get deals in place to bring them to Italy for the 2028/29 season.

As hard as Cooper was working to bring players to the club he was working double time to move on some of the deadwood in an effort to bring in some funds. Serie A operated with a foreign player limit and this was something Derek had not experienced in previous roles, it would require him to rethink some of his recruitment policies and take the unfamiliar regulations into consideration.

Juventus had some players at the club currently who were classed as "foreign" and Cooper would be weighing up their roles in the first team squad and his plans to overhaul the club. It was important for Cooper that he settled quickly, there was an unrelenting fixture programme as well as countless changes and modifications being made behind the scenes. If he wasn't out on the training pitch working with the squad he was holed up in his office on the phone trying to sign off on various deals for the club.

In the week after the Bologna win Juventus travelled to Rome to face Lazio and played host to Napoli in an Italian Cup Quarter Final tie. In Rome a very early Martial goal put Juve ahead, but there was another first half red card as winger Peguy Nllend was sent off after just twenty-two minutes. Fortunately Cooper was once again able to shut up shop and hold out to secure the win (1-0).

Napoli were likely to provide the toughest test to date and Cooper was keen to make an impression on a domestic cup competition having been left frustrated at his failure to do so in Holland. Juventus flew out of the blocks in front of a slightly bigger home crowd of 41,475 and the game was effectively all but over by half time. Coopers side were 3-0 up with goals from Dutch attacker David Smit, Striker Kevin Didriksen and that man Martial again. The second half slid by with little in the way of incident and no change in the score. Cooper saw Juventus reach a cup semi final in just his third game in charge.

There were two more games before the end of January and the closing of the transfer window. On Monday the 24th of January there was a big home game as INTER came to the Juventus stadium. A third first half goal in as many games for Anthony Martial would be enough to secure a win (1-0), marking a fourth victory in a row for Cooper and Juventus.

A trip to Cagliari closed out the month and Juventus put in another stellar performance running out 3-0 victors with an early brace for David Smit and a late goal for Peguy Nllend who was back from his suspension. Cooper had settled in well; five games played with five games won, ten goals scored and just the one conceded it was the sort of start he had hoped for, but never expected to get.

January ended having been a successful month on the pitch with Juventus picking up some fantastic results on their way to a five match winning streak. Off the pitch it had seen Cooper secure the services of several members of backroom staff as well as reaching agreements with a couple of exciting players to join the club in July when their contracts expired with their current clubs.

Swiss attacking midfielder Jurgen Hoxha would be joining from AS Monaco, French central midfielder Maxence Gonalons would arrive from Manchester United and in the biggest and most exciting deal South Korean winger Ik-Hyun Moon would link up with Juventus after agreeing to leave Mexican outfit Monterrey.

Cooper also managed to conclude two permanent transfers that represented very little risk for the club. Michal Hosek would join for £500k and Ladislav Kudela for just £200k. Hosek was a promising central midfielder whilst Kudela was an exciting winger with both players regularly appearing in the Czech U19 international side.

Derek agreed to move on a couple of players who were either unhappy at the club or unlikely to break into his first team, especially given that he was already looking to bring in players with ability that would surpass that of his current starting eleven. He would move on a selection of players that brought in a combined £22.5m for the club, a much needed boost to rapidly deteriorating funds.

The biggest sale was that of Mexican central defender Cesar Montes as he was shipped out for £12.5m to Chinese side Huaxia Xingfu. Portuguese duo Carlos Costa and Ruben Dias were both headed for the Premier League as Stoke paid £4.5m for Costa and Leicester coughed up £5m for Dias. Cooper wished each player well, but ultimately the club needed to sell to improve and he had deemed them surplus to requirements. Football could be a brutal industry.

Deals concluded and transfer window shut it was back to matters on the field and another run of fixtures in both the league and cup. February kicked off away to Serie A strugglers Salernitana and the game saw Coopers side lose late on in a match that had it all. An early goal put the home side ahead before Didriksen levelled the game on the hour mark. There was then yet another red card for Cooper who was beginning to question his instructions to "get stuck in" in his tactical plans. Orel Mangala was the player to see red this time as Juventus were reduced to ten men with seventy-seven minutes on the clock.

That red card sparked a frenetic end to the match with two goals coming just seconds apart in the seventy-ninth minute. Memphis Depay struck for Salernitana before Didriksen added his second to level the game again. Cooper would have taken the 2-2 draw, but sadly it wasn't to be and on the eighty-first minute Italian striker Claudio Sabelli put the home side ahead for the third time in the match. It proved to be too much for the ten men of Juventus who didn't have enough left in the tank to come back again. Cooper had been handed the first defeat of his Juventus reign.

Up next was Roma in the first leg of the Italian Cup semi final and the perfect opportunity to bounce back. It was becoming clear to Cooper that Italy had a greater depth to their domestic football with every other game seeming to be against a recognisable name such as INTER, Napoli, Lazio or Roma. Holland in contrast had provided stern tests for sure, but more often than not he came up against clubs that were yet to become household names outside of Holland. FC Twente, FC Utrecht and FC Groningen were examples of this type of club.

Roma were difficult opposition and the first leg of the cup semi final finished goalless. Juventus were simply unable to break the stubborn resolve of Roma. A draw wasn't a disaster and it left it all to play for in the second leg at the end of the month.

Before then Juventus faced three Serie A fixtures as they looked to get back to winning ways in an effort to climb the league table. It would see a return to form for Cooper as his side recorded straight victories against

Parma (1-0), away to Empoli (2-0) and finally at Juventus Stadium against Ascoli (3-0). It had been four clean sheets in succession for Cooper and he was delighted with his back five, but it was a concern that Martials goals had dried up with him having started so well.

February 2028 ended with nearly 70,000 fans in the Olimpico to watch the second leg of the Italian Cup semi final with a final spot against either Foirentina or INTER up for grabs. Cooper was once again desperate for cup success, but his team failed to show up when it mattered as a rampant Roma tore through his previously impenetrable backline. By the time the referee blew for half time Juventus found themselves four goals behind. Luigi Cabrini, Lorenzo Bertacchini (2) and Paolo Lazzaroni scored for Roma and it left Cooper staring an embarrassing defeat in the mouth.

He told his side to go back out and win the second half; fully aware that his cup dream was likely sidelined for another season. Juventus responded in the second half, but a lone Didriksen goal wasn't enough to stave off a humbling defeat (4-1). The return to good form had not been enough to see Juve reach a cup final and they would now focus solely on Serie A.

There were ten remaining Serie A fixtures culminating with the end of the campaign at home to Udinese on the 14th of May. Cooper started the run in hopeful that he would be able to get up the league table and push for European football. Serie A was a tough league and chasing down those teams above him would be a tall order.

The run in would not start well as Juventus dropped five points in the first two fixtures drawing away to Pescara (1-1) and losing at home to AC Milan (1-0) with Brazilian attacking midfielder Gerson getting the only goal. Not an ideal start, especially when Cooper looked at the remaining fixtures and saw tough games against Napoli and Roma up next.

He needn't have worried as his Juventus side turned in two exceptional performances to beat Napoli (2-1) with goals from Martial and Didriksen either side of a familiar foe in Moises Otero who had found the net against Coopers Ajax side in previous contests. That win was then followed by another as Juventus got revenge on Roma with a late goal in injury time to steal the three points   (3-2). Marital had put Juve ahead before Lorenzo Bertacchini and Leo Andre turned the tie on its head with just twenty minutes to go. Passlack then started the comeback off from the penalty spot before David Smit pounced in the ninety-first minute to win the match.

The run of wins stretched to five games with yet more impressive wins and plenty of goals. Didriksen, Smit and Martial (2) sealed a derby win against Torino (4-2) before the Martial show rolled into town as he scored all four goals in another victory, this time at home to Atalanta (4-2).

The fifth consecutive three points were won in a win away to Sassuolo (3-1) with Ceballos, Smit and the other Norwegian striker at the club, William Johansson cancelling out an early own goal. Juventus had positioned themselves nicely in the league table and a continuation of this form could see them sneak into the top four.

Sampdoria at home was seen by Cooper as a winnable game, they were considered a top ten side, but Juventus were on a hot streak and looking to finish the season strongly. A terrible start for Juve meant Luca Montanari was able to put Sampdoria ahead after just five minutes before they added a second through Sabatino Campana with twenty minutes gone. Juventus responded well and William Johansson scored in the thirty-fifth minute before drawing Juventus back on level terms with his second seven minutes later.

It looked like another impressive comeback was on, but indiscipline reared its ugly head again with the dismissal of defender Hamza Boussaid on the stroke of half time. Juventus weren't able to sustain the momentum from their first half recovery having gone a man down and Corentin Jean completed a miserable day for Cooper with a winner for Sampdoria in the sixty-second minute. Juventus tried to get themselves back in the game, but it wasn't to be and the winning streak was ended by the defeat (3-2).

That loss against Sampdoria was then followed by another loss as Cooper recorded back to back defeats for the first time at Juventus. Palermo surprised Cooper and pundits alike as they ran out 2-0 winners with a brace from striker Corrado Ferraro. The back to back defeats had killed off any hopes of a top four finish and meant it was now increasingly likely that European qualification would only be possible with both Roma and Foirentina qualifying through their league position and not the Italian Cup qualification spot.

Cooper still wanted to sign off with a win and finish the season in the right manner and Juventus did just that as they beat Udinese (3-0) with an own goal and a Martial brace to cap off a sombre end to the season. The Sampdoria and Palermo defeats had come at the worst possible time for Juventus and really brought home to Derek Cooper just how much work there was ahead of him.

Juventus finished sixth in the 2027/28 campaign with a points total of sixty-five, a full fifteen points off AC Milan's league winning total of eighty. It was a smaller gap than the one he had closed in Holland and he had no doubts he was capable of repeating that feat, but there were five impressive clubs ahead of him this time in AC Milan, INTER, Napoli, Roma and Foirentina. It was a tough ask, but Derek Cooper was a manager who relished a challenge.

Martial had ended the season as the clubs top scorer and whilst his total of twenty-one goals in thirty-nine appearances wasn't terrible it wasn't up to the standard Cooper had expected of Ramos, Zuberski and Cetin back at Ajax. Kevin Didriksen was the next highest scorer with thirteen before you were down to David Smit with nine. It was an area of the squad the Derek may need to look at investing in to make Juventus more competitive in the seasons to come.

The older players in the squad had done nothing to deter Derek Cooper from his plans to move them on with both Domenico Berardi and Dani Ceballos performing well below the required standard with average ratings of 6.52 and 6.92 for the season. Cooper was sure that younger players would be available and could offer more to the side. Alex Meret in goal was probably the exception to the rule when it came to the older members of the squad and Cooper felt confident moving forward with Meret as the established number one.

As the 2027/28 season drew to a close Cooper looked back on a reasonable start to life in Turin, but was rueful of the missed opportunities of a cup final and a potential top four finish. Those two accomplishments would have pushed him past the threshold of where he expected to be after just half a season in charge, but he was an ambitious manager and he never liked to lose football matches.

His early assessments had been correct and Juventus were a football club in need of a revamp, aging players would need to be let go or moved on and replaced with younger blood who would be capable of developing along with the club to challenge back at the top of Serie A. Cooper was now more sure than ever that he was the right man for the job and that he had a big summer ahead.

Throughout his time at Juventus Cooper had begun assembling a backroom team that he felt would offer the depth of knowledge and experience required to assist him in the project. Where possible Cooper liked to work with ex-pro's who could offer personal insight into the game and had a real world understanding of professional football. If those former players were also connected to the club he was in charge of then that was even better, having an affiliation with the club and its fans could only strengthen their determination to see the club doing well.

Former Juventus and Switzerland wing back Stephan Lichtsteiner returned to the club as an U18's Coach alongside other ex-professionals Freddy Guarin (U20's Coach), Sokratis Papastathopoulos (U18's Coach), Javier

Mascherano (U18's Assistant Manager), Brad Friedel (U20's Manager), Quincy Promes (U20's Coach) and Alexandre Lacazette (U18's Fitness Coach).

There was also a reunion for Derek Cooper and Kanga Ndiwa, a scout he had first worked with back in England at Kirkley and Pakefield. Ndiwa had been Chief Scout for Cooper during his time in the lower reaches of English football and both were pleased with the opportunity to work together again.

With a half season of Italian football under his belt Cooper had made the necessary assessments going into the summer transfer window. There was a plan in place regarding player departures and he was chasing a number of selected targets to bring into the club. Some arrivals would depend on certain players leaving the club, but Derek remained confident the summer of 2028 would be a productive one for Juventus.

Cooper had held meetings with prominent squad members in the days following the final league game allowing players to go away on holiday knowing where they stood. Big earners Dani Ceballos, Domenico Berardi, Sergi Samper and Julian Weigl had all been informed that they would not be offered new deals with the club. All four players were vastly experienced, but had wages that surpassed the £100k per week mark and that was something Derek Cooper was keen to address.

As the window opened and pre-season got underway Anthony Martial agreed a return to Manchester United in an £8.5m deal which again was orchestrated by Cooper to move on another aging player with lucrative wages. Orel Mangala had been good for Juventus under Cooper, but an £18.5m offer from AC Milan for the thirty year old had been too good to turn down and would again see another high earner leave the club.

French winger Peguy Nlend also left the club in a deal that came about as Cooper wanted to avoid paying a costly clause to the players' former club Real Madrid. Should Nlend make another appearance for Juventus they would be required to pay R.Madrid around £12m, which was something Cooper was reluctant to do given that he was only likely to be a squad player. Hoffenheim coughed up £17m for Nlend, which was less than his market value, but saved the club shelling out for the clause payment.

Coopers reunion with Rafa Mendez was short lived as the Chilean central defender was moved on by his manager for a second time to help comply with foreign player limits as he joined Atlanta for £7.5m. Other notable sales saw Leicester pay £12.5m for centre back Filippo Cortesi and Swansea pay £6.5m for left back Hamza Boussaid.

With many of the high earners either released or sold on, Derek Cooper moved onto the recruitment side of his squad redevelopment. Having already agreed a number of pre-contract deals he now looked to invest the money he had brought in through player sales.

As with his policy at Ajax Derek Cooper would continue to look for value in the market, players that were available for a reasonable price and may well develop enough for the club to sell on and make a profit. Young players were his preference, but he would not turn down the chance to sign any player available at the right price.

Swedish right back Haris Eriksson was very much a player who Cooper saw a great deal of potential in and at £400k from Malmo FF represented a very low risk deal for the club. In comparison, Austrian left back Hannes Pentz was a player that had been on Coopers radar since his time at Ajax and a bidding war resulted in Cooper getting his man, but paying what looked a costly £16.75m for the pleasure. Pentz had been attracting interest from across Europe and Juventus had to fight off interest from Chelsea and Arsenal amongst others to persuade him that they were the right club for him. He was only twenty, and the fee represented a much greater risk for the club, but he still had plenty of room to develop and reach his impressive potential.

Derek Cooper also returned to former club Ajax to bolster his squad with players he knew and could trust. Jose Luis Camarasa had been on loan during Cooper's time in charge there and the centre back joined Juventus permanently in a £5.25m deal from A.Madrid. Marek Janda had been an exciting prospect Cooper picked up in the Czech Republic and Ajax had made him available for just £1m, which Cooper was more than happy to pay for a player he believed still had plenty of room to develop. Marcel Groot had been a promising Dutch central midfielder from the Ajax academy that had been on the fringes of the first team under Cooper and when he became available for £3.5m he took the gamble on him too.

Despite attempts to secure other permanent deals for former players Ajax were understandably looking to make Juventus and Cooper pay a premium for any further permanent transfers so loan deals for wingers Rui Ferreira and Frederico Antunes alongside striker Rocky Homoet were agreed as a compromise for both parties.

Derek Cooper and his recruitment team had worked extensively throughout South America previously, but with the foreign player limits in place in Italy Portugal was proving to be another option and they looked to exploit what could be a market with great value within it. Deals to sign players from clubs such as Academica, Vit. Setubal, Arouca and Braga saw players with a great deal of potential join the club with fees ranging from £150k to £800k.

Ahead of the opening pre-season fixture on the 11th of July 2028 Cooper managed to secure another couple of big deals for the club. Norwegian central midfielder Svein Harald Harket joined on a season long loan from Manchester United and fellow midfielder, twenty-five year old Argentinean, Matias Sanchez joined on a permanent deal from Boca Juniors for £5.25m. Cooper was particularly excited by the deal for Sanchez. The last player he had signed from Boca had been Ignacio Varennes during his time at Ajax and he had turned out to be a fantastic acquisition.

Pre-season allowed Cooper to bed in his new players and spot any deficiencies within the squad. He began the friendlies as he always did with an in house match against the U18's before a packed programme which included games against former clubs Ajax and Ross County as well as Arsenal, Bra , Legnano, Juventus U20's and a testimonial in Sampdoria.

The beginning of August saw the club jet off for a quick training camp in South Korea. There they would compete in a couple of exhibition matches to increase the clubs exposure and maximise the commercial income following the signing of South Korean international Moon Ik-Hyun. It was a plan devised by Cooper to hopefully allow some growth within the Asian market as well as good preparation for the season opener at home to Salernitana on the 20th of August.

Juventus lost just one match of their busy pre-season schedule with defeat coming against Ajax (5-2) in an exciting match. Arsenal held Juve to a draw (2-2) whilst they won the other eight matches scoring plenty of goals in the process. Legnano and Bra were both beaten 6-0, Sampdoria lost 5-3 and the two games over in South Korea saw consecutive 4-0 wins for the Old Lady. Moon Ik-Hyun failed to find the net in either match, but the games had hopefully served their purpose and raised the profile of the club in the Asian market.

Cooper was continually active in the transfer market during the non-competitive matches and agreed the biggest deal of the summer when he decided to sell Norwegian striker Kevin Didriksen to Liverpool for £27m. Didriksen had performed well for Cooper at the tail end of last season, but he was unlikely to get a better offer for the twenty-seven year old. On the same day he agreed to sell Didriksen he also signed off on the £10m transfer of back up goalkeeper Guillermo Prieto to English side Aston Villa.

Those two deals had seen Juventus receive £37m and allowed Cooper to further invest in the squad. Impressive eighteen year old winger Abdoulaye Sy signed for an incentivised £4.5m from FC Sochaux-Montbe, striker Kwabena Diallo also signed from Ligue 1 in France joining for a fee of £7.5m from AS Monaco and Ezra

Kok was another ex-player who signed on loan from Ajax to join the raft of former players at Cooper's disposal once again.

There was also a deal agreed that Cooper saw as potentially the best of his career to date. Spanish defensive midfielder David Arce had been spotted by a member of Coopers scouting staff playing youth football for Espanyol and was available for just £95k compensation. The eighteen year old had bags of potential and was already showing signs that he could well develop into a potential superstar. Cooper was delighted to get the deal over the line and bring him to the club.

With his squad now formed and the transfer window closed until January Cooper was keen to get stuck into his first full season in charge of Juventus. There was a sixth place finish to be improved upon and a fifteen point gap to be reduced on last season's Champions.

Cooper had achieved similar feats in the past and he was hopeful he would be able to do the same again. Winning Serie A was obviously the ultimate goal, but his objectives for this season were to finish higher than the sixth from last campaign, break into the top four and secure a return to Champions League action. Only then could Cooper say the season had been a successful one.

Cooper had what he considered to be a kind opening to the Serie A campaign with fixtures against Salernitana, Crotone and Bologna ahead of their opening Europa League fixture in mid September. Juventus started well, with an opening day win at home to Slernitana (3-0). New boys Diallo and Pentz signed on with debut goals either side of a David Smit strike.

Crotone were up next and Diallo had a real mixed bag in the disappointing draw (2-2). He opened the scoring in the first minute before adding a second just before half time. Crotone then somehow got back into the match scoring in the fifty-third and sixty-first minutes before Diallo received his marching orders after allowing frustration to get the better of him. He was subsequently banned for the visit of Bologna, but his goals weren't missed as Juventus won (3-1) with Smit, the on loan Homoet and an own goal on the score sheet. Serie A had started with two wins, one draw, eight goals scored, three conceded and one red card. All things considered Cooper was relatively happy with that heading into Europa League action.

Juventus had been drawn in Europa League Group D alongside AZ, Dinipro and Dinamo Bucharest. It was a group that Cooper considered winnable and he fully expected to qualify without much of a problem. AZ represented familiar opponents, but little was known about the other two clubs and scouts were dispatched to do due diligence.

AZ were up first in gameweek one and Cooper travelled to Holland confident of getting a positive result. Back in the familiar surroundings of AFAS Stadion Cooper was surprised by the home side as they took the lead through Haruna Onuegbu, a Nigerian defender Cooper had signed as an eighteen year old for Ajax and subsequently sold to AZ. Juventus were surprised, but not stunned and a quick fire double from David Smit just before half time carried them to the break with a 2-1 lead.

Derek Cooper warned his side not to be complacent, telling them that AZ would come at them in the second half. It took just five minutes for AZ to prove him right as Juve failed to heed his warnings. Polish front man Dariusz Gawllik drew them level at 2-2. Again Juventus responded and midfielder Maxence Gonalons struck to put the Italians back in the lead with sixty-six minutes gone. AZ were proving to be much more resilient than anticipated and looked more than capable of trading blows with Coopers side. Just three minutes after the restart the game was level again with Ricardo Barbosa netting for AZ. Juventus had been the better side, but they had been unable to shake off the dogged Dutch side until Moon Ik-Hyun weaved some magic down the right hand side and slotted home the winner with five minutes of normal time remaining. The game finished 4-3 to Juventus and Cooper was pleased at the character shown by his side whilst admiring the determination of an impressive AZ that had been more than capable of going toe to toe with the attacking nature of his tactics.

The perceived easy start to Serie A continued on the return to domestic action with games against Ascoli and Palermo ahead of what Cooper considered their first real test in Roma. Having just two days between the AZ and Ascoli fixtures was not ideal and it showed as Juventus failed to put their opponents away having led at the break. An early second half equaliser for their opponents meant Juventus maintained their unbeaten start in the draw (2-2), but would not take all three points back to Turin.

Palermo were up next and nothing much happened for the opening hour of the match before it burst to life. Raphael Guerreiro put the visitors one up on fifty-nine minutes before Moon Ik-Hyun levelled in the sixty-second. Palermo were back in the lead after seventy-six minutes through their home-grown striker Guiseppe Farina. Cooper responded by demanding more of his players and he was rewarded with an immediate reply from Rocky Homoet in the seventy-eighth minute. Juventus smelled blood and wanted the win, they were in the ascendancy and looked the more likely to go on and get all three points. It was to be another eighty-fifth minute winner for the second time in three games as midfielder Matias Sanchez grabbed the late winner this time.

Once again Cooper was pleased with the winning mentality and the attacking power of his side, but he had cause for concern over the number of goals they were conceding, seven goals in three games wasn't ideal and was certainly not the norm for a stereotypical Italian side. Roma were up next and Cooper could not afford to lose ground to a side he considered a rival so early in the season. An improvement defensively was a must ahead of the game.

A trip to the Olimpico was never easy and Cooper suffered a heavy defeat there last season in the Italian Cup semi final. Roma had finished fourth last season in comparison to Juve's sixth and Cooper wanted to make sure that wasn't the case this campaign. Juventus had been persisting with Cooper's usual brand of attacking football, but he would tone it down for the trip to Rome in an attempt to sure up what had been a very leaky defence.

The game kicked off and it quickly became apparent that neither side wanted to lose the match. It made for a very cagey affair with very little in the way of highlights. The match slowly meandered towards a drab 0-0, which Cooper considered a better result for his side than their opponents. The clean sheet was a welcome one, and a point away at a rival to continue the unbeaten start was another positive to be taken from the result.

The next big test for Cooper and Juventus would come with the visit of INTER to Juventus Stadium in a months' time. Between the Roma and INTER fixtures Juventus continued their unbeaten runs in both the Serie A and Europa League with wins against Cesena (2-1), Sassuolo (1-0), Dinipro (4-0) and Dinamo Bucharest (4-2). Kwabena Diallo had returned to the side and was back amongst the goals scoring four in four matches. Abdoulaye Sy and Ezra Kok also scored their first goals for the club in league wins which was pleasing to see.

As with Roma, INTER were a side Cooper considered to be direct rivals for a top four finish having finished as runners up to their Milan rivals in last season's Serie A. The draw away to Roma had been a good result, but Cooper hoped that with home advantage he would be able to grab all three points against INTER.

As such Cooper would revert back to his attacking philosophy and attempt to outscore the opposition. INTER were also unbeaten in Serie A coming into the match at Juventus Stadium and were fresh off the back of a 4-0 win against Foirentina. Kwabena Diallo was up top following his return to goal scoring ways and he led the line impeccably scoring the only goal of a fairly tight affair in the thirty-second minute. Juventus held onto the win (1-0) and brought an end to INTER's unbeaten start to the season.

As Cooper and Juventus ended October and headed into November the games continued to come thick and fast ahead of the short winter break over Christmas and New Year. October continued to be a good month for Juve as the remaining two fixtures of the month bought wins and six Seire A points.

Brescia put in a very spirited performance and were ahead going into the final twenty minutes of the match, but Coopers men rallied late on to overpower the hosts and secure the win (3-1) with Smit, Ik-Hyun and Homoet on target. Foirentina were also beaten, but they were the side who finished the game strongest in the Juventus win (2-1). A Viola goal in the eighty-third minute threatened to undo the good work and goals of Smit and Ezra Kok, two of Juve's strong Dutch contingent.

Cooper was experiencing the best form of his time in Italy thus far, unbeaten this season notching eleven wins and three draws across their Serie A and Europa League fixtures. November would see five fixtures contested including the return fixtures against Dinamo Bucharest and AZ in the Europa League. Juventus were in control of their group and wins against Dinamo and AZ would secure them top spot.

A rotated side started the first fixture of the month away in Bucharest and Italian striker Alfredo Fava made the most of his opportunity taking home the match ball having scored a hat-trick in the easy win (5-2). Fellow striker Marek Janda also grabbed himself a rare goal before Smit scored the fifth.

Before gameweek five and the visit of AZ there was the matter of domestic ties against Sampdoria and Atalanta. Juventus notched up another impressive win away to Sampdoria (4-0) before they dropped their first points in the league for nearly two months with a draw away to Atalanta (1-1).

The game away to AZ had been a goal fest with Juventus running out narrow winners 4-3. Cooper hoped for a much tighter defensive performance this time out as beating AZ here would guarantee Juventus could not be caught and would qualify from their group as winners. That was incentive enough for Derek to task his side to attack from the off and really take the game to their opponents.

His players duly delivered and Moon Ik-Hyun in particular stood out as it was his turn to take home a Europa League hat-trick ball. It ended 5-1 on the night with Moon (3), David Smit and Jurgen Hoxha on the score sheet. Hoxha was an attacking midfielder by trade, but he had adjusted to play in one of the deeper roles in the middle of the park and he was beginning to reap the rewards of his manager's tutelage. With this win Derek Cooper had secured safe passage from Group D for Juventus and could now look forward to knockout European football in the New Year.

November began with a win and the visit of Pescara to Juventus Stadium would see them close out the month with another (4-0). Smit (2), Fava and Rui Ferreira were on target in the match in which Derek had rotated his players and still managed to sweep the opposition aside. David Smit had enjoyed a particularly fruitful month scoring in all but one of the matches and taking his season total to twelve in all competitions ahead of Diallo and Moon Ik-Hyun who had nine goals each.

December rolled into town with Derek looking to keep the good run of form going and maintain their place at the sharp end of the Serie A table. A brace from Alfredo Fava was enough to cancel out the own goal of team mate Jairo Riedewald and start the month with a home win against Lazio (2-1).

It was then onto gameweek six of the Europa League and a trip to the Ukraine to face Dinipro, it was 1-1 after nine minutes, but the match would be unable to sustain that pace and there was just one more goal in another win for Juventus (2-1). Ukraine was a tough trip midweek and Cooper had left a number of his regular starters at home in preparation for the match away to Napoli who had only one Serie A defeat to their name this season.

Napoli had lost that match last time out in a defeat at the hands of Foirentina leaving Juve as the form team coming into the fixture. A visit to the intimidating San Paolo was never easy, especially after a gruelling midweek trip. The match itself was a very tight affair and neither side wanted to drop points to a rival. Sadly it was Cooper's men who blinked first and allowed Napoli's classy Belgian attacking midfielder Grant Phuthego to put the hosts ahead. Juventus were unable to break their resolve and the twenty-fourth minute strike was enough for a 1-0 win to end the Juventus unbeaten run which had gone on to last fifteen games.

As always Cooper was keen to see his side respond to the set back and show the character required to bounce back in their next game. Thankfully the next game was against weaker opposition in Cagliari who were very much relegation candidates having finished in seventeenth for the last two seasons.

Coopers task was made easier on the night when left back Nicola Vesconti was sent off halfway through the first half for Cagliari, reducing them to ten men away from home. Amazingly and against the run of play the ten men would take the lead just before the interval prompting Cooper to aggressively address his players questioning their passion and desire. The chat would illicit the required response and goals from Fava (2), Sy and Smit saw Juventus end up winning comfortably (4-1).

Udinese were the final opposition before the Serie A would resume again in 2029 and Diallo fired Juventus into the lead inside the opening minute. A mad ten minutes midway through that first half saw Juventus concede twice and throwaway what could have been another vital three points by losing 2-1.

Juventus went into the winter break in a strong position, better than Cooper could have hoped for in pre-season as he looked to bed in a number of new recruits. He was however troubled by the recent dip in form and hoped it was just a blip rather than the wheels coming off what had been a very impressive campaign to date.

It was a much shorter winter break in Italy than Cooper had become used to in Holland so there was no need to arrange friendlies or training camps. It was simply a time for Cooper and his players to continue their training as they looked to recuperate with friends and family over the Christmas break. Derek allowed his players Christmas and Boxing Day off and he returned home to Lowestoft to be amongst his nearest and dearest ahead of the end to his first full season in charge.

It was back to action on the 7th of January 2029 and reigning champions AC Milan offered Cooper the chance to measure his current squad against the current league champions. Juventus were helped by another early red card as Italian defender and former Juventus player Edoarado Goldaniga was sent off on twenty-nine minutes. The ten men of Milan struggled to contain a Juve side that Cooper was encouraging to push forward and go for the jugular. A quick fire double on the stroke of half time effectively killed the game as first David Smit and then Ezra Kok found the back of the net. It was a blow Milan couldn't recover from and Juventus were largely untroubled in a second half that was of no consequence to the result. Juventus had won at the San Siro (2-0) and Cooper was delighted to start the second half of the season with a win.

Four victories followed the win in Milan as Juventus took on Salernitana (3-1), Novara (1-0) in the Italian Cup, Crotone (2-0) and Bologna (1-0). Milan aside it had been another kind opening for Juve and Cooper was once again pleased with the start his side had made. The three clean sheets were particularly pleasing having not kept back to back clean sheets since late September in the games against Roma and Dinipro.

January ended with anItalian Cup quarter final tie against Atalanta and a chance for Derek to try and win the domestic cup he had been craving since winning the Nathaniel MG Cup back in 2021 with TNS. The game with Atalnta started at a frantic pace with Luc Stoll opening the scoring in the very first minute for the away side. Hoxha pulled Juventus level ten minutes later, but again the visitors got themselves in front with goals either side of half time. Cooper made some changes and freshened things up in the hope of coming back into the game and he looked to have done it to perfection as goals from strikers Fava and Janda drew Juventus back on terms at 3-3 with eighty-two minutes gone. Juventus were now in the ascendancy and headed into extra time as the side most likely to nick a winner.

Atalanta had other ideas and Andrea Pinmonti scored his second of the game as the clock hit eleven minutes of extra time played. Juventus again pushed for a way back into the game and Hannes Pentz pushed a little too hard getting himself sent off with ten minutes of the game to go. Being down a man as well as a goal proved too much for Juve and they crashed out of the Italian Cup a round earlier than they had in 2027/28, much to the disappointment of their manager.

The January transfer window closed the day after cup elimination, but there was very little to report for Derek Cooper and Juventus. There were some signings made with all but one coming from clubs in Portugal, but they were all considered players for the youth section sides to sell on after some development with the club. Cooper was happy with the balance of the first team squad and there were no players available that he felt were worth bringing in. To that end there were also no outgoing sales and Derek worked hard to keep his squad intact and pulling in the right direction.

Cup disappointment put to one side it was back to Serie A action ahead of the Europa League first knockout round and another trip to Holland to face old title rivals Feyenoord. A win against Ascoli (3-0) and a poor performance in a draw with Palermo (2-2) preceded the first leg of the Feyenoord tie and trip to Rotterdam.

Cooper always wanted to make a winning return to old clubs and their league rivals and this was no different, it also had the added incentive of it being knockout football, which added that extra bit of spice. Feyenoord had always proven tough opposition for Cooper whilst at Ajax and had been the number one Dutch side prior to his arrival in the Eredivisie. They proved to be stern opposition once more and his Juventus side although superior on paper failed to prove that on the pitch. In the end a solitary David Smit goal on his return to face his former club would be enough to secure the 1-0 away win.

Before the return leg against Feyenoord Cooper had a tough Monday night fixture against Roma, a side who were hot on their heels in Serie A and looking to capitalise on the Europa League distractions of Cooper and Juventus. The game started badly for Juve as Kok put the ball past his own keeper to send Roma ahead, before Abdoulaye Sy levelled the game after thirty-six minutes. With half time approaching Roma would strike again to see them lead at the break.

Juventus struggled to recover and made a tired effort of dragging themselves back into the game. Roma sensed the fatigue within the legs of their Juventus counterparts and extended their lead in the seventy-ninth minute. The game was done and Juventus lost their third Serie A game of the season (3-1) against a direct rival for the top four and possibly the title at this point.

A week after the first leg in Rotterdam Feyenoord were the visitors to Juventus Stadium looking to overturn their home loss. David Smit who had scored against his old club at his old home, scored again for his new side in his new home, putting Juve 1-0 up on twenty-eight minutes. Moon Ik-Hyun would add a second on forty minutes and it was effectively game over at 2-0 on the night and 3-0 on aggregate.

Only an unlikely Juventus collapse and three away goals from Feyenoord could save the Dutch club. With neither likely to happen the second half petered away with little of note for either side. Juventus progressed into the Second Knockout Round and Cooper began to cast his mind back to the Europa League victory he had in 2024/25 in his first full season in charge at Ajax. What a remarkable coincidence it would be were he to achieve the same feat in his first full season with Juventus.

European progression secured it was back to domestic duty, whilst players and staff waited to see who they would be paired against in the second knockout round of the Europa League. Cooper wanted to continue the sides' good form against Cesena and Sassuolo. Having played twenty-five matches so far Juventus had managed seventeen wins, five draws and just the three defeats. A strong end to the campaign could see them challenge the likes of INTER and a very strong Napoli side at the top of the table.

The trip to Cesena started well with goals from Smit and Diallo, but Juventus let their lead slip not once, but twice and allowed the home side to rescue a point in the ninety-first minute. Dropping vital points against weaker opposition was always a disappointment, but drawing so late on made it particularly galling for Cooper.

They had the chance to put things right a week later against Sassuolo with another game that looked winnable on paper. Smit put the Old Lady ahead once again, before Marek Janda added a second. Unfortunately for Cooper his Juventus side were yet again unable to hold onto a lead and allowed inferior opposition back into the game to earn a share of those valuable points. Another day to forget for Cooper who was left incredibly frustrated at his sides wastefulness and lack of concentration when in front.

Ahead of the Sassuolo stalemate Juventus had watched the Europa League draw to see they would come up against league rivals Napoli. It was one of the tougher draws of the round with slightly easier sides such as Palermo, FC Kobenhaven and Dynamo Kyiv drawn elsewhere. Cooper was reluctant to put all his eggs in one basket as was the case with some managers in the past and he felt he was able to compete across both the Serie A and the Europa League. Winning Serie A was unlikely, but he was not willing to concede the fact until it was mathematically impossible.

It was back to the San Paolo for the first leg of the Europa League tie against Napoli. Cooper and Juventus had suffered their first defeat of the season there earlier in the campaign, a defeat that ended a fifteen match unbeaten run. Form heading into the fixture hadn't been great, throwing away leads and failing to convert dominance into goals had proven to be their undoing in recent displays.

Late goals had also proven a pain for Cooper in recent matches, but he was to be the beneficiary of one here as experienced full back Felix Passlack notched in theninety-second minute to silence the home crowd. The game had started in much the same way as previous fixtures against Napoli had with Moises Otero scoring for the hosts. David Smit then continued his fine goal scoring form with the leveller ten minutes after the break. Napoli were probably the better side and certainly created the better chances, Cooper would have been satisfied with the draw and an away goal, but Passlack and his dramatic late goal meant it was advantage Juventus heading back to Turin.

There was no rest for Juventus as they faced a tough league match with INTER between the ties with Napoli. It was an unrelenting week of football that could potentially see them fall behind in the league and be eliminated from Europe too. Coopers gamble to try and be competitive on both fronts could backfire spectacularly. Although he hadn't given up on a tilt at the title he was fully aware that it was increasingly unlikely. Napoli were simply too strong and they had opened up a gap at the top.

INTER however were right in the thick of the chasing pack along with Juventus. Both sides were eyeing up that runners up spot and Champions League football, which was still the primary objective for Cooper. The trip to Naples had taken a lot out of the Juventus lads and Cooper rotated slightly in the hope he could win the match and save a few legs for the Napoli game in two days time.

INTER had the benefit of no European football and a longer rest ahead of the match and it showed in the first half. Portuguese striker and £42.5m man Robim Schaufelberger and French attacking midfielder Houssem Aouar put the home side ahead with goals in the thirty-second and forty-sixth minutes. The goal from Aouar was the worst possible start to the second half for Cooper, but it did at least illicit the right response from his players as they began to show signs of life. South Korean winger Moon Ik-Hyun pulled one back in the fifty-eigth minute, but it was to be the only reply from Juventus as they were left unable to score an equaliser. Their case wasn't helped in the eighty-fifth minute as Ezra Kok was sent off, reducing Juventus to ten men.

It had been a poor display against INTER, but there was little time to dwell on it as Napoli arrived looking to overturn the deficit of the first leg. With more Serie A points dropped Cooper was more determined than ever to see his side go deep in the Europa League. Getting past Napoli would see them progress into the quarter finals and any side that made it that far had a real chance of winning it.

Juventus Stadium wanted to see a performance from Cooper's men to dump a rival Italian side out of the competition. Alfredo Fava made the most of his start with the opener on thirty-nine minutes sending Juventus into the break 1-0 up on the night and 3-1 to the good on aggregate. Napoli responded well and were almost immediately on terms following the half time break. Emmanuel Kamga broke through the Juventus back line to score with just one minute of the second half having been played and Coopers men clearly still in the changing room.

Letting Napoli back in and allowing them to get their away goal so easily angered Cooper, but it also unnerved him with the game now finely poised at 3-2 on aggregate. Another goal for Napoli would see them gain the advantage through the pesky away goals rule. Juventus held firm and weathered the early second half pressure from Napoli. Slowly, but surely Juve regained control using their home advantage. Pushed on by the crowd David Smit added a second before Fava grabbed his second and Juve's third to make it 3-1. The game finished that way and Juventus progressed through to the Europa League quarter final 5-2 on aggregate.

There was a real buzz around the place in the days and weeks following the Napoli result. The win had buoyed not just the players, but Derek Cooper too and it showed in their Serie A performances. They went on a three match winning run beating Brescia (5-2), Foirentina (3-0) and Sampdoria (1-0).

Cooper was particularly pleased with the final win against Sampdoria with the winner coming in the eighty-eighth minute courtesy of a Kwabena Diallo penalty. It showed Cooper that his side had what it took to dig deep and win a game that they hadn't played particularly well in. That was a skill that his players hadn't always shown they were capable of in recent months and the tough 1-0 was hopefully a sign that they had found a bit of resilience. David Smit was taken out of the firing line for the Foirentina and Sampdoria matches for a rest. He had become a vital component of the team and his eight goals in his last nine appearances were testament to that.

The quarter final stage for the Europa League had been drawn and Cooper was delighted to be facing off against boyhood club Liverpool. He had been interviewed for the job whilst at Ajax, but the Merseyside club had ultimately decided he wasn't the man for them opting for William Kvist instead. Kvist had not lasted long at Anfield and found himself out of the job by December 2027.

They were now under the management of Ralph Hassenhuttl with the Austrian having taken charge in January 2028. He had improved league performances in his time there and had now led them to a Europa League quarter final against Derek Coopers Juventus. It was once again a chance for Cooper to return to his home country and show the fans there what one of their exports was capable of. The chance to stand on the touchline at Anfield was also making the hairs on the back of his neck stand up, even if it was only as a visiting manager.

Cooper would have to wait for his Anfield debut as Liverpool were to visit Turin for the first leg. David Smit returned to the side fresh from his two game break and the Dutch forward looked completely rejuvenated. The rest had clearly worked and Smit helped himself to two goals in a 3-0 victory for Juventus. The early damage had been done with the first half brace from Smit before Alfredo Fava sealed a comfortable home win and saw Juventus head to Liverpool on the right end of a 3-0 aggregate score.

Atalanta followed Liverpool at Juventus Stadium just two days later to suffer the same fate albeit by a slightly smaller score line (2-0). David Smit was once again amongst the goals grabbing the second to add to the Jurgen Hoxha opener. It was a fourth straight win for Juventus in the Serie A and meant that they were still very much in and amongst it at the top of the table. With the Atalanta result put to bed and three points in the bag Cooper could allow his mind to move on to the impending trip to what he considered the home of football.

As a young lad Derek Cooper dreamed of playing football for Liverpool and running out to touch the "This is Anfield" sign. As a young man he dreamed of one day managing his club and leading them to domestic and European glory as Shankly, Paisley, Dalglish and Benitez had done in years gone by.

His Anfield debut would come as the manager of Italian side Juventus, but Cooper would not let that diminish his desire to make a winning start on the ground. To win at Anfield would be a real buzz for Derek and he was determined to see it happen. The side travelled to Merseyside ahead of the fixture and whilst they were out training on the pitch Cooper used the time to make his way around the venue, soaking up the history of the club and imagining what it would be like to one day walk the corridors as manager of Liverpool Football Club.

Come 19:45 on the 19th of April 2029 it was purely business for Cooper as his side looked to extend their lead from the first leg. Hassenhuttl had his men fired up for the game and they looked to start strong and force their way back into the tie. They managed to do just that as impressive Uruguayan striker Santiago Lietes put them ahead in the thirty-first minute. Juventus managed to stop them building any momentum following the Lietes opener and made it to halftime losing on the night but still in control on aggregate.

Liverpool again looked to assert themselves in the second half with that man Lietes looking like the real deal and posing a considerable threat to Juventus. Liverpool managed to break the Juventus resolve for a second time on sixty-five minutes, but it was to come from their French striker Brian Houssein rather than the lively Uruguayan.

With Juventus 2-0 down and facing an inspired Liverpool comeback Derek Cooper implored his side to show some passion from his technical area. Going out of the competition having won the first leg 3-0 at home would be a bitter pill to swallow and one Cooper was desperate to avoid. Felix Passlack was proving to be a real asset in his role as fullback and he stepped up once more to stop the Anfield rot in the sixty-eighth minute and score a vital away goal to make it 4-2 on aggregate.

The final twenty minutes saw a deflated Liverpool fail to recover from the Passlack goal and although the game ended in defeat for Juventus (2-1), it saw them progress through to the semi final over the two legs. Coopers Anfield debut had ended in defeat, but ultimately he had been the winner as his side made it to the next round and celebrated in front of the travelling support.

Derek Cooper had lifted the Europa League with Ajax and he had now made it to the semi final as manager of Juventus. He, like the players and the fans were now starting to believe that Europa League success may well be a possibility. They had been handed a relatively kind tie having been drawn against Danish side FC Kobenhavn instead of Real Sociedad or Hamburg who would contest the other semi final. This only added to the feeling that it could be their year to win a European trophy.

The recent run of fixtures had taken a toll on the Juventus players and their return fixture in Serie A saw them travel to Pescara and contest a thrilling 4-3. All seven goals came in the first half as Pescara and Juve flew out of the blocks with each team looking to kill the other one off as quickly as possible. It was a breathless, end to end start to the game which didn't suit Juventus who looked leggy given their European exploits. It was a clever ploy from Pescara who looked to capitalise on their freshness in comparison. Goals from Diallo, Passlack and an own goal were all in vain as ultimately Pescara had enough in the tank to claim all three points.

Udinese were up next ahead of the opening Kobenhavn fixture and Cooper was hoping his players were capable of contesting two games in four days again. He had allowed a brief respite from training in an attempt to keep condition and match sharpness as high as possible. Having missed out on three vital points last time out Cooper wanted to rectify their domestic form in an attempt at making one last push for that runner up spot. It was Napoli's title to throw away, but he wanted to push them as hard as he could. Diallo, Smit and Moon Ik-Hyun all rewarded Cooper's team selection with a goal each in a comfortable win (3-0). Now attention turned back to the Europa League and Danish champions FC Kobenhavn.

Cooper had faced Kobenhavn in the Europa League earlier in his career, back in 2023/24 whilst in charge at Ross County. He had failed to get the better of them twice in Group F losing away and drawing at home. This time out Cooper was at the helm of a much bigger club, with vastly superior players and he fancied his chances. As confident as Cooper was he had to ensure that there was no element of complacency creeping in to the preparation of either himself or his players.

Juventus were a club that had been used to big European occasions, but it was now fourteen long years since their last European final when they had taken on and lost to Barcelona in the Champions League final of 2014/15. The club and its fans were desperate to see the Old Lady back in a European final and Cooper was acutely aware of the pressure mounting from the terraces. Derek was confident in his players and footballing philosophy, the two games against FC Kobenhavn represented a real shot at making the final.

FC Kobenhavn arrived at the Juventus Stadium on the evening of the 3rd of May 2029 looking to thwart Cooper's plans and put a kibosh on his hopes of adding another Europa League to his trophy cabinet. Cooper started the same eleven that had dismantled Udinese three days earlier with Kwabena Diallo retaining his place up top alongside David Smit.

Diallo scored again, his third in as many matches, in the ninth minute and got Juventus off to the best possible start. Kobenhavn rallied well and found a way back into the match from the penalty spot on thirty-six minutes with Luka Illic converting to score what could be a vital away goal.

Cooper took the chance at half time to reassure his players, telling them that they were doing fine and he knew there was much more to come. He hoped his positive and reassuring words would inspire his side to kick on and win the game. Kwabena Diallo had obviously been paying attention to the manager as he took the chance to add his second of the game when it came his way in the sixty-third minute. A 2-1 lead with twenty minutes to go was enough for Cooper to be satisfied and he looked to shut up shop and take the victory to Denmark in a weeks' time.

Before Derek and his lads travelled to Denmark there was a trip to the capital to face off against Lazio. Juventus were favourites for the match, with Lazio very much a mid table side at best, but Cooper's team had been in patchy form domestically with their minds possibly elsewhere. That proved to be the case again in Rome with Juventus unable to shake off the European cobwebs as his side slumped to defeat (1-0) courtesy of a Matheus Pereira goal.

The defeat to Lazio was Juventus' sixth of the season, but it was also their second in three league fixtures which was a concern for Cooper. There were only three Serie A fixtures left of the season and it was still possible that Cooper would be able to guide Juventus to a second place and Champions League qualification, but a drop off in form could see that all come under threat.

A Europa League win would see Juventus lift that trophy as well as compete in the playoff round of next seasons Champions League irrespective of where they finished in Serie A. All that stood in the way was the second leg in Denmark and a final against either Real Sociedad or Hamburg in Turkey.

The Lazio result had not been ideal preparation, but once again Cooper had the feeling that his team would come good in the Europa League when it mattered. They had only been beaten once in the competition thus far, losing away to Liverpool in the last round.

There was a crowd of 38,076 in Telia Parken to watch the second leg of the Semi Final with Juventus contributing 1,900 away supporters to add to the occasion. Derek Cooper felt that scoring an away goal to cancel out the penalty Kobenhavn got in Turin was paramount to making it to the final and set his side up to take the game to their opponents rather than sit back to protect their narrow lead.

The game kicked off and Juventus went straight on the front foot looking to score an away goal of their own. They came close early on before South Korean winger Moon Ik-Hyun found the back of the net in the thirty-first minute. It was now advantage Juventus and it was their game to lose. 3-1 up on aggregate Cooper told his team to keep their concentration and not let complacency get the better of them. Juventus went out for the second half and carried out their managers instructions perfectly. Kwabena Diallo grabbed himself another goal in the final ten minutes to put the tie beyond doubt and book Juventus their spot in the 23rd of May final in Turkey.

Ahead of the second European final of his managerial career Derek Cooper returned to league action and a potential title decider against Napoli. If Napoli won the fixture the Scudetto would almost certainly be theirs with INTER and Juventus left to fight for the runner up spot. Juventus were in the driving seat for that spot as it stood, but INTER were hot on their heels hoping to achieve back to back runner up spots and Champions League qualification.

It was a tough game to come back to and Juventus were slow out of the blocks. Napoli had been very good all season and it was a familiar face that once again found the back of the net against Derek Cooper. Peruvian striker Moises Otero scored his third goal against Juventus since Cooper's arrival at the club to put the visitors ahead. Juve's case wasn't helped when left back Hannes Pentz was sent off with just under half an hour of play remaining. Cooper continued to instruct his side to push for an equaliser, but with a man less and having just played a big European fixture there simply wasn't enough left in the tank. Napoli saw out the remainder of the match and held on to the three points that all but secured their second title in three years.

The game against Cagliari a week later was scheduled to be played just three days before the Europa League final against Real Sociedad, who had beaten Hamburg over two legs in the other semi final. With such a limited rest period between fixtures Derek took the decision to rotate his side as much as possible. The title was out of reach and although he obviously wanted to finish in that runner up spot, he wanted to win his second Europa League that much more.

Sant Elia and its 15,000 spectators were treated to a proper game of football that Juventus won late on with a ninety-second minute goal from Serbian right back Vlada Sreckovic. Sreckovic had made the most of a rare start since his £2.7m move from Partizan at the start of the season. David Smit and Greek centre back Asterios Gaianopoulos were the other scorers for Juventus in the win (3-2).

Annoyingly there was still one Serie A fixture left to be played and unusually it was to come after the Real Sociedad match. It wasn't ideal, but it was what it was and Cooper would have to deal with the situation. He had his first final as manager of Juventus to prepare for. The awkward league scheduling meant that preparations had been kept to a minimum and there was no time to take the squad away for a warm weather break as he had done with Ajax in 2024/25.

The squad had arrived in Turkey on the Monday following the Cagliari fixture and trained for the two days ahead of the Wednesday evening final to acclimatise and familiarise themselves with the impressive venue. Team spirit was good and Cooper was confident going into the match.

Real Sociedad were a side performing below expectations in La Liga this season and looked likely to finish well below their sixth place of last season which had seen them qualify for the Europa League. Although their league form had been poor they had produced impressive European performances and had beaten Hamburg, Villareal, AC Milan and Lille in the knockout stages of the competition to reach the final. Former INTER manager Ingo Dominguez was in charge of the Spanish side and he hoped to win them their first ever European trophy. Juventus and their European pedigree meant that Derek Cooper and his side entered the match as favourites with the bookies and pundits predicting a tight game, but a victory for the Old Lady.

Cooper started the game with his now customary 4-2-4 that he had developed at Ajax and had tweaked during his time with Juventus. Alex Meret would start in goal with a back four of Hannes Pentz, Jairo Riedewald, Ezra Kok and Antonio Salvaggio. The midfield two would be Jurgen Hoxha and Svein Herald Harket who had impressed whilst on loan at the club. The front four would see young Abdoulaye Sy start on the left hand side, Moon Ik-Hyun down the right with David Smit and Kwabena Diallo through the centre. It was a side that Cooper felt was his strongest eleven and he still had players such as Felix Passlack, Rui Ferreira, Alfredo Fava and Marek Janda on the bench who he knew were capable of making the difference.

The match was a 41,981 sell out being broadcast around the world to a global audience. Cooper had come a long way since managing his local semi-professional side back home in Lowestoft. Wearing a tailored club suit he led his side out to shake hands with the Turkish Prime minister and UEFA representatives before taking his place in the dugout alongside his trusted assistant Massimiliano Farris who had been invaluable since Cooper had arrived at the club.

The game kicked off with both sets of fans in full voice and an atmosphere worthy of a European showpiece. It was a tight opening quarter of the game as each side felt their way into the match. Juventus looked dangerous in attack, but they were also allowing Sociedad their fair share of chances.

As half time approached Cooper was planning what needed addressing ahead of the second half when Sociedad forced him into a rethink as striker Xabier Zablaza fired them ahead. The Juventus players sat in the changing room listening to Cooper telling them that he was disappointed in their performance so far, but that he knew there was more to come from them. Freshly motivated and with a European trophy as their reward the players headed out to make amends and get themselves back in the game.

The breakthrough just wouldn't come for Juventus as they toiled to get themselves an equaliser. They were now the better side and Sociedad had been limited to the odd counter attack. As the minutes ticked away Cooper looked to the bench to change things bringing Alfredo Fava and Rui Ferreira on to liven up the attacking options. The goal they had been looking for finally arrived in the seventy-third minute with David Smit on target to draw Juventus Level. Cooper shouted for his side to push forward and capitalise on their dominance.

With seventy-five minutes on the clock a rare Sociedad attack brought about a defensive error resulting in a penalty against Juventus. It was a nightmare for Cooper, coming just two minutes after his side had got themselves back into the game. Xabier Zablaza coolly slotted home the penalty with no signs of the pressure he surely must have been feeling. His second goal of the game had fired his side back into the lead and given himself the chance of a European final hat-trick. How would Juventus respond? It had taken them seventy-three minutes of hard work to get themselves level and just two further minutes for them to undo it all.

Things then went from bad to worse for Cooper as Sociedad, who were spurred on by the vociferous support, added a third goal through David Aranbarri in the 80th minute. The pressure of the occasion was getting to Coopers lads and they were beginning to sink without trace. Despite having most of the play and creating the better chances Sociedad had been much more clinical in front of goal and had capitalised on Juventus mistakes in the defensive third.

There were still ten minutes to play and Cooper urged his side to show some passion, there was still time, they had scored late goals before. The Juventus fans sensed their sides' chances slipping and upped the noise level to rival the Spanish fans and it had the desired effect. Jurgen Hoxha took the game by the scruff of the neck and managed to grab another goal for Juventus on eighty-six minutes. He was then instrumental as Cooper pushed men forward, throwing Ezra Kok up front and instructing Alex Meret to go forward should there be a late corner. Sociedad had all but retreated into their own eighteen yard box putting all eleven men between the ball and the goal.

For the remaining minutes Juvenuts looked to mount attack after attack, but they simply couldn't penetrate the layers of Sociedad's defence. The final whistle blew, Real Sociedad had held on to win 3-2. Juventus had given it their all and as Cooper shook hands with his opposite number, players dropped to their knees with some using their shirts to hide their tears.

It had been a tough result to take; they had played well, but ultimately come up short in the moments that really mattered. Derek Cooper led his side on a lap of the pitch to thank the travelling support and formed a guard of honour for the Real Sociedad players as they went to collect their winner's medals and the Europa League trophy. There was to be no second European trophy for Derek Cooper, at least not yet, but he was pleased to have made it to yet another final. He was heading in the right direction with Juventus and he was confident the future was bright for the club.

Juventus returned to Italy for their final game of the season against AC Milan which was still to be played. A win would guarantee finishing the season in second place behind Napoli and ahead of INTER in third. It wasn't much of a consolation for a side that had returned from Turkey immediately after their final loss to prepare for the game.

Cooper faced an uphill task motivating his players for the match and it showed in a home defeat (2-1) bearing all the markers of a European hangover. Italian international striker Andrea Frau grabbed a brace for Milan before Fava managed a late consolation to complete the scoring. It was a disappointing result which had opened the door for INTER to nick the runner up spot and compound a miserable five days for Derek and the Juventus squad.

After the Sociedad and Milan defeats Cooper retired to his office to look back on a season that at times promised so much, but ended up delivering so little. There was no trophy to show for their season's efforts and even the third place finish felt like a kick in the teeth. Derek looked back on his decision to try and compete across all competitions and couldn't help wondering whether it had been the right decision. Should he have prioritised one competition ahead of the others? He couldn't complain too much, he had surpassed the board expectations and had met his own objective of Champions League qualification. The board were evidently happy with progress under his management and he was offered a new contract that he had absolutely no hesitation in signing. Big things would happen here under his leadership, he was determined to return Juventus to the top of Italian football.

Individually there had been some pleasing performances and many of the younger players within the squad had taken great strides forward in their development. David Smit was probably the pick of the players making fifty-two appearances across all competitions, scoring thirty goals and attaining an average rating of 7.38. Fellow strikers Kwabena Diallo and Alfredo Fava had also played their part in the campaign scoring eighteen and twenty-one goals respectively.

Moon Ik-Hyun had settled well in Italy following his move from Mexico and achieved a 7.14 average rating across fifty appearances with the bonus of thirteen goals from right wing. Abdoulaye Sy had also settled well with the club and the eighteen year old had scored five goals in his twenty-seven appearances. Sy's development had been pleasing for Derek and it looked like being £3.5m well spent for the club.

Svein Herald Harket had played well in the middle of the park and Cooper was keen to get a permanent deal agreed over the summer. Initial contact with Manchester United had not been overly promising with them now wanting to offer him first team football at Old Trafford instead of loaning him back out or selling permanently.

The season hadn't been a complete disaster and the seventy-six points of 2028/29 was an eleven point improvement on their sixty-five points and sixth place finish of 2027/28. Coopers first full season in charge had seen Juventus move in the right direction, that was clear, but there was still plenty of work to be done and a fourteen point gap on Napoli to be overturned for starters. Winning Serie A was now Cooper's primary objective moving forward with Champions League qualification considered an absolute must.

Derek Cooper knew where it had gone wrong for them domestically. The second half of the Serie A campaign had been pockmarked by defeats that had scuppered any shot at the title and cost them their runners up spot. In the second half of the season Juventus suffered six of their eight defeats for the season with four of those losses coming in their last six games.

For Juventus to have any chance of challenging Napoli for the 29/30 Scudetto then they would need to make sure that they would be able to replicate the excellent league form from the first half of the season after the winter break. Without that being done they would be unable to mount a serious challenge for the title, there was simply too much competition in the league to get away with subpar performances at such an important time in the league campaign.

Throughout the season Cooper had kept tabs on potential recruits as well as monitoring the progress and decline of his current crop of players. Staffing wise Cooper was satisfied with the current set up and barring any major departures he doubted he would be adding to his staff. Player wise he was always looking at ways he could improve not just the first team squad, but the squads of both the U20's and U18's. That was an important part of Coopers plans for the club as a whole.

The summer window saw Cooper once again invest heavily as well as moving on a number of players that he felt were no longer of use to him, or had begun to decline and needed to make way for younger players to step up and develop. Derek Cooper was a manager who wasn't afraid to make tough calls and he had shown that already in his time at the club moving on senior players such as Martial, Samper and Weigl.

Having worked with limited resources since joining Juventus Cooper was now able to spend bigger with the club back in the Champions League. Cooper was taking a gamble as they would need to make it through to the group stage of the competition before the real revenue would kick in, but he was confident that with the right recruits it would be a risk he was comfortable taking.

By the 1st of August and the first competitive game of the season against FC Viitorul of Romania in the Champions League best placed playoff Qual.3 Cooper had concluded all of his incoming deals. Moving to get the players in place ahead of the competitive fixtures had been a priority for Cooper and he was absolutely over the moon with the business he had been able to get done. He ranked it up there as probably the best transfer window of his career to date.

Cooper had gone big on his defence splashing a combined £39m on two new starting centre backs. Derek returned to former club Ajax again as he went back and spent £17m on Ignacio Varennes who had been an absolute rock for him there having signed him from Boca Juniors. The other £22m was spent on a young Belgian who was showing signs of becoming a real world class centre back in the near future. Arne Bruyninckx joined from AA Gent and would be partnering the Argentinian Varennes in the heart of a new look back line. Portuguese left back Jose Cristo joined on loan from Manchester United having been deemed surplus to requirements there and Brazilian centre back Thyago also came in on loan, this time from AS Monaco, as cover for the two new centre backs.

Alex Meret had been a Juventus stalwart between the sticks since joining the club in 2021, but Cooper had deemed it was time for him to leave Juventus with Crystal Palace his destination in an £11m deal. Meret leaving cleared the way for there to be a new first team goalkeeper behind the expensively assembled back line.

Derek turned to another Belgian and Alexander Guillaume of Zulte Waregem. The twenty-one year old stopper was young and represented a risk with an outlay of £20.5m, but as with Bruyninckx he had the potential to go

105

on and become a world class player. Cooper also signed another young goalkeeper as understudy to Guillaume and become a starter across both the U18 and U20 teams as Serbian Dusan Vukomanovic joined for an initial £250k from Partizan

Federico Antunes once again linked up with Derek Cooper as he made his loan from Ajax permanent for the unbelievable fee of just £2m. At that price Cooper was unable to turn the deal down and Antunes would provide competition for Moon Ik-Hyun down the right hand side. Another attacking option was brought in to provide competition for Sy down the left had side. Mikel Goni was signed on a season long loan from Barcelona, with Rui Ferreira having returned to Ajax and Sy in need of some competition. Despite a reasonable first season Derek was acutely aware that Sy was still only young and would need taking out of the firing line every now and then, Goni would provide him with that option.

There were a number of other deals concluded for a range of promising players from across Europe to come and develop at the club. None of those deals broke the bank and Derek Cooper was confident he could have them develop enough to either turn out for the first team or be sold on for a profit at a later date.

Cooper had also been ruthless with the outgoing deals and prominent players Jario Riedewald (Cordoba, £1.8m), Alex Meret (Crystal Palace, £11m) and Asterios Gianopoulos (AS Saint-Etienne, £10m) all left the club on permanent deals. Cooper had been unable to arrange a permanent transfer for the ageing Felix Passlack with his large wages and Coopers asking price putting potential suitors off. Passlack was in the last year of his contract now and Cooper was keen to have him off the wage bill. A loan move was an option Cooper explored and the German full back ended up joining Liverpool for the season with them paying £300k per month and 50% of his wages for the season long loan.

There were also deals agreed which would see youngsters Marcelo Pires (Verona, £1.3m) and Emiliano Hyka (Genoa, £500k) leave for pastures new in search of first team football having failed to make the grade at Juventus.

Pre-season had gone well off the pitch with Cooper more than happy with the transfer business he had done and results on the pitch had been just as pleasing. Ahead of the FC Vitorul match Juventus had played seven friendlies winning five and drawing two. Wins came against the U20's (5-2), Spezia (3-1), Luzern (2-1), Anderlecht (2-0) and Venezia (3-1). The draws came against Young Boys (0-0) and West Ham (1-1).

New additions had settled in well and there was a good atmosphere around the club. Cooper was happy with the work done over the summer, but it was down to business earlier than usual this season as his side looked to progress into the Champions League group stage. Should they progress through the FC Vitorul tie there was then the best placed playoff to be contested before securing their place in the groups

FC Vitorul shouldn't have posed too many problems to a side of Juventus' stature and on paper the Italians had the much better side and were obvious favourites to progress. The first leg was to be played away in Romania with the return leg back in Italy a week later.

The game was a nervy affair and Juventus failed to find their rhythm in the early stages. It took until early in the second half for Juve to break the resolve of the Romanians with Jurgen Hoxha grabbing the first competitive goal of 2029/30. It remained 1-0 until the final whistle and Cooper would return to Turin with a solitary away goal and a clean sheet to kick off the season.

Between the Vitorul games Juventus sent a heavily rotated side to contest a friendly draw with Sparta Rotterdam (2-2) whilst the first team stayed behind to concentrate on the second leg.

Juventus started the return fixture much better than they had done in Romania and raced into a commanding three goal lead inside the opening half an hour. Vitorul couldn't live with the home side and Diallo opened his account for the season with a brace before Hannes Pentz completed the scoring on twenty-six minutes. The game was done by half time with the three goals on the night making it 4-0 on aggregate. Cooper gave minutes to some younger members of the squad in the second half and Juventus took their foot off the gas coasting to a comfortable win (3-0).

Juventus completed their pre-season in Spain with a draw against Espanol (2-2) and a win against Villareal (3-2) in a testimonial for their long serving player Augusto Batalla. They had been the final two fixtures ahead of a return to competitive action in the form of Serie A and the Champions League best placed playoff, which stood between them and the Champions League group stage.

In a cruel twist of fate Juventus had been drawn against their Europa League final opponents Real Sociedad, offering Cooper and the players the chance to exact revenge for that defeat at the end of last season. Sociedad had only qualified for the Champions League by beating Juventus in that final, so it would be poetic justice for Cooper to deny them their place in the groups.

The first leg of the best placed playoff was contested at Juventus Stadium with Ingo Dominguez bringing his Europa League champions to Turin looking to get one over Derek Cooper on his own patch. Cooper still had that final defeat fresh in his memory and that was driving him on to do better here.

Juventus got off to the best possible start in front of their home fans with Kwabena Diallo notching the first of the game after just three minutes. It felt like a tonne of pressure had been lifted off Cooper as the ball hit the back of the net, so desperate he was to avenge that loss. The goal also allowed his players the freedom to relax into the game and express themselves. Mikel Goni added a second and grabbed his first for the club after thirty minutes and Jurgen Hoxha made it three on the stroke of half time to put Juventus firmly in control of the tie.

Cooper was delighted with the first half and asked for more of the same in the second forty-five. Sadly with the game all but over the second half passed without incident. Sociedad were beaten and clammed up trying to keep the score down whilst Juventus took it easy knowing that they had the game won. No more goals followed and the final whistle sounded with Juventus the 3-0 winners.

Having got that particular monkey off his back for the time being Derek turned his attention to the opening fixture of the 2029/30 Serie A campaign keen to carry the good pre-season form into the league. For the second season running it would be Salernitana at home up first for Juventus. The game last season had seen Juventus run out 3-0 winners with Diallo, Smit and Pentz on the score sheet that day. A similar result to kick off this season would do just fine for Cooper.

Juventus started strongly again and went full throttle from the first minute. They found the back of the net after just three minutes for the second game running with Maxence Gonalons the man on target this time out. As with the Sociedad game there were two more added before the break with Alfredo Fava and Kwabena Diallo scoring in the sixteenth and forty-first minutes.

Once again Cooper spoke to his side with them 3-0 up at home by half time; more of the same was once again the message from the manager. The game threatened to drift away, but Salernitana delivered a wakeup call on the hour mark as Renato Megalo pulled one back to try and make a game of it. Juventus responded by adding a fourth through Abdoulaye Sy with ten minutes to go. Juventus had kicked off 2029/30 with a 4-1 win and three points.

Juventus had kicked the league off with a win and now it was time to put the final nail in the Real Sociedad coffin. Cooper and his lads travelled to Spain with a 3-0 aggregate lead, but once again Cooper was hoping to beat Sociedad on their own patch and banish those Europa League demons once and for all.

Derek had taken a gamble on his side qualifying for the group stages, spending big on squad improvements. Failure to reach the group stage would mean he had potentially risked the long term financial security of the club. The first leg result had put them in the ideal position to qualify and it was now just a case of getting the job done. With a 3-0 deficit to overturn the onus was on Real Sociedad to come out and attack, but in truth they looked a shadow of the side from that May final and very rarely offered any sort of attacking threat. Kwabena Diallo scored a fourth aggregate goal to ensure no way back for Ingo Dominguez's side. It ended 1-0 in Spain and 4-0 on aggregate with Champions League group stage qualification and the financial future of the club now secure.

As his side returned to Turin Derek Cooper jetted out to UEFA HQ to learn who Juventus would be competing against in the group stage. Whilst there Cooper took the opportunity to speak with Manchester United manager Jose Mourinho wanting to discuss the possibility of a deal for Herald Harket whilst Mourinho was asking after his player, Jose Cristo, who was on loan at Juventus.

Once the draw had been concluded Juventus had been pulled out in Group B alongside Borussia Dortmund, FC Porto and FK Austria Wien. A tough draw, one of the toughest he had faced, but he still fancied Juventus's chances. Derek had been keen to avoid English opponents and luckily the draw had been kind to him. Juventus would play FK Austria Wien on the 18th of September in their first game of the group stage.

Before that game with Austria Wien Juventus faced a trip to the San Siro to play last season's runners up INTER as well as a game against Bologna at home. Both games ended in 1-0's and fortunately for Derek Cooper Juve would be on the right side of both score lines. An own goal from the fantastically named Anne Mark Goolkate was enough to beat INTER in front of their own fans and a solitary goal for Abdoulaye Sy got the three points at home to Bologna. That meant a perfect start in the Serie A with three wins, six goals scored and just the one against.

FK Austria Wien were the next team to visit the Juventus Stadium and Juventus secured their third consecutive 1-0 win. In fact it was almost a carbon copy of the Bologna result as Sy was once again the scorer of the only goal of the game. It was a good start to the group for Juventus, but Cooper was left slightly underwhelmed that they hadn't been able to win by more. A win was a win of course, but Cooper had wanted to win convincingly and send a message to Dortmund and Porto who he considered the stronger members of the group. It hadn't quite panned out that way, but Juventus had the winning start they wanted.

A return to domestic action saw the frugal wins continue and Juventus played out their fifth 1-0 win on the trot against newly promoted Cremonese. It would be Kwabena Diallo rather than Abdoulaye Sy grabbing the goal, but it was a familiar feeling for Cooper who was glad to get the win, but was left feeling like he wanted more from his side. Winning with style was of course preferable and maybe it was the aesthetic aspect of the performances that left the manager disheartened. He certainly couldn't complain at his sides efficiency with nine wins from nine so far this season across both the Serie A and the Champions League.

Gameweek two of Group B took Derek Cooper to a stadium and atmosphere that he had dreamed of experiencing when he started out on his managerial career. The Signal Iduna Park and its "Yellow Wall" had a reputation that few stadiums in world football could match.Leading a side out here was another career high for Cooper and he hoped to crown the occasion with a win.

Juventus came into the Dortmund game having won at home to Udinese (2-1) and away to Cagliari (3-1) to see out September. Cooper had been boosted by his side scoring more than one goal in a game and in particular the return to form of striker Diallo who managed three goals in the two wins.

Diallo found the net again in Dortmund as his strike in the second half opened the scoring and put the visiting side ahead. Another form player for Juventus was Abdoulaye Sy who had all but matched his tally of five from last season by scoring his fourth of this campaign on seventy-four minutes to make it 2-0.

BVB responded thanks to their impressive German attacking midfielder Sead Dizdarevic as he found the net with ten minutes still to play. Cooper dropped his wide men back and looked to hold on to what would be an impressive away win for the team. Juventus managed to do just that making it two wins in Group B and twelve wins across all competitions so far this season.

It had been a fantastic start for Cooper and Juventus. They were sat at the top of Serie A and had back to back wins in a competitive Champions League group. They returned from Dortmund to take on newly promoted Verona and both Derek and his players were guilty of underestimating their opponents. The complacency cost Juventus not only the three points, but also their unbeaten run.

Francesco De Luca put the visitors ahead in the eighth minute and Juventus failed to formulate a response. They were the much better side with more of the ball and plenty more efforts on goal, but they were unable to use their dominance to grab the goals needed. Verona stunned Juventus Stadium with the 1-0 win to abruptly end what had been an impressive start to 2029/30.

Derek and his side had an international break to stew on the result before their return to action in the Olimpico nearly two weeks after the Verona defeat. His players responded in the right way and the Lazio game saw a return of the familiar third minute opener courtesy of Alfredo Fava this time out. Juventus added a second through Jurgen Hoxha but it was a game to forget for on loan centre-back Thyago as he would send the ball past his own goal keeper before being dismissed late on. A win (2-1) was just what Juve needed and it was a good result for Derek who was happy to return to winning ways.

The trip to Portugal to face FC Porto followed the Lazio game with their hosts having won one and lost one of their group games so far. The result against Dortmund in front of their own fans had raised his expectations to a level where Derek considered anything but a win at the Estadio do Drago a poor result.

That opinion changed fairly quickly as central defender Arne Bruyninckx was sent off with just sixteen minutes on the clock. It forced Cooper to sacrifice one of his strikers to plug the gap left by the Belgian and re-evaluate what he considered a good result. Getting out of Porto with a point was now the aim and anything beyond that was a bonus.

Juve held firm until half time and made it through a large portion of the second half before the Portuguese side finally managed to breach the backline. Goals in the seventy-sixth and eighty-sixth minutes saw off the ten men of Juventus and sent a disappointed Cooper back to Turin with no points. There would be repercussions for young Bruyninckx who was fined a week's wages for his lack of discipline in the fixture.

The inconsistency continued through to the end of October as Juventus followed up the loss in Portugal with a win at home to Sampdoria (4-2) and a catastrophic derby loss to Turin rivals Torino (2-1). Every win in October had been followed by a loss and Cooper hoped that November would see his side recapture their early season form and manage to string a run of wins together. If the inconsistency continued there was a real danger Juventus would drop behind Napoli who had once again started very strongly.

Cooper was hoping that November would be a better month and Juventus were able to eradicate the losses that had punctuated each win during October. AC Milan were the first opponents of the new month and Juventus dispatched them with ease (4-2) on their way to four matches that saw them score four goals in each.

After Milan Juve exacted revenge on Porto (4-0), beat Fiorentina (4-1) and finally Sassuolo (4-0). Juventus closed out the month away to FK Austria Wien in Gameweek five of the Champions League. Abdoulaye Sy and Kwabena Diallo had been in fine form during November with Sy grabbing five goals and Diallo six, including a Champions League hat-trick against FC Porto. Both men found the net again in Austria with Diallo helping himself to back to back Champions League hat-tricks adding another match ball to the collection. Maxence

Gonalons and David Smit also scored in an impressive 6-1 victory to conclude what had been a very successful month for the Old Lady and its manager.

Juventus faced the toughest possible start to December, travelling to Naples to take on the reigning champions. Morale was high off the back of their high scoring winning run, but Napoli themselves were also in good form and had lost only two league games so far this season. Cooper had had mixed results against Napoli during his time in Italy and this was a fixture between two sides who hoped to lift the Scudetto come the season's end.

Dieter Hecking had his side well drilled and they suffered no fools, especially at home in the San Paolo. The game got off to the worst possible start for Cooper as Italian right back Luca Rinaldi fired the home side ahead inside a minute. Juventus struggled to get going following the early blow and Napoli added a second just after the hour mark as Tobias Svendsen slotted home. It was a win for Napoli which handed them the advantage in the race for the title.

The tough games kept on coming and gameweek six of the Champions League followed the Napoli defeat. It would be a straight shootout against Borussia Dortmund for the right to be crowned as winner of Group B and progress as top seed. It was a shootout Juventus would win with Dortmund blinking first and losing 2-0, the Germans going down to two more Kwabena Diallo strikes. Diallo had been just one goal away from a hat-trick of Champions League hat-tricks which surely would have been some sort of competition record. Including the qualifying rounds Diallo had now scored thirteen goals in the Champions League so far this season which was a very impressive return. Juventus topped the group following the win and qualified for the knockout stages as group winners having won five and lost one of their six matches.

The Dortmund win was the catalyst for the side to go on another unbeaten run spanning a further eight games and the short winter break. There were wins against Crotone (5-0), Atalanta (1-0), Cremonese in the Italian Cup (3-0), Roma (1-0), Pescara (2-0), Salernitana (4-0) and INTER (2-0) with a draw against Palermo (0-0).

The nine match run which stretched from Dortmund in early December to INTER in late January included yet another Diallo hat-trick in the win against Crotone and saw Juventus charge to the top of the table and progress through to the quarter final of the Italian Cup, a competition Cooper was still desperate to win. The most pleasing aspect of the run was not just the wins, but rather the amount of clean sheets the side had managed to keep. Cooper had invested heavily in the defensive areas of the squad bringing in Varennes, a man he knew and trusted from their time together in Ajax, alongside young Belgians Guillaume and Bruyninckx. Cooper was delighted with the impact and progress of all three players, with the investment clearly paying dividends for the club.

Whilst his side were embarking on their impressive run of form, Derek was working hard away from the pitch. The manager and his recruitment staff worked tirelessly throughout the season, not just during the allocated windows and January would see yet more promising talent join the ranks. Exciting sixteen year old Hamza Mohamed joined from Lazio for £3m in the biggest of the deals.

During his career Derek had worked with far less than was now available to him at Juve, but that experience was still serving him well and during January he held preliminary talks with a number of exciting transfer targets over a possible free transfer in the summer. One of the players who signed a pre-contract agreement was long term target Svein Herald Harket who had decided to leave Manchester United at the end of his current contract. Derek Cooper was only too happy to offer him the chance of a return to Turin.

There were two more deals concluded which meant twenty-one year old French right winger Prince Nsiala-Ekunde, would be joining from OGC Nice and twenty year old German attacking midfielder Johannes Spittler from 1860 Munich in Germany. All pre-contract deals would see the players join in the summer of 2030 when the window re-opened on the 1st of July.

Back to matters on the pitch and a game against Udinese in the Italian Cup quarter final. Failure to make his mark on not only the domestic cup of Italy, but also those of Holland and Scotland had begun to eat away at Derek who was left questioning his shortcomings. In the build up to the game Cooper had every right to be confident of progressing past Udinese. His side were the better team on paper and came into the game in fantastic form.

As the game kicked off it became apparent that the pre-match confidence of Derek Cooper had been misplaced and his side did nothing to staunch the flow of the hosts' early attacks. By the half hour mark Juventus were 2-0 down and sinking without a trace. They say form goes out of the window in the cup competitions and that was certainly true as Udinese comfortably saw off Juve with a 2-0 victory which could have been more had they not missed a second half penalty. His quest for a domestic cup win would have to wait for at least another season as the cup woes continued.

Following the cup disappointment it was vital that league form wasn't disrupted. A cup exit, whilst frustrating for Cooper was only a minor blip, but a loss of form in the league could leave the door open for Napoli who were intent on matching Juventus blow for blow at the top of the table.

Luckily for Cooper the league form hadn't been compromised and the side picked up where they had left off against INTER. Six league ties saw Juventus win all six, scoring fifteen and conceding two, keeping four clean sheets along the way. The wins came against Bologna (3-1), Cremonese (5-0), Udinese (2-0), Cagliari (2-1), Verona (2-0) and Lazio (1-0).

Alfredo Fava had played particularly well and scored the ninety-first minute winner against Cagliari as well as goals against Verona and Bologna. Juventus were still sitting pretty at the top of Serie A and they had been handed a tough draw in the Champions League as they would travel to Manchester to face Mourinho's Manchester United.

Manchester United was a tough draw for Juventus, probably the toughest that they could have been given. United had won the Champions League last season in 2028/29 and were favourites to retain their crown. They had been playing well and were being led by their talismanic German striker Soren Mayer who had joined the club for a deal totalling £108m in 2025/26.

The £108m Manchester United deal took the combined cost of transfer fees for the twenty-six year old striker to a whopping £239m having joined Wolfsburg from Mainz for £56m before Bayern snapped him up for a cool £75m two and half seasons later. To put that into context Coopers most expensive signing to date had been Arne Bruyninckx for £22m. There was a huge gap in the finances available at a club like Manchester United who had also paid £103m for Harry Kane in January 2021.

Coopers plan involved keeping it tight at Old Trafford with hopes of a draw and dreams of snatching an away win. Derek didn't have a great record in England and still considered their club sides amongst the most dangerous opposition in the Champions League.

The plan to sit back and catch United on the counter attack did not start well as Soren Mayer proved the pundits right by finding the back of the net just sixteen minutes in. Juventus constantly failed to pick up the German who was a real thorn in the side of the relatively inexperienced Varennes and Bruyninckx.

Mayer lost his marker once more on twenty-five minutes and converted his second of the game. Counter attacking was no longer a viable option and Juventus faced being out of the tie before the return leg at Juventus Stadium. Cooper tweaked the set up at half time looking to play on the front foot a little more, but without over committing. Juventus failed to get that elusive away goal and were punished late on when another expensive import added a third for United. £105m Man Fernando Gurrieri sealed the victory with seventy-four minutes on the clock to further highlight the gulf in class between the sides. Mourinho had a wealth of expensively assembled talent at his disposal that Cooper could only dream of, but Derek knew that his players were capable of more than they had shown on this occasion.

Juventus had been working hard and the whole squad were disheartened by the manner of their defeat in Manchester. Cooper called a meeting to discuss the result and ensured his side that they had been playing well and it had just been a bad day at the office for the team. Everyone knew that qualification was now extremely unlikely being 3-0 down to the reigning champions, but they were determined to save face when the sides met again in a week's time and show the footballing world that they were capable of better.

In the weeks between the United ties Juventus contested a routine win against Sampdoria (1-0) with David Smit on target from the penalty spot. That win took Juventus to nine straight wins in the league and fouteen games unbeaten since the loss to Napoli back on December the 1st.

That unbeaten run was then ended in the worst possible way as Torino beat Juventus on their own patch to complete a league double over their city rivals. The Torino defeat had obviously affected the team who recorded back to back defeats for the first time since May 2028 with another loss to AC Milan (1-0).

The back to back defeats were hardly ideal preparation for the United game and meant Juventus had lost three of their last four in all competitions. Cooper was praying that this was just a stumble and not a collapse that would see them hand Napoli another Scudetto.

The return tie of the United game was more about saving face than progressing with the latter almost impossible given the quality of opposition and the 3-0 score line. Showing that they were no pushovers and were more than capable of mixing it with the perceived big boys of European football was the prize on offer tonight and Cooper told his players as much.

It was a night to remember for Cooper and the Juventus faithful as they went toe to toe with Manchester United, the reigning European champions. The game was end to end and Juventus traded blows with United for the entirety of the match. Goals from Fava, Antunes and Bruyninckx had Juventus 3-1 up with Mayer on the score sheet again for the visitors. With eighty minutes on the clock it became 3-2 as Mayer added his fourth goal across the two legs, but Juventus held on for the final tenminutes and although they didn't progress they had won on the night and Cooper was pleased that they had at least managed that.

The slip up in the league between United games was not ideal. Napoli had drawn a lot more games than Juventus and were managing to avoid defeat more often than not. Every time Cooper and his side dropped three points and Napoli avoided defeat they slowly reeled them back in.

There were now eight games left in Serie A and both Juve and Napoli had been knocked out of the Italian Cup and the Champions League, so it was all both clubs had left to play for. Juventus were in the driving seat, but Napoli were now arguably the form side. It was all to play for in the final few fixtures.

The run in started well for Juventus as they won at Foirentina (2-0) on their return to domestic action, but the wheels looked set to come off again with back to back defeats against Sassuolo (4-3) and worryingly to title rivals Napoli (2-1). The Napoli game had been huge and the pressure seemingly got to the younger Juventus squad.

Peruvian Moises Otero scored against Juventus again before Goni levelled for the home side. Juventus weren't level for long and Napoli were back in front on twenty-four minutes with their players more than up for the occasion. Jose Cristo saw red for Juventus in the eighty-first minute, but by that point in the match Coopers boys never looked like finding an equaliser. Napoli had been the better side and had capitalised on an impotent Juventus showing that had been paralyzed by the fear of losing to win 2-1.

Juventus needed to recover and rescue their season. Derek was determined to stop the rot and prevent throwing away all their hard work in the first part of the campaign. They were so close now and it would be heartbreaking to let Napoli in through the back door in the last matches of the season.

Following that Napoli defeat Juventus embarked on a mission of recovery as they won their next four matches. Crotone were dispatched first (3-2) with an eighty-seventh minute winner from Diallo. The next wins against Atalanta (1-0) and Roma (3-0) meant that Juventus had two shots at securing their first Scudetto since 2020/21 when Jorge Jesus was in charge.

A win in their next match at home to Pescara would see them crowned champions in front of their home fans. Surely that was incentive enough for them to get the job done? Derek Cooper wore his club suit for the occasion, but he also wanted to instil the attitude in his players that it was business as normal. They got the perfect start when just ten minutes into the game Diallo scored to settle the nerves of the crowd and players alike.

With a one goal lead the team grew in confidence and wouldn't look back. Diallo added a second just before half time and David Smit secured the win and the 2029/30 Serie A Scudetto with the third on seventy one minutes. As the final whistle sounded Cooper managed to shake hands with his opposite number, Pierluigi Casiraghi, before he was mobbed by his players and staff, hoisted into the air and carried in a lap of honour around the Juventus Stadium pitch.

The stadium chanted his name as Cooper addressed them in broken Italian promising them that this was just the start for the club and there was more success to come in the future. He thanked them for their support and asked them to continue to get behind the team in upcoming seasons.

It was then time to follow his team up onto the staging that had been erected in the centre circle and lift the Serie A trophy high above his head with the club captain, Ignacio Varennes. Juventus and Derek Cooper were Serie A champions with one game to spare.

Juventus and Turin partied long into the night. It had been too long since the fans had tasted success and been able to celebrate their side winning a Scudetto. There was still one game left to be played, but there was now nothing riding on it and Cooper was powerless to stop the flow of champagne as he himself was swept up on the waves of emotion following securing the title.

The celebrations had taken their toll and it showed when the side returned to action against Palermo a week later. With nothing left to play for Juventus went down 1-0 to a side looking to secure Europa League qualification. The defeat didn't matter and the celebrations continued after the defeat with an open top bus tour through the streets of Turin planned for the weekend following the end of the season.

There had been clear and steady improvement during his time at Juventus, with Cooper taking them from a sixth place finish and sixty-five points in his first half season to the title and eighty-eight points in his second full season. The 2028/29 season in the middle had seen a jump, but the seventy-six points gained that season weren't enough to beat Napoli to the title.

The club as a whole was in a much healthier place than when Derek had arrived too and the league title was testament to the work that had been put into the club as a whole. The youth and reserve sides now had much greater depth, a depth that was able to supplement the first team with progression from within now a viable option. The first team squad was much younger, with the older members of the squad having been moved on after failing to bring success to the club. Juventus had a much healthier wage balance as a result and were investing their money smartly to secure the clubs long term future.

Kwabena Diallo had been in fine form throughout the 2029/30 season and his thirty-six goals in forty-five appearances were key to the side winning the league title. His average rating of 7.36 wasn't quite enough to win him the player of the year award and he was beaten by both Italian right back Antonio Salvaggio (7.38) and Argentinean club captain Ignacio Varennes who topped the average ratings charts with 7.49 marking him out as the sides top performer.

Abdoulaye Sy had built upon an impressive 2028/29 season by almost trebling his goals tally of five from last year with thirteen in forty-four appearances this term. Derek Cooper had brought Mikel Goni in on loan to provide competition for Sy and the young Senegalese winger had risen to the challenge limiting Goni to just seventeen appearances.

David Smit and Alfredo Fava had been steady throughout the season adding goals to supplement those of Kwabena Diallo, but both players were showing signs that they may have reached their peak and Cooper was contemplating whether it was time to look at bolstering his attacking options having redeveloped the defence last summer.

With his first Italian silverware in the bag and duly celebrated Derek Cooper immediately turned his attention to adding more. He had spent time in the aftermath of securing the title holed up in his office with his staff discussing what they had done well, but also the areas that they felt needed improving. There would be another busy summer with much to do ahead of 2030/31. Cooper had never failed to defend a top league title having won back to back titles with TNS and Ajax in his time at those clubs.

Coopers summer business began with him moving on the last of the big earners already present when he arrived as Felix Passlack was allowed to leave the club on a free transfer. Cooper had tried to agree a deal for Passlack last summer, but a loan move had proved to be the only possibility, now with his contract expiring he was free to leave in search of pastures new.

Cooper had already moved to reinvest the Passlack wages having secured pre-contract deals for Harket, Nsiala-Ekunde and Spittler in January with them arriving when the transfer window opened on the 1st of July. Cooper was always keen to exploit this facet of the market and it had once again provided him the opportunity to bring in three very good young players who would really add to the squad.

Alongside the free transfers that Cooper had previously arranged there were a number of big money deals secured to improve the squad. There were also a large number of departures as Cooper ruthlessly cut the players he felt were unlikely to have any impact on the first team squad moving forward.

Portuguese left back Jose Cristo made his loan move from Manchester United permanent for the tiny fee of just £3.7m. Cooper considered the deal to be one of the best of his career with Cristo having showed he was more than capable during his year on loan at the club. He couldn't believe they were willing to let such a talented player leave for so little, but their loss was most certainly Juventus's gain.

There were three more deals that stood out as Cooper spent £20m plus on three new recruits. Dutch striker Henk Theuns joined from Feyenoord for £27m which was the most Cooper had ever spent on a player. Mexican centre-back Luis Carranco signed for £25.5m leaving Leon in his homeland and Belgian central midfielder Ferre Declerck made the move from Club Brugge. Cooper had returned to Belgium for the signing of Declerck following the successes of both Arne Bruyninckx and Alexander Guillaume last season. It had proved a fruitful location for his scouts and the £21m midfielder looked destined for great things in the future.

Derek and his recruitment team had extensively scouted France in the summer and had identified a number of young sixteen year old lads who had been making appearances for the French U19's side recently. Pablo Peron (AS Monaco), Morgan Clement (Montpellier) and Jean Guy-Bougrissi were the brightest of those talents and joined Juventus in the hopes of developing through the U18 and U20 sides to make the grade as a first team player in the years to come.

Maxence Gonalons was a French central midfielder brought to the club by Cooper back in 2028 on a free transfer from Manchester United and the signings of both Declerck and Nicolas Andreozzi, an Argentinean midfielder who possessed an Italian passport, were necessary to cover Gonalons who looked set to leave Juventus.

Bayern Munich had begun their pursuit of Gonalons back in January, but Cooper had persuaded his man to stay on and help the side win the league title. Now that they had accomplished that together Cooper was powerless to stop Gonalons pursuing his move away. Bayern Munich made several offers before meeting the £30m price tag Cooper had placed on his midfield star. It was with a heavy heart and a cool £30m profit that Derek signed off on the deal and wished him well for the next chapter of his career.

There were a few other outgoings that summer as Cooper trimmed his squad to allow for the new arrivals. Midfilder Marcel Groot left to join West Brom for £6.5m and others departing the club included Marek Janda (Salernitana £2.4m), Jose Luis Camarasa (Brighton £11m), Juan Carlos (Barcelona £4m) and Flavio Guimares (Atletico Madrid £4m).

Each of those players left Juventus for more than Cooper had paid for them, further adding to the clubs profits. Groot and Janda had followed Cooper from Ajax, as had Camarasa, but Juventus had now outgrown them and he didn't want to stand in their way of regular first team action.

Cooper also moved on a number of other players that he and his staff had deemed surplus to requirements having never made it to the first team. It was important that players who hadn't progressed as hoped were moved on to make way for the next batch of hopefuls to try and take their chance. Cooper always looked to achieve the best deal and many of those players were also moved on for more than they had cost.

The squad was now beginning to take shape ahead of the 2030/31 season and Derek was satisfied with the summer business. He was a manager who was used to a high turnover of players with his recruitment plans the way they were. He was constantly looking to improve the squad and wasn't a manager who shied away from a big name departure, provided he got the money he was looking to get for the player.

There were arrivals behind the scenes too as Zlatan Ibrahimovic joined from Ajax (Coach), Maarten Stekelenburg from Tottenham Hotspur (U18's GK Coach) and Pepijn Lijnders who was offered a route back into football having previously worked at Liverpool and Ajax amongst others.

On the pitch pre-season had gone very well and Juventus had remained unbeaten. They kicked off against the U20's before embarking on a tour of America and several other friendlies ahead of the Italian Super Cup curtain raiser against AC Milan. In the nine pre-season games played Juventus scored twenty-nine goals and conceded just one with Cooper hoping to carry that form into the competitive fixtures.

The Olimpico was the venue for the Italian Super Cup as Derek Cooper looked to kick off the campaign with a win and add another piece of silverware to his resume. AC Milan were the opponents and they took the lead just before half time despite Juventus having been the slightly better side.

Abdoulaye Sy was the player to respond to the half time team talk as he pulled Juventus level five minutes into the second half. In an even game it looked as though it would be heading to extra time before it went horribly wrong for Juve. Right back Antonio Salvaggio was sent off for a second yellow card in the eighty-seventh minute having given away a penalty handing Andrea Frau a chance to win it from the spot for AC Milan. It was a chance the striker would take and with so little time left in the match Cooper was unable to rally a comeback. It was a disappointing start to the season, but it wasn't the end of the world. Defending their Serie A title and progressing deep into the Champions League were the objectives for the season.

There was a gap of nearly three weeks following the AC Milan game and the opening Serie A game against Udinese. Juventus returned to non-competitive action during the break and immediately recaptured their devastating form beating Besiktas (5-0), Bari (5-0) and AA Gent (3-0). Plenty of goals and clean sheets heading into that season opener where they would look to lay down a marker as to their intentions for the season.

Udinese were the visitors to Juventus Stadium to open the 2030/31 Serie A campaign. Cooper didn't get that start he was looking for and Udinese sprung an opening day surprise by beating their hosts 1-0 with a fortieth minute goal from Cristian Moisa.

Yet again Juventus had been unable to translate their excellent friendly performances into a competitive fixture. Cooper hoped it was nothing more than opening day nerves as new players settled into the club. He remained confident that his men were more than capable of winning another Serie A title. They would get the chance to put it right against Sampdoria in two weeks time following an oddly timed international break.

Over the international break Cooper worked hard with the players who remained at the club fearing that the overhaul in the summer had had more of an impact than he realised. There was also a trip overseas to attend the draw of the Champions League group stage, Juventus were handed a tough group with Paris Saint-Germain, Villarreal and FC Red Bull Salzburg. PSG in particular would provide very stiff opposition for Derek Cooper.

Juventus returned to action and travelled to Sampdoria knowing that they needed a win to get their campaign up and running. It was a nervy first half which ended 0-0, but goals from Sy and Smit in the second half settled the affair and secured their first three points for Juventus.

Not only had Juventus been drawn in a group with PSG, but they were to travel to Paris to face the toughest member of their group in gameweek one. Just three days after their opening win of the season Derek and Juve travelled to the French capital looking to secure their first three Champions League points for the campaign. Goals in the sixth and eighty-seventh minutes at the Parc des Princes bookended a poor display from Juventus and PSG deservedly won the game 2-0.

It hadn't been the ideal start to the new season and Cooper addressed the squad on their return to Italy. He told them that although the opening games hadn't gone to plan they needed to find the form he knew they were capable of. The players seemed to respond well leaving Derek confident that they weren't far off hitting top gear once everything clicked into place. The new members of the squad were settling in well and looking stronger with every session.

What followed was an unbeaten run of nine games, winning six and drawing three. Whilst it wasn't setting the world alight it was a steady improvement with Prince Nsiala-Ekunde and Henk Theuns showing their class as they began to establish themselves in the first team. The draws against Salernitana (1-1) and Atalanta (2-2) were both very nearly defeats, only late goals saved Juventus on both occasions and Cooper was pleased with the fighting spirit shown if not the end result.

Towards the end of October Juventus faced back to back games against INTER and Napoli who finished behind them in second and third in the league last season. INTER were beaten (2-1) at the San Siro and Napoli were dispatched (3-1) at the Juventus Stadium thanks to a couple of late goals from Kwabena Diallo and Prince Nsiala-Ekunde. Juventus had recovered well from their three defeats in the opening four competitive fixtures.

Following the excellent wins against both INTER and Napoli, who were widely considered as the main threats again this season, Cooper was confident that his side had found top gear to set aside the earlier patchy form.

Those statement wins against two title rivals couldn't be underestimated, but it was vital that Juve continued to push on and really drive home the advantage.

Pescara were up next, but Juventus were unable to capitalise on their recent form and slipped to a narrow defeat (2-1). Svein Herald Harket put the old lady ahead in the first half, but a complacent performance in the second forty-five allowed young Italian striker Alberto Montesi to score twice in a five minute period. It was exactly the type of result Derek had been keen to avoid with his side having seemingly turned a corner.

There were then three days before Juventus were back in action with gameweek four of the Champions League. Villareal travelled to the Juventus Stadium as Cooper looked to illicit a response from his side. It was important that the Pescara result was put to one side rather than allowed to disrupt their European campaign.

After the opening loss to PSG Juventus had worked hard to turn things around and had managed to do so by beating both Villarreal away (2-1) and RB Salzburg at home (2-1). A win here would all but cement their progress through to the knockout stages leaving them to fight it out with the Paris giants for top spot.

Derek Cooper challenged his side pre-match asking them to put in a better showing than they put in last time out and they duly delivered. It was a scintillating display of attacking football in the first half and the Old Lady were three goals to the good by half time. Dutch striker and £27m man Henk Theuns set the team on their way in the twenty-second minute before Carranco and Spittler added two more on thirty and thirty-nine minutes. Cooper told his side not to get complacent, assertively reminding them of their second half display earlier in the week. There was to be no switching off this time and Theuns added his second on forty-nine minutes to quell any hopes of a Villarreal comeback.

The Villarreal result kick-started another run of form that stretched from the 5th of November through to the 2nd of February 2031. In those weeks and months Juventus would contest no fewer than fourteen matches across three competitions with them winning ten and drawing the other four.

Those fourteen games saw Juventus keep an impressive nine clean sheets with seven of those coming off the back of the Villarreal result. Cooper attributed this upturn in shut outs to the adjusted shape he had been working on. Cooper had switched from his attacking 4-2-4 opting for a more solid 4-1-2-2-1 with a defensive midfielder operating just in front of the back four.

Juventus still operated with an attacking mentality and many of the fundamentals remained the same, but Cooper hoped that by dropping one of the strikers in favour of an extra defensive body he could eliminate some of the erratic results that had hampered the opening fixtures.

Victories against Verona (2-0) and Palermo (2-0) preceded the gameweek five visit of Group B rivals Paris Saint-Germain. The game followed a familiar pattern as Juventus once again won by a 2-0 score line. In front of a capacity home crowd Moon Ik-Hyun and Matias Sanchez got the goals to secure the victory.

The wins then continued for Juventus against Fiorentina (3-0), Cagliari (1-0) and RB Salzburg (2-0). The win against Salzburg meant that The Old Lady and PSG had almost identical records with Juve missing out on top spot by virtue of away goals scored during the group stage.

After the Champions League fixture in Austria Juventus returned to a tough run of fixtures, but remained unbeaten despite failing to win. In a minor blip Juventus drew three matches on the spin against Empoli (0-0), Roma (2-2) and AC Milan (1-1). The draw against Roma was symbolic to Cooper as it showcased his sides never say die attitude as they twice came from behind in a game they would have lost a few short months ago.

It was back to taking all three points just in time for the Turin derby as Juventus beat Torino (4-2) to make up for the two defeats of last season and restore some bragging rights for the Juventus fans. The match following the derby victory marked the halfway point of the Serie A season and delivered another win against Sassuolo

(2-0) with a brace for Henk Theuns who was now more than justifying his transfer fee with fifteen goals to his name.

Halfway through the season and Cooper was pleased with his sides title defence efforts overall. Juventus had played nineteen, won eleven, drawn six and lost just twice. It was a few too many draws for Coopers liking and he would have ideally turned a handful of those into wins to really pull away from Napoli and INTER.

The first team squad had been boosted in September by the arrival of young Ghanaian centre back Yaw Ansong from Cordoba for £4m and in January by impressive French central midfielder Pierre Millet who signed from Nantes for £25m. The deal for Millet was more than Cooper originally planned to spend for a player of only twenty-two, but he was impressed with the number of appearances Millet had made at the club since his senior debut in the 2026/27 season. The recruitment team were also excited by the young Frenchman, believing him to have the potential to become a world class talent if given the chance to develop.

The main dealings of Juventus in the January window saw players on the periphery allowed out on loan to garner some first team experience. There was however a disappointing departure from the youth ranks as exciting youth prospect Graziano Brovarone decided to join Manchester City for £3m in compensation rather than sign a professional deal with his boyhood club.

On the pitch January ended with an Italian Cup win against Sampdoria (4-1) which included a goal for new signing Pierre Millet and a Serie A win away to Udinese (1-0). Sampdoria then exacted some form of revenge by denying Cooper all three points and scoring a ninety-first minute leveller in a 2-2 league draw. Matias Sanchez didn't help the Juventus cause by getting himself sent off with ten minutes remaining and his side 2-1 up.

Having secured the Serie A title last campaign Cooper hoped he would be able to add the Italian Cup to this seasons Serie A. Domestic cups had proved a constant source of frustration for Cooper in his managerial career to date and he was desperate to rectify that in Italy. He travelled to Palermo for the Italian Cup quarter final hoping to progress having lost at this stage for the past two seasons.

Palermo had other ideas and yet again it would be elimination for Juventus and Cooper in the quarter final. Giuseppe Farina put the Rosanero ahead just after the break and Cooper couldn't find a way back into the tie for Juventus. Despite becoming the dominant force in the league Juventus and Cooper had yet again failed to translate that into a decent run in the Italian Cup. Not only did the 1-0 defeat eliminate Juventus it also brought an end to their fifteen game unbeaten run that stretched back to early November.

Juventus were now entering the business end of the season and without the distraction of the Italian Cup Derek was free to concentrate on retaining the Scudetto and making progress in the Champions League. Manchester United knocked Juventus out of the Champions League at the First Knockout Round stage last season and Coopers primary objective was to improve on that this time out. Qualifying behind PSG had not helped his cause however and progression looked tough having been drawn against another Premier League side in Chelsea.

Before the first of those Chelsea matches Juventus faced off against Cesena, Salernitana and Atalanta in the league. Wins against Cesena (3-0) and Salernitana (5-1) were spoiled by an unexpected defeat away to Atalanta with an Andrea Pinamonti goal the difference in the 1-0 loss.

The Atalanta game was hardly ideal preparation for the visit of Pep Guardiola's Chelsea side. Chelsea had topped a group that included Malmo, Bayern Munich and French side AS Saint-Etienne. It was a sell out crowd at the Juventus Stadium and they were suitably entertained by two sides looking to win the game. Spanish striker Dario Moreno put Chelsea ahead on eleven minutes before Moon and Theuns scored for Juventus to send the home side in at the break winning 2-1. A home win would have been a good result to take into the second leg, but it wasn't to be and a penalty from former Wonderkid Martin Odegaard just after the hour mark was enough to secure a draw and two vital away goals for the London club.

Before the second leg match against Chelsea Juventus faced a tough run of fixtures including games against title rivals INTER and Napoli. Juventus were in the driving seat in Serie A, but that could all change if they lost ground to their direct rivals. After the first leg Juventus faced off against and beat Crotone (4-1) before a disappointing draw against Brescia (1-1). It was then onto the incredibly tricky run of games that saw Juventus face INTER at home before Chelsea and Napoli away.

It was a strange game as INTER came to Turin with two own goals and two red cards for the visitors. Dutch defender Wesley Hoedt scored the first of INTER's own goals in the second minute, but that was immediately cancelled out by Guglielmo Schitoin in the third minute in what was a blistering start to the game. Swiss midfielder Jurgen Hoxha then restored the lead for Juve making it 2-1 on twenty-one minutes swiftly followed by the first of INTER's red cards on thirty minutes for Czech midfielder Libor Macek. Hakan Bozkurt then followed his team mate down the tunnel on the hour mark before Jerome Onguene completed the self inflicted INTER misery with their second own goal of the game on eighty-seven minutes. A 3-1 home win against INTER was a good victory, but Cooper now looked to build on the result with further wins against Chelsea and Napoli.

One game of the big three down it was on to Chelsea and a trip back to England for yet another knockout match in a European competition. Stamford Bridge wasn't considered one of the more atmospheric stadiums in England, but Cooper knew that on its day it could be a formidable place to visit. He was once again relishing his chance to show the English media what he was capable of and hoped to see off the challenge of Chelsea and Pep Guardiola, arguably one of the best managers club football had ever seen.

It was a capacity 60,000 crowd inside the recently expanded Stamford Bridge to witness the visit of Juventus and once again they were not let down by the football on show. The home side raced into a two goal lead inside the opening fifteen minutes through Chilean Alejandro Reyes and Norwegian Aksel Halvorsen. Jurgen Hoxha continued his fine form in front of goal and clawed one back before the break. 2-1 down on the night and 4-3 behind on aggregate Cooper demanded more from his side knowing they were more than capable of causing Chelsea problems. Pep looked to control the game and Chelsea got their reward on sixty-four minutes as £47m striker Dario Moreno made it 3-1.

Cooper rallied his troops and Jurgen Hoxha got his second of the night just three minutes later. Momentum had swung and Juventus needed just one more goal to see them through on away goals. They pushed and pushed without reward and their fate was all but sealed on eighty-four minutes as left back Jose Cristo was sent off for an overly enthusiastic tackle as Chelsea looked to break.

It ended 3-2 at Stamford Bridge and 5-4 over the two legs in favour of the Premier League side. Cooper and Juventus had failed to make it past English opposition in the First Knockout Round for the second season running.

Having been eliminated from the Champions League and Italian Cup it left just the Serie A title defence as Juve's only chance of silverware in 2030/31. Juventus were in a commanding position in the league, sitting top with a small cushion between them and Napoli who were up next for Derek Cooper. A win away at the San Paolo against their nearest rivals would be the best possible start to the eleven game run in and help to put European disappointment behind them.

The Napoli game was a tight affair and it took Juventus a long time to get going in the game. Napoli were the much better side and there were clear signs of fatigue affecting the Juve players. There had been only three days between the second Chelsea fixture and the trip to Naples, with the players looking leggy in the first half.

It was 0-0 at half time, a score line that suited Juventus more than it did Napoli with the impotence on them to attack the league leaders.

Napoli did just that as the second half got underway and the brilliantly named Stanley Stans put them ahead on forty-eight minutes. Juventus continued to struggle to find any sort of rhythm, their usually slick attacking football seemingly impossible to replicate on the day. The clock ticked past the ninetieth minute and it looked for all the world like Napoli were going to get the three points and put pressure on Juventus in the title race. Cooper had all but given up hope and was preparing a rousing post match team talk when the ever reliable Moon Ik-Hyun stole a yard on his marker and fired home the most unlikely of equalisers. It felt like a victory for Juventus, snatching a point from the jaws of defeat against their nearest title rival was a wonderful feeling. Post match Cooper urged his side to use that as the catalyst for the remaining ten games, propelling them to their second Scudetto in two years.

Pescara at home followed the Napoli game and it was an emphatic win (6-0) which set Juventus on the way to a fantastic run of results. It was a brilliant team display with goals from five different players offering a threat across the entire pitch. Moon scored again with Pierre Millet, Jurgen Hoxha, Abdoulaye Sy and Kawbena Diallo (2) joining the South Korean amongst the goals.

More impressive results followed as The Old Lady cruised to back to back league titles winning nine and drawing one of their final ten matches. After Pescara Juventus beat Verona (4-2) and Palermo (2-0) before the draw against Foirentina (1-1) where a Viola own goal was required to get a point against their historic rivals. It was then back to winning ways as Juventus and Cooper closed out the 2030/31 campaign with another unbeaten run including wins against Cagliari (3-1), Empoli (2-0), Roma (2-0), AC Milan (3-1), Torino (5-0) and Sassuolo (3-0).

They had done it, Juventus had retained their Scudetto with games to spare, although that hadn't stopped them from putting all comers to the sword in the final weeks as Derek was impressed with his sides' ruthlessness. It would have been easy to take their foot off the pedal with the title in the bag, but they wanted to keep pushing and putting points on the board. Juventus hadn't won back to back titles since 2019/20 and 2020/21 under the management of Antonio Conte and Jorge Jesus.

2030/31 had been another good season, the transition from 4-2-4 to 4-1-2-2-1 had gone well and it had successfully limited the inconsistency that had dogged previous campaigns. New signing Henk Theuns had finished the season as the sides top scorer with twenty-four goals in all competitions boasting an average rating of 7.21 and justifying his £27m transfer from Feyenoord.

Other new signing Prince Nsiala-Ekunde had also settled well in Turin and the Frenchman made forty appearances in his debut season displacing right wing regular Moon Ik-Hyun who was used on the left more often than not. Nsiala-Ekunde got himself an average rating of 7.21 scoring seven goals in the campaign and was now valued at somewhere in the region of £35m, which wasn't bad for someone who had arrived at the club on a free transfer.

The pick of the bunch however was not a new signing, but rather Jurgen Hoxha who had a very good season in the centre of midfield attaining an average rating of 7.47 and scoring fifteen goals on his way to winning the coveted player of the season award for 2030/31.

Cooper had good competition for places throughout the squad now, but was alarmed at the drastic drop off in the performances of David Smit who had his worst season since Cooper joined the club. Smit only managed seven goals in all competitions and failed to break the seven barrier on his average rating, falling just short with 6.99 across his twenty appearances.

Juventus ended up winning the title by nine points from runners up Napoli thanks to that excellent run of form to close out the season. Of their thirty-eight league fixtures Juventus won twenty-five, drew ten and lost just three times as they amassed eighty-five points and a goal difference of plus fifty-eight.

Coincidentally Juventus also scored eighty-five goals, conceding just twenty-seven which was comfortably the lowest in the league. By comparison Napoli won twenty-four, drew just the four games, but tellingly lost ten which really cost them in their quest for the title. Napoli did manage to score four more goals than Juve, hitting eighty-nine, but they also conceded more, nearly double in fact, as they let in forty-eight achieving a goal difference of plus forty-one.

Cooper had certainly raised the bar at the club since arriving midway through the 27/28 season having led them from sixth and sixty-five points to top spot with eighty-eight and eighty-five points respectively in 29/30 and 30/31. Juventus had also consistently scored more and conceded fewer year upon year under Cooper, which was another sign that he was having a positive impact on the squad, signing the right players and taking the club forward.

As with TNS back in Wales and Ajax over in Holland Cooper had successfully managed to retain a top league title. He had now won back to back league titles in three countries and it was a record he was especially proud of. Achieving this particular feat in Italy had probably been his most impressive to date, with teams such as Napoli, INTER, AC Milan and Roma all trying, and failing to stop the Juventus momentum.

Once the dust had settled on anther stellar season Derek Cooper reflected on what had been an excellent three and a half years in Turin. He could speak passable Italian and loved the culture of the city, with it beginning to feel like home off the pitch. However, in footballing terms Derek Cooper was beginning to get itchy feet. He had conquered the Serie A not once, but twice and although he hadn't won on the night he had taken them back to a major European final. He would have liked to have gone further in the Champions League and he believed that in time he would be able do just that.

However, his domestic cup struggles still irked him and although he felt that he would rectify that in time, there was a nagging feeling that maybe there was a new challenge out there for him. There were few clubs bigger than Juventus in world football and Cooper would only leave for the right club or project. He still dreamed of managing in the Premier League with Liverpool his preferred destination.

Derek decided to talk things over with his agent asking him to put some feelers out to gauge his standing in the game and his suitability for some of the top jobs in European football should they become available.

As always Derek Cooper was busy throughout the summer as he and his staff put their plans for next season into action. The 2031/32 season was fast approaching and they were working hard behind the scenes to ensure another successful season for the club. Juventus legend and former Italian central defender Giorgio Chiellini re-joined the club as an U20's Coach and he was followed by football royalty in the eyes of Derek Cooper as his hero Steven Gerrard agreed a deal to become the U20's Assistant Manager.

Transfer business was a priority as ever and Cooper was dealt a massive blow during pre-season as club captain and defensive rock Ignacio Varennes agitated for a move away. Numerous clubs had shown an interest and Varennes had had his head turned over the summer. Cooper was effectively powerless to stop the central defender as he began to unsettle other members of the squad. Juventus wouldn't be held to ransom and the manager would only allow his captain to move if a suitable offer came in. Dortmund were the club pushing hardest and after several back and forth's a deal was agreed for the permanent transfer of the Argentinean international. Dortmund paid £42m to get the deal done and that was the highest fee Juventus had received for a player since Barcelona paid £49.75m for Daniele Rugani in 2018.

Other notable departures saw striker Alfredo Fava leave to join Al-Hilal (£6.5m), youth graduate Adriano Magnani left for Spurs (£7m), Ladislav Kudela joined Aston Villa (£2m) and Michel Hosek who had been Coopers first signing for the club back in 2028 joined Pisa (£1.5m).

With Varennes the only key player departing Cooper was able to keep the bulk of the squad together, with just a few additions planned to hopefully compete across more than just the Serie A. There were three big signings announced in June as Cooper reinvested the Varennes money and looked to plug the gap he left in the squad.

Derek Cooper and his scouting staff identified two central defenders as potential replacements and ended up agreeing deals for both players. There was another Belgian addition as twenty-two year old Ange Zogbo put pen to paper on a £26m deal from Standard whilst nineteen year old American Bill Sarachan signed from New York City Football Club for just £6.75m in line with his minimum release fee. Cooper felt that both players were more than capable of filling the Varennes shaped hole with Zogbo slightly ahead in terms of development although Sarachan was considered capable of developing beyond both Zogbo and the departed Varennes.

The final big money arrival saw Cooper sign Javier Perez, a striker that he had been watching for a while, but had decided not to make a move for. Cooper had opted to sign Theuns instead last summer as he was considered more affordable for the club at that time. The chance to sign Braga striker Perez had only come about this summer as the player had become unsettled in Portugal. He had now been listed for transfer by his club and at just £23m, way below their asking price of twelve months ago.

Perez would be joining a squad that was looking overloaded with strikers as Smit, Theuns and Diallo were all competing for the now lone starting spot up front. Cooper had noticed a worrying drop off in the performances and goals of both Smit and Diallo last season, with Theuns easily the side's top performing striker. He hoped that Perez would offer him yet more firepower in a squad that were hungry for more trophies. It was rare that a player Cooper had been following became available at such an affordable price and he felt it was a deal worth taking Braga up on.

On the field it was another successful pre-season for Cooper and Juventus. He continued, as always, to work on the team's cohesion in training to get the newcomers up to speed and fully integrated as soon as possible. Impressive performances saw Juve go unbeaten in the lead up to the Italian Super Cup Final on the 9th of August 2031. Juventus had big wins against Man City (3-2), Anderlecht (7-3) and Espanyol (7-1) with the team gelling well and scoring plenty of goals.

Cooper was once again experimenting with his formation in an effort to get the best out of the attacking midfield options he now had at his disposal. Jurgen Hoxha had been playing as a central midfielder, but had been predominantly used as a number ten before joining the club and young Johannes Spittler had so far failed to live up to his potential playing mainly from the left wing in as opposed to his preferred central role.

The tactical switch up saw the defensive midfielder scrapped and replaced with an attacking midfielder playing just behind the lone striker. As a result the formation was now a more attacking 4-2-3-1instead of the 4-1-2-2-1. It was a risk as the defensive midfielder had helped to solidify the team and limit the inconsistent form, but results in pre-season had been promising with the added attacking threat helping the side find the back of the net with regularity. That being said there were also a number of goals conceded and that offered some food for thought for Cooper who would need to refine the defensive aspects of his new tactical approach.

The 9th of August soon rolled around and it was time for Cooper and his team to travel to the Olimpico in Rome again, this time to face off against Palermo in the curtain raiser of the 2031/32 Italian football season. Cooper was yet to win the Italian Super Cup having been beaten in last season's final by AC Milan and he travelled hoping to redeem himself.

Palermo were reigning Italian Cup champions, another competition Cooper was yet to win during his time in Italy, and they were not to be underestimated. Juventus were the overwhelming favourites amongst pundits and the pre-match odds reinforced that view.

It was an underwhelming performance from Juventus as they failed to find the fluidity that had been shown throughout pre-season. Johannes Spittler was given an opportunity to play in his preferred position as he operated in the central attacking midfielder role and the German rewarded Derek Cooper's faith midway through the first half with the opening goal.

Juve enjoyed almost total dominance in the game, but they consistently failed to capitalise and were often wasteful in front of goal. The Spittler goal proved to be enough for Juve as they saw the game out to lift their first silverware of the season with the win (1-0). Cooper was delighted to add a domestic trophy to his league titles and this now took his career tally to a total of fifteen league and cup victories in his sixteenth season as a manager.

With the Super Cup victory under their belts Juve returned to non-competitive action to fill the gap before Serie A got underway on the 23rd of August. In an unusual move for Derek Cooper he played domestic opposition in pre-season as he took on Venezia and AC Milan wanting to minimise travel and disruption ahead of the league beginning.

The Milan fixture in particular was out of the ordinary as Cooper had never previously faced off against a league rival in a friendly. It was a move that backfired and having comfortably beat Venezia (4-0) Juventus were well beaten by Milan (2-0). The defeat in the San Siro was far from ideal preparation for the Serie A opener at home to Brescia.

As always the primary aim for 2031/32 was to retain their domestic league title, but Cooper also wanted to compete for the Italian Cup and get to the final stages of the Champions League. Derek Cooper had enjoyed his time so far in Italy, but he had been left frustrated by his lack of cup success and failure to make his mark with this side in Europe. The Serie A title was the bread and butter for the club and winning the league was now the minimum requirement for them, a far cry from when he arrived in 2028 which was testament to the transformation he had overseen.

The 2031/32 season kicked off with a comfortable home win against a very lacklustre Brescia side (5-0) who failed to capitalise on any possible frailties in the Juventus side after their final pre-season defeat. The visitors didn't help themselves as they scored a hat-trick of own goals to add to the strikes from Millet and Moon Ik-Hyun.

The home win on the opening day set the tone for the opening half of the season and Juventus went on a rampage that saw them lose only once in their next twenty-five fixtures across all competitions. Sadly that loss came in the Italian Cup first round with an extra time defeat at the hands of Lazio.

Following the first game of the season against Brescia there was a bore draw against a stubborn INTER side (0-0) that Juventus tried, but ultimately failed to break down. Coopers side responded well as they embarked on a five match winning run beating Sampdoria (3-0), Zenit (2-1), Udinese (2-0), Pescara (4-0) and Roma (1-0).

Juventus took on all comers in Serie A and the Champions League alike, winning eighteen games and drawing six. By the time they reached the halfway point of their season in mid January 2032 Juventus sat top of the Serie A with a commanding lead over the chasing pack as well as qualifying top of their Champions' League Group ahead of Anderlecht, Monaco and Zenit St. Petersburg.

Confidence was high and Juventus were a team that looked more than capable of beating anyone. AS Monaco set out to frustrate Juve from the off and as with the INTER result Juventus simply couldn't find a way to break through the French sides rear guard. The game ended 0-0 and whilst not a disaster left Cooper frustrated at negative opposition tactics as well as his sides lack of an answer in a game they really should have won.

Wins against Atalanta (4-0) and Bari (3-2) followed in October before another side came to park the bus at the Juventus Stadium. Anderlecht had been comfortably dispatched 7-3 in pre-season, but the Belgian champions had seemingly learned from their humbling defeat and had seen Monaco's defensive tactics, opting to follow the French sides lead. It was the third frustrating 0-0 of the season and Cooper was left to lament another two points dropped at home.

Juventus always seemed to bounce back from their disappointing 0-0 results and they did the same after Anderlecht as they comfortably beat Sassuolo (3-0). However the return to winning ways only lasted one game this time as they went on to record two further draws; against both Crotone (2-2) and AC Milan (2-2). Juventus were lucky to come away with a share of the points against Crotone and it was thanks to late goals from Theuns (78mins) and Moon Ik-Hyun (87mins) that they secured a share of the spoils.

Derek Cooper was a manager who was satisfied, but not pleased with his sides form. Too many points were being dropped in games in which they were the dominant side. He had taken Juventus back to the top of Italian football and they were now very much the dominant side he had grown up watching, but most of the draws could and should have added to their wins tally. He doubled his efforts to motivate his players, speaking to individuals and praising their conduct in one on one meetings to raise their morale in a bid to overturn those stalemates.

It seemed to have the desired effect and his rejuvenated squad went on a six match winning run which included a victory against their closest league rivals Napoli at home (3-1) having already exacted revenge on Anderlecht in Belgium by the same score line   (3-1). Further wins against Catania (1-0), Zenit (4-0) Empoli (3-1) and Lazio (3-1) followed to complete the six game winning streak.

By the time Juventus had beaten Lazio it was early December and Juventus had remained unbeaten in all competitions. For all of Derek's frustrations at the dropped points he was not blind to the fact that he had built an impressive side that were probably on their best run of form under his stewardship. Like every manager he dreamed of emulating the Arsenal "Invincibles" he had watched as a young man and going unbeaten for an entire campaign. It was a dream that he knew was most unlikely, but every win took him that little bit closer to writing his name into the history books

After six wins on the trot confidence was high as Juventus travelled to Monaco and the Stade Louis II looking to take all three points and show the French side their ruthless side. Monaco had other ideas and flew out of the traps catching Juventus by surprise and racing into a rapid three goal lead inside twenty minutes.

Juventus then finally settled into the game and made it to half time without conceding any further goals. 3-0 Down away from home was cue for Derek Cooper to let his players have it. He aggressively told his men that they were well below the levels of what he expected, telling them they didn't look like a side that wanted to win the game and questioning their passion.

Now it was the turn of Juventus to stun their opponents with a quick fire double to start the second half. Coopers words had hit home and Theuns (54mins) and Moon (55mins) scored two goals in as many minutes to pile the pressure on Monaco. The game was poised at 3-2 and Juventus were the team in the ascendancy. Monaco had retreated to the edge of their own penalty area and were only sporadically trying to counter the Juventus dominance. It took until the eighty-seventh minute for substitute Javier Perez to find that third goal and ensure they wouldn't be travelling back to Turin empty handed.

The draw in Monaco meant that Juventus topped the group ahead of Anderlecht with Monaco claiming the Europa League spot in third ahead of Zenit. It also meant that Cooper had never failed to make it out of the

Champions League group stage when his teams had competed in that round, which was a record he was immensely proud of.

The short winter break and re-opening of the transfer window were now just around the corner for Cooper and his side would be in domestic action for a while before they discovered their opponents for the next round of the Champions League, scheduled to be played in February. Juventus were still unbeaten in Serie A this term and Cooper wanted to keep that going in the hope of going unbeaten for the entire season.

Cagliari were up next in a Serie A match that was comfortably won by Juventus away from home (2-0). It was then onto Lazio and Italian Cup duty. Derek picked a rotated, but strong side to contest the tie and despite going behind in the first half Juventus were the stronger of the two sides again. Abdoulaye Sy got them back into the game with the equaliser on seventy-one minutes, but Juventus were unable to build on it and the game would enter extra time. Tiredness began to show in some of the lads who had not been afforded a rest and it ultimately cost Juventus as Lazio took the lead with one hundred and twelve minutes on the clock. Juventus pushed, but it was all in vain and Lazio held on to send Cooper crashing out of the cup with his tail between his legs in the first round of the competition.

There was just one more league game to be contested before the winter break and that saw historic rivals Foirentina travel to Turin. The manager was determined to get back to winning ways and the players duly delivered a win (1-0) albeit courtesy of an Oliver Kristic own goal. Juventus had now played seventeen of their league games, remaining unbeaten, winning fourteen and drawing the other three sitting top of the pile and on course for their third successive Scudetto.

When the players returned to training following their Christmas and New Year festivities there was a new young and exciting player within their ranks. Cooper had been in ongoing negotiations with the French side FC Metz for a number of weeks looking to secure a deal for their promising winger Alassane Diop. Coopers scouting team had spotted a then sixteen year old Diop playing first team football whilst out on loan at Ligue 2 side USL Dunkerque. He had displayed impressive physical attributes as well as a developing technical ability. Cooper had seen enough to make his move and eventually a £9.5m deal was agreed for the now seventeen year old to join up with his new manager and teammates.

There were only a couple more January signings including Japanese forward Asuka Minami for £3.5m from German side Hoffenheim and Spanish central defender Juan Francisco who signed from Bilbao for £2.5m, but neither showed the promise of the young Diop who Cooper was sure was destined to go right to the very top.

Cooper and his players returned to work looking to continue the unbeaten run. The intensity of football would now increase as his side looked to compete on domestic and European fronts once more. Juventus returned to action on the 6th of January 2032 and duly picked up all three points away to Palermo (1-0). However just five days later their unbeaten run came to an abrupt end at the hands of Brescia. Juve suffered a 2-0 defeat to end Cooper's dream of an unbeaten title winning campaign. Derek Cooper tried to lift his men following the unexpected loss not wanting there to be any lingering effects from the result.

Juventus responded in almost perfect fashion thumping an impressive INTER side for five (5-0). INTER were more than in the game for the opening thirty minutes, but then striker Guglielmo Schito was shown a straight red card and the Nerazzurri fell apart in the second half as goals came from Nsiala-Ekunde, Millet, Sanchez as well as an unexpected brace for right back Antonio Salvaggio.

The INTER victory was yet again the catalyst for another inspired run of results that stretched to seven matches and saw Juventus right up to their Champions League first knockout round match away to Schalke. On the way to that match in Germany atthe VELTINS-Arena Juventus took on and beat Sampdoria (3-1), Cesena (2-1), Udinese (3-0), Pescara (2-1), Roma (1-0) and Atalanta (1-0). Moon Ik-Hyun and Javier Perez had both been in particularly good form, scoring ten goals between them in the seven matches.

Last season had seen Cooper and Juventus eliminated from the Champions League at the hands of Chelsea in the First Knockout Round. It was a defeat that still annoyed Cooper as he felt he had built a team that were capable of making it much further in the competition. There was just under a year between that first leg match with Chelsea and the upcoming match with this year's opposition Gelsenkirchen. His side were better for the experience and Cooper was convinced that the Germans were less formidable opponents than Chelsea had proven to be.

Cooper had a reasonable record in the Champions League, he had made it as far as the quarter final stage during his time at Ajax, but since then had failed to make it past the first knockout round with both Ajax and now Juventus. Derek had the 2024/25 Europa League title to his name, but he was desperate to upgrade that to a Champions League title.

Schalke had qualified as runners up from Group E behind PSG and ahead of Shakhtar and Olympiakos. Juventus had come through an equally tough group and were considered the favourites to progress through the tie. The first leg was to be contested in Germany on the 18th of February 2032 a week after Derek Cooper turned forty-four.

Juventus had trained well and had been in a fantastic run of form leading into the match. Cooper was confident his side would attain a positive result to take back to Turin and the second leg in just under a months' time. The game was slow to catch light and it took until the half hour mark for there to be any real action. Sadly for Cooper it was at the wrong end of the pitch as veteran German playmaker and former Wonderkid Kai Havertz pounced to put the home side ahead.

Juventus huffed and puffed with Derek Cooper trying his best to inspire his charges during the half time break, but try as they might they simply couldn't break through the typically efficient Germans. There was yet more misery for Cooper and the Old Lady as Argentinean central defender Lautaro Almada added a second for Gelsenkirchen in the eighty-fifth minute. That late goal proved to be the final action of the match and Juventus had slumped to a disappointing and out of character defeat (2-0). It wasn't game over for Cooper, but it was certainly looking like mission improbable back at Juventus Stadium.

There was no time to dwell on the midweek disappointment and it was straight back to it in the quest for their third consecutive Serie A title. Bari were the visitors to the Juventus Stadium three days later with Cooper set to field a rotated side in a bid to fend off fatigue. It worked and a rare start for Kwabena Diallo was rewarded with a hat-trick and all three of the side's goals in the win (3-0).

Wins against Sassuolo (4-2) and Crotone (2-0) followed and led the side perfectly into their second leg tie. Kwabena Diallo had played his way into a starting spot after his Bari hat-trick having repeated the feat against Sassuolo bagging back to back hat-tricks in the process. He had very nearly done the impossible and made it a hat-trick of trebles, but had to settle for just the two goals and a brace against Crotone.

In the three matches Juventus as a team scored nine goals with Diallo netting eight of them, a quite unbelievable achievement. In fact the only negative in this run of fixtures had been a lack of discipline from some of the younger players with Millet and Spittler both receiving straight red cards in the Sassuolo and Crotone games respectively.

Once again form boded very well as Cooper prepared his side for a Champions League match. Diallo was red hot in front of goal and the team had bounced back well from the first leg loss. Cooper called on the fans to make it an intimidating atmosphere for the visitors whilst using his press duties to tell his team that he believed they were more than capable of overturning the deficit.

Juventus Stadium was a sea of black and white as the game kicked off, but it failed to inspire a Juventus side who lacked quality when it really mattered. Diallo's recent goal scoring streak came to an untimely end with Juventus failing to score in a match for the first time since they faced Gelsenkirchen back in Germany.

The Germans were disciplined and whilst they rarely threatened they knew the onus was on Cooper's men to try and win the game, they were more than happy to see out the 0-0 and claim the tie 2-0 on aggregate. A full house turned out to try and motivate the home side and the vast majority of those fans left lamenting a very lacklustre performance in the draw (0-0) that followed. Cooper knew it wasn't going to be his night when Moon Ik-Hyun missed a very early penalty. It was a familiar feeling for both Juventus and Cooper who found themselves out of the Champions League at the first knockout round. Again.

The league title was all but sewn up by this point and failing a dramatic drop off in form Juventus would have their treble of titles. European frustration was tougher to shake for Cooper and whilst his side returned to league action he was consumed by questions as to what his squad lacked to compete in the latter Champions League stages.

AC Milan were the first opponents of the nine remaining Serie A fixtures left to be played in the 2032/32 season. A solitary Moon goal on the hour mark was enough to see of the Rossinieri (1-0), grabbing a win ahead of the next match which was against nearest title rivals Napoli. Should Juventus beat Napoli then they were almost certain to claim the title with matches to spare for another season

Cooper was confident going into the match having easily beaten Napoli earlier in the season and the game started well with Juventus the better side. Pierre Millet scored the opener for Juve on twenty-six minutes and all looked set for them to kick on through the gears as they had done countless times already this season.

Try as they might that second goal simply wouldn't come and Napoli remained in the game at just 1-0. In a mad six minute spell in the second half Napoli scored twice to take the lead and wrestle the three points back from the likely champions. Juventus continued to draw a blank and the game concluded with Napoli winning (2-1). The result would do little but delay the inevitable and yet Cooper let his side have it in the dressing room post match damning the performance as unacceptable in a game they should have won.

Just seven games remained and Cooper was desperate to get the required wins on the board as soon as possible. By the time Juventus faced Cagliari in early May Juventus had won their five fixtures following the Napoli defeat and were due to be presented with their latest Serie A title in front of a capacity home crowd.

Juventus had beaten Catania (3-2), Empoli (6-3), Cesena (4-1) and Lazio (1-0) on their way to that home match against Cagliari and they ensured the good times continued rolling by winning 2-1 ahead of their trophy presentation. Cooper was once again paraded around the Juventus Stadium turf on the shoulders of his players as they saluted the man who had yet again led Juventus to the very top of Italian football. The club hadn't won three consecutive Scudetto's since they won seven consecutively from 2011/12 to 2017/18.

Turin and Juventus celebrated long into the night as Cooper savoured another title, his third in Italy and the tenth of his career to date. The two remaining fixtures almost didn't matter now and it showed as Juventus struggled to a draw with Fiorentina (2-2) and fell to a defeat against Palermo (2-1).

With the league title clinched and games left to play Cooper had used the time to blood some of the younger squad members and Asuka Minami, Hamza Mohammed, Bill Sarachan and Alassane Diop all made the most of their chances to get amongst the goals during their time on the pitch.

As the curtain came down on another successful season Derek Cooper couldn't shake the nagging feeling that he had achieved all he could in Turin. An Italian side hadn't won the Champions League since Roma in 2019/20 with the vast majority of wins coming from either the wealth of PSG or the Premier League sides.

Derek Cooper felt that this squad weren't that far off being good enough to win the Champions League and yet each season he felt no closer to doing so. During his time in Turin he had been offered jobs elsewhere, most notably in Spain with Valencia asking him again to become their new manager and Sevilla laying down a firm offer of their own. Although Cooper could see himself managing in Spain there were only two, maybe three, jobs that he saw himself willing to consider and Valencia or Sevilla weren't one of them.

Germany was another possibility and Cooper had looked at Dortmund in the past, but the timings had never quite worked out. Of course England was where Derek saw himself managing long term, returning home to test himself in what was still the best league in the world, the Premier League. Could the time now be right for him to make that leg of his journey, he had applied for the Liverpool job in the past and it was his dream to one day manage there, but that still looked unlikely for now. There was much to ponder as he and his agent sat and weighed up their possible options.

Coopers CV was impressive and included league wins in the lower leagues of England, the Welsh Premier, Eredivisie and now Serie A. Cooper could also list manager of the year awards in England, Scotland, Holland and Italy with him having been named Serie A manager of the year in both 2029/30 and 2030/31.

Right back Antonio Salvaggio had been the Juventus player of the season with an average rating of 7.49 across thirty-nine appearances whilst new boy Javier Perez had been named top scorer netting eighteen times in twenty-seven matches. It was a modest return considering how many goals Juventus scored, but it was a testament to how much strength in depth Cooper had at his disposal.

Moon Ik-Hyun once again hit double figures with fifteen goals and Diallo's late surge also saw him convert ten times. Arne Bruyninckx and Luis Carranco had been imperious at the back with thirty-seven and thirty-three appearances each and average ratings of 7.39 and 7.25. Pierre Millet had also really come of age and established himself as regular in the midfield two alongside Matias Sanchez. Across thirty-three appearances twenty-three year old Millet scored six goals and amassed a 7.28 average rating.

On the 11th of June 2032 the news broke that R.Madrid manager Carlo Ancelotti would be retiring from football management. He had completed the Spanish league and cup double ahead of his exit, deeming it the right time to call it a day and the club were now actively seeking his successor. Derek Cooper was in his office when he heard the news and immediately contacted his agent to register his interest in the vacancy. There would be many top managers in the running and Cooper hoped to get ahead of the pack.

Pre-season preparations were well underway for Cooper who had already organised a small friendly tournament which he had named the "Turin Cup" ahead of the 2032/33 season. Manchester United, Manchester City and Red Bull Leipzig had all agreed to compete and it was something different for the club in the run up to the season starting. It now looked like there was every possibility that Derek Cooper wouldn't be around to bear the fruits of his labour as the news broke that his name had been shortlisted as a possible frontrunner for the R.Madrid role.

Cooper and his agent flew out to Madrid to attend a meeting with the club's board which served as an interview, but was more like an informal discussion on Cooper's vision for the club and his achievements both in Italy and Holland. As always Cooper once again stated his preference to build around youth, which was a risk this time as it seemingly went against the R.Madrid policy of signing high profile players, Galactico's as they had long been called by the clubs fans and media alike.

All in all the interview went well, Cooper left knowing that it was the next step he wanted to take in his career and he hoped that the Madrid board had been impressed with his plans for their club. It was now a waiting game as other candidates were to be interviewed and evaluated.

It was almost a week since the meeting in Madrid and a full fourteen days since Ancelotti had retired, but Cooper and the footballing world were still yet to learn who the new boss of Real Madrid would be. There were many illustrious names from across the world of football being bandied about and as yet Cooper had not made it to the top of the bookies list.

Cooper wasn't too concerned; the only opinion that mattered to him was that of the Madrid board and the current club president. It was mid-morning in Turin when the phone rang in Derek Coopers office, the conversation with his agent was short and very sweet. Real Madrid had been suitably impressed, and had made a very nice offer for Derek Cooper to become the new manager of the Spanish giants. Pending the signing of paperwork and the relevant parties agreeing the compensation for his departure Derek Cooper would be named as the new Real Madrid manager.

CHAPTER SEVEN.

The 25th June 2032 signalled the ushering in of a new era at Real Madrid. Derek Cooper arrived fresh off a flight direct from Turin and straight into the media spotlight. It was intense, like nothing he had experienced to date and a complete contrast to his first ever job at Kirkley and Pakefield sixteen years ago. Then it had been just one man and a notepad from the local paper, now it was every media outlet from across Europe waiting to hear what he had to say.

The airport was not the place to speak to the press and that would have to wait until Cooper had been given the chance to meet with his new boss and the current members of the backroom team. Only then would Cooper be ready to take centre stage and unveil his grand plans to the world.

As ever the change had come quickly and after four years and one hundred and sixty-seven days in Turin Derek had said his goodbyes to his staff and the few players who were back from summer holidays. It was then time to clear his desk and vacate the office for the next manager of Juventus football club. They were thankful for all Derek Cooper had done, and he had done a lot, but he was quickly becoming old news and as with in Madrid it was now all about who would come in to take the vacant managerial spot.

Derek Cooper had not taken a pay rise to be here, in fact his contract was identical to what he had been on back in Turin. This move wasn't about the money at all, for him it was all about the prestige of being able to manage at one of the most historic football clubs the world had ever seen. That famous white strip, the Bernabeu, everything about the club was dripping in history and he wanted to add to that and have his name attached to such a formidable club.

When Cooper arrived at Real Madrid he was faced with a threadbare backroom staff and plenty of vacancies to be filled. There were also a few members of staff who Derek deemed not capable of hitting the levels he required of them, so there would be changes in their departments too.

Squad wise Real Madrid were obviously a very decent team. They had completed the Spanish league and cup double under Ancelotti the previous season and although he would be making changes it wouldn't be to the same extent as his backroom plans. Clubs in Spain had to abide by the La Liga ruling of no more than three Non-EU players registered in the twenty-five man squad and this would need to be factored into any changes Cooper was planning on making.

The first scheduled match of pre season wasn't until the 13th of July against the U19's side and Cooper had much to do between now and then, starting with facing the waiting media as the new manager of one of Europe's biggest football clubs. He addressed the assembled journalists in broken Spanish where possible utilising what little he could remember from his school days.

Derek Cooper was following in the footsteps of recent managers like Ancelotti, Unai Emery and Max Allegri. All had come to the Estadio Bernabeu and won trophies and Derek Cooper planned on doing the same. After outlining his plans for the club, his recruitment plan and what he felt he could bring to the role Derek posed on stage holding the Los Merengues shirt with the club president. He signed off his first appearance as Real Madrid manager with the words "Hala Madrid" and headed to his office to get things started.

The first couple of weeks were all about recruitment and putting the foundations for success in place. Derek Cooper always wanted to work with the best backroom staff available to him and that would be no different here in Madrid. His first port of call was to find an assistant manager he felt comfortable working with. He had worked with many different assistants over the years and he now knew exactly what he wanted from a right hand man. With that in mind the first call Cooper placed was back to his old club Juventus to lure away his old number two Massimiliano Farris. Within two days it was a done deal and Farris was in Madrid to continue their working relationship.

More ex-colleagues arrived from Juventus in the form of Quincy Promes as a first team coach, Giancarlo Pariscenti as a scout, Marco Luison as a sports scientist and Cooper once again linked up with a scout he had lost to Manchester United during his time in Turin when Roberto Brovarone made the move to Spain. There were vacancies littered within the setup and Cooper aimed to have them all filled come the end of pre-season. It would be a laborious task, but he now had an established network of contacts within the game and finding suitable applicants shouldn't pose too many problems.

As well as ex-colleagues in the backroom staff there were two notable former players within the first team set up. Both Michael Roodenburg and Quissama had played under Cooper during his time at Ajax. Both players had been sold by their new manager whilst in Holland, but only because the offers from Madrid had been too good to turn down or triggered release clauses at £30.5m and £32m respectively. Both players were established squad members and Cooper was looking forward to working with them both again.

The squad was a very strong one, packed full of world class talent and Cooper knew it would be a case of supplementing the existing quality during his first season in charge. It would be counterproductive to come in and start tearing apart a side which had been successful in the previous season.

Derek aimed to implement the same tactical approach that had worked in Turin. Real Madrid were a more dominant force in Spain with the league arguably lacking the depth of Serie A so Cooper planned to continue with the attacking midfielder operating the in number ten role behind the front man. Coopers reasoning was sound and it felt that it gave the side the best opportunity at breaking down the leagues inferior sides.

Cooper moved swiftly to secure his first signing, a Uruguayan forward who had been plying his trade in Brazil with Gremio. At twenty-two years old Enzo Moreira had an impressive goal tally of thirty-seven across his last fifty-four appearances for the club. He was a player Cooper had been aware of whilst at Juventus, but had been unable to make a move for the front man due to the non-EU player restrictions and a lack of funds to meet the £17m release clause in the player's contract at the time. Cooper felt that he was a player suited to Madrid and filled a current gap in the squad, the deal was done swiftly and Moreira arrived on the 5th of July to be unveiled to the press.

By the time Enzo Moreira arrived Cooper had worked hard to move on several players who after careful consideration had been deemed surplus to requirements. The biggest deal was a £25m move for Brazilian right midfielder Jair who joined Bundesliga outfit Wolfsburg. By selling Jair Cooper had freed up one of his allocated non-EU spots to accommodate the arrival of Moreira.

Central midfielder Miroslav Caktas moved to West Ham United for £13.5m, central defender Youssouf Traore left for Red Bull Leipzig for £10m and Graziano Cortazzi moved to Napoli for a fee of £11.75m. There was also a small £225k deal agreed with Juventus for a promising central midfielder by the name of Victor Rizzi who looked as though he may develop into a half decent player if given the game time he was unlikely to get in Madrid. Cooper didn't mind taking the hit on Rizzi's fee if it meant helping his former employers out.

Pre-season went well on the pitch as the side settled into life under Derek Cooper. There was an impressive demolition of the U19's (13-0) to get them started and the wins continued as they faced Anderlecht (2-0) and Grenada (5-0) before heading off on tour to the United States. Madrid played three friendlies whilst stateside, winning all three comfortably. There was a win against Portland Timbers (3-1) as well as against Orlando City (2-0) and Philadelphia (2-0) to end the tour.

It was now the end of July 2032 and there were just over two weeks before Derek Cooper's first competitive game in charge and his first shot at adding some silverware to his record. There were some more additions to the club as promising French defensive midfielder Cedric Renaud joined for £775k from Toulouse and exciting American defender Bill Sarachan arrived on loan from Juventus. Cooper had been keen to tie up a permanent deal for Sarachan, but Juventus were adamant they weren't interested in selling one of their brightest prospects. A loan deal was agreed and Cooper hoped it would be a potential back door to securing a permanent deal further down the line.

The £775k deal for Renaud was a small one when compared to the Moreira fee, but Cooper was equally excited feeling Renaud had the potential to push the senior members of the squad for a starting position within a year or two. Cooper was still trying to tie up a couple of other deals, but he would only enter the market for the right player.

There were also a number of departures during that time as Brazilian striker Everton Rafael left for £11m (Bochum), left winger Orlando Dominguez for £10.75m (Red Bull Leipzig) and Italian striker Matteo Medici for £9m (Sporting Lisbon). By the end of July Cooper had added an impressive £100m to the club coffers through player sales.

On the 15th of August 2032 Derek Cooper travelled to Sociedad to play his first competitive fixture in the first leg of the Spanish Super Cup. It had been an impressive pre-season and Derek looked to carry that positivity into the game. Real Madrid made a good start and were rewarded in the tenth minute when twenty-three year old Swiss striker Richel Friedli put Los Blancos ahead.

Real looked to have mastered the Derek Cooper tactical blueprint and thirty-three year old attacking midfielder Ezequiel Barco put them 2-0 up on thirty-five minutes. There was little to be done at half-time as Cooper reminded his side not to lose their concentration. They didn't, and Barco popped in his second of the game in the dying minutes to cap off an excellent 3-0 first leg win in the Super Cup.

It was back to Madrid just three days later for the return leg and in all likelihood the first trophy of Cooper's time in Spain. The first half passed without any real action of note, but the nearly 79,000 strong crowd were rewarded for their patience in the second half with goals from Richel Friedli from the spot and Michael Roodenburg from the wing. A 2-0 win on the day saw Madrid lift the Spanish Super Cup with a comprehensive 5-0 aggregate victory. Cooper was pleased to get his first wins and trophy under his belt, now it was on to securing domestic and European titles.

The first success story of Cooper's short time in charge had been the emergence of Swiss striker Richel Friedli. He had scored in both legs of the Super Cup and was a shoe in to lead the line in the first league game of the season away to Mallorca. Friedli was keeping more experienced members of the squad out based on his current form and he didn't disappoint again as the La Liga campaign got off to a winning start for Madrid. Friedli was on fire and completed a hat-trick in the victory (4-0) to take home the match ball. Spanish central midfielder and academy graduate Roberto Cobo was the other player on the score sheet on the opening day.

Ahead the second La Liga match and first Madrid derby Real were drawn in Group H of the Champions League alongside AS Monaco, Bayern Munich and Basel. There was never an easy group in the competition and Bayern represented very tough opposition, but as always Cooper was confident in his ability to navigate his side through to the latter stages.

Cooper had experienced football rivalries and derby matches in his time as a manager, but the Madrid derby would represent the biggest and fiercest to date. Games like these could make or break a reputation so early on in a career and Derek was keen to be remembered for being on the winning side in this derby.

He was on home soil at the Santiago Bernabeu and looked to seize that advantage. Real were the better side early on and veteran attacking midfielder Ezequiel Barco scored his third of the season in the tenth minute. The game remained at just 1-0 until the half time break as Derek Cooper tried to inspire his men. Both teams played out a fairly tepid second half which saw neither side really play their best and resulted in a 1-0 win for the hosts. It wasn't their best performance by any means, but it was a win against their city rivals and for that Cooper was thankful.

A timely international break followed the Madrid derby which allowed Cooper to close out his summer transfer dealings. With the influx of cash from player sales Cooper was able to loosen the purse strings a little more and agree deals for a young Belgian attacker and a classy German attacking midfielder.

Sebastian Marie joined from Belgian side Charleroi for an initial £7m, but that fee could rise as high as £19m depending on performance and appearances. He was a player Cooper liked the look of and hoped to integrate into the first team as soon as possible.

The other signing, Manuel Siewert represented the biggest outlay at a pricey £38m, but Cooper saw him as his new first choice number ten. Despite starting the season well Barco wasn't getting any younger and was a player set to decline in the coming months and years. Siewert represented Cooper's attempts to fill that spot for the long term. He was already a fantastic player, but at twenty-three years old there was still plenty of room for development.

Cooper was happy with his summer dealings, bringing more money into the club than he had spent and trimming down the squad without diluting the overall quality. Staff continued to arrive throughout this time and his backroom staff were now operating with much healthier staffing numbers across the board. The foundations for success were now in place and it was time to kick on for Derek Cooper.

Following his first Madrid derby Cooper was looking ahead in his calendar to the visit of bitter rivals Barcelona and his first El Clasico match. Barca manager Leonardo Jardim would bring his side to the Bernabeu at the end of September with Cooper desperate to lay down a marker to the competition. Before then Madrid had four fixtures to contest starting with a trip to La Liga side Atletico Pamplona. A late Stefan Meusburger goal was all that stopped Pamplona causing an unlikely upset and secured a narrow win for Cooper's side (1-0). Wins against Basel (4-1) featuring an Enzo Moreira hat-trick and Real Sociedad (2-1) preceded a poor result with a draw away to Getafe (0-0).

After five La Liga matches Madrid had thirteen points, winning four and drawing one, but now came the visit of their biggest rivals, Barcelona. Cooper had grown up watching El Clasico on the TV and here he was stood in the Real Madrid dressing room as the manager of Los Merengues.

Madrid started the stronger of the two teams and Enzo Moreira made the most of his Clasico debut to open the scoring on nineteen minutes. A second goal for Madrid came just before half time as twenty-nine year old German striker Stefan Meusburger netted with forty-three minutes on the clock. Cooper asked for more of the same in the second half and Meusburger delivered once more scoring his second and Madrid's third of the game on sixty-eight minutes. Massimilliano Allegri had paid £82m back in 2026 to secure the services of Meusburger and on today's showing Cooper was sure that the German was worth every penny. Barcelona did manage to save some face with a consolation goal on seventy-nine minutes, but the game was done by then and Cooper had the statement win he was looking for.

The next month presented some tricky fixtures for Cooper with European ties against Monaco and Bayern woven in alongside La Liga fixtures against Real Betis and Villareal amongst others. The Barcelona result was the beginning of a decent run of form which stretched to seven games, winning six and drawing one. Madrid travelled to Monaco and won (3-2) with both Moreira (2) and Meusburger on the score sheet again. From there the side recorded wins against Betis (4-0), Bayern (4-1), Valladolid (6-1), Eibar (3-0) and Cadiz (2-0).

That run of form had taken Madrid through October and into November where they faced Bayern again in gameweek four of the 2032/33 Champions League. Madrid were top of Group H having won all three previous matches, including a demolition of their German opponents.. Madrid couldn't repeat their impressive home win in Munich, but Cooper was more than happy with a 0-0 draw away from home against a side like Bayern. Madrid were almost certain to qualify and more than likely to do so as group winners.

November proved to be a bad month for Cooper and Real Madrid. Whether that was down to the managers willingness to accept a draw away to Bayern or whether complacency had started to creep in it was hard to say, but what was evident was a marked loss of form. Madrid failed to register a single win in a month which saw them draw four matches and lose one, their first defeat of the season. After the draw in Germany Madrid failed to break down Valencia (1-1), Celta Vigo (0-0) and Basel (0-0) whilst Athletic Bilbao came from 2-1 behind with twenty minutes to go to win the match 3-2.

Things could only get better in December, especially if Cooper wanted to maintain any sort of lead at the top of La Liga. As always Barcelona were topping the chasing pack and the dropped points had allowed them to get back within striking distance. December arrived and the November curse was seemingly lifted. Madrid started the month with a favourable tie in the Spanish Cup as they began the defence of their trophy against Castellon of Spain's second tier. Madrid secured a comfortable away win (2-0) in the first leg of the fourth round tie.

More wins followed and in fact it would be an unbeaten December across three competitions for Madrid as they won all six matches. They took on and bested Espanol (3-1), Monaco (3-0), Sevilla (2-1), Castellon again (5-0), and Elche (1-0). The good form continued through into January following the short winter break and Cooper recorded a further eight victories in their nine matches in a jam packed schedule. The one fixture Madrid failed to win was the Spanish Cup quarter final second leg away to Sociedad which ended 2-2, but was still enough to see them through to the semi after a 2-0 home win earlier in the month.

Victories against Grenada (3-1), Sevilla (5-0 & 2-0), Cordoba (3-0), Mallorca (4-1), Atletico Pamplona (4-1) and the previously mentioned Sociedad (2-0) led the side perfectly into the second Madrid derby of the season away in Estadio de Madrid. Since the defeat to Bilbao on the 27th of November Real Madrid had gone fourteen games unbeaten, winning thirteen with a solitary draw. Cooper hoped to add another win to that figure against his city rivals on the 29th of January.

Real Madrid had been triumphant the last time he had come up against Fernando Torres and his Atletico Madrid side. It had ended 1-0 at the Bernabeu and Derek would settle for the same result here. Torres was failing to inspire as a manager in the same way he had managed as a player and Atleti were languishing in mid-table and well off the title pace. Cooper and his Real side were here to pile on the misery for El Nino and Enzo Moreira did just that scoring both goals in a comfortable win (2-0). The white half of Madrid went home the happier of the fans for a second time this season as Cooper completed a Madrid derby double.

Ahead of a Spanish Cup semi final Cooper had some January transfer business to conclude before the window slammed shut. Cooper had once again chosen not to upset the apple cart too much in his first transfer window and opted to only sign players that either represented excellent value for money, or looked too good to pass up on now and risk losing them to another club.

With that in mind the club moved to agree deals for forward Markus Rossi from Freiburg for £325k, Roman Oliver who was an exciting left winger for just £70k from Portuguese side Braga and Goalkeeper Goran Sabov from Borussia Monchengladbach for £3.8m. With the squad lacking a decent understudy goalkeeper, Sabov was signed to act as immediate back up to the first choice keeper, Raulen Luiz.

There were also a couple of notable outs as Belgian centre back Thomas Riviere was sold to Manchester City for £28m and the aging, but still impressive Ezequiel Barco was allowed to join INTER for just £3.5m. Barco was unimpressed with his diminished role since the arrival of Siewart and ultimately Cooper gave in to his requests to find more regular first team football elsewhere. As the January window closed Cooper had netted the club an impressive £154m in transfer fees whilst he spent shrewdly and kept his expenditure to a fraction of the income at just £69m.

Coopers failure to add any domestic cups since his time in Wales over a decade ago had been the single biggest frustration of his career so far. He had never managed to win one of the cup competitions of Scotland,

Holland or Italy and hoped to rectify the situation here in Spain. Madrid had experienced a pain free run to the semi-final and a draw against Celta Vigo meant avoiding Barcelona until the final, should both clubs make it that far of course.

Form had been fantastic leading into their semi-final tie, but that counted for nothing on the night as Celta Vigo upset the odds with a 1-0 victory. A solitary goal from Turkish striker, and former Atletico Madrid man, Bartu Asci was enough to get the unlikely first leg victory against favourites Real Madrid.

The shock defeat at Vigo was then followed by another surprise defeat, this time in La Liga, as Madrid registered just their second defeat of the campaign. Their loss against Bilbao in late November was joined by the latest defeat at the hands of Real Sociedad. A goal from Coopers Bulgarian left winger Borislav Mihaylov levelled the game at 1-1, but it wasn't enough and Sociedad scored their winner just ten minutes later.

Back to back losses had become a very alien thing to Derek Cooper and he was in no mood to see his side lose three on the bounce. Celta Vigo travelled to the Bernabeu with their one goal lead from the Spanish Cup first leg hoping for a repeat performance. What followed was a Stefan Meusburger master class as he inspired his teammates to an impressive and emphatic home win (7-0). Meusburger opened the scoring in the thirteenth minute and the game remained at 1-0 until the floodgates opened when he added his second on seventy-two minutes. An own goal and a Roberto Cobo brace came before Meusburger completed his hat-trick in the eighty-first minute. Madrid weren't done and ruthlessly added their seventh goal when fellow German Siewert completed the rout on eighty-seven minutes.

Cooper had qualified for a domestic cup final, his first since his time with Ross County back in the 2023/24 season when he lost in the Betfred Cup final to Celtic. He was more determined than ever to banish his cup demons and ensure Real Madrid held onto their Copa del Rey trophy. The final wouldn't be until the 14th of May so there was plenty of time for Derek to prepare his side for another battle with Barcelona who had triumphed in their semi-final against Valencia.

Between now and then there was the small matter of tying up his first La Liga title and progression in the latter stages of the Champions League. In a cruel twist of fate Cooper had been drawn against former club Juventus in the first knockout round of the Champions League which meant returning to Juventus Stadium for the second leg in the middle of March.

El Clasico was up next in La Liga and Barcelona still represented the biggest threat in the race for the title. Madrid were unable to reproduce the heroics of their home win, but still managed to stifle Barca into a dull 0-0 in front of a packed Camp Nou. It was a draw which suited Cooper and Madrid more than the Jardim led Catalans.

Cooper turned forty-five the day before the Barcelona match and his side delivered a belated present in the form of a four match winning run which included a 2-1 first leg victory away to former club Juventus in the Champions League. The run began with an impressive win over Getafe (5-0) before the Juve win and further victories against Real Betis (3-0) and Valladolid (6-1).

There were familiar faces aplenty when Madrid visited Juventus Stadium with Cooper's replacement Torsten Frings fielding a side full of players signed by Derek Cooper and one of those players, Prince Nsiala-Ekunde, found the back of the net for the Old Lady. It was a tight game with away goals from Moreira and Meusburger enough to secure the important away win for Madrid.

There was a draw against Villareal (2-2) and a win against Cadiz (2-1) ahead of the second leg of the Champions League tie. Cooper had successfully rotated his side in the Cadiz match, resting players and giving opportunities to some other members of the squad. Spanish right winger Mohamed Oudghiri particularly impressed scoring both of the games goals.

The rotation also meant Cooper had a refreshed squad for the visit of the Italians. Juventus were still very much the dominant force in Serie A, as they had been when Cooper left in the summer and he was prepared for a very tough match. Madrid definitely had the upper hand with their 2-1 away victory making them the bookies favourites to make the quarter finals. Whilst manager of Juventus Cooper had never managed to take them past the first knockout round, and he hoped it would be the same case for his ex-players this evening.

Real started the better side, like a team that had benefitted from a week off and were soon two goals ahead as Enzo Moreira scored again before Brazilian centre back Conrado scored the second. It was effectively game over, Madrid were 4-1 up on aggregate with two away goals in the bag. There was no way back for Juventus, but they did score a consolation through a late ninetieth minute penalty which Nsiala-Ekunde stepped up to score against his former manager again. Madrid progressed and Cooper triumphed 4-2 over the two legs against his old club. Failure to make his mark on the Champions League whilst in Italy was one of the main factors in Cooper seeking pastures new and he felt this victory had vindicated the decision.

Victory against his old club set up a reasonably kind quarter final tie against Benfica. Cooper had avoided the remaining Premier League clubs Manchester United and Manchester City as well as fellow La Liga sides Villareal and Barcelona. Cooper was happy with the draw and after a good showing against Juve was confident of progressing past the Portuguese Champions.

Before those Benfica matches in April there was a month of La Liga action. Disappointing draws against both Eibar (2-2) and Valencia (1-1) kicked off the domestic fixtures and allowed Barcelona to keep pace at the top of the table. Two victories followed to finish strongly ahead of the Champions League action as Madrid beat Celta Vigo (1-0) and A.Bilbao (2-1).

Form hadn't been scintillating, but all the big players were scoring goals with Moreira, Siewert and Meusburger amongst the goals in recent matches. Benfica weren't to be taken lightly, but Derek was confident as his side travelled to Lisbon.

Estadio da Luz was an impressive sight filled with nearly 65,000 people and Cooper enjoyed the pre-match build up watching the sides as they warmed up. The game got underway and Madrid started brightly with £17m striker Enzo Moreira opening the scoring after twenty-seven minutes. Benfica responded and within five minutes striker Juan Pozio had them on level terms. Benfica weren't done and there was a late blow for Madrid as they took the lead through Pozio's strike partner Diego Suarez in first half added time.

Coopers team talk became less positive than he had envisioned with his side 1-0 up. He was disappointed with the overall performance of his players and told them as much. An improved second half performance stopped Benfica adding to their two goals and Spanish midfielder Jose Vicente spared Coopers blushes as he popped up in the ninetieth minute to rescue a draw for Real Madrid (2-2). Benfica had proved they were no pushovers, but Cooper was returning to Madrid with two away goals and home advantage for the second leg.

Cooper rotated where possible for the victory against Espanyol (5-2) which came between the two Benfica ties. Oudghiri and Roodenburg both got themselves on the score sheet and turned in impressive performances in the wide areas. Once the Espanyol game had been put to bed all eyes focussed on the visit of Benfica and qualification to the Champions League semi finals.

The Santiago Bernabeu was packed to the rafters with an 80,000 capacity crowd with all except a small section of away fans hoping for a Madrid victory. The game started in the worst possible way for Cooper as his side conspired to give away a penalty in the opening five minutes. Diego Suarez duly dispatched the spot kick to put Benfica 1-0 up. Madrid were unable to find a way back into the game in the first half and Cooper once again gave his side a kick up the bum during the break.

Madrid responded, but it took them until the hour mark to find the back of the net as thirty year old Spanish midfielder Roberto Cobo handed the advantage back to the home side. Away goals would now see Derek Cooper and his team progress, but it was a dangerous game to try and defend a narrow victory on a technicality. Madrid continued to attack, it was how Derek wanted them to play, they looked to seize the initiative and win the tie outright. It was a decision that always allowed Benfica a way back into the match and it was an opportunity that they took as Suarez found the back of the net for the third time across the two matches.

Benfica won 2-1 on the night and took their place in the semi final with a 4-3 aggregate victory. Cooper had blown it, he had been so close, but once again he had come up short in the latter stages of the Champions League. Although he had finally made it past the first knockout round for the first time in years Cooper wouldn't be getting his hands on the trophy he coveted so badly this season.

Real Madrid needed to put European disappointment behind them and finish the La Liga season strongly. Winning and retaining their league title was more important than European success, but that didn't make it hurt any less for Derek Cooper and his players. They returned to domestic action away to Cordoba knowing that a victory would seal that La Liga title and give them the perfect platform going into the Spanish Cup final against Barcelona.

Failure to beat Cordoba would leave the possibility that Madrid would need a final day victory against Granada, or failing that, hope that Barcelona choked when it mattered. As it happened Cooper needn't have worried about the possible permutations as his side comfortably saw off Cordoba (2-0) to seal the league title victory.

For now though the celebrations were put firmly on hold until the final game of the season at home to Granada where they would hopefully get the chance to celebrate not only the 2032/33 La Liga title win, but also a Spanish Cup victory. Barcelona would not want to be runners up to their big rivals in the two biggest domestic competitions, but that was exactly what Derek Cooper and Madrid had planned for them.

There was nearly a week between the Cordoba fixture and the cup final which was to be held at Mestalla, the home ground of La Liga club Valencia. 75,000 spectators were in the crowd on Saturday the 14th of May 2033 to witness Derek Coopers Real Madrid side completely dominate Barcelona.

The final finished 2-0 to Madrid with goals either side of half time from Brazilian centre back Conrado and Bulgarian winger Mihaylov. Barcelona had simply been unable to live with a rampant Madrid and in truth it could, and probably should have been a much bigger win for them. The stats told the story of the game and the better side had won meaning there would be a carnival atmosphere inside the Bernabeu for the final game of the season in eight days time.

The final match had become irrelevant now, the result didn't matter at all, but there were fans desperate to get into the Bernabeu to see Cooper and his side celebrate retaining both the league title and Spanish Cup that they had won the year before with Ancelotti. Cooper gave some of the talented youngsters at the club a chance to show the home fans what they were capable of and both Sebastien Marie and Cedric Renaud did just that as they both found the back of the net in the 2-0 final day victory. The sounding of the final whistle was cue for the celebrations to begin and trophies to be presented.

Club captain Conrado led his side up to lift the La Liga trophy before leading the players and staff on a lap of honour with their families in tow to celebrate the incredible success of the season with the clubs fans. Derek Cooper soaked it all up, enjoying the party in the stadium before heading out on an open top bus tour of the city later in the day.

The first season in Madrid for Derek Cooper had gone to plan, although he was still disappointed by their Champions League defeat at the hands of Benfica. He had a fantastic team here at Madrid, there was no denying that, but he had asked a lot from his players this season with some playing as many as fifty-eight times. In fact all of what he considered his first choice eleven had played over forty times with four of those lads breaking the fifty game mark.

Despite playing so many games every player, from Raulen Luiz in goal to Enzo Moriera up top, had maintained an average rating above seven. Raulen Luiz had the lowest which was 7.11 from his fifty-eight appearances and French right back Stephane Jacquot narrowly beat Moreira to the best rating with 7.62 from fifty-four appearances. The fact Jacquot beat Enzo Moreira who top scored not only for Real Madrid, but also in La Liga with his thirty-five goals in forty-nine appearances was testament to just how consistently good the right back had been.

Having looked at the number of games he was asking his regular first teamers to play Cooper decided to add depth to what was already an impressive squad. He would, as ever, look to sign up any promising young players who were available at the right price, but he also needed to try and find those one or two world class players who would reduce the number of games certain regulars were having to play.

There were decent lads already at the club, and maybe Cooper needed to trust some of them more in games where he would usually stick to his strongest eleven. Wingers Michael Roodenburg and Mohamed Oudghiri had both had good seasons with thirty-four and twenty-six appearances respectively. Roodenburg scored six times and got an average rating of 7.24 whilst Oudghiri found the back of the net eight times and managed a 7.23 average rating.

However there were other players in an around the first team squad that still had to convince Cooper they had the quality or potential to dislodge those regulars ahead of them. Striker Richel Friedli had started the season on fire, but failed to maintain that form and finished the season with just five goals from twenty-one appearances and a disappointing average rating of 6.83.

With his transfer plans settled and a pre-season programme in place Derek Cooper and Real Madrid headed into the summer with the intention of coming back even stronger in 2033/34 to not only retain their league and cup titles for a third season, but also to mount a charge for that Champions League trophy that Cooper wanted.

Because of the earlier start in Spain and the two legged Spanish Super Cup there would be limited time for his squad to get up to match fitness. Cooper arranged six friendly fixtures in under a month to really push his lads ahead of the Barcelona Super Cup matches and bed in his new arrivals.

Whilst things were going very well on the pitch for Cooper including pre-season wins against the U19's (4-1), Anderlecht (2-0), Standard (3-0), Almeria (3-1) and Boca Juniors (5-0) with a draw against affiliate side Cadiz (0-0), finding players of the required standard to immediately improve his first eleven was tough. His situation wasn't helped by two prominent first team players being distracted by the bright lights of the Premier League.

Conrado was club captain and had been a rock at the back for Derek Cooper last season. The Brazilian international was now thirty and in the form of his life, so it was no surprise that Manchester City had been sniffing around doing all they could to unsettle the Madrid player. Arsenal were the other guilty party and their interest was focussed on Dutch winger Michael Roodenburg. Cooper was more open to this transfer as he had plenty of depth in that position with Meusnurger, Oudghiri and Quissama all vying for the same spot, but Cooper would not be selling for the sake of it. He would only sell if a suitable bid was made for either player.

Very early in the summer it became clear that Conrado would do all he could to get his move. Derek really didn't want to lose a player of his quality, but constantly turning away bids from Man City was proving to be detrimental to the morale of the squad. The English club came in with several offers and eventually Cooper and Real Madrid managed to negotiate them up to £60m which was considered good money for a thirty year old central defender.

The Roodenburg deal soon followed and Cooper once again drove a hard bargain forcing Arsenal to pay out £55m to get their man. Madrid had paid Ajax £30.5m for Roodenburg back in 2028/29 following Cooper's departure from the club, and now here he was selling his former winger on for a profit of nearly £25m after five seasons in Madrid.

The Conrado sale in particular left Cooper with a huge hole he needed to fill and he knew exactly who he wanted. Arne Bruyninckx was now twenty-four and well on his way to becoming a truly world class centre back. Cooper knew him and he trusted him, which were two factors in his decision to try and bring him in.

Whilst he had an open line of communication with Juventus established Cooper enquired about another central defender, Ange Zogbo, as well as their goalkeeper, Alexander Guillaume who he was also very interested in bringing into the Madrid set up. Juventus proved to be tough negotiators and they weren't doing their ex-manager any favours in this transfer window.

Cooper would eventually come to an agreement for the transfer of all three players, but it would come at a hefty price with him paying out £125m up front with fees potentially rising as high as £142m for them to join up with Real Madrid. Of course a large portion of those fees had been paid for with the departures of Roodenburg and Conrado, but it still represented the biggest outlay of Cooper's career.

Roodenburg and Conrado weren't the only departures of the summer and the sales of striker Maurizio Mastelli to Napoli for £17.5m, goalkeeper Raulen Luiz to Everton for £17m and full back Pablo Gonzalez to Red Bull Leipzig for £12m also brought in some money for the club. Raulen Luiz was only allowed to leave as the signing of Alexander Guillaume would see him lose his spot as the first choice goalkeeper and Mastelli was incapable of performing to the required level to dislodge Enzo Moreira as the number one striker in the team.

There were a few other signings in the summer window, but many of those were considered players for the future with young lads like seventeen year olds Mohamed Yao and Sebastian Clerc joining from Olympique Lyonnais for £85k and £51k, which was peanuts compared to the deals concluded for the established players.

German left back Alexander Frank was the final signing made by Real Madrid as they paid his £6.25m release clause to effectively steal him from Greek champions Olympiakos. Frank was worth more than the fee paid the minute he became a Madrid player and would act as more than reliable back up to regular left back Luis Claudio.

Derek Cooper had also been working on a new tactic throughout the pre-season scheduling, but he was unsure as to whether he would test it out competitively against Barcelona in the Spanish Super Cup. He was working on a strikerless formation that utilised Meusburger and Moriera on the wings with Manuel Siewert the main attacking threat through the centre, arriving in the box late from an attacking midfield position. It was effectively a 4-1-2-3-0 with a holding midfielder reinstated at the cost of the lone striker. It was something different and Cooper was keen to see how this tactical experiment would play out for him.

Real Madrid lined up in their more familiar formation for the first leg of the Spanish Super Cup, with Moriera up top, Siewert in behind and Mihaylov and Meusburger out on the wings. There were competitive debuts for the Juventus trio of Zogbo and Brunyinckx in the centre of defence with Guillaume between the sticks. Barcelona had paid £73m to Arsenal for Dutch striker Budiman Setaiwan and £17m to Wolfsburg for Thyago, a central defender Cooper had managed previously, and both started the game for Barca.

Madrid had a good record against Barcelona since Coopers arrival having beaten them twice and drawn with them once to remain unbeaten in the Clasico's to date. It was a precedent that Cooper hoped to maintain and a fast start in the Camp Nou was rewarded with a Meusburger goal just four minutes in for Madrid. Barcelona were determined to not let Real have it all their own way and Setaiwan began to pay back his hefty fee with his first goal for the club on nine minutes to level the score.

The game then settled down as both sides looked to establish dominance over the other. Madrid were slightly the better side and Brazilian midfielder Robson put the away side back in front ten minutes before half time. Advantage Real Madrid. Cooper encouraged his side at the break and asked for more of the same going into the second half. Los Merengues continued to play the better football with an attacking intent that kept their hosts on the back foot for most of the second half. Arne Bruyninckx got himself a debut goal to instantly endear him to his new clubs fans on seventy-four minutes before Sebastien Marie came off the bench to replace Enzo Moreira and complete a humiliating 4-1 defeat for Leonardo Jardim.

The second leg was only three days later and Barcelona rolled into town looking to be much harder to beat. They had changed formation to a 4-4-2 that utilised the two central midfielders in defensive midfielder territories, sitting just in front of the central defenders and looking to stifle Manuel Siewert who was the creator in chief of Real Madrid.

The defensive block was successful in the sense that it limited the home side to just a 1-0 victory courtesy of another Robson goal. Barcelona's case wasn't helped when one of their defensive midfielders, Portuguese midfielder Daniel Braganca, was sent off in first half injury time. They never looked like troubling Madrid and managed only three shots in the match, with none on target to trouble Guilluame. Real Madrid had been comfortably the better side over the two legged final and the 5-1 win reflected that. Derek Cooper could now add a second Spanish Super Cup to his list of honours.

With the season officially underway Real Madrid headed into the 2033/34 La Liga and Champions League campaigns with wins against Cordoba away (3-1) and Valladolid at home (2-0) before draws against A.Bilbao (0-0) and Arsenal (2-2). Stefan Meusburger had put Real Madrid 2-0 up at the Emirates, but they had been unable to look after their lead and the Gunners scored two goals either side of half time to earn a share of the points. The draw was even more galling for Madrid as the recently departed winger Michael Roodenburg grabbed his first goal for his new club to kick-start their comeback.

Alongside Arsenal Real Madrid had been drawn in Group A with Red Bull Salzburg and Italian side Napoli who Derek Cooper was well aware of following his time in Serie A. Before the Salzburg game at the end of September Madrid got back to winning ways in La Liga beating Betis (2-1), Valenica (4-0) and Grenada (4-0). Manuel Siewert was in devastating form in the Grenada victory scoring all four of the side's goals in a player of the match performance from the German.

The 4-0 wins continued against the Austrians in the Champions League with goals from Borislav Mihaylov, Enzo Moreira, Sebastien Marie and Stefan Meusburger. Madrid closed out September 2033 unbeaten having made a decent start to the season with seven wins and two draws across the Spanish Super Cup, La Liga and UEFA Champions League.

Meusburger, , Moreira and Siewert were proving to be the standout performers in front of goal whilst nineteen year old Belgian striker Sebastien Marie was beginning to make an impact from the bench in a few of the early season games which was pleasing for Derek Cooper having agreed to pay up to £19m for the lad.

As always Derek Cooper hoped to keep the run going and dreamed of an unbeaten season a la Arsene Wenger and his Arsenal "Invincibles". Sadly this dream was yet again cut short as Eibar dealt out a surprise and humbling 3-1 defeat, which could have been four had they not missed a second half penalty. Ange Zogbo was particularly poor in the loss and was taken off to face the wrath of the manager. The defeat wasn't the end of the world, more of a bump in the road, but it was still frustrating for Cooper when Madrid had dominated the ball and gone ahead early in the game.

The side recovered well and wins against Elche (4-0), Napoli (3-1) and a Madrid derby victory against Atletico (3-0) came before the first league meeting against Barcelona on the 26th October 2033. Barcelona once again lined up to stop R.Madrid with a 4-5-1 formation that included a defensive midfielder.

Despite the match stats being in Madrid's favour with more posession, fifty-nine percent to Barca's forty-one, and more shots on goal, eighteen to seven, Barcelona delivered their game plan perfectly and inflicted Derek Coopers first Clasico defeat (1-0). Cooper was worried by the recent trend that saw his sides dominating games and having more shots than their opponents, but failing to convert them in to goals. Against both Eibar and Barcelona less than half the Madrid shots had managed to find the target.

A trip to Malaga followed the Barcelona match and Madrid managed to get the win, but only just. Malaga took the lead with just twenty minutes remaining and it was once again looking like being one of those games where Madrid were left unable to turn their shots in to goals. Manuel Siewert had missed an early penalty, which looked to have been a sign of things to come, but Enzo Moreira came off the bench to level the game before Stefan Meusburger added the winner in the eighty-ninth minute.

November started with a trip back to Italy and to Naples to face off against a familiar opponent in the Napoli side of Italian Davide Lanzafame. Napoli had emerged as the closest rivals in the group with Arsenal having dropped points elsewhere and they would be keen to try and peg back Coopers Madrid. In the last encounter back in gameweek three Real Madrid had been victorious winning 3-1, but there was to be no repeat here with Napoli much the better side in a 1-0 win. There was a late red card for Madrid as Mohamed Oudghiri received his marching orders in the eighty-eighth minute.

The Napoli loss on the opening day of November would be the last time Real Madrid were beaten as they progressed through December and into January. There were wins in La Liga against Villareal (1-0), Getafe (2-1), Zaragoza (4-1), Levante (4-1), Celta Vigo (6-0), A.Pamplona (3-0), Espanol (2-0), Cordoba (2-0) and A.Bilbao (3-0) with a solitary draw against Real Sociedad (2-2).

Madrid also progressed through the early rounds of the Spanish Cup as they looked to defend their title for the third consecutive season. Victories against Barakaldo (3-1) in the fourth round, city rivals Atletico Madrid in the fifth round (2-1) and Villareal in the quarter final (2-0) saw them through to a semi final clash against Grenada in February.

Champions League form was also good and there were some impressive victories in gameweek five and six to finish off the group stage and progress through to the knockout stage as group winners. Arsenal were totally outclassed on their visit to the Bernabeu and were sent packing back to England with their tails between their legs after a 7-0 win. Red Bull Salzburg fared slightly better but were still swept aside by Coopers men as Madrid won 5-2 with Stefan Meusburger scoring four of the sides five goals.

Away from the pitch January had been a busy time for the club with both incoming and outgoing transfers. Some of Coopers established first team players were being tracked by clubs in England with their wealth an obvious draw for players. Stephane Jacquot was one of the best full backs Cooper had seen and the Frenchman was a virtual ever present in the side under his management, but with the players contract running down and a feeling that he had achieved all he could at the club Cooper was forced to relent and sell to Chelsea in a deal worth £25m, which wasn't bad money for a thirty year old.

Borislav Mihaylov was the next player to have his head turned by an English club as Manchester United tried to unsettle the Bulgarian winger. Cooper never liked to sell his big names, but he was also of the mindset that no-one was unsellable and when Manchester United offered £85m upfront for the left winger Cooper agreed to accept their proposal.

Roberto Cobo was another senior player allowed to leave as Juventus invested some of the funds garnered through sales to Madrid in the summer and paid £25m for the thirty year old Spanish central midfielder who had been at the club since coming through the academy in 2019/20.

Third choice right winger Stefano Ferrasi left to join Sunderland for £10m and twenty-nine year old backup centre half Ruyman Guerra headed to China and Guangzhou for £18m to help take the total money made from player sales in 2033/34 up to the £328m mark. Once again this was a clear strategy by Cooper who liked to bring as much money into the club as possible to be reinvested in the playing staff as well as the club and ensuring the club finances were left comfortably in the black.

With player sales Cooper was able to draw on a very healthy transfer budget and he once again returned to former club Juventus to complete the biggest of his winter deals agreeing to pay £58m for the French midfielder Pierre Millet. Cooper had signed Millet from Nantes a few years ago and had watched him develop into one of the finest midfielders in Europe. It was a no brainer to go and pay big money for a player he knew so well and was confident would improve Real Madrid.

As well as Millet there were transfers agreed for Swedish right back Fredrik Arvidsson from Monaco for £14.5m, Belgian defensive midfielder Bert Beernaert from Manchester United for £14m and Turkish central midfielder Erkan Tasar for £12.75m from Munchen Lions in the Bundesliga. Deals for first team regulars aside there were also a number of young players signed from across the world with fees ranging from £100k up to £5m.

As January approached its end Cooper was integrating his new players and looking to maintain the clubs excellent run of form. Unfortunately January ended with a surprise defeat away to Valladolid whose goal in the twenty-third minute proved to be enough to grab a 1-0 win. New boys Millet, Beernaert and Tasar all played some part in the fixture and Derek Cooper hoped his transfer dealings hadn't led to the defeat. It was unlike Cooper to change so many members of his squad at this point of the season, but he was optimistic that the right decisions had been made for the clubs long term future.

February arrived and with it another Spanish Cup victory as Real Madrid beat Granada 4-0 in the first leg with two goals each for Meusberger and Marie. Madrid were looking like a side capable of retaining their crown once more and were now just one step away from another final.

A disappointing draw followed in the league as Real Betis stood firm to deny Madrid a return to winning ways in La Liga. Left back Alexander Frank got himself on the score sheet to give Cooper's side the lead, but they were unable to hang on and a goal in added time in the first half pegged them back to earn Betis a share of the points.

Another draw then came as Madrid travelled to Granada looking to cement their place in the Spanish Cup final in May. The 4-0 victory from the first leg meant that the bulk of the heavy lifting had been done and the 0-0 at Nuevo Los Carmenes had no impact on the overall outcome of the tie, Madrid were in the final and would be facing off against a familiar foe in Barcelona who had come through their semi final against Real Sociedad.

With their place booked in the cup final it was back to La Liga before travelling to Germany to play Wolfsburg in the Champions League first knockout round. Real Madrid travelled to the Mestalla to take on Valencia on the day their manager turned forty-six and they marked to occasion with an impressive 3-0 victory. Bert Beeraert joined Meusburger and Moreira on the score sheet to score his first goal for his new club. The Valencia win was then followed by another win, this time at home to a now familiar Granada side (2-0).

It was then off to Germany to face their Bundesliga opponents for the first leg of their encounter. Real Madrid travelled without both Millet and Beernaert who were deemed ineligible to play because of their involvement with Juventus and United in the group stage of the competition. The side put out by Cooper was still more than capable of getting a result and he had no concerns despite losing two key members of the side.

His confidence was vindicated by his men as they set about winning the game and taking two away goals back to Madrid for the next leg. Wolfsburg started the better side and took the lead through attacking midfielder Max Durrschnabel in the twenty-fourth minute. It took Madrid until the fifty-fourth minute to get back on level terms as midfielder David Perez found the back of the net. There was then a disastrous three minutes for the home side which saw Florent Morisse put the ball past his own keeper to hand Madrid the lead before right back Paul Bier was dismissed having been shown a straight red card. Down to ten men Wolfsburg failed to threaten Real Madrid who headed back to Spain on the right end of the 2-1 score line.

There was nearly a month before Wolfsburg travelled to Madrid looking to overturn the deficit and in the intervening period there were league games to be played to ensure they remained in top spot with the final months now on the horizon. There were comfortable wins against Eibar (4-1) and Elche (3-0) which led into a run of three big games. Atletico, Barcelona and then Wolfsburg.

Real had to settle for a share of the points in the Madrid derby as Atletico refused to beaten in front of their home support. Atleti could consider themselves a little unfortunate not to have claimed the victory with them in the ascendancy for much of the game, recording more shots than Coopers side managed in the ninety minutes. Barcelona then came to town and Pierre Millet was the hero of the game as he more than paid back his large fee with a last gasp winner in time added on at the end of the ninety minutes to secure the 1-0 win. It was the type of goal that instantly guarantees you hero status, scoring a last minute winner in front of a home crowd to defeat your bitter rivals.

After the euphoria of that late goal against Barcelona Madrid needed to ensure they didn't get carried away and carry out a professional performance against Wolfsburg. The German side were looking to overturn the 2-1 defeat they suffered at home and they got off to the best possible start as impressive German striker and former Manchester United man Soren Mayer scored after five minutes. The early goal woke Madrid up and from that point on they delivered the performance that was required to progress into the next round. Enzo Moreira equalized after eighteen minutes before adding his second before half time. It remained 2-1 on the night and Madrid won 4-2 on aggregate to set up an exciting quarter final with Manchester United and their manager Peter Niemeyer.

There was a ten day break before Madrid were next in action and Cooper used the time to work hard on the strikerless formation he had developed in pre-season. It was based around his three attacking players stretching the opposition backline and drawing them out, whilst his inverted wingbacks tucked in to offer stability alongside the defensive midfielder, allowing his midfielders to make lung bursting third man runs from deep to get behind the opposition. Real Madrid had used this tactic on and off for the last few weeks and Derek Cooper was confident it was time to make this the default way for his team to set up.

Malaga were the visitors to the Berabeu as Madrid returned to action ahead of the Manchester United matches and it was an easy 4-0 win for Real as Manuel Siewert scored an impressive hat-trick playing as the central attacking midfielder which was now the focal point of the teams set up with there being no striker.

Manchester United were an impressive side and were still one of the dominant forces in the Premier League, although they hadn't won a league title since the 2030/31 season. Madrid badly missed Millet on the night and looked completely off the pace losing 2-0 to United and failing to really threaten their English opponents. Just four shots on target was disappointing and Millets creativity was definitely a miss for Derek Coopers side.

Between the ties with Manchester United Cooper took his side to play Villareal in La Liga and it started well for them at El Madrigal with centre back Bruyninckx putting them one goal ahead early on. Real had looked in control as the game reached the hour mark, but then Argentinean striker Matias Crosa, who had played for Cooper at Ajax, pulled one back before his strike partner Stefan Middel added what proved to be the winner just seven minutes later. It was a poor result coming at a bad time for the side who now departed for England and an unforgiving Old Trafford.

Two goals down from the home leg Cooper knew it would take a minor miracle to see his side through to their first semi final together. Three goals away from home was never easy, especially in the Champions League, but to try and do that at Old Trafford whilst keeping the home side at bay was going to be very tough. There was a capacity crowd of 94,777 in attendance to see if Madrid could accomplish what seemed impossible.

Manuel Siewert got the game off to the best possible start for the Spanish champions scoring the opening goal after ten minutes to reduce the arrears to just the one goal. The hopes of players and fans alike where then almost immediately dashed as United were awarded a penalty on thirteen minutes that Fernando Gurrieri stuck away to make it 1-1 on the night and 3-1 on aggregate. Things then got worse for Cooper as United took the lead through Donat Brun after twenty-two minutes of play. Madrid were now playing for pride, there was of course still a chance that they could recover from 4-1 down, but it was a very unlikely outcome. On the stroke of half time as the game ticked into the forty-fifth minute Manuel Siewert once again found a way past Alain Olivier in the Manchester United goal to at least make the second half a little more nervy for the English side.

Sadly there was to be little more of note in the match despite Coopers attempts to inspire his men at half time. Manchester United had done the damage in the opening leg of the tie and defended stubbornly in that second forty five to curtail any hopes of a Madrid revival. It was a close game, but United edged possession and controlled the game in a manner that suited them more than their visitors who needed to try and force the issue. Real Madrid would be exiting the Champions League at the quarter final stage for the second time in two seasons and the wait for another European cup win would extend to twelve years with their last victory coming in 2021/22 against Arsenal.

Games in April and May would now be devoid of any European fixtures and it left the Spanish league and cup champions looking to successfully defend both titles. A Spanish Cup final in May was already booked against Barcelona and Madrid were in the box seats of La Liga leading their rivals comfortably with seven games to go. Two wins from those remaining La Liga fixtures would be enough to end the chase of Barcelona and secure back to back titles in a fourth country for Derek Cooper. Narrow wins against both Getafe (1-0) and Real Sociedad (1-0) immediately after the clubs return from England meant that Real had done it again and secured consecutive titles under Cooper and their third in as many years.

The remaining fixtures against Zaragoza (3-0), Levante (3-0), Celta Vigo (2-1), Atletico Pamplona (4-1) and Espanol (2-1) were irrelevant although they contributed towards the fifteen point gap that had opened up between league winners and runners up. Portuguese winger Roman Oliver was handed some game time in the final few fixtures and managed to grab himself a couple of goals. Pierre Millet continued to settle into the side and prove he was becoming a world class midfielder with two goals to his name against both Celta Vigo and Atletico Pamplona.

The fifteen point gap was a massive boost to the players heading into the Spanish Cup final with Barcelona. It was their biggest winning margin in La Liga since 2028/29 when they finished with ninety-one points to Barca's seventy-five. Derek Cooper hoped that the psychological benefits of such a victory would lift his side as they attempted to defend the cup element of the 2032/33 double.

Barcelona and Real Madrid met at Nuevo Mestalla on the 25th of May 2034 in a repeat of the final from a year ago when Real had triumphed 2-0. Both scorers on that occasion had since left the club with Mihaylov and Conrado now plying their trades on separate sides of Manchester. Coopers side were considered the favourites by both the bookies and the pundits prior to kick off, but he was taking nothing for granted, Barcelona were still a very good side.

Cooper was able to pick from virtually a full complement of players and he named his strongest eleven to start the match. Barcelona wanted nothing more than to end the recent spell of Madrid dominance and that was typified by the display of La Masia graduate and Spanish international striker Joan Moreno who opened the scoring on six minutes before killing the game off in the seventy-ninth minute with his second of the game. Madrid had good possession and managed ten shots to Barca's three, but with only two of those ten on target it was a game to forget for Cooper as his side succumbed to a 2-0 defeat. Barcelona and Moreno had scored with their only shots on target in the match as the Catalans made the most of the chances they created to walk away as Copa Del Rey champions 2033/34.

2033/34 had been a satisfactory season for Derek Cooper and Real Madrid. They had retained their La Liga crown, but they had lost out to Barcelona in the Spanish Cup and had yet again failed to make it to the final four in the Champions League. The change in formation had largely gone well, but it had possibly come up short in the biggest games of the season against Manchester United and Barca. Cooper would be looking at ways he could tweak the strikerless tactics to reduce the number of wasted efforts on goal and refine the player roles and instructions.

The decision to sell some big names in January may also have been a rare error of judgement by the manager considering it left them slightly short in Europe with new signings Millet and Beernaert ineligible to play. French right back Stephane Jacquot, who left for Chelsea for £25m, had arguably been the standout performer going into the winter transfer window boasting an average rating of 7.69 from his twenty-three appearances. Mihaylov had also contributed a number of important goals and impressive appearances during his time with the club, but it was the absence of Jacquot that seemed to really hurt despite Alexander Frank filling in incredibly well on his weaker side.

Stefan Meusburger and Enzo Moreira both managed twenty-seven goals each, but Meusburger was named top scorer by virtue of having made five less appearances over the course of the season. The German international also beat his Uruguayan team mate in terms of average rating as he achieved 7.53 to the 7.36 of Moreira. The third member of the attacking trio, Manuel Siewert, also posted impressive figures, matching the 7.53 average rating of his compatriot, but falling slightly short in the goal charts with twenty-one. The contribution from Siewert had seen a massive improvement from his debut season and Cooper recognised him as an instrumental part of his new tactical plan.

Defensively the team had been as sound as ever, despite the loss of Jacquot, and Guilluame (7.10), Zogbo (7.28), Bruyninckx (7.53) and Claudio (7.59) consistently turned in decent performances throughout the season with them all making over forty appearances each, over fifty in the cases of centre backs Zogbo and Bruyninckx.

As with the previous eighteen campaigns Derek Cooper was busy throughout the summer months when his players were off resting and recuperating as he planned for pre-season and looked to recruit in the areas he thought the club were lacking. As always he was looking for ways to improve not only the first team squad, but also the U19 and B sides to develop players for the future or achieve some profit.

By the time the transfer window opened on the 1st of July 2034 Derek Cooper had agreed deals with SPO in Brazil for their U20 number one Felipe Renan (£5.25m), Torino for Italian right back Felice Mair (£12.5m) and America in Mexico for an Argentinean central defender named Hugo Rodriguez (£9.5m). Felipe Renan would come in and act as understudy to Alexander Guilluame with Cooper hoping to see the Brazilian stopper develop sufficiently to challenge his mentor. Mair was a player Cooper was aware of during his time in Italy, but was never able to tempt across Turin to Juventus. Derek saw the twenty-two year old right back as the long term successor to Jacquot and his arrival would free up Alexander Frank to challenge Luis Claudio in his favoured role at left back. Rodriguez was brought in to act as cover for Zogbo and Bruyninckx with current back up Victor Lucas looking likely to leave the club in search of regular first team action. At £9.5m Rodriguez was worth the chance and Cooper felt there would be room for a profit should the Argentinean fail to make an impression with the first team.

As expected Victor Lucas left for pastures new as the thirty-four year old agreed to join Juventus for £7m. There were also deals concluded for central midfielder Jose Vicente who joined Marseille for £21m whilst Jose Ramon Contreras (£2m) and Ayman Soliman (£8m) also left the club. Despite interest in many of his players they were the only ones Cooper was willing to let go permanently although there would be a number of young players heading out on loan to gain some first team playing time across Europe.

Frustratingly Paris Saint-Germain had made several attempts to unsettle Stefan Meusburger who had once again been a standout performer for the side in his ninth year with the club. Cooper had no intention of selling one of his star players having struggled to replace Jacquot, so moved to agree a new contract with the German hoping to dissuade any further PSG bids. Thankfully Meusburger agreed to the contract extension and PSG cooled their interest allowing Madrid to hang onto their talismanic striker.

Throughout pre-season there were more transfers agreed as Cooper continued to bolster the clubs with promising players from across the world. Right winger Mauro Carra signed from River (£7.25m), striker Nickthiel Matias joined from Santos (£2m), Roar Fossen from Norwegian club Start for up to £1m and striker Facundo Ibanez from Lanus for a fee which could reach £3.4m.

There were also some arrivals behind the scenes as club legends Fernando Hierro and Guti returned to Real Madrid. Guti arrived back from Manchester City to work as a coach whilst Hierro took on the role of Director of Football to work alongside Cooper and his trusted recruitment team. Derek Cooper also decided to hire a former player in Adam Campbell who had played for TNS back in Wales. Campbell had turned into a fine attacking coach despite his modest playing career and he joined the club from Premier League side Crystal Palace.

Away from his work behind the scenes pre-season had gone well for Real Madrid with them winning all seven of the non-competitive matches arranged ahead of the Spanish Super Cup first leg against Barcelona in late August. Plenty of players were given run outs in the freindlies and there was an impressive win at home to Manchester United (3-1) with a hat-trick for Enzo Moreira. Some of the other victories came against the likes of Anderlecht (3-0), Newcastle (4-1) and Burnley (5-2).

Derek Cooper planned to approach the upcoming 2034/35 season slightly differently with him taking the decision to make the Champions League his priority. Their La Liga victories in the past two campaigns had been achieved with relative ease and Cooper felt that provided he could take points off Barcelona, who were likely to emerge as their only title rivals, his side would once again retain their crown. The Spanish Cup was a competition that Cooper was proud to have won, although he would trade those wins for his first Champions League title.

The Santiago Bernabeu had been chosen as the stadium to host the 2034/35 Champions League final and Derek Cooper was desperate to take his side all the way and win his first European Cup in front of his home fans. It would be a tough ask without question, but Derek Cooper felt that with the final being in their home stadium it just might be their time. It would take a lot of hard work and luck along the way, but to win that final would be truly brilliant.

By the time the first leg of the Super Cup rolled around Real Madrid were ready to face the long season ahead. Pre-season had gone well both on and off the pitch and it was now time to take on their main rivals for yet another piece of silverware. Derek Cooper had not yet lost the two legged final during his time in Spain and he didn't want to start with a defeat here.

The first leg was held at the Nou Camp and it was an evenly contested affair, neither side was able to establish a spell of dominance although legendary French striker Willy Charpentier put the Catalans ahead after two minutes to worry the Madrid faithful. The players however weren't fazed and slowly Real Madrid clawed their way back into the game. It was their own legendary front man who levelled the score with Stefan Meusburger opening his account for the season on twenty-eight minutes. With parity restored both sides were unable to break the other down and it looked to be heading for a 1-1 draw. That changed in the eighty-fourth minute when the home side were awarded a penalty to hand them the advantage. Luckily for Madrid Alexander Guilluame was on his game and managed to save the effort from Jan Baron who was a second half substitute for Barcelona. The penalty miss meant that the game did end 1-1 and it was all to play for in the second leg three days later.

Barcelona travelled to Madrid for the second leg hoping to catch them out early in the game again, but this time it was Real who grabbed an early goal through Meusburger. Whereas no team had managed to dominate in the Nou Camp, here and in front of their home support Real Madrid turned in a performance of the highest quality to really put Barcelona to the sword. Goals from Manuel Siewert, David Perez, Pierre Millet and Sebastien Marie followed the early opener without reply as a dominant Madrid ran out 5-0 winners in the Bernabeu and 6-1 winners overall. It was Cooper's best Clasico result to date and he was delighted with the way his side dismantled their fiercest rivals.

The good times continued for Real Madrid and Derek Cooper as win after win rolled in for them in both domestic and European action. In the Champions League Madrid had been drawn alongside Borussia Dortmund, Besiktas and Malmo FF in Group H and it wasn't until Derek and his side travelled to face Besiktas in Turkey on the 8th of November that they dropped their first points of the season.

Besiktas was never an easy place to go, but having already recorded three wins in the group, including a home win against the Turkish side Cooper approached the fixture in gameweek four with his usual optimism looking to make it sixteen consecutive wins. It wasn't to be and Besiktas got the unlikely win for their home fans scoring a goal either side of half time with their only shots on target to win 2-0.

Prior to that loss and following the 5-0 drubbing of Barcelona, Real Madrid won fourteen on the bounce including wins against Borussia Dortmund (2-1), Malmo FF (3-0) and Beskitas at home (1-0) in Group H as well as La Liga wins against Cordoba (4-1), Espanol (5-1), Villareal (1-0), Deportivo La Coruna (4-1) and Real Betis (2-0) amongst them. Stefan Meusburger was in particularly good form and he had notched fourteen goals already including back to back hat-tricks in the games against Cordoba and Espanol.

Real Madrid sat top of La Liga and top of their Champions League group and having won all but two of their competitive games in 2034/35 thus far, but it was Barcelona up next and they would be looking to avenge the thrashing that kick started the season for Cooper's side. Leonardo Jardim was still the man in charge at the Nou Camp and he sent his side out to frustrate Real Madrid playing a 4-1-4-1 formation that used a defensive midfielder and a flat four across the middle to try and nullify the attacking threat of their opponents.

Derek Cooper's side slipped into old habits and found themselves unable to make the most of their efforts on goal with just one of the thirteen shots mustered making it on target. This had been a common theme with the defeats of last season as Madrid laboured to find a way through a stubborn opposition defence. Barcelona were the much more effective team on the night taking the lead through Jordi Garcia before striker Joan Moreno added a second from the penalty spot on twenty-seven minutes. Barcelona had regained some credibility with the 2-0 win and it meant that Derek had to be careful with La Liga results in future to ensure they didn't let their rivals back into the title race.

Back to back defeats had become very rare for Derek Cooper and Real Madrid and it was now important that everyone refocused and weren't distracted by the disappointing results. Thankfully the side managed to do just that and made their way through November, December and into January notching impressive victories along the way. There was a Champions League win at home to Dortmund (4-1) to go with a win against Malmo FF in gameweek five (4-0). Impressive wins in La Liga against Sevilla (1-0), Valencia (2-1) and city rivals Atletico (3-0) as well as progression to the Spanish Cup semi final after wins against El Ejido (7-0 agg), Espanol (8-0 agg) and Alaves (4-0 agg). In fact Madrid had made it seventeen games unbeaten winning fifteen and drawing two by the end of January.

The end of January also saw the transfer window close once more. Derek Cooper decided he would refrain from allowing any players to leave the club on permanent deals still feeling that the departures of last January proved costly in the second half of the season. He was however persuaded to get out the chequebook once more and there was a £4.4m deal agreed with OB in Denmark for their exciting central midfielder Christian Olsson and a £2.5m initial fee agreed with Bremen for their Swiss attacking midfielder Ramazan Holzknecht which could rise to £6m in the future. A number of other young players joined the club with fees ranging from free transfers up to £1.1m.

Real Madrid had been drawn against Athletic Bilbao in the Spanish Cup semi final and another Turkish side, Fenerbache, in the first knockout round of the Champions League and with both ties on the horizon Derek Cooper was keen to keep the momentum they had built up leading into February 2035. A win away at Cordoba (4-1) meant the winning run continued ahead of the first leg with Bilbao which Madrid duly won as well (4-0) to all but seal their place in the clubs fifth consecutive final.

In between the Bilbao ties there was a shock defeat which curtailed the now nineteen match unbeaten run and was a very unwelcome birthday present for Derek Cooper. Real Betis really turned up on the day and blew Madrid away to win 4-0 with the home side managing four different goal scorers and Manuel Siewert picking up an ankle injury that would rule him out for a month. The ankle injury meant Siewert was almost certain to miss both legs of the Fenerbache tie which was a disappointment for both manager and player alike.

With a 4-0 victory already in the bag Cooper took the opportunity to rest some of his first eleven and handed starts to some of the clubs bright young stars with Felipe Renan starting in goal, Czech full back Jiri Michalek started at right back and Hugo Rodriguez partnered Zogbo. Both Christian Olsson and Ramazan Holzknecht also made appearances off the bench in what turned out to be a 1-1 draw on the day.

There was then a win against Valladolid (1-0) in La Liga before the side headed back to Turkey hoping for a better result than the last time they visited the country back in November. The game at Sukru Saracoglu did not start well for the visitors and Luis Claudio was shown a straight red card after eighteen minutes having already gone a goal behind to French striker Christophe Audard ten minutes earlier. Cooper sacrificed a central midfielder in the form of David Perez to bring on Alexander Frank and Madrid slowly began to find their feet with ten men. Real were actually on top approaching half time and Cooper urged them for more of the same in the second half. Sebastien Marie who was deputising for the injured Siewert pulled Madrid level on fifty-two minutes before Enzo Moreira put them ahead and secured an unlikely and vital away win in the eighty-eighth minute to break Fenerbache hearts. Surely Madrid would now finish the job off in the second leg scheduled for a months' time and make their way into the quarter finals.

Four league matches needed to be played before the return leg and Real won three and drew one beating Levante (1-0), Sporting Gijon (7-0) and Celta Vigo (2-0) before the draw with Eibar (0-0) in which Madrid had more than enough chances to put the home side to the sword and take all three points.

Real Madrid held a narrow lead over their Turkish visitors, but Derek Cooper was more than confident the hard work had been done in the first leg. His side would not be stupid enough to get another man sent off and they had the home advantage on their side this time out, Fenerbache had missed their chance to strike. The manager's confidence was misplaced and in an uncomfortable evening his side managed thirty-one shots on goal with ten on target and fifty-nine percent possession yet somehow failed to find the back of the net. As it was another lone goal from Christophe Audard wasn't enough for the visitors and their 1-0 victory on the night meant Real Madrid only progressed by virtue of away goals after a 2-2 draw over the two legs.

With their Champions League dream just about still alive Derek Cooper hoped to return to the form his side displayed earlier in the season to close out the campaign and secure his first treble. The wins returned in the league which included another Clasico win as Barcelona succumbed to defeat again (3-0) to all but surrender the league title to Madrid. There were other wins against Coruna (5-0), Malaga (2-0) and Granada (4-0). It was shortly after the league victory over Barcelona that Real Madrid learned they would be facing off against the Catalans at least three more times this season having drawn them in the Champions League quarter finals and scheduled to face them in the Spanish Cup final for the third year running.

The draw was definitely better for Cooper and Madrid who by now held an impressive record over Jardim and Barcelona. In this season alone Madrid had won three of the four meetings and had scored nine to Barca's three. Real had been drawn away for the first leg and they made the comparatively short trip to Barcelona looking to secure an away win and a couple of goals to help their cause. Jardim once again set out to stop Cooper's side by playing the defensive 4-1-4-1 formation that had succeeded back in early November. Both defences proved to be on top form and it was a game that afforded little in the way of entertainment for the neutral fans. Madrid dominated possession, but Barcelona perhaps created the better of the chances with Belgian centre back Arne Buryninckx picking up the player of the match award for an impressive display at the heart of the Madrid back line. The game ended 0-0 and it was not a fantastic result for Cooper, but not a poor one either. Barcelona had been unable to make the most of their home advantage as they were more concerned with nullifying the attacking threat their opponents offered.

The league was tighter than in other years which was a surprise considering Madrid had only lost twice so far all season which was testament to the improvement in Barcelona's form to maintain a title challenge, although with the seasons end in sight it was unlikely that they would realistically usurp Real Madrid. A 2-0 league win against Sevilla courtesy of an unexpected brace from young midfielder Christian Olsson ensured that Madrid kept Barca at arm's length yet again as the sides prepared to face off for the sixth time this season in the Champions League quarter final second leg.

Jardim and Barcelona adopted a slightly different approach for the second leg with a variation of 4-4-2 which saw the two central midfielders sit deep as defensive midfielders to help out the defence. The change in formation didn't help their chance and instead allowed Real Madrid to go one better than their 5-0 victory earlier in the season. A hat-trick from Enzo Moreira as well as goals from David Perez (2) and Luis Claudio meant Madrid emerged as 6-0 winners, a score line that no-one saw coming in the quarter final of a Champions League. Madrid were simply brilliant on the night with their clinical attack and stingy defence who also played their part with Barcelona failing to manage a single shot on target and just two in total during the ninety minutes. Cooper was delighted, he had made it past the quarter finals for the first time and was now just one round away from a potential final at their home ground.

The other teams left in the Champions League were Bayern Munich and Wolfsburg of Germany and Manchester United of England. Ideally Cooper would like to avoid both Bayern and Manchester United as he felt they were the strongest two sides remaining, but of all the teams it was United he feared the most and he would take either German opponent over the English side. As luck would have it Cooper was handed his best case scenario and Real Madrid would play Wolfsburg with the first leg to be played on the 9th of May away from home.

Cooper rewarded many of his first team with a rest for the Valencia game which followed their heroics against Barcelona. With just three days to rest between the games there were starts for Renan, Michalek, Rodriquez, Pantovic, Frank, Tasar, Olsson, Friedli, Renaud, Oudghiri and Siewert who was still trying to play his way back into form following his ankle injury. The stand ins played very well and managed a decent 3-1 win with a hat-trick from Friedli who had failed to really make an impact since Coopers very first few games with the club back in 2032. There was then a draw with Villareal (1-1) as the first team lads returned to action before Cooper once again rotated the side ahead of the semi final with the fringe players managing another win, this time against Elche (2-1) with Oudghiri and Holzknecht on the score sheet.

Wolfsburg had finished as runners up in the Bundesliga under Unai Emery, but he had since departed the club and it was now Jurgen Klopp who was in charge at the newly built Dzeko Park. Derek Cooper was very much a fan of the charismatic Jurgen Klopp and he had read books on the German as a young manager hoping to learn from them. Now he found himself headed to compete against one of his managerial idols in a semi final of the Champions League, it was a quite unbelievable turn of events for the Lowestoft born manager.

The German side were certainly no mugs and they proved that in the first leg as they matched Real Madrid stride for stride in the 0-0 that showed there was nothing between the two sides. Once again it was a result Cooper was satisfied with, Wolfsburg had been unable to capitalise on their home advantage and whilst Madrid hadn't scored any away goals their task was still simple, win at home and they were in the final. The Bernabeu Champions League dream was still very much on.

A rotated side once again played in the league as Cooper hoped to keep his first choice eleven injury free and in good condition ahead of the second leg. It was a risky move given that the game was against Atletico Madrid, but thankfully it didn't backfire, although they were unable to replicate the recent wins against Valencia and Elche and only managed a 2-2 draw with Atletico rallying late on to come from two goals behind in the final twenty minutes. The result was irrelevant as Barcelona were already unable to catch Madrid with just one league game left to play now. Madrid had asked to save the presentation of the trophy until their last game of the season at home to Bilbao in order to avoid any potential distractions from their Champions League run in.

Real Madrid were determined to make the most of their home crowd once again, as they had done in the 6-0 win against Barcelona in the last round and they looked on course for a repeat performance following two goals inside the opening ten minutes. Meusburger scored against his former club to make it 1-0 after four minutes before Pierre Millet added a second on ten minutes. Things then got better for the home side as Meusburger further tormented his ex-employers with his second of the game before the half hour mark to make it 3-0. Half time allowed Klopp a chance to regroup and try to stem the flow of Madrid attacks. They continued to be the better side, but Wolfsburg had a newfound resolve that made them much tougher to break down. German striker Soren Mayer then pulled one back on sixty-four minutes to ensure a nervy final half an hour for the home crowd. Those nerves were then further tested as Brazilian winger and former Madrid man Jair came off the bench to score for Wolfsburg and make it 3-2. Madrid were in danger now and just one more goal would see them out and their Bernabeu dream dashed, but luckily the defence held out for the remaining twenty minutes and Cooper was able to celebrate with his players as they made their first Champions League final together. Klopp was humble in defeat and offered Derek Cooper the best of luck for the final as well as signing an old Liverpool shirt post match for the fan boy that remained in the Madrid manager.

Derek had fulfilled his pre-season hopes of taking his side all the way to the Champions League final at their home ground and he hoped it was a sign that this was their year. Manchester United had come through their tie with Bayern and would travel to Madrid to try and nick the trophy from under the noses of Cooper, Real Madrid and their fans come the 9th of June.

Just three games remained of the 2034/35 season and two of those were finals, with the other seeing them handed the La Liga title, potentially the first of a historic treble. Awkwardly the league match was scheduled between the two cup finals, the Spanish Cup coming before the Champions League to close the season out. Once again it was a trip to the Nuevo Mestalla to face Barcelona for the third consecutive year. It would also be the seventh time the clubs had come up against each other in four different competitions this season. Derek Cooper and Real Madrid had triumphed more often than not and they were hoping for more of the same in this final.

As was now customary Barca set up the more negative of the two finalists playing a defensive 4-1-4-1 as Jardim often did when playing against Madrid. Los Blancos were the much better side in the opening exchanges looking to take the game to their opponents and they were rewarded on thirty-four minutes when Enzo Moreira slotted away the game's first goal. There wasn't much of a wait for the second and a rare Barcelona attack was rewarded with an equaliser three minutes after they had fallen behind with midfielder Felipe Ormeno grabbing the goal. The game remained level for the duration of the ninety minutes with Madrid finding it tough to break through the defensive block of Barcelona.

The final went into extra time and by this point Barcelona were a side playing for penalties, in fact in the entire one hundred and twenty minutes of play they only managed two shots on target compared to nine from Madrid. In truth Derek Cooper's side had once again proven to be wasteful with their opportunities managing to get just the nine of their twenty-three efforts on goal on target. Penalties would now decide who would win the Spanish Cup and Barcelona had elected to go first having won the toss. Early saves from Guilluame handed Madrid the advantage, but misses from Meusburger and Moreira threatened to hand Barcelona the victory. Luckily the big Belgian came up trumps again and made a third save in the shootout to allow Ange Zogbo to slot home the winning penalty and send the Real Madrid fans into raptures.

Eight days later Real Madrid hosted Athletic Bilbao in the final game of the league season and Meusburger and co really put on a show for the fans who had turned out for the chance to see their side crowned league champions again. Meusburger, Marie and Moreira all scored two goals each with Arne Bruyninckx scoring another to make it a 7-1 thriller and ensure the party atmosphere lasted long into the night in Madrid. That was now two trophies in the hands of Derek Cooper and he was now hoping to make it three and add that Champions League that he had been coveting since the moment he embarked on his managerial journey.

Attention now turned to the Champions League and the week leading up to the final was spent in familiar surroundings, training in their own facilities and spending time with their families ahead of the biggest match of their seasons and possibly their careers to date in some cases. It was a relaxed build up, but Derek Cooper and his team were fully focussed on bringing home the final instalment of a potential treble.

There were a couple of familiar faces in the Manchester United squad and Derek managed to grab a brief word with Borislav Mihaylov, the Bulgarian winger he had sold for £85m as well as the Belgian midfielder Philippe Petit who Cooper had signed on loan whilst manager of Scottish side Ross County. Since the Ross County days Petit had been signed by PSG for £27m and then Manchester United for a further £23m.

Philippe Petit took his place in the Manchester United starting eleven alongside a wealth of talent that wanted to deny Cooper and Madrid the Champions League title and make it two in a row for them having beaten Juventus in the final of 2033/34. Manchester clubs had monopolised Europe's premier competition with Manchester City winning four consecutive titles between the victories of Manchester United in 2033/34 and 2028/29. Cooper hoped to break their dominance and he felt that he could do just that at home in Madrid.

Madrid started with Guilluame in goal, Mair, Zogbo, Bruynincxk and Luis Claudio at the back, Bert Beernaert would anchor the midfield against his old club with Millet and Perez operating in front of him, Sebastien Marie started ahead of Manuel Siewert with Meusburger and Moreira operating out on the wings. It was a strong side and Cooper felt confident as the game got underway in front of 80,304 spectators.

The media had been saying the game was too close to call with little between the two teams and that proved prophetic as both teams looked to ease their way into the game. There was very little action of note before English striker Ronnie Walker put United ahead with forty minutes gone. Madrid were behind at the break, but they weren't out of the game and were more than capable of kicking on in the second half. Derek Cooper used the interval to demand more from his team, they had done ok, but he knew they were capable of so much more.

The second half minutes slowly ticked away and Derek introduced Manuel Siewert for the largely ineffective Marie and Friedli for an unusually off colour Stefan Meusburger, but neither change had the desired effect and although Real Madrid had proved to be more than a match for United they were unable to find a way to break down their English opponents. The first half goal for Ronnie Walker proved to be enough to see his side retain the Champions League and send Derek Cooper back to the changing room with a runner up medal.

Cooper was immensely disappointed, his side had fallen at the final hurdle and it hurt all the more to have been so close to what would have been an almost unbelievable treble. As it was he had guided his side to a third consecutive La Liga title and a second domestic Spanish Cup win in three seasons. It took his trophy haul in Spain to eight and his overall career total to an impressive twenty-four league and cup wins.

His players had been impressive throughout the season and during the gala dinner the manager hosted at the end of every campaign he thanked all the players and the staff for giving it their all. Bert Beernaert made fifty-two appearances during the course of the season with Millet, Meusburger, Moreira and Bruyninckx also making it to fifty appearances as well. He had asked a lot of his squad and they had repaid him with impressive average ratings and plenty of goals. Meusburger top scored with thirty-one, Moreira made it to twenty-five and whilst Millet and Perez chipped in with fifteen and eleven apiece from central midfield. Felice Mair led the way in terms of average rating with his score of 7.88 from thirty-seven matches ahead of his opposite full back, Luis Claudio who attained a decent 7.71 from thirty-nine outings. The final loss did not take away from what had been an impressive season, the players were told to go and enjoy their summer holidays before coming back ready to do it all again.

After a brief holiday the pain of the final defeat slowly subsided and Cooper returned to Madrid to begin planning a way to take his side to victory in all competitions in 2035/36. Manuel Siewert had been disappointing following such an impressive season in 33/34 and Cooper considered it an area he may need to strengthen in the summer window having not been convinced by Sebastien Marie in the attacking midfield role either.

Whilst Cooper was keen to bring in new faces that would improve the squad he once again chose to hang on to the majority of his senior squad with central midfielder Robson and right back Arvidsson the only exceptions. Robson had failed to agree a new deal with the club and had decided to leave on a free transfer signing a pre-contract deal to join Italian side Roma. Madrid were well stocked in that area and a lack of playing time was the reason for Robson's decision to leave. Swedish full back Arvidsson had failed to make an impact since joining from Monaco in a £14m move so he was allowed to leave for Sunderland in a rare deal that actually saw Cooper fail to make a profit on a player. Sunderland paid £11m to secure the services of the Swede who had been unable to dislodge the impressive Felice Mair.

Bringing the right players in proved to be a source of frustration for Derek and he was being quoted some simply ridiculous prices for some of his transfer targets. He had been working hard on the darker arts of trying to unsettle the coveted players, but their clubs were standing firm with little progress being made Derek was left looking at other options.

July saw the arrival of French attacking midfielder Abdul Youssouf from Lille for an initial £17m which could rise to a costly £31.5m. The transfer was an expensive one for the club, especially when you consider the inexperience of the twenty-one year old who had made less than one hundred appearances in senior football. Egyptian central defender Amr Samir was the other standout deal of the month when Real Madrid agreed to pay Sporting Lisbon the £34.5m release clause in the player's contract. At twenty-five and with over fifty caps to his name Samir represented less of a risk with Cooper feeling the player was more than up to challenging regulars Zogbo and Bruyninckx for their starting spots.

There were a number of other deals completed for some young Portuguese players with the club hoping to develop them in the U19 and B sides before either making the step into the senior side or being loaned out and sold on. South American midfielders Marcus Vinicius and Sebastian Ortiz were signed as young players capable of operating as back up members of the first team squad and both players joined for a combined £10m which could rise to £18m. The final pieces of business for the summer were concluded on the morning of the Spanish Super Cup first leg, Swiss attacking midfielder Alexander Renevey arrived in a clause heavy deal which could hit the £10m mark and Brazilian midfielder Jose joined for £4.8m with Cooper hopeful that both players had a bright future ahead of them.

Real Madrid had performed well in pre-season winning all seven of the friendlies that had been arranged for July and August 2035. There were wins against Everton, Red Bull Leipzig, River Plate and Jeonbuk, Ulsan and Pohang on their tour of Asia. Derek Cooper and his side headed to Barcelona for their first competitive game of the season wanting to carry that winning feeling on their way to yet another Spanish Super Cup victory.

The season got underway on the 19th of August 2035 with Amr Samir making his debut in the first leg of the Super Cup tie. Barca started the better of the two sides and took the lead early on through Joan Moreno, but Madrid grew into the game dominating possession and they found an equaliser on thirty minutes through Stefan Meusburger. The game remained tied at 1-1 as it had done in the same match last season. Real Madrid went on to win the second leg 5-0 in 2034/35 and Derek Cooper would welcome another thrashing of their opponents this season.

The second leg this time out was much tighter and extra time was needed to find the eventual winner. It was a game Madrid really should have won in normal time with their incredible domination; they managed thirteen shots on target to the one of Barcelona and achieved sixty-one percent possession. Barcelona's one shot on target was rewarded with a goal on thirty-seven minutes as Moreno once again beat Guilluame in the Madrid goal. Enzo Moreira levelled the game almost immediately, but Real would have to wait until a Pierre Millet winner in the ninety-seventh minute before they turned their domination into victory. It was Cooper's fourth straight Spanish Super Cup victory and he was delighted that the last three had come at the expense of Barcelona.

With the Spanish seasons curtain raiser done and dusted for another year it was back to La Liga and Champions League action and a run of fourteen games that would take Real through to early November. In that period there would be only one defeat as Madrid succumbed against Real Sociedad (1-0) and one draw against Manchester City (1-1) in Group C of the Champions League. The other twelve fixtures all saw wins for Real Madrid and included victories against Marseille (2-0), Espanol (3-0), FC Steaua (3-1) and Villareal (3-0).

The remainder of November saw the club fail to win in three matches most notably losing 1-0 to title rivals Barcelona who had started the season incredibly strongly looking to end the Madrid domination of recent years. Prior to the Clasico defeat there was another loss, this time in the Champions League away to FC Steaua with the Romanians profiting from a wasteful Madrid who slipped into the old habit of failing to convert numerous chances into goals. There was the same issue in the 0-0 draw with Valladolid that came sandwiched between the two losses. Real Madrid's wastefulness had handed Barcelona the early advantage in the race for the title.

November of 2035 ended with a nervy 3-2 win away to Marseille in the Champions League, but a win was a win and that was just what Cooper and Madrid needed to get their season back on track. They were in the unfamiliar position of chasing Barcelona rather than leading them, but everyone at the club were more than confident of keeping their run of titles going.

Another win followed in the league as Bilbao were brushed aside (2-0) before Real Madrid really turned on the style in front of their home fans to beat Manchester City (4-0) and cement their place as winners of Group C. Goals from Millet, Oudghiri (2) and an own goal from Luis Carranco, who had played for Cooper at Juventus saw the Spanish side inflict a heavy defeat on one of the favourites to lift the Champions League.

With their season seemingly back on track Madrid and their manager were then left frustrated as they once again failed to see off inferior opposition with Levante coming to the Bernabeu and only managing one shot in ninety minutes. Madrid managed seventeen in the match, but failed to find a way past Fernando Arregi in Levante's goal. The club couldn't afford to drop points when they had been so dominant, it was becoming a constant frustration for Cooper and he hoped it wouldn't cost them silverware come the end of the season.

Although there would be no defeat until the 9th of February 2036 Madrid did not look wholly convincing, especially in La Liga and there were more dropped points in games against Celta Vigo (0-0) and Villareal (0-0). In fact the majority of fixtures in the period from the end of November until early February had come in the Spanish Cup with wins against R.Majadahonda (7-0 agg), Racing Santander (6-0 agg) and Villareal (2-0 agg) seeing them through to a first leg semi final win against Cordoba (2-0).

Although not entirely happy with their league form, Cooper did lead his side to victories against Atletico Madrid (2-0), Cordoba   (2-0), Grenada (4-0), Racing Santander (3-0), Deportivo Coruna (5-0) and Real Sociedad (4-0). On Paper the sides form didn't look bad at all, but Cooper wasn't happy with the performances despite the results. He couldn't help but feel the early dropped points against Barcelona coupled with the sporadic draws would cost them come May.

Manuel Siewert had been vital with Real Madrid moving to their strikerless system, but form had dropped off after a brilliant first season in that role. The Germans poor performances combined with a failure to convert domination into wins was forcing Derek Cooper to reconsider the approach that had won them leagues and taken them so close to the Champions League last time out. There were players at the club more than capable of occupying that lone striker role and that may well be the approach for the manager moving forward.

January had been a quiet window for Madrid and there were no signings of any note either in or out. In fact the only player signed was young Brazilian centre back Jailton Lopes who arrived from Santos for £1.1m. Derek Cooper was in a strange position where although frustrated with some of his sides performances he was very happy with the players at his disposal and was finding it very hard to identify any suitable transfer targets with Real Madrid being held to ransom more often than not.

The defeat that ended Madrid's resurgence inevitably came in La Liga causing them more problems in their efforts to chase down a Barcelona side who looked to have the bit between their teeth this campaign. Madrid were one goal down away to Espanol and chasing the game when Belgian midfielder Bert Beernaert got himself sent off in the seventy-fourth minute to curtail any hopes of a comeback. Swiss attacker Richel Friedli came off the bench to try and rescue something for Madrid, but he failed to convert an eighty-ninth minute penalty before Espanol put the final nail in the coffin in the ninetieth minute adding their second and securing the 2-0 win against the reigning champions.

There was a break from La Liga action as Cordoba hosted the second leg of the Spanish Cup semi final trailing by two goals, but looking to capitalise on the deflated Madrid. A sixty-sixth minute goal from Cordoba's Spanish winger Alexis Ramirez ensured a nervous finish to the match for Madrid and their fans, but they held on to their advantage and made it to yet another domestic cup final winning 2-1 on aggregate. Inevitably it would see another final where they would go up against Barcelona, their fourth in a row.

The Champions League remained the ultimate prize for Derek Cooper and he knew realistically that he was at one of only a few clubs in the world that were capable of lifting that prestigious trophy. He had come so close last season, and Madrid had sailed through the group stage this season seeing off Manchester City 4-0 along the way. However topping the group had seen them drawn against very tough opposition in PSG who had finished behind German side Wolfsburg in Group A. The first leg would be played in Paris on the 20th of February and would come off the back of a league victory away to Valencia courtesy of an eighty-fifth minute goal from Erkan Tasar to keep the pressure on Barcelona.

Madrid travelled to Paris wanting a win to take back to the Bernabeu, but it was important for them to avoid defeat. Losing an away leg and failing to score against opposition such as PSG would amount to Champions League suicide and Cooper knew his side had what it takes to go one step further than they had last season and lift that trophy. It was a tight match in France, but Madrid were handed the advantage by their hosts early in the second half when their Italian right back Emanuele Lelj was sent for an early bath and saw Madrid awarded a penalty. Friedli had missed a late penalty in the defeat to Espanol and the responsibility fell to Pierre Millet this time out. Yet again it was a chance Madrid failed to take and Millet saw his spot kick saved by Canadian Kyle De Rosario. Ironically the Canadian stopper had nearly become a team mate of Millet at Juventus, but a potential deal fell through with Juventus already having the maximum number of non-EU players in their squad.

Madrid failed to capitalise against the ten men of PSG, who were always a threat on the counter attack and still managed six shots on the Madrid goal. It was all to play for in Madrid, but Cooper was disappointed that his side hadn't managed to make the most of their opportunity from the spot and their hosts having to play over half an hour with a man less.

Before their Champions League fate could be sorted Madrid needed to keep the wins coming in the league and apply more pressure on Barca in the race for the title. Real went unbeaten between PSG matches winning three and drawing one of their four La Liga matches. The draw with Betis (2-2) was yet another sore point, but wins against Eibar (3-0), Getafe (3-1) and Elche (6-0) kept Barcelona within touching distance.

PSG arrived in Madrid looking to add a Champions League win of their own to the four they had won since their first in 2020/21. They were certainly no pushovers and the French side stunned the home crowd with an early goal, scoring before there was a minute on the clock. Winger Fatih Mert put his side ahead and gave them a valuable away goal that certainly handed them the advantage. Real Madrid reacted well and were dominant for large periods of the game, but looked unable to find the back of the net. Time was ticking on and Cooper was throwing more and more men forward in the hopes of rescuing their European hopes. With just five minutes left a hopeful ball was tossed into the PSG box and Egyptian centre-back Amr Samir rose highest to nod Madrid level. The 1-1 score line still favoured the away side and would see Madrid eliminated, but just three minutes later there was a carbon copy as Amr Samir once again popped up in the box to poke home and nick a 2-1 victory for Derek Cooper and Real Madrid. Derek Cooper dared to dream once more.

Madrid were through to the quarter finals and they were handed a slightly kinder draw this time out, taking on Portuguese side FC Porto over two legs in April. Porto had come through their first knockout round match against Croatian side Dinamo, but only just, sneaking through 1-1 but winning courtesy of away goals. Cooper wouldn't be underestimating them, having lost to seemingly inferior opponents in the past, but it was considered one of the better draws for the club.

The FC Porto ties came at an inconvenient time for Real Madrid with the games coming either side of a Clasico against Barcelona that could well determine the destination of the La Liga title for 2035/36. Madrid had reeled in Barcelona, but they were now out of the Champions League, having lost to Manchester City, and Leonardo Jardim could focus solely on winning just his second title with the club in his five years there. Wins against Villareal (2-1) and Zaragoza (5-0) as well as the now customary disappointing draw with a 0-0 against Valladolid meant Barcelona and Real Madrid would go into that match neck and neck with the implications of a victory potentially huge for either club.

Before taking on Barcelona Cooper took his side across to Portugal looking to get a win and hand them the advantage for the return leg back in Spain. Madrid turned in an impressive performance on the night and cruised to a comfortable 3-0 victory with goals from Millet, Samir and Perez giving Real the best possible chance of making it to another Champions League semi final. It was also an important win when it came to the La Liga title race and Cooper hoped his side would keep the good form going into the biggest Clasico of recent times.

Barcelona had triumphed 1-0 at the Bernabeu earlier in the season and Cooper knew he would need to inflict a home defeat on them in the Nou Camp if he was to win a fourth consecutive La Liga title. Whilst a defeat wasn't the end for either side, it certainly put them at a disadvantage and neither side wanted to rely on the other slipping up. Madrid dominated at the Nou Camp managing fifty-nine percent of the possession on the night, but they fell behind in the only stat that mattered twice losing by three goals to two. Barcelona took the lead before goals from central defenders Zogbo and Bruyninckx flipped the score line in Madrids favour. Coopers side were unable to hold on and a brace from Joan Moreno secured the important win for the Catalans.

Cooper was not yet willing to concede the title, but he knew he was now relying on Barcelona slipping up, whilst he continued to win games in the hopes of chasing them down. The Champions League was still very much on Coopers mind and a European victory would certainly alleviate the disappointment should they fail to catch their rivals. To ensure progression in Europe and keep their dreams alive Madrid needed to finish off Porto and capitalise on their 3-0 lead from the first leg.

Derek Cooper saw an improvement in the sides' performance since the defeat to Barcelona, but he was not entirely happy as once again Real Madrid failed to convert their dominance into a win. Porto somehow held on to a 0-0 draw, which although frustrating for Madrid, it was not enough to stop their progress into the semi finals for the second year running. Disappointing score line aside there was more concerning news post match when it was revealed that key player Stefan Meusburger, who had been forced off in the game through injury, was suffering with a hip problem that would keep him out of action for two months, ending his season.

There was now only a maximum of ten fixtures left of 2035/36 with that dependant on Real Madrid making it past Juventus who had been confirmed as their opponents in the Champions League semi final. It was a really interesting draw for the club with the media all over the narrative of Cooper facing off against his former club for a place in the final. Torsten Frings who had replaced Cooper in Turin had since left the club to lead the German national side and his successor Yohann Pele was making Juve a real force in Europe again having beaten Wolfsburg in the quarter finals to set up the tie with Madrid.

There were three La Liga matches to be played before Derek returned to Turin on the 30th of April. It was important that Real Madrid continued to win their remaining league matches in the efforts to reel in Barcelona. His side duly delivered with three wins, including an impressive 5-1 victory in the Madrid derby in the last of the matches before returning to European action. Erkan Tasar helped himself to two goals with David Perez, Abdul Youssouf and Mohamed Oudghiri adding the others on a night where Atletico were totally outplayed by their city rivals. There was yet more injury concern for Derek Cooper as both Tasar and more worryingly Enzo Moreira were forced off in the win. Tasar was robbed of his chance to grab a hat-trick by a pulled hamstring which would sideline him for two weeks, whilst there was relatively good news with Moreira only suffering a bruised shin and a potential five day layoff. With a Champions League semi final and possible final as well as the La Liga run in and a Spanish Cup final Derek was hoping to avoid any serious injuries to key players.

There were a lot of familiar faces present on Derek Coopers return to the Juventus Stadium. His opponents lined up with a starting eleven that was nearly full of players he had brought to the club. As well as players such as the American Bill Sarachan, French winger Prince Nsiala-Ekunde, German playmaker Johannes Spittler, Italian full back Antonio Salvaggio, Swiss midfielder Jurgen Hoxha and one time record signing Henk Theuns there was Dutch winger Andre Ablas who Derek Cooper had handed a senior debut to at Ajax back in 2024 to make him their youngest ever player. There were some ex-Real Madrid players also present with Roberto Cobo and Victor Lucas having been sold to Juventus by Cooper since his arrival at the Berabeu.

Despite the friendly faces Derek Cooper was keen to put the tie to bed as soon as possible, starting with an away win to hand them the advantage for the return leg back in Madrid. He also needed the win over the two legs to justify his decision to leave Turin in search of the Champions League victory that had eluded him so far in his career. Juventus started the stronger and looked to make it a miserable return for the former boss. Henk Theuns put the hosts ahead reminding Cooper why he paid Feyenoord £27m for his services back in 2030. Real Madrid got back into the game by way of a second half penalty that was duly converted by one of the four ex-Juventus players in the Real Madrid squad, Pierre Millet slotting home from twelve yards to make it 1-1. Real had found their feet now and were beginning to apply serious pressure dominating possession and working Eduardo Benitez in the Juventus goal. It took them until the eighty-eighth minute, but Madrid finally found a way past the Uruguayan stopper with Belgian Sebastien Marie grabbing the winner.

Real Madrid hadn't made it through the first leg unscathed and influential midfielder David Perez was now facing a race against time to recover from a sprained ankle that he picked up in Turin. The clubs medical staff were estimating a four week recovery period and that meant that he could be a doubt for the Champions League final should Madrid make it through the second leg in a weeks' time. Moreira was also not yet fully fit, playing through the pain barrier at the risk of aggravating the existing injury.

Between Juventus fixtures there was a La Liga game against Celta Vigo that Cooper played a rotated side in, resting the players who needed the recovery, but playing a core of regulars to keep momentum and morale high going into the most important game of their season so far. With the league title still not yet out of reach the 2-0 win against Vigo with goals from Moreira and Millet was the ideal result for the club. They were now level on points with Barcelona and boasted a better goal difference, should they go unbeaten for the remainder of the season in the games against Cordoba and Granada the league title would be theirs, which had seemed unlikely just a few weeks ago.

Juventus came to town looking to overturn their first leg defeat and take the Champions League final spot for themselves. Cooper and his Madrid side were in no mood to let that happen and turned in one of their most dominating performances of the season to send a message to both Manchester City and Bayern Munich who were contesting the other semi final. Sebastien Marie turned in a player of the match performance scoring two goals and helping Real Madrid to a 5-0 drubbing of their Italian opponents. Enzo Moreira, Manuel Siewert and Mohamed Oudghiri grabbed the other goals on a night that couldn't have gone any better for Derek Cooper. Real Madrid had cruised through to their second Champions League final in as many years and everyone associated with the club hoped it would be a different outcome than that of 2034/35 when they had cruelly lost on home soil to Manchester United 1-0.

In a strange twist of fate Real Madrid would play the 2035/36 Champions League final at Old Trafford, the home of current champions Manchester United, who had won their title at the Bernabeu, home of Real Madrid. They would also be contesting the final in Manchester against a Manchester club, but it was United's rivals City rather than the Red Devils themselves. Cooper had beaten and drawn with the Citizens already this campaign having competed alongside them in the group stage, but they were very much the bookies favourite to win the trophy that they had won four times consecutively from 2029/30 through to 2032/33.

The Real Madrid players had their tails up, they had just recorded their most comprehensive performance in the biggest game of the season and they now had four games left of their season to secure the treble. Getting wins against Cordoba and Granada in the league, Barcelona in the Spanish Cup final and Manchester City in the Champions League final was all that stood between them and making history. Four games and effectively four cup finals, nothing but wins would be enough, unless of course Barcelona slipped up in one of their final league matches, but that was unlikely to happen.

Form was good and morale was as high as it had been all season when Madrid travelled to Cordoba to begin their run in. Madrid were playing well, but their recent potency in front of goal entirely deserted them and it was an injury time goal at the end of the first half that broke the deadlock in the favour of their hosts. Real continued their dominance, but could only find one goal in reply through the resurgent Sebastien Marie. That solitary goal was only enough for a share of the points and it looked like Madrid had fallen at the first hurdle handing the title advantage back to Barcelona who had won in their game against Zaragoza.

It went to the final day of the season. Barcelona were at home to Getafe whilst Madrid travelled to Granada. Both Madrid and Barcelona were pre-match favourites and should those predictions come true Barcelona would lift the La Liga title for the first time since 2030/31 by a margin of just two points. Cooper urged his players to focus on the job at hand and forget what was happening at the Nou Camp. He needed them to hold up their end of the bargain and get all three points in their match.

His players listened and after an early flurry of goals, three in the opening sixteen minutes, Madrid ran out 4-2 winners with goals from Erkan Tasar and an Enzo Moreira hat-trick. Sadly it was to be a hollow victory as Barcelona emerged victorious in a narrow 1-0 victory against Getafe. Joan Moreno had put Barcelona ahead midway through the first half and they held on for the remainder of the game to get the win they required to take the title back to the Nou Camp. The treble was now unattainable, but there was still a Spanish Cup and that Champions League that Derek Cooper had been so desperate to win up for grabs. Losing both would be a disaster, but Cooper was confident that his side had enough about them to win both competitions.

The draw at Cordoba had ultimately cost Madrid their title and the squad travelled for yet another Spanish Cup final in the Mestalla against Barcelona looking to deny their rivals a domestic double. Yet again it was a packed house with 75,000 fans packed into the stadium to witness El Clasico, it was still a big draw for football fans across the world. Madrid seized the initiative looking to play the attacking style of football that people had come to expect under Derek Cooper. In contrast Barcelona set up in their 4-1-4-1 formation looking to stifle their opponents and hit them on the break. It was a tactic that had failed in the past with Madrid simply blowing them away, but this season in particular Barca seemed to have refined their approach and Cooper had failed to beat Jardim's side in their last two encounters.

Real Madrid dominated possession throughout, but in truth neither side really consistently threatened the other. It was a poor game with limited chances for both sides, Madrid restricted Barcelona to just one shot on target whilst they only managed two on target themselves. A poor final was inevitably settled by a solitary goal and it came in the form of a penalty early in the second half which was put away by the ever reliable Joan Moreno for Barcelona. Their Spanish striker consistently found the back of the net against Real Madrid and he had done so again here securing a domestic double for his side and rubbing salt in the wounds of their historic rivals.

There was now just one game remaining in the 2035/36 season and it was the biggest game of the season without a doubt. Of the four "cup final" fixtures Cooper ear marked as season defining the Manchester City game at Old Trafford was now the only shot Real Madrid and Derek Cooper had at winning silverware this season. They already had the Spanish Super Cup in the bag, but failure to win either the La Liga title and the Spanish Cup meant that another final loss here would force Derek Cooper to view his season as a failure. A club such as Real Madrid should not only be competing for trophies, but winning them, that was what was required, just making the final or being involved in a title race was rightly not enough for the club and its fans.

Madrid were considered the underdogs by the bookies going into the final and there was a good reason for that. Manchester City had displayed their European pedigree with a spell of domination that saw them win four consecutive Champions League trophies, an impressive feat when you consider no other club had managed more than two consecutive titles previously. City were a global superpower and Cooper was fully aware of the pool of talent at manager Diego Simeone's disposal. In fact there were a number of players named in the squad for the final that Cooper had previously managed or had signed at other clubs.

Portuguese goalkeeper Henri Goncalves had joined Ajax on a free transfer before City paid £31.5m for his services. Brazilian central defender Conrado had left Real Madrid to play in the Premier League for £60m in 2033. Colombian left back Edwin Gutierrez had been spotted playing for Envigado FC and Cooper paid £500k to bring him to Holland whilst manager of Ajax before City forked out £28.5m on the full back. Norwegian central midfielder Svein Harald Harket had signed on loan and then permanently for Derek Cooper at Juventus, he arrived on a free transfer before going on to join City in a deal worth £35.5m. Mexican central defender Luis Carranco was also amongst their ranks, but was unavailable to play in the final. Carranco had signed for Juventus from Leon for £25.5m and left for an eye watering £63m to link up with Manchester City.

All but Harald Harket and Carranco took to the field for Manchester City in the final with Harket named amongst the substitutes. Real Madrid went as strong as possible with David Perez having won his fitness battle to make it back in time to start the game. Cooper named a side that had Guillaume in goal, a back four of Luis Claudio, Bruyninckx, Samir and Mair. Bert Beernaert anchored the midfield with Perez and Millet operating behind an attacking three of Siewert, Moreira and Oudghiri who was deputising for the absent Meusburger.

City lined up with a very English 4-4-2 whereas Cooper was belying his English roots by playing a very continental strikerless formation that had been developed during his time in the Spanish capital. Real Madrid benefitted from the fluidity their system allowed and managed to maintain possession for large periods of the game. Whilst dominating possession was not always guaranteed to bring them a victory it denied their opponents time on the ball and allowed Madrid to assert themselves on the game.

As to be expected in a Champions League final it was a tight match with little between the two sides. Goncalves was the much busier keeper and he had kept Madrid at bay for the first forty-five, but an early second half strike from Enzo Moreira found its way past the City stopper and put Real Madrid 1-0 up. Derek Cooper felt the one goal was enough and introduced defensive midfielder Cedric Renaud for a flagging David Perez with ten minutes to go dropping the young Frenchman into a defensive midfielder role alongside Belgian Bert Beernaert.

The change worked and it allowed Madrid to see out the final ten minutes relatively untroubled. Manchester City managed just three shots on target, which considering the attacking talent in their squad was a sign of just how well Derek Coopers side had defended. As the final whistle sounded Manchester City players collapsed to the floor whilst their Madrid counterparts found reserves of energy they didn't know they had to run and jump on each other in celebration. Cooper offered condolences to Diego Simeone as well as his former players before he allowed himself to get swept up in the emotion of the evenings events. He had led a team to the Champions League title and was now considered the best club manager in Europe. Derek Cooper who had started his career at little old Walmer Road with a capacity of just 3,000 had just won the Champions League against Manchester City at Old Trafford in front of 94,777 spectators, it was simply unbelievable.

Derek Cooper woke up the morning after the night before with the European Cup sat at the bottom of the bed in his Manchester hotel room and reflected on what had been the biggest win of his career. Eight of his starting eleven against Manchester City had played the year before when United had dashed their hopes in the Bernabeu, Ange Zogbo and Sebastien Marie were on the bench this time around whilst Stefan Meusburger missed out through injury, but the faith Cooper had shown in his men had more than been repaid out on the Old Trafford pitch.

The squad flew back to the Spanish capital the following day to parade the clubs thirteenth European Cup through the centre of Madrid as fans lined the streets to get a look at the historic trophy. Despite the European glory and all the cheering faces out in the crowd Derek was frustrated that he had let Barcelona take both his La Liga and Spanish Cup crowns and he had every intention of winning them both back in 2036/37 whilst trying to retain the Champions League and complete a historic treble.

The 2035/36 season had been a productive one for a number of the squad; collectively they had been superb and had triumphed against the odds. Individually Enzo Moreira, Pierre Millet and Mohamed Oudghiri had been particularly impressive, but the player of the year award went to the Italian full back Felice Mair who attained an almost unbelievable average rating of 7.70 from fifty-two appearances. Mair continued to go from strength to strength and Derek Cooper genuinely believed the Italian was one of the best players he had signed during his career.

Moreira, Oudghiri and Millet all top scored for the club with eighteen goals each, which again showed the strength of the team, but also highlighted the drop off in the side's ability to convert their chances, especially in games where they were entirely dominant. Millet in particular had proven himself to be a truly world class player and the Frenchman had fully justified his £58m price tag whilst Mohamed Oudghiri was beginning to step out of the shadow of club legend Stefan Meusburger who had suffered a frustrating season on and off the pitch. Despite having been in Madrid for ten years now, since arriving in 2026, the German forward had begun to complain about feeling homesick whilst simultaneously flirting with PSG about a potential summer transfer. It was confusing for Cooper, but the homesickness and desire to leave coupled with the injuries and emergence of Oudghiri meant that Meusburger's place in the squad was under consideration.

Derek Cooper returned to Madrid after a short break fully recharged and with a clear plan of action laid out for the season ahead. There was a pre-season tour of China organised with a series of friendly fixtures arranged alongside games against the U19's and Gremio of Brazil. Some European based players were late returning to pre-season following the summers European Championships in Germany, and Cooper allocated the recommended extra rest for those in need of it.

There was no "Galactico" signing to unveil and Cooper chose to invest in some exciting young players, having been particularly excited by two of his scout's recommendations. Igor Obradovic could operate through the middle, predominantly as a striker, but also as a central midfielder or central attacking midfielder. The eighteen year old Serbian joined for an initial £2.5m from Paritzan and was someone Cooper looked forward to working with and seeing develop at the club; a spot in the first team was not beyond him this season. Polish left winger Bartosz Korzeniewski was another player that greatly excited Cooper and when a deal of £1.8m up front was agreed there was no hesitation on getting it done. He was another player that the manager felt could make a few first team appearances this year, provided he developed as expected.

The biggest deal of the window came in the form of French central defender Eddy Landre who joined for £16m rising to £25.5m from Auxerre. There had been a bidding war with interest from both PSG and Barcelona, but Real Madrid had paid the money to get the deal done and get their man in the door. Landre showed a lot of promise and Cooper hoped the inflated fee would not weigh heavily on the young man.

Whereas Madrid were on the end of a seemingly expensive deal with the signing of Landre they more than recouped the money they had spent with some inflation of their own. Real Madrid were now European champions and with that title there seemed to be a lot of interest in not only the established first team members, but many of the fringe players too. Erkan Tasar, who had joined the club back in 2033 for £12.75m had made steady improvements in his limited appearances last campaign, so much so that Red Bull Leipzig were willing to pay £45m to secure his services for the upcoming campaign. There were two further big money departures as squad members Richel Friedli and Christian Olsson both agreed deals to join the French club AS Saint-Etienne for a combined £59m. The French club were benefitting from a recent tycoon takeover and were seemingly willing to pay whatever it cost to get the Swiss attacker and Danish midfielder.

Tactically Cooper had decided to stick with the 4-1-2-3-0 choosing to refine it and tweak some of the player roles rather than reinvent his side's philosophy. He had been disappointed with the goals output of his side last term, with the exception of Pierre Millet who notched eighteen from central midfield. He was looking to Moreira, Siewert, Oudghiri and Meusburger, who was still at the club, to improve on their goal tallies from last season.

Performances in the friendlies both at home and in Asia had been impressive with five wins from five scoring twenty-two times and conceding just the twice. It was a much shorter pre-season than Cooper and his players had been used to and they were back in competitive action as early as the 12th of August as his side travelled to Telia Parken in Denmark to take on Schalke in the European Super Cup. Cooper had competed in the competition once before taking his Europa League winning Ajax side to Germany to take on PSG. Cooper was beaten on that occasion and he was keen to avoid the same outcome here and add another trophy to his cabinet.

Cooper named a strong side, stating his intentions for all to see, he wanted to win the match. The game set off at a frantic pace and by the time the clock hit the half hour mark there had already been six goals. Schalke took the lead in the opening minute and Madrid levelled after nine, the Germans then got themselves back in front three minutes later only to be pegged back again after twenty-one minutes. By thirty minutes Madrid had added a further two to their tally and led the game 4-2 at half time. Once in front Madrid never looked back and scored a further two goals in the second half to secure a 6-2 win and add the European Super Cup to Coopers burgeoning list of honours.

The increase in goals was notable throughout pre-season and Cooper was delighted to see his side carry it on into the first competitive fixture of the season. Real Madrid managed a total of twenty-seven shots on goal in Denmark which was a huge number when compared to the six of Schalke. Hopefully the free scoring form would continue as Real Madrid prepared for their now annual clash with Barcelona in the Spanish Super Cup to kick off their domestic season.

Leonardo Jardim was now no longer in charge at the Nou Camp having left to take charge of Manchester United for the new season. Unai Garcia was his replacement having managed Sporting Lisbon and the Spanish national side in recent times. Cooper hoped the new manager would favour a more attacking approach than that often adopted by his predecessor for the Clasico ties.

Sadly that was not the case and if anything Garcia set his team to be as defensive as Jardim had. He started the first leg of the Super Cup at the Bernabeu with a 4-4-2 variation that deployed the two in the middle of the park as defensive midfielders sitting right on the toes of the central defenders. It became clear early on that the Catalan club had come to suffocate the Madrid side whilst showing very little creativity or attacking intent themselves. In the ninety minutes of the first leg Barcelona managed three shots on Guillaume's goal, with none managing to hit the target. Real Madrid hit the target with eight of their fifteen shots, but they were made to wait until the ninety-second minute for Sebastien Marie who was on off the bench to find a way past the stubborn Barcelona backline.

Cooper was beginning to think the win his side deserved wasn't coming, but they stuck at it and eventually made it count. There was nothing better for the Real Madrid fans than scoring a late goal to beat Barcelona and they would enjoy the feeling before heading to the Nou Camp in three days time looking to finish the job.

This time Garcia showed a little more intent and chose an entirely different set up using a 4-2-3-1 system with a player in behind the striker. It made for a much more even contest and Barcelona managed to test Guillaume this time out forcing him to face five shots on target. Madrid were still the slightly better side and showed their strength by creating more than their hosts and crucially managing to find the back of the net through central defender Ange Zogbo with forty-four minutes gone. Madrid were now 2-0 up over the two legs and they never really looked troubled in the second half, holding on to secure their fifth straight Super Cup victory under Cooper with all but one of those victories coming against Barcelona.

Super Cups out of the way it was down to the business of kicking off their La Liga campaign and reinstating themselves as the Champions of Spain. Failure to convert dominance into goals and therefore wins had cost them last time out and Derek was keen to ensure that it was not the same this campaign. His players seemed to agree and Real Madrid opened their 2036/37 season on fire in front of goal. There were back to back 4-0 wins to open the season at home to Racing Santander and away to Valladolid, before an even more emphatic win (6-1) at home to A.Bilbao. Oudghiri helped himself to a hat-trick and the match ball against Santander, but there were six different scorers in the Bilbao win which was pleasing for the manager.

Madrid had been drawn in Group C for the defence of the Champions League crown along with Manchester United, Lille and PAOK of Greece. The Greeks were up first and faced Madrid off the back of a stunning start to the league. They were no match for a rampant Real Madrid and goals from Pierre Millet (2) and Sebastien Marie secured a 3-0 home win to kick start their European season.

Cooper was impressed and he had every right to be, his side had scored seventeen goals in four games and they had come from all over the pitch. The side were playing out of their skins and Derek hoped it was a sign of things to come for the duration of the season with hopes of that historic treble still occupying his mind.

Getafe away were up next and after a frustrating first forty-five Cooper was sure his side would click through the gears and continue their devastating form. It looked even more likely once the home side went down to ten men with over half an hour left to play, but try as they might Real Madrid couldn't find a way past the home sides goal keeper. In truth Cooper's side didn't do enough and failed to create as many chances as they had been in the opening month, it was just one of those bad days at the office. The 0-0 draw was disappointing, but Cooper saw it as a blip and was sure his side would bounce back in the coming games.

The Madrid derby followed the Getafe draw and it was a derby to forget for the white half of the City as Atletico held on to an eleventh minute goal to claim the unlikely 1-0 win. Cooper knew it wasn't going to be his day when Millet failed to convert a penalty in the final couple of minutes to rescue a point. Two poor results on the spin meant the next game against Celta Vigo was vital to getting their season back on track, especially as the following game was a trip to Old Trafford which was always a very tough game.

Uruguayan attacker Enzo Moreira turned up when it mattered against Celta Vigo and it was his two goals that secured a routine 2-0 win for Madrid. They had put the recent bad performances behind them and had created plenty of opportunities whilst severely limiting their opponents. In fact Celta joined Barcelona on the list of teams who had failed to register a shot on target against them in games this season.

Madrid travelled to Old Trafford, the scene of their recent Champions League victory, looking to get one over a number of familiar faces. Leandro Jardim was now in charge there of course and as well as Borislav Mihaylov who had played under Cooper in Madrid there was Rodrigo Godoy who Cooper had signed at Ajax as well as their latest signing, Johannes Spittler, the German attacker signed on a free by Cooper for Juventus and recently sold on to the Red Devils for a whopping £73m. Further vindication that Cooper and his recruitment teams over the years knew how to spot and nurture talent.

It was a slightly less defensive formation from the former Barcelona manager but he did choose to play a 4-2-3-1 with both central midfielders playing as defensive midfielders just in front of the back four in a nod to his defensive set up back in Spain. In truth United were the better side on the night and were worthy winners (2-1). Young winger Roman Oliver made an appearance from the bench replacing an ineffective Moreira and he grabbed himself a stoppage time goal to make the final few seconds slightly uncomfortable for the English side, but it wasn't enough to earn a share of the points.

Barcelona had suffered a shaky start to their title defence under their new manager and ironically it was Madrid rivals Atletico who had beaten them alongside A.Bilbao to keep Coopers men in pole position at this early stage of the season. Cooper was acutely aware that his side would need to buck their ideas up and quickly rediscover the Midas touch from the opening month of action.

Once again the Real Madrid players responded to what Derek Cooper asked of them and they made it to December and the Club World Championships in South Africa having gone unbeaten in fourteen games, although it had not been all plain sailing with a run of four La Liga draws on the spin marring the otherwise impressive run. Those draws came against Valencia (1-1), Barcelona (0-0), recently promoted Sabadell (0-0) and Villareal (1-1). But there were plenty of wins in both La Liga and the Champions league and they included victories against Deportivo Coruna (4-0), Lille (3-0 and 4-0), Sevilla (2-1), PAOK (3-0), Cordoba (3-0) and Granada (3-0) before finishing off in style against Manchester United at home, exacting revenge in a dominant 4-1 win over the English side.

Cooper had been making the most of his squad this season and with the clubs impending trip to South Africa to compete in the FIFA World Club Championships it was pleasing to see that so many of the squad players had been stepping up to grab the odd goal during their time on the pitch. This competition was a distraction in many ways and it came at an already busy period in the season, it would leave Madrid with games in hand on their return, but they were only of use if Madrid managed to win them. Despite that Derek Cooper was keen to add more silverware to his trophy cabinet and he fully expected his side to triumph in the competition.

Real Madrid had been drawn against South African outfit Kaizer Chiefs in the semi final with Mexican side Tigres and Argentinean side San Lorenzo contesting the other semi. Real Madrid were the biggest side in the competition and were the bookies favourites by quite a margin. Kaizer Chiefs proved no match for Madrid in a game that they should have won by more than the 2-0 score line, but a win was a win and saw them through to the final three days later against Tigres.

Cooper took the decision to go with the same side that had beaten Kaizer Chiefs despite the fact that a couple of players were beginning to show signs of tiredness creeping in and he was limited by the fact he could only name a twenty-three man squad. On paper the side he named should have been more than capable of beating what was obviously a fairly competent Tigres side. Eight of the starting line up had started against Manchester City in May and Enzo Moreira duly put the favourite's ahead midway through the first half. Tigres responded well and replied with a goal of their own before half time before adding a second early on in the second half. Coopers men were flagging and many were turning in sub standard performances, Cooper tried to freshen things up and introduce fresh legs, but it didn't work and the Mexicans held on to win 2-1 and deny Real Madrid their third trophy of the season.

Whilst Cooper viewed the World Club Championships as a missed opportunity Real Madrid returned to Spain with ground to make up and a packed schedule that included league and Spanish Cup matches, provided they continued to progress, before returning to European action in February.

The January transfer window was also looming and although Cooper didn't foresee any major transfer activity he wouldn't pass up the chance to sign a promising youngster or two when the window opened in just a few days time. Before that could happen there was a Spanish Cup fourth round second leg to be played on New Year's Eve with Madrid already 1-0 up from the first leg. They won the second leg against R.Majadahonda by the exact same score line with Felice Mair getting a rare goal in the win.

By the time Real Madrid lined up for their first match of 2037 away to Real Betis Cooper had already moved to agree deals for five South American lads who would come in and join up with the clubs youth and reserve sides adding yet more depth to the clubs ranks. Although the deals hadn't been confirmed yet they were all but done and the players would join up with the club in the days following the Betis game.

Real Madrid kicked off the year with a comfortable win although the 2-1 score line made the game look a little closer than it had been. Moreira and Oudghiri put Madrid ahead in the first half, but Madrid failed to widen the deficit and a late goal from Betis meant Cooper was forced into a nervous last ten minutes.

There were then three games in seven days for Cooper's men as they played catch up following their trip to South Africa. Wins came in both the league and Spanish Cup, but Cooper was forced to rotate his side and use the most of the players at his disposal. Racing Santander were beaten 3-0 over the two legs of the Spanish Cup fifth round and between those matches Pierre Millet scored a double in a win away at Levante (2-1) in La Liga.

In the midst of the packed schedule Cooper had dipped back into the transfer market to sign a twenty-one year old Serbian defensive midfielder. Nikola Srdanovic was a full international for his country and had been made available by Liverpool after not getting the required game time under their manager Solomon Rondon. Srdanovic had been with the Reds for a couple of seasons, but had failed to make an impression on the first team and was made available for £15m. Cooper could see bags of potential and he would provide excellent cover for Bert Beernaert who was the only senior defensive midfielder in the squad.

Srdanovic was involved in the squad for the next game at home to Valladolid and he made his debut from the bench in the 5-0 win. It was an impressive team performance, but Enzo Moreira put on a real show for the fans scoring four of the teams five goals including a first half hat-trick from the Uruguayan who had been in fine form in front of goal this campaign.

For the last month La Liga and Spanish Cup fixtures had come thick and fast, alternating between the competitions with games almost every three days. It was a punishing schedule and there was no let up on the horizon having been drawn against Barcelona in the Spanish Cup quarter final. Madrid had won their last six and travelled to the Nou Camp looking to keep that run of wins going. Barcelona were the holders of the Spanish Cup and they would want to hold onto their crown as much as Derek Cooper wanted to take it back. It was a tight game in Barcelona and Madrid shaded it with more efforts on goal than their opponents, but Barca managed to grab two goals from their three shots on target and they would travel for the second leg in Madrid with a two goal advantage (2-0).

Between the Barcelona clashes there was a nervy win against R.Santander (1-0) as Madrid were made to wait until the ninetieth minute before Stefan Meusburger finally broke the deadlock and the hearts of the home crowd who thought they were going to see their side grab an unlikely point. Luckily for Cooper his side got the three points and were back to winning ways in time to host Barcelona and try to overturn the defeat of the first leg.

Cooper was once again forced into a bout of rotation and handed starts to younger players Eddy Landre, Juan Martin Gomez and Nikola Srdanovic. The stars aligned perfectly in the Bernabeu and everything Cooper's side tried to do came off. Argentinean central midfielder Juan Martin Gomez was in the form of his life and helped himself to a fourteen minute hat-trick to go with an Enzo Moreira strike that had Madrid 4-0 up with thirty-one minutes played. Joan Moreno pulled one back for Barcelona to give them a glimmer of hope, but midfielder

Carlos Andrade then got himself sent off for the away side allowing Pierre Millet and Alexander Frank to complete what was a miserable evening for Barcelona. The 6-1 victory was more than enough to see Real Madrid through to the semi finals winning 6-3 over the two legs.

The emphatic victory over Barcelona was the final game of January and meant the transfer window once again closed with Cooper more than happy with the business done. Srdanovic was the only big purchase and he had slotted in nicely taking part in every game since his arrival either starting or from the bench. The only out was for third or fourth choice goalkeeper Dusan Vukomanovic who had only arrived at the club in the summer on a free transfer from Cooper's former club Juventus. He left to join FC Kobenhavn in Denmark for £1.7m with Cooper happy to sign off on the deal rather than stand in the way of a player who clearly wanted to leave for first team football.

Real Madrid now knew their opponents for the first knockout round of the Champions League and they would be travelling to France to take on AS Monaco at their new Ettori Stadium on the 18th of February. That left five games to contest before then including a Madrid derby and a Spanish Cup semi final against Real Betis. The five games in a two week period once again stretched Coopers squad, but yet again they passed with flying colours winning the three La Liga matches against A.Bilbao (4-1), Getafe (3-0) and their city rivals Ateltico (2-0) avenging the defeat of earlier in the season. The Spanish Cup semi final matches were less convincing and a 0-0 draw in the first leg was followed by a 1-1 draw away from home in the second leg that saw Real Madrid into their seventh consecutive final on away goals.

With that victory in the Madrid derby it was off to France and their knockout round tie with AS Monaco. They had come through a group that had included Bayern Munich, Napoli and FC Kobenhavn finishing as runners up behind Bayern Munich. The principality outfit had consistently finished as runners up in Ligue 1 behind the wealthy PSG, and Cooper was certainly expecting a tough game. It turned out to be anything but as Real Madrid emerged from France unscathed with a comfortable 4-0 win under their belts. Goals from Moreira, Oudghiri and a Perez double meant their side would face AS Monaco at home with a comfortable buffer that would probably be enough to see them through to the quarter final.

Real Madrid were in a comfortable position in La Liga come the end of February, but draws against Celta Vigo (0-0) and Elche (1-1) before a win against Sporting Gijon (3-0) meant that they were not out of reach of Villareal who were emerging as the main title challengers ahead of reigning champions Barcelona.

March started with another win at home to Coruna (3-0), but then there was another draw, this time coming against Valencia (1-1). AS Monaco then arrived hoping to complete the impossible and turn around the four goal defeat they suffered a couple of weeks ago. Real Madrid were yet again too strong and emerged as 2-1 winners on the night with a 6-1 win over the two legs. Derek Cooper and his side were into the quarter final as they looked to defend their European crown.

Before the first leg of that quarter final there were six La Liga matches that began with a trip to the Nou Camp and a ninety-second minute leveller from the home side to cancel out Pierre Millet's goal and stop Madrid nicking a narrow win. The 1-1 draw wasn't a terrible result, it kept Barcelona at a distance in the race for the title, but it also meant Cooper's side weren't able to pull away from Villareal. Thankfully wins followed against Real Sociedad (5-2) and Sevilla (6-1) with Mohamed Oudghiri impressing his manager by scoring five goals in the two matches, grabbing a hat-trick in the Sevilla match.

Villareal then arrived in town and with them looking to take Madrid on in the race for the title it was important for Cooper and the team that they didn't get beaten. A late goal from that man Oudghiri again looked to have given Real Madrid all three points and cemented their title credentials, but there was more late drama as the defence switched off and allowed Villareal's Belgian striker Nico Plessers in to score with ninety-four minutes on the clock. Luckily it only earned the Yellow Submarines a share of the points rather than all three, but

Cooper was furious that his side had yet again switched off late in a match, it was starting to become something of a habit.

Real Madrid returned to winning ways for the final two La Liga matches ahead of the Champions League quarter final ties with Manchester United. A comfortable win against Cordoba (3-0) was followed by a big 6-0 victory against lowly Sabadell which included a brace for Manuel Siewert and a hat-trick for Sebastien Marie. Cooper played a second string side against Sabadell and the visiting side didn't help their cause when one of their defensive midfielders was sent off just three minutes into proceedings. With the Manchester United match up next Derek had decided to take some of his regular eleven out of the starting line up in the hopes of keeping them fresh for the visit of United.

The reigning Champions of England weren't having their best season domestically and trailed to both Manchester City and surprise package Liverpool who looked like they may finally get their first Premier League title and their first league win since 1989/90. Former Barcelona man Jardim was still in charge, but he was under pressure to do well in the Champions League with the Premier League title looking like it was beyond them for 2036/37. Real Madrid and Manchester United had already met twice in this season's competition with one win each, although Madrid had won 5-3 over the two group games which included an impressive 4-0 home win. The same outcome over the two legs of the knockout stage match would be ideal for Cooper and would see Madrid through to their third semi final in as many years.

Manuel Siewert got Real off to a flyer and put the home side ahead with ten minutes played, but Madrid were unable to kick on from there and allowed United to grow into the game before they found an equaliser on thirty-six minutes through Ronnie Walker, the man who had scored the winning goal in the Champions League final between the two sides back in 2034/35. The Red Devils continued to play with a growing confidence in the second half and they took the lead, scoring another away goal, as the Swiss attacking midfielder Donat Brun beat Guillaume in the Madrid goal. Coopers side battled back and a very even game eventually ended all square as legendary midfielder David Perez scored in the eighty-fifth minute to level the tie. There was nothing between the two sides come the end of the game and it remained all to play for in the second leg in a weeks' time.

A trip to Granada fell in between the European ties and a rotated side duly did the business with goals from Marie (2) and Meusburger securing all three points in the 3-0 win. Mesuburger was thirty-three now and playing a reduced role in the squad having lost his place to Mohamed Oudghiri for much of the season, but Cooper knew he was able to rely on the German and more often than not Meusburger chipped in with a goal or an assist to show he still had enough quality about him.

It was a capacity crowd at Old Trafford, which had of course been the scene of Madrid's final victory over Manchester City less than twelve months ago, with fans aplenty coming out to see who would make it through to the semi final. The game was finely balanced and there had been nothing between the two sides back in Madrid. It was advantage Manchester United however as they not only had home advantage, but also the two away goals scored seven days ago in the 2-2 draw. The home side seized the early initiative and took the lead through another Ronnie Walker goal on twenty-eight minutes. It stayed 1-0 until half time and Cooper demanded more from his men saying he knew they were capable of better. They returned to the pitch for the second half and Pierre Millet grabbed an away goal for Madrid on fifty-four minutes, back in the tie at 3-3 but trailing on away goals it was now vital they built on their performance so far keeping it tight at the back, but pushing for a winner. Sadly a defensive lapse just seven minutes later allowed Walker to add his and United's second of the night. 2-1 down Cooper knew he had to go for it and began to push players up the pitch telling them to operate in a more attacking manner, but that backfired when Lewis Andrews and then Philippe Petit added numbers three and four for United. It finished 4-1 on the night and 6-3 on aggregate, but it had been much closer than the score line suggested. United weren't that much better than Madrid, but they had taken their chances when it mattered and would go through to play German side Wolfsburg in one of the semi finals.

Derek Cooper and his squad returned from England dejected at their failure to see of Manchester United and defend their Champions League crown, but knowing that they needed to pick themselves up off the floor to see off the challenge of Villareal and beat surprise package Elche in the Spanish Cup Final. Many of the first eleven that had started the game against United were tired upon their return to action and a rotated side failed to beat their cup final opponents in the league match drawing 0-0 in what was a pretty uninspiring performance from the side. It was slightly better against Betis next time out, but yet again they failed to win only managing a 1-1 draw. This allowed Villareal to catch Madrid and instead of celebrating a title victory it left them needing to win their remaining games or risk throwing away their season.

Awkwardly the Spanish Cup final was scheduled to fall right in the middle of Madrid's final two league games against Real Sociedad and Levante. It was a distraction, but Cooper wanted to win that trophy just as much as the league title so he was going all out for three wins from three to finish the season. Game one against Sociedad yielded a 2-0 victory with Moriera and Oudghiri getting the Madrid goals which took them nicely onto Elche and the Spanish Cup final at the Mestalla.

Real Madrid were the obvious pre-match favourites although Elche had done well this season surprising many by only just missing out on a Europa League spot and looking like finishing seventh in La Liga. Cooper picked pretty much a full strength side as he wanted that trophy back. As predicted Madrid were the strongest side, and by quite a margin. Elche failed to register a shot in the first forty-five and Madrid failed to find the back of the net with one of their countless efforts, Derek was beginning to think it might be one of those games. Enzo Moreira alleviated those fears just past the hour mark when he finally beat the Elche keeper to make it 1-0. Madrid were then awarded a penalty, but Pierre Millet continued his indifferent record from twelve yards and missed from the spot. Madrid then went back to wasting good opportunities to build on their lead and Elche continued to do next to nothing in front of goal. In fact it took until the ninetieth minute for Madrid to extend their lead through David Perez and at that point Elche still hadn't registered a shot on goal, but as they kicked off with next to no time left they mounted one last attack and beat Guillaume with their first shot to make it 2-1 and ensure a nervous minute for all in white. As it was that was all Elche could muster and Derek Cooper had once again won the Spanish Cup, his third trophy of the season and hopefully his first of two in a week if all went to plan on the final day of the La Liga season.

Derek Cooper ensured celebrations were kept to a minimum, there was still a league title to be won and with the chance to win their fourth La Liga together he needed his players to focus on the task that lay ahead, Levante at home. Villareal were now the only team in with a shot o stopping Real and they faced a trip away from home to play Celta Vihgo. The Villareal result would be rendered irrelevant should Madrid beat Levante as expected, but anything less than a win would leave the door open for Gabriel Paulista's men to pip them at the very end.

The squad benefitted from a week's rest prior to the final game of the season and Derek Cooper had virtually a full compliment of players to choose from. He named a strong line-up which included new man Srdanovic as well as Juan Martin Gomez who had really come into his own as the season had progressed turning in some very fine performances. With a league title on the line it was important that the players really turned up when it mattered and that was just what Mohamed Oudghiri did against Levante. The Spanish right winger was simply unplayable at times and turned in a player of the match performance that not only won the match for Madrid and Cooper, but the La Liga title too. Oudghiri scored a hat-trick and all three goals at the Bernabeu in the 3-0 win that allowed the players and staff to celebrate out on the pitch in front of a packed stadium.

Of all the league victories during his time in Spain the 2036/37 win was one of the sweetest, wrestling their crown back from Barcelona by playing the Derek Cooper way was special and although they had won titles by more points it was actually strangely enjoyable to have had Villareal breathing down their necks until the very end, they had thrived under the pressure and risen to the occasion and that hadn't always been required in title wins gone by.

In fact as Cooper paraded around the pitch he began to contemplate whether he had achieved all he could with Real Madrid. He had won the Champions League that he had chased so desperately, comfortably won league titles and almost every other competition available to him, in fact the only trophy he had missed out on during his tenure was the FIFA World Club Cup which was a symbol of just how good his sides had been.

2036/37 had seen the emergence of Mohamed Oudghiri, he had taken his game to the next level and ousted arguably the finest player Madrid had seen in the last decade in Stefan Meusburger. Oudghiri posted figures of twenty-six goals and twenty assists in forty-six appearances with an average rating of 7.69. Those stats were even more impressive when you consider that just one of those forty-six appearances came as a substitute, he had made himself a virtual ever present which was an indication as to just how good he had been on the right hand side of the front three.

More often than not when Mohamed Oudghiri got himself a goal his partner in crime from the other side of the front three got in on the act too. Enzo Moreira hadn't been at his lethal best in the previous campaign, but this time out he had more than contributed, adding thirty goals and twenty-one assists to the teams cause in his fifty-five appearances. As with Oudghiri, Moreira had been a virtual ever present in the starting line ups with only two of his appearances coming from the bench. Derek Cooper had been delighted with the way his wide men had operated this season and they had comfortably been the sides' best performers in terms of goals and assists.

Felice Mair continued to get better and better at right back comfortably filling the void that the departure of Stephane Jacquot had left in the side. Coopers attacking brand of football allowed the Italian to get forward and in his fifty appearances he made eleven assists and forty-nine key passes, which was easily double of any other defender in the side. These contributions helped him pick up the player of the year award for a second season running with an impressive average rating of 7.77.

The emergence of Juan Martin Gomez in the second half of the season had taken the pressure off the aging David Perez who at thirty-four needed to be managed more carefully than in years gone by. Manuel Siewert had improved on a disappointing 2035/36, but had still struggled to hit the numbers of his debut season, although thirteen goals and seventeen assists in 2036/37 certainly weren't bad stats.

The future was bright for Real Madrid, they had claimed another league and cup double and had a wealth of talent at their disposal, players like Felipe Renan in goal, Igor Obradovic, Bartosz Korzeniewski, Abdul Youssouf and Belgian forward Sebastien Marie who was still only twenty-two years old having played over one hundred games for the first team already scoring twenty-eight goals along the way.

As bright as the future looked in Spain Derek Cooper felt that the time was right to embark on a new challenge, but the problem he faced was choosing the right destination. There were only a limited number of clubs that could be considered a step up from managing Real Madrid and all of those were based back home in England. The next stumbling block he faced was that realistically there was only one club he really saw himself managing in the Premier League and they were very, very unlikely to be looking for a new manager anytime soon with Venezuelan Salomon Rondon having just won Liverpool their first league title since 1989/90. Cooper considered International management and was intrigued rather than interested in the vacant Belgium post with the Belgian FA looking to appoint a permanent successor to Paolo Sousa.

As leagues across the world reached their conclusion Derek had decided to ask his agent to begin ascertaining what jobs were available and should any pique his interest it would be something he would look into. If nothing became available over the summer Cooper wasn't opposed to another year with Madrid whilst hoping that Rondon made a hash of Liverpool's title defence and they began to look at alternatives. As unlikely as that was to happen it was looking like Coopers only real option.

Jardim was sacked in Manchester, the Champions League defeat to Bayern Munich the final nail in the coffin for the former Barcelona and Monaco manager. His City counterpart Diego Simeone had also been handed his P45 with failure to win either the Premier League or Champions League deemed sufficient grounds for termination. Belgium were still looking for a manager and Cooper had agreed to attend an interview despite not being fully sold on the idea that international management was for him. Liverpool were still jubilant and had declared their manager as untouchable which was a blow for Derek's hopes of one day managing his boyhood club.

Derek Cooper knew as he sat in front of the Belgian FA answering questions on his lack of international management experience that the job wasn't for him. He had managed in six different countries, could speak a number of languages and had worked with players from Costa Rica to Scotland, but he was being grilled on a perceived lack of experience. Upon his return to Spain Cooper informed his agent that should Belgium offer him the role he would be politely declining, even if told he could remain in charge of Real Madrid, the job wasn't for him.

Cooper needn't have worried, just days after his interview he was informed that he had not been successful and they had chosen to go with Jean-Francois Gillet instead despite him having never managed internationally either. Although he had some sort of reputation within the country having managed there with AA Gent for the last seven years.

Unai Emery was the man chosen by Manchester United to replace Jardim, there had been countless links to Derek Cooper in several media outlets, but every time the question was asked he stated in no uncertain terms that he had no interest at all in becoming manager of the Red Devils. There was also constant speculation naming him as the heir to the Manchester City throne that had been vacated by Diego Simeone, but again Cooper denied his interest, although less vociferously than he had done with their city rivals.

Shortly after the players had all departed for their summer breaks word reached Cooper that Manchester City would like him to go over for an interview with the board, they were big fans and wanted to be formally introduced. Cooper had an honest chat with his agent and they both agreed that the Liverpool job simply wasn't an option at this point in time which left Manchester City as the next best option, should Cooper feel it was the right time to leave Spain. Cooper attended the meeting and enjoyed what was a largely positive discussion. They liked his attacking style of football and were more than willing to back him with his plans to develop youth and sign young players for the first team, which had been prominent parts of his plan with all former clubs. They wanted to win back the Premier League title and Cooper felt it was something he would be more than capable of doing. All parties shook hands and agreed to be in touch in due course.

A few days passed before Derek Cooper heard from the chairman of Manchester City, but when the call came it was a positive one stating that they had been impressed by his attitude and of course his track record of winning titles. A job offer would arrive within the hour and should he choose to accept he would become the new manager of Manchester City in the Premier League.

To manage in the Premier League, the top league in the world had been his ambition when he set out to take Kirkley and Pakefield to the top of the football pyramid twenty years ago. That dream was now on the verge of becoming a reality, albeit with Manchester City rather than his local semi-professional outfit as he had first planned. Coopers agent rang to confirm that the contract was in and all it now required was the crossing of the T's and the dotting of the I's and they would be off to England in the morning, but there was something else, something that his agent felt Derek should know and it would have a huge impact on what he chose to do next.

Derek Cooper had interviewed very well and he was the first choice of Manchester City's board, but word had leaked that another candidate had impressed and had come a very close second. That man was Salomon

Rondon, current manager of Liverpool Football Club. If Derek passed up on the opportunity to manage Manchester City they would logically turn their attention to their number two candidate, which in this case was Rondon. If the Venezuelan chose to accept the offer of City it would leave Liverpool managerless and open up the vacancy that Derek had been desperate to fill for as long as he could remember. It was a risky strategy no doubt, and with so many variables it could backfire massively, but that wouldn't be the end of the world, it would just mean another season in Madrid, where he was happy enough anyway.

The chance to have a shot at managing Liverpool was simply too good to pass up and he set the wheels of his bold plan in motion, informing Manchester City that he would be declining their offer of employment in favour of staying in his current role. Now it was a waiting game as he hoped the various pieces of his managerial puzzle fell into place.

Within the week Salomon Rondon had been unveiled as the new manager of Manchester City and Derek Cooper had lived out a childhood fantasy by sitting in the Anfield boardroom to discuss his visions for the club he loved. They could have told him that there would be no money to spend and would have to sack all the staff and he still would have taken the job had it been offered to him. The interview went well, they were receptive to his footballing ideology and he was of course delighted to be interviewing for the role. Derek Cooper felt he had given a good account of himself, but Liverpool were reigning Premier League champions and there were sure to be a lot of established managers throwing their names into the hat too.

The days that passed felt like weeks for Cooper as he badgered his agent and constantly refreshed his inbox hoping to hear something from the club. On the 28th of July, almost exactly five years to the day since Derek Cooper arrived in Madrid, he received the call he had been waiting for. Liverpool Football Club wanted Derek Cooper to become the next manager of the club and follow in the footsteps of Roy Evans, Gerard Houllier, Rafa Benitez, Brendan Rodgers and Jurgen Klopp who he had grown up watching manage his team. The terms of the contract were irrelevant, he just asked his agent to get whatever was put in front of them signed and sealed, he couldn't wait to get started.

Real Madrid had been a fantastic club to work for and Cooper had thoroughly enjoyed his time there. He penned an open letter to the players, staff and the fans thanking them for all their support over his five years and explained that Madrid would always have a place in his heart. He hoped that they could accept his decision and he wished them all the best for their futures. Cooper had so many wonderful memories of the Bernabeu and his time in La Liga, but the time had come to pack his bags and return home to manage the club of his dreams in the best league in the world. Derek Cooper was off to the Premier League.

CHAPTER EIGHT.

The gamble had paid off and Derek Cooper found himself in a room full of media once more facing questions on why he had chosen to leave Madrid, was he happy to be back in England, was it a problem that he hadn't managed in the Premier League or the Football League before? No matter what the questions Cooper couldn't help but answer with a big smile and the enthusiasm of child. It was tough to leave Madrid, but he couldn't turn down the chance to manage Liverpool, he was delighted to be back in England it was his home and he had been away for a good few years now and of course it wouldn't be a problem having never managed in the Premier League, he was a Champions League winning manager who had amassed thirty league and cup wins in his career to date. In all honesty he just wanted to go get stuck in and meet all the staff members and his playing squad.

Liverpool had won the Premier League title in 2036/37, but that had been a bit of a surprise given that the club had come very close to relegation in both the 2024/25 and 2025/26 seasons finishing in seventeenth and sixteenth position. The club had improved since then, but it had been up and down with finishes ranging from tenth to a third place finish the year before the title win. They had stopped being a top four side for the most part and were usually found around fifth to seventh place as a rule.

A trophy-less Jurgen Klopp left Anfield in December 2016 and that set off a barren run for the club that saw the likes of Bielsa, Pochettino, Paolo Sousa and Zinedine Zidane all try and fail to win a trophy before Ralph Hasenhuttl finally broke the drought with an FA Cup win in 2032. Liverpool went through eleven permanent managers between Klopp and Hasenhuttl with none able to win any silverware. Things had gotten slightly better since 2032 and Hasenhuttl's replacement Diego Simeone led them to a Europa League victory in 2033 and the European Super Cup just three months later. Simeone then left the club and was replaced by Massimiliano Allegri, but he was sacked after less than a year in the job. Salomon Rondon then arrived to win the club an unlikely EFL Cup and Premier League double in the 2036/37 season to take Liverpool back where they belonged at the summit of English football. It was a tough act to follow, the manager who won the club their first title in nearly fifty years, but Derek Cooper felt confident he was the right man for the job. He had restored both Ajax and Juventus to the top of their respective divisions and he had maintained Madrid's dominance in La Liga, now he just needed to repeat the feat with his club, the club he had grown up supporting.

Liverpool had obviously had a fantastic season under Rondon playing his adventurous 3-4-3 tactic. Forwards Andre Santos and Santiago Leites had been the standout performers in front of goal scoring thirty-one and twenty-seven respectively. Midfielder Miguel Ribiero had also shone with his fourteen goals, an impressive return from the centre of the park. Club captain and Romanian international Alin Marginean was also dependable and offered cover throughout the middle of the pitch. There was a lot for Cooper to work with, but he wanted to bring his strikerless system that had worked so well for him in Madrid with him and that would require a summer reshuffle. The only negative Cooper could see in his new squad was the average age; there were a lot of players either the wrong side of thirty or approaching that landmark. Cooper was used to working with a much younger squad, more often than not the youngest in the league, and that was something he may need to look at going forward.

Upon his Man City departure Salomon Rondon had taken seven members of his backroom staff with him, including the clubs director of football Christian Eriksen. That meant that staffing numbers were a little light and Derek Cooper always liked to work with a full complement of backroom staff behind him. Derek now had a rolodex full of contacts from his twenty year career and he moved quickly in his opening weeks in the post to secure many of those he had worked with previously. His right hand man from both Juventus and Real Madrid, Massimiliano Farris, came in to be his assistant manager once more. He took scouts from Juvents and Ajax as well as bringing in Fredy Guarin, Ard van Peppen and Zlatan Ibrahimovic who he had worked with in Turin. As well as staff he knew from past roles Derek liked to bring in ex-professionals to work alongside him and

Liverpool was no different. Sead Kolasinac, Giorgio Chiellini, Rickie Lambert, Roberto Carlos, Kelechi Iheanacho and Gabriel Barbosa all joined the club in various roles.

With his staffing issues well under control Cooper turned his attention to the playing side of things. There was a pre-season schedule to be sorted, new formations to be worked on and plenty of player arrivals and departures to signal the end of the Rondon era and announce the beginning of the Cooper revolution. There were non-competitive matches arranged against Orlando, Bayern, Juventus, Ajax, Roma and Bristol City who were one of the club affiliates and therefore entitled to a pre-season match at their Ashton Gate stadium. They were tough friendly fixtures, and five of the six were played away from home to really test his sides' resilience. A draw in Munich (1-1) and a defeat to Roma (2-0) were the only blots on their copybook and Cooper recorded victories against his old clubs, 4-0 against Ajax and 2-0 against Juve.

Whilst the players focussed on learning their new managers style of play and getting themselves fit for the new season Derek was busy signing and selling players to finalise his squad for 2037/38. One of the major hurdles facing the new man in charge was the unwanted interest in some of his stars from other clubs. Inevitably the players stock had risen following their league victory and some had seemingly had their heads turned by the glances of some other clubs. The most notable of these was Portuguese top scorer Andre Santos who was beginning to cause problems within the squad amid interest from a number of clubs from across Europe. It was obvious that Santos wanted to make the move away from the club and Cooper began a bidding war amongst the interested parties. Derek was willing to sell the clubs star striker, but only if a suitable offer came in. French side PSG seemed the most intent on signing Santos and duly forked out £95m for the pleasure. It was the biggest sale of Cooper's career to date both literally and figuratively, Cooper was now committed to his strikerless way of playing having sold the clubs top striking talent.

Derek Cooper then doubled down on his footballing ethos by selling the clubs other main striker to West Ham for £40m. Uruguayan Leites was thirty-two years old and incapable of playing anywhere but as a central striker, a role that was now redundant in the team's new formation. The sale of the clubs main two assets for a combined £145m meant that Cooper had plenty of wiggle room in both his transfer and wage budgets, especially when the sales of Alain Koffi (Napoli, £15m), Nick Blake (Stuttgart £40m) and Jean Kouagou (Cordoba, £8m) added a further £63m into the club coffers.

With as much as £200m available to him Cooper began his recruitment in an effort to imprint himself on the Liverpool squad. Left back Alexander Frank, attacking midfielder Mohamed Yao and goalkeeper Felipe Renan all signed from Real Madrid for a combined total of £42.8m. Central defender Drazen Musa signed for £20.5m from AS Monaco and seventeen year old defensive midfielder Gregory Buisson also arrived from France with Derek paying an eye watering £30m which could rise as high as £41m for the teen. Buisson was highly rated by Cooper as well as AS Saint-Etienne who had been so reluctant to let their teen sensation leave for Anfield. Brazilian winger Anderson Miguel signed from Corinthians for an initial £21.5m and his countryman, twenty year old attacking midfielder Durval, joined from Atletico Paramaense for £14.5m which could rise to £23m.

 Liverpool were scheduled to kick off their competitive season against Tottenham on the 2nd of August as they contested the Community Shield at Wembley for an early chance of silverware to begin Derek Coopers Liverpool career. Before that game there was time for one more major transfer as Belgian international midfielder Thibo Parmentier arrived for a fee of £37.5m from Lille, again in France. Parmentier was another lad who Cooper felt had a bright future in the game and Lille fought tooth and nail to keep hold of the twenty-one year old, which was a sign of how highly rated he was.

Parmetier was one of four debutants named in Derek Coopers first Liverpool starting eleven for the Community Shield against Tottenham. Brazilian stopper Neeskens started in goal with a back four of Serbian right back Igor Rusalic, two English central defenders in Tony Watson and Frank Seddon and new boy Alexander Frank at left back. Thibo Parmentier anchored the midfield behind Captain Alin Marginean and another debutant in Mohamed Yao. Miguel Ribeiro stepped forward from his midfield role to play the number ten with Brazilian Anderson Miguel on his right and Italian Ange Kouassi on his left in the new look front three for Liverpool. Spurs lined up in a 4-4-2 with a Kante in midfield, although it was Malian international Ibrahim Kante and not the long retired N'golo.

Suit on and having picked his first competitive starting eleven Cooper led his side out at Wembley with another shot at silverware in his first game at a club. He had a similar opportunity after taking over at Real Madrid, an opportunity had made the most of beating Real Sociedad over two legs to lift the Spanish Super Cup. Ange Kouassi scored the first goal of Derek Coopers Liverpool reign as he put Liverpool ahead after twenty-eight minutes of play. The game remained 1-0 until half time despite Liverpool being almost completely dominant. Spurs looked like a different team in the second half and pulled one back almost immediately to make it 1-1. Anderson Miguel got himself a debut goal to make it 2-1 on sixty-one minutes before Tony Watson added a third for Liverpool four minutes later. Liverpool looked to have the game sewn up, but a momentary lapse late on to allowed Mike Coxall to score a second Spurs goal. The Liverpool mistake was almost instantly put right by Kouassi who added his second and Liverpool's fourth almost straight from the kick off. It finished 4-2 to Liverpool and Derek Cooper had already matched the trophy haul of Ralph Hassenhuttl and beaten the likes of Klopp, Pochettino, Bielsa, Allegri and Zidane.

The Premier League kicked off the week following their victory at Wembley and oddly the first visitors to Anfield would be Jimmy Dunne and his Tottenham Hotspurs side. Liverpool had been much the better side in that meeting and Cooper hoped his side would perform similarly this time out. The home fans were made to wait by the players, but Liverpool emerged victorious again, winning 4-0 with all four goals coming after the hour mark. Cooper started with the same eleven, but it was subs Josip Matesan and Peter Jarvis who seemed to inspire the victory by scoring from the bench.

Cooper was off and running, a Community Shield win and an opening day Premier League victory, but in England there was always another tough match just around the corner and that came in the form of an away trip to Stamford Bridge to take on Chelsea. Cooper had further strengthened the squad ahead of the Chelsea fixture with the arrival of Luis Espinoza. The twenty-two year old Mexican would provide further competition and youth to Cooper's midfield options.

Espinoza made the bench for the Chelsea match, but it was a game Liverpool lost despite the best efforts of experienced midfielder Marginean whose two goals actually put Liverpool ahead heading into the break. Unfortunately they didn't hold on and Chelsea's Spanish striker Dario Moreno pulled one back on forty-four minutes. In a complete turnaround following half time Chelsea and Dario Moreno added two more to the delight of the home crowd. It was a poor second half performance from Cooper's side having been in a commanding position, but it was still early and there was plenty to play for.

The side recovered well and went on to win their next three games which took them up to their first Champions League group match. Victories at home to West Ham (4-1), Crystal Palace away (2-1) and a commanding victory at home to Aston Villa (6-0) with a Marginean hat-trick, meant that they had four wins and one defeat from their opening five games which wasn't a bad start by any means.

By the time of the Aston Villa match Derek and Liverpool had finalised all the clubs transfer activity for his first window in charge. He had facilitated the sale of some big name players which had generated roughly £200m for the club, reinvesting around £160m of that on new players to reduce the average age and improve squad depth to suit their new tactical direction. The arrival of nineteen year old winger Aya Diouf from OGC Nice for £8.5m signalled the end of Liverpool's transfer business for the summer of 2037. All in all Cooper was happy with the clubs signings both on and off the pitch with the club in a healthy position for the present as well as long term with players such as Buisson and Durval now part of the set up.

In the 2037/38 Champions League Derek Cooper and his Liverpool side had been drawn against Dortmund, Ajax and Dynamo Kyiv in Group E. This year would see Derek compete with his fifth side in the competition - if you include the preliminary rounds contested during his time with TNS. That was something that Cooper was proud of and he hoped to mimic his success with Real Madrid in bringing the famous trophy back to its spiritual home of Anfield.

The European campaign didn't get off to the best start in Germany and despite taking the lead when Miguel Ribeiro found the back of the Dortmund net a brace from their striker Celalettin Celik in the second half rescued the hosts and gave them the win. There was more bad news for Liverpool as the imperious Alin Marginean was stretchered off with what was confirmed as strained knee ligaments and ruled out of action for the next six weeks which was a big loss for the side.

The footballing schedule in England was known for its relentless pace and there was no let up following the defeat in Dortmund with games coming thick and fast. A disappointing draw with QPR (2-2) followed as Liverpool once again failed to hold on to their advantage having led at both 1-0 and 2-1 in the game. Cooper then played a heavily rotated side in the EFL third round against Sheffield Wednesday and nearly came undone drawing 0-0 before winning 3-1 on penalties as Wednesdays players choked to miss three of their four spot kicks. Two more wins followed against Nottingham Forrest (1-0) and Ajax (3-0) in the Champions League before Liverpool faced a tough start to October with back to back visits away from home to face Manchester United and Manchester City.

It had been nice to welcome Ajax to Anfield and play host to his former side and their new manager Ricardo van Rhijn. Of the starting eleven there was only two names Cooper recognised from his time at the club and both those players had rejoined the club having been sold on by him. Winger Frederico Antunes had returned following his £10m sale to Crystal Palace and Nigerian defender Haruna Onuegbu had come back to the club for a second time following spells at both AZ and Shakhtar Donetsk.

September gave way to October with the difficult start looming large on the horizon. Both Manchester clubs were still very much the dominant forces in the English Premier League despite Liverpool unseating them both in the previous campaign. Both clubs had sacked their respective managers following that campaign and both Unai Emery at United and Salomon Rondon at City would like to put Liverpool back in their place, especially with Liverpool being the former club of Rondon.

Cooper had been dreading travelling to the Manchester clubs in successive weeks, it had been a cruel twist of fate that the games should come one after the other and there was no respite for Liverpool in either fixture as they were completely outclassed on both occasions. Liverpool were simply unable to live with both United and City who ran out easy winners in what was an embarrassing time for Derek Cooper. Manchester United hit his Liverpool side for four winning 4-0 as the Red Men were barely able to lay a glove on the Red Devils. A goal from one of Cooper's former players rubbed salt in the wound as Johannes Spittler looked to have settled into his new club very well. Things then went from bad to worse as Liverpool visited the Etihad only to be humped 5-0 by Solomon Rondon and his new team. There was yet another familiar face on the score sheet again as former Madrid man and Brazilian centre back Cornado got amongst the goals for the Citizens.

No-one played well against either Manchester club and Cooper rang the changes for the trip to Dynamo Kyiv in the Champions League. Durval was handed a start in the number ten role and Felipe Renan was asked to step up and replace the more experienced Neeskens in goal who had conceded nine in two games. The changes worked and Liverpool managed a win in the Ukraine (2-0) keeping them on course for qualification from the group with two wins from their first three matches.

Having performed terribly in the Manchester matches the Liverpool fans were desperate for a win in the Merseyside derby, a game that still mattered very much to both the blue and red halves of the city. Everton had dropped out of the Premier League twice in the last ten years, but since returning for the second time in 2033/34 they had managed solid mid table finishes making Liverpool the strong favourites for the clash at Anfield and Coopers first taste of a Merseyside derby.

Felipe Renan remained in goal at the expense of Neeskens again with Mohamed Yao given the nod ahead of Durval as the main attacking midfielder. Yao did not disappoint and put in a player of the match performance scoring the opener after eleven minutes. English midfielder Ashley Fletcher scored a second for Liverpool in the first half before Everton tried to find a way back into the match through their French striker Mounir Chafik on the hour mark. A second goal from Frenchman Yao on seventy-six minutes killed the game off and all but sealed the 3-1 victory for Liverpool.

First Merseyside derby victory under his belt Cooper was back in EFL Cup action facing Manchester United away from home less than a month after their 4-0 defeat in the league. A rotated Liverpool side put in a good performance and held United to a 2-2 draw at the end of ninety minutes, but the full strength United team showed their ability and experience during extra time to win 4-2 after the full one hundred and twenty minutes of play. Elimination from the League Cup wasn't the end of the world and it allowed Cooper to focus attention and resources on other, seemingly more important, competitions.

Mohamed Yao had scored in consecutive games with goals against Everton and Manchester United and he continued his fine form in front of goal scoring the only goal of the match as Liverpool triumphed away at Swansea (1-0). Yao was also the central figure of the attacking three for the next two games playing well, but not finding the back of the net in a victory against Dinamo Kyiv (3-0), before rediscovering his finishing touch in front of goal scoring the first of four in an Anfield victory over Arsenal (4-0). Goals from Espinoza, Kayala and Rusalic completed the scoring in the Arsenal game in what had been an impressive display from Cooper's young team.

The final three games of November were a mixed bag for Liverpool and following a run of three victories there was a disappointing draw with Fulham (0-0) before a second defeat of the season in the Champions League as Dortmund once again proved too strong for Cooper's men winning at Anfield (2-0). The full set of results was then completed by a home victory against Leicester (2-0) with goals from Kayala and Fletcher coming either side of a red card for the visitors when Samy Peeters was sent off just before half time. Cooper was becoming frustrated by the inconsistency, they were falling away in the race for the title and they were now only capable of qualifying as runners up from their Champions League group ensuring a tough first knockout round match.

Cooper was now into his first Christmas period in the Premier League and in the month of December Liverpool were tasked with seven fixtures which yielded his sides best run of form to date. There were wins against Norwich (1-0), Ajax (3-1), Brighton (1-0), Stoke (1-0), Tottenham (2-0) and Burnley (2-0) as well as draws against both Southampton (0-0) and Chelsea (1-1) on New Years Day to see out December and usher in January and 2038. Liverpool and Felipe Renan kept six clean sheets in those eight matches and the solid defence was built upon the foundation of the improving twenty-two year old Brazilian stopper.

The home draw with Chelsea not only signalled the first day of 2038, but also the opening of the January transfer window for clubs across Europe. Cooper had been beavering away throughout the season so far working hard with his recruitment team to secure the signings of a number of promising young players. Croatian defensive midfielder Hrvoje Miletic (Zagreb, £1.5m rising to £3m) and right back Antonio Stilinovic (Partizan, £2.5m rising to £3.9m) had shown great promise with their clubs and respective countries at youth level convincing Derek to take the plunge and bring them in to improve the clubs depth across all age levels.

There was also a deal for South American defender Juan Jose Sosa (Belgrano, £10m rising to £13.5m), but the deal was further complicated by the fact that the club had been denied a work permit for the new acquisition.

Cooper revised his developmental plan for the player deciding to go ahead with the signing and planning to loan him out for first team football until he qualified with the required criteria for the work permit he needed.

As well as deals agreed for new arrivals there were several outgoing deals that looked like being completed before the end of the window. Former number one Neeskens was looking to leave the club having lost his place to Felipe Renan and a couple of other fringe players were beginning to voice their discontent at a lack of playing time. Cooper had no interest in keeping unhappy senior players about preferring to give an opportunity to a young prospect. Prior to the opening of the window striker Danny Pearce had already agreed a deal to join Southampton for £10m whilst thirty year old Italian central defender Massimo Schietroma was signed by Burnley as they paid the £9.75m fee that had been inserted into his earlier loan deal with the club. Various other deals were ongoing and Cooper was sure there would be further departures.

Back to matters on the pitch Liverpool were drawn away to League Two side Preston in the FA Cup third round, a historic day in the English football calendar that Cooper had never managed to experience in his roles at Kirkley and Pakefield and Maidenhead. Cooper viewed Preston as an easy draw for his side and took a very heavily rotated side to Deepdale leaving out a whole host of first team regulars. Preston were buoyed by the perceived lack of respect from their visitors and pulled off a memorable "Cupset" by winning 2-1 to make it a very bitter third round experience for the Liverpool boss.

With elimination from the FA Cup at the hands of lower league opposition complete it was back to Premier League action for the remainder of January and into late February. A draw away to West Ham (2-2) got them back in action before wins against Crystal Palace (1-0), Aston Villa (4-0), QPR (2-1) and Nottingham Forrest (4-1) followed. Cooper celebrated his fiftieth birthday after the Forrest victory ahead of a daunting run of fixtures which included both Manchester clubs, Everton and the cash rich AS Saint-Etienne in the Champions League.

The transfer window had also closed and there was only one more addition to speak of since the opening flurry of signings. Brazilian central defender Assis had joined for £2.7m from Santos and had been denied a work permit in a similar fashion to that of Argentinean Juan Jose Sosa earlier in the window. Assis was signed by Cooper despite the lack of work permit and the managers plan for him mimicked that of Sosa with him heading out on loan to Valencia for at least the remainder of the 2037/38 season.

There were further departures as expected with Neeskens joining West Ham for £15.5m as well as central defender Vlade Visinka who left for £11.5m to join Sheffield Wednesday whilst attacking midfielder Erdem Malkoc signed for Zenit for £8.25m. The January sales added to the summer departures took the clubs income from transfers to £258m, which Cooper had begun to reinvest back into not only the playing staff, but the clubs facilities and youth set ups as well.

Last time out Cooper had visited both Manchester United and Manchester City and was sent packing with his tail firmly between his legs on both occasions. He was keen to show Emery and Rondon that his side had improved and were not the pushovers they had been back in October. Liverpool went ahead in both games this time out, but unfortunately couldn't capitalise on their leads and were forced to share the points in 1-1 draws against both clubs. Rulasic had put Liverpool ahead against United, but a Donat Brun penalty just three minutes later levelled the match. Angelino Kayala put the Red Men ahead against City and Liverpool went into the break one goal to the good, but a fifty-sixth minute equaliser from English striker Jamie Tierney once again denied Liverpool the victory.

AS Saint-Etienne now represented a real threat in European competition with the recently acquired French club spending over £300m on players since the takeover had been completed. They were buying themselves a seat at the top table of Champions League football and were a tough draw for Liverpool in the first knockout round. Cooper usually preferred to play away from home in the first leg, but finishing second in the group had robbed him of that chance and he would play host for the first leg instead.

AS Saint-Etienne arrived in Liverpool as yet another side littered with players signed by Derek Cooper in his previous roles. Dragan Vukcevic, Richel Friedli, Christian Olsson and Alassane Diop were all in the match day squad of former Liverpool manager Diego Simeone who had followed the money over to France with many of his players. Unfortunately for Cooper it would be one of those former players who turned it on against his side to grab two important away goals for his new club in the 2-2 draw at Anfield. Richel Friedli had helped Cooper out on numerous occasions during his time playing for the Englishman in Madrid, but he did the business for his new manager this time securing a player of the match award to go with his brace. Kayala had cancelled out the first Friedli goal before former AS Saint-Etienne man Gregory Buisson put Liverpool ahead just after the hour mark. It was a lead that lasted until the eighty-second minute when Friedli grabbed his second to take the 2-2 draw back to France for his side.

Liverpool returned to domestic action just across Stanley Park as they took on Everton at Goodison. It was a tough game to come back to having played out the hard fought draw with AS Saint-Etienne just four days earlier. Cooper stuck with the majority of the eleven that started the Champions League tie and it showed as the side laboured to a very poor 0-0 draw. It was a very even game which lacked quality with both sides managing just seven shots on target over the ninety minutes. Cooper knew that his side were capable of more, but he had come through the run of difficult fixtures without being beaten and that was an improvement on some of the performances from earlier in the season.

Mohamed Yao rediscovered the goal scoring touch at the start of March, albeit from a slightly deeper central midfield role as Liverpool hosted Swansea, beating the Welsh side 1-0. From there it was down to the Emirates Stadium to take on Yohann Pele and his Arsenal side. It wasn't a vintage performance by Liverpool and failure to convert their chances allowed Arsenal to take the lead before Peter Jarvis finally found the back of the net to earn a share of the points with the 1-1 draw.

With the Swansea victory and the draws against Arsenal and Everton out of the way it was back to Champions League action and the second leg of their first knockout round match against Saint-Etiene. Liverpool travelled to France having held on to a 2-2 draw at home and needing to win or better the previous draw in order to progress. The evening didn't start well for the hosts as full back Alexander Frank was stretchered off after twenty-nine minutes with a serious achilles injury that would rule him out for the remainder of the season. It looked like the game was heading to the break goalless, but with just two minutes remaining of the first forty-five Polish striker Rafal Szalek found the back of the net for the hosts. Cooper told his side to keep going and the result would come, they were actually playing relatively well and had looked to be in the ascendancy before the opening goal.

If Cooper hoped to inspire his side he seriously misjudged the situation. Liverpool turned in an abject second half performance that saw them concede goals at will with Szalek adding a second as well as Richel Firedli grabbing three of his own to complete an impressive hat-trick and walk away with the match ball. Liverpool did manage a seventy-ninth minute consolation through central defender Drazen Musa, but by then the damage had been done and Liverpool had been well beaten 5-1 on the night and 7-3 on aggregate. AS Saint-Etienne had been lethal in front of goal clinically finishing five of their six shots on target with the impressive Szalek showing his class in the match. Szalek was a player Cooper had tried to sign whilst with Madrid, but had been unwilling to pay the £59m eventually put up by his current employers.

Champions League elimination meant that it was nothing but Premier League action for the remainder of the season. There were seven matches left of the 2037/38 season and although Liverpool were still mathematically in with a shot of successfully defending their title it would mean going the remainder of the season unbeaten and hoping Manchester United slipped up along the way. Manchester City were still in the hunt for that top spot, but Rondon's men were still competing across a couple of competitions and had fallen slightly behind both their Manchester rivals as well as Coopers Liverpool.

Liverpool had a kind run in when looking at the fixtures they had left to play and they kicked off their run in with a routine win at home to Fulham (3-1). More wins followed as they beat Leicester away (2-1), Norwich at home (3-0), Brighton away (4-1) before another win at home against Stoke (2-0). With just two games left Liverpool had dragged themselves back onto the same points total as Manchester United. Against the odds it looked like there was a possibility that the club could successfully defend a title for the first time in over fifty years. It was all to play for going into the final fixtures and although level on points Manchester United had a far superior goal difference which handed them an advantage. Liverpool would need to win both theirs and hope that United dropped points or else they would need a dramatic goals swing, the likes of which had never been seen before.

Burnley and Southampton remained with Burnley needing points in their fight against relegation and Southampton riding high and fighting for a surprise European spot. Two games that had looked easy on paper were now beginning to look a bit tougher for Cooper and his team. Cooper and Liverpool travelled to Turf Moor on the back of five victories hoping to make it six and pile the pressure on United to get a result in their game. Anderson Miguel got Liverpool off to the best possible start giving them the lead midway through the first half, but they were unable to hang on until the break and conceded a Burnley equaliser in added time at the end of the first half. The goal was a blow for Liverpool who had looked comfortable up until that point. Burnley improved after the interval and Liverpool fell asleep conceding what would prove to be the winner for the Clarets on sixty-eight minutes. Liverpool had switched off and it was likely to cost them even if they managed a result in the final game of the season at home to Southampton.

United had indeed won as Liverpool dropped points with the Red Devils dispatching already relegated Fulham 4-1. They too had one game remaining and that came away to Crystal Palace. Cooper fully expected them to win that match, but he would still be doing all he could to get a positive result against the saints. Liverpool totally dominated at Anfield, but their fans were made to wait for the victory that eventually came courtesy of an eighty-second minute goal from substitute Durval. Liverpool had been the much better side and had limited Southampton to two shots on target, but their defence had proven stubborn and there was a time when Cooper didn't think his side would get the win their performance deserved.

The 1-0 win against Southampton was all in vain as Cooper had predicted with Manchester United winning by the same score line down in London. Johannes Spittler had scored the winner for United to secure them the 2037/38 Premier League title, but Liverpool had run them closer than even Derek Cooper had expected given the humbling defeat suffered back in October. There was a three point gap come the end of play with City stumbling in the second half of the season to finish fifteen points behind United and twelve behind Liverpool.

 The 2037/38 season was a tricky one for Derek Cooper to evaluate. His side were very much a team in transition with a new manager, new players and adapting to a new way of playing. With all that considered Cooper was relatively happy with the runners up spot, but he was concerned by some of the results, most notably the heavy away losses to both Manchester clubs as well as the defeat to Saint-Etienne in the Champions League. Derek Cooper had arrived to win trophies with Liverpool and the performance in all cup competitions this season had been very poor, he would be looking for an improved performance in the FA and EFL Cups next time out.

There had been some impressive individual performances from various players throughout the season. Felipe Renan had established himself as the clubs number one goalkeeper playing thirty-nine times with an average rating of 7.10, which wasn't bad for a keeper. Full backs Alexander Frank and Igor Rusalic had revelled in their roles as inverted wingbacks playing over forty games each. Rusalic chipped in with five goals and an average rating of 7.59 whilst Frank managed just the one goal, but a fractionally higher average rating at 7.60. The full backs had outshone the central defenders with Cooper not entirely convinced by the options available to him in that area.

There had been no outstanding goal threat and winger Angelino Kayala emerged as the sides' top scorer with nineteen for the season. Mohamed Yao and Peter Jarvis were the other main goal scorers as they contributed ten and twelve goals respectively. Club captain Alin Marginean had notched eight from the centre of midfield in a season that had seen him make thirty-nine appearances. Miguel Ribeiro had been disappointing in front of goal for Liverpool this season with the attacking midfielder only finding the back of the net six times in forty appearances. Ribeiro was Coopers best attacking midfielder option on paper but had often been outperformed by the younger Yao, which was a concern for Cooper going forward. In fact Cooper was beginning to question the depth of his attacking options, for his system to work he needed his front three to be the sides best players and he wasn't sure that was the case with the current squad. There was no Enzo Moreira, Stefan Meusburger or Mohamed Oudghiri that he could rely on to carry the team when others were having a bad game.

Cooper was already planning for the season ahead, looking at potential signings whilst sticking to his ideals of signing younger players that still had time to develop. His way of working had got him results at all of his previous clubs and he backed himself to get it right at Liverpool once again. Preparations for the 2038/39 season weren't helped by Massimiliano Farris who had decided to call it a day on his time in football. Farris had first linked up with Cooper back in Italy and he had accompanied the English manager onto jobs in Spain and then England. As an assistant manager Farris had been extremely good and he would be a huge loss to Cooper going into the new season. Farris had notified Cooper of his decision privately well in advance so the search for his replacement could be sorted in time for the new campaign.

The man Cooper had chosen to bring in as his new assistant manager was Spaniard Aitor Olmo. Having bounced around clubs in the Spanish lower leagues as a player Olmo had gone on to hold various positions with clubs such as Barcelona, Villareal and Manchester City. His most recent role had been as the assistant manager at Spanish club Elche working under their manager Oriol Romeu, the former Chelsea and Southampton midfielder. Olmo would bring a wealth of experience to the club and as sad as Cooper was to be losing his long term right hand man and friend, Massimilano Farris, he was just as excited to start life with Aitor Olmo by his side.

As well as hiring a new assistant manager Cooper looked to add numbers and improve the quality of his backroom staff in other areas. Real Madrid icon Guti arrived to work as a coach with the first team whilst former players Adam Campbell and Marcel Groot joined the club as first team and U19 coaches respectively. Campbell had played for Cooper at TNS before working under him as a coach at Real Madrid whilst Marcel Groot was a player who had come through the academy at Ajax during Cooper's time there before playing for him again at Juventus.

Pre-season began in July as Derek Cooper took his squad over to China for a series of friendly matches in an effort to capitalise on the Asian market and bring some extra revenue into the club. The spending power of Manchester United and Manchester City was a worry for Cooper and he was looking to boost club finances in any way possible. There was a testimonial match arranged for Alin Marginean with Derek using his connections with Real Madrid to get them to bring a side over to celebrate with several ex-Liverpool players also turning out for their former teammate. There were other matches arranged against a range of opposition including Red Bull Leipzig, AC Milan and Portuguese sides Leiria and Cova de Piedade.

Cooper and his recruitment team had been working quickly to secure a number of new signings for the club. Meeting home-grown player rules whilst working in England was something Derek was having to take into consideration and he put a long term plan in place by investing heavily in young English players, poaching them from other clubs such as Crystal Palace, West Ham, Bournemouth, Reading and Fulham. Some of these players had cost the club more than Cooper had anticipated, but if one of the players picked up could eventually make the first team and qualify as a home-grown player then they would be worth their weight in gold.

As well as stocking his U18 and U23 sides with the best English talent available Cooper also signed players from further afield for both the senior and youth set ups ahead of the Premier League opening weekend on the 14th of August. There were deals agreed for eighteen year old left winger Jean Menga who joined for £10m from Stade Brestois 29 over in France and Gustavo Penalba, a twenty year old Argentinean attacker, joined for his £8.25m release fee from Racing Club over in his homeland.

Big money moves were also made by the club as they backed their manager in signing another German left back to provide competition for Frank with twenty-one year old Fresno Kitoko joining from Borussia Monchengladbach for £30m. Kitoko was a player that Cooper had been looking at for a while, but had failed to prise away from Gladbach until now. He was a German international of Congolese heritage and at six foot five was already an absolute specimen with his physical attributes a real asset in his role as either a full back or wing back on that left hand side.

Another £30m was spent on Honduran winger Lesther Cordova who had been playing his football over in Portugal for Sporting Lisbon. Cordova's fee could eventually rise as high as £43m depending on targets being met, but at twenty-one years old and with plenty of room to develop he was just the type of player Cooper was now renowned for signing. He was comfortable operating off either wing, although preferring to work as a winger on the left hand side, and would provide competition for the attacking players already at the club moving forward.

Cooper hadn't been entirely convinced by his options in central defence last time out and he moved decisively in the summer window to secure the signing of highly rated Spanish central defender Jose Rodriguez. The twenty-one year old had come through the ranks at Lyon over in France and they had allowed him to leave to join up with Cooper's side for an initial £26m although that was likely to rise to £30.5m over time. As with Cordova and Kitoko Rodriguez had plenty of first team football under his belt and lots of room left to develop into a potentially world class talent and whilst they weren't brought in to be automatic starters Cooper expected them to be challenging the established members of the current squad.

Cooper raised some of the funds for his summer spree through the sale of a couple of the fringe players he deemed not up to the required standard moving forward. QPR were willing to pay £32m for Marco Teixeira and whilst the centre back was a decent player he had struggled for game time and Cooper was delighted to accept such a fee for a back up player. Central midfielder Peter Eccles was allowed to leave and join Bournemouth for £4.7m, he was a player who wanted first team football and Cooper simply couldn't promise him that at Liverpool. Milos Djorovic was another who asked to leave the club in search of minutes elsewhere and he left to join Werder Bremen for £17m in another deal in which the size of the fee surprised Cooper.

Juan Jose Sosa had extended his loan at Vitesse for another season and Assis had returned from Valencia before joining his team mate over in Holland signing with PSV on loan for the duration of the 2038/39 season. Both players were hoping to get the required amount of first team football that would either boost their reputation enough to get the required work permit or earn an international call up that would also see them meet the relevant criteria. Both players were improving slowly and whilst Cooper would ideally be overseeing their development personally he had eyes on his players constantly and was in contact with the managers of the clubs they were on loan at.

Having played and beaten his former club in pre-season Cooper had made contact with Real Madrid over the availability of their player Igor Obradovic. The attacker was a player Derek had been a massive fan of and was keen to link up with again at Liverpool, but the feedback from Madrid was less than positive and he was being stonewalled on any potential permanent deal. There was a possibility of a loan deal mentioned and it was something Cooper felt was worth considering as he could offer cover in a number of positions. He also hoped that by working together again he would be able to convince the Serbian international that he should join him at Liverpool, unsettling the attacker enough to force through a move further down the line.

Derek Cooper was happy with his summer business but he knew both Manchester clubs had also been active ahead of the 2038/39 Premier League season. Manchester City had made just one signing of note, but it was a huge transfer for the club as they laid out £78m on Ukrainian central midfielder Oleg Kravchenko from German champions Bayern Munich. The twenty-five year old was already a world superstar and that was reflected by the fee and the £225k per week City were willing to pay to secure his services. Manchester United had spent a little more freely than their city rivals splashing £47m on Belgian right back Timothy Goossens from Southampton as well as an initial £31m for Aston Villa's English striker Kane Davis who could end up costing the Red Devils as much as £56m in the long run. There were also strong rumours in the press that they were close to agreeing a £33m deal for Atletico Madrid's twenty-one year old Spanish left back Victor Cruz which would take their window spend to around £145m.

Ahead of the Premier League opening weekend it was predicted to be business as usual with the two Manchester clubs made favourites for the title with Liverpool considered by many to have an outside chance of improving on their second place finish of last season. With transfer business all but done and with a decent pre-season under their belts all eyes turned to the opening fixture at home to Sheffield Wednesday. Cooper was looking to persist with his strikerless approach having strengthened where possible in the summer window to hopefully provide more firepower for the team.

Liverpool had been afforded a kind start to the new season with games against Sheffield Wednesday, Brighton and Watford before playing Chelsea and their first group game of the Champions League. Cordova, Rodriguez and Kitoko all made their full home debuts with Penalba and Obradovic appearing from the bench against Sheffield Wednesday, but it was a lacklustre Liverpool performance that saw them fail to break down the opposition defence. Wednesday were a constant threat and on another day could have taken advantage of a wasteful Liverpool. The match ended 0-0 and sent the Anfield faithful home disappointed with their sides start.

Cooper and his players hoped to turn it around on their visit to Brighton and the American Express Community Stadium. He went with the same starting eleven expecting a better performance in front of goal this time out, but sadly Liverpool once again drew a blank whilst their opponents made the most of their opportunities. Goals from Amine Adjaoud and Fabien Marie secured a 2-0 win for Brighton to once again send the Liverpool fans home unhappy. It was turning into a nightmare start for Derek Cooper and he had already lost ground on the Manchester clubs, although United had dropped points on the opening day too, drawing with Nottingham Forrest.

The Watford game was now a must win in the eyes of Derek Cooper, morale was taking a hit and there were games against Chelsea, Bayern Munich and Manchester United fast approaching. Failure to win at home to Watford could see the club head into a very tough month of football on the back of their worst run of form since Cooper arrived at the club last summer.

Derek Cooper made one change with Ange Kouassi coming in for new boy Lesther Cordova on the left side of the attacking three. A team meeting prior to the Watford game had been productive with the manager telling his side he knew they were capable of more than they had been showing. The pep talk seemed to have the desired effect and first half goals from Mohamed Yao, Ange Kouassi and Luis Espinoza sent them in 3-1 up at half time. It had been a much better all round performance from Liverpool as they managed to turn their shots into goals with substitute Gustavo Penalba adding a fourth in the eighty-ninth minute following a red card for the visitors with ten minutes of the game remaining. The 4-1 win was much needed as the next month saw games away to Chelsea, Bayern and Manchester United, whilst there was also a home match against the reigning champions three days before Cooper took his side to Old Trafford.

Following the victory against Watford and registering their first three points of the season Coopers side travelled to Stamford Bridge looking to add to their total of four points. Chelsea had suffered a drop off in recent years but had finished in the top four last season as they looked to regain a seat at the top table.

Giovanni van Bronkhorst was now the man in charge of the Blues with the Dutchman a former adversary of Cooper during their time in Holland with Ajax and Feyenoord respectively. As with in Holland it was Cooper who would emerge with the bragging rights as Liverpool held onto a first half Gustavo Penalba goal to win 1-0 and kick off the tough run of fixtures.

Next up for Liverpool was the trip to Germany to face Bayern Munich in Group G of the Champions League. It was a tough group that included FC Basel and AC Milan alongside Liverpool and Bayern. Cooper hoped to get off to a winning start in gameweek one, but the Allianz Arena was a notoriously difficult place to go and there was no guarantee of coming away with any points at all. Liverpool rode their luck in a first half that was largely dominated by the home side. Bayern had much more of the play and should have been at least one goal ahead, but striker Bosko Juric missed a twenty-eighth minute penalty for the home side. Former Liverpool man Nikola Srdanovic lined up for the German side having been sold by Cooper's successor at Real Madrid. Liverpool were much better in the second half and goals from both widemen, Kouassi and Kayala, got the 2-0 win for Derek Cooper.

Back to back victories away from home against both Chelsea and Bayern Munich was a stark contrast to the early season results against both Sheffield Wednesday and Brighton. The games kept on coming for Liverpool and the side now faced back to back games against Manchester United as they faced them at Anfield in the League before making the trip to Old Trafford to play them three days later in the EFL Cup third round. Of the two matches Cooper was keen to do well in the league fixture with taking points off a title rival the incentive for his players.

Liverpool were the better side at Anfield, but fortune favoured the visitors and despite recording just one shot on target they left with a 2-0 victory. A Fresnel Kitoko own goal put United ahead after twenty-one minutes before Italian striker Alessandro Rossi added a second before half time. The home side continued to have more of the ball and the better of the chances, but there was no end result once more and Liverpool failed to score for the third time in their opening six matches. Now it was on to Old Trafford and an EFL Cup rematch with the Red Devils that Cooper could really do without.

Cooper used the EFL Cup match as a chance to rotate his squad and allow the majority of his starting eleven to have the night off. It was virtually a totally different match day squad with only Marginean and Rodriguez reprising their starting spots. United also rotated, but they played more of their regulars as they looked to make it two wins against Coopers side in three days. Manchester United were the much better side throughout the cup tie and that was reflected in the 2-1 score line, with a consolation goal for Igor Obradovic not enough to take Liverpool through to the next round.

It was a disappointing return to Premier League action at the end of September as Liverpool travelled to the City Ground to face Nottingham Forrest throwing away a two goal lead to draw 2-2. Goals from Mohamed Yao and Lesther Cordova looked to have all but sewn up the three points, but goals from Chokri Mejri, who had played for Cooper at Ajax, and Pierre Huart saw Forrest battle back to earn a share of the points.

The start to the season had left Cooper immensely frustrated, his side had dropped valuable Premier League points in games that they really should have won, whilst there were also some disheartening defeats against title rivals United in both the league and the EFL Cup. Derek needed his side to hit their rhythm and put together a run of form that would get them back challenging for the title, which is where the club should be.

September closed out with a decent victory at home to AC Milan (2-0) with goals from Kayala and Rusalic securing the win and making it two wins from two in Group G. Wins against Bournemouth (5-0) and Crystal Palace (3-2) followed with Kayala grabbing a hat-trick and the match ball against Bournemouth and Palace scoring two late goals to make it a nervy end to proceedings at Selhurst Park. The winning form was then briefly interrupted by FC Basel as they held on for a 0-0 draw in Switzerland to frustrate the travelling supporters.

Liverpool hosted Arsenal on their return from European action and Mexican midfielder Luis Espinoza put on a show for the home crowd scoring a memorable hat-trick in the 3-1 win against the Gunners. Back to winning ways Derek took his side across Stanley Park to Goodison and returned with another win (3-1) with early goals from Buisson and Cordova the foundation of their derby victory. Angelino Kayala added a third in the second half to secure the win after Vladmir Dobes had pulled one back for the Toffees. With five wins in their last six Liverpool welcomed Basel to Anfield for gameweek four of the Champions League. Liverpool were able to see off their Swiss opponents having failed to do so earlier in the month and Derek Coopers side strolled to a comfortable victory (3-0) to all but secure qualification through to the knockout stages of the competition.

Liverpool travelled to New White Hart Lane on the 6th of November as they returned to domestic action having won six of their last seven in all competitions. Tottenham had criminally underachieved in recent years and had actually been relegated to the Championship three times since 2027/28. They had fallen a long way from the title contenders they had been as Cooper kicked off his managerial career over twenty years ago. Spurs turned in a half decent performance against Derek Coopers side and were able to come from behind twice to take a share of the points. Kouassi and then Espinoza had given Liverpool the lead on two separate occasions, but they had been unable to hold on and take all three points back to Anfield.

Liverpool were now unbeaten in nine games across all competitions and they further extended that run with wins against Southampton (1-0), Bayern (4-1), Norwich (2-0) and Leicester (2-1). The win against Bayern was particularly impressive and meant that Liverpool would now top the group with one game remaining. It was also looking increasingly likely that FC Basel would surprise both AC Milan and Bayern Munich by beating them to the runners up spot and securing passage through to the Champions League knockout stages.

AC Milan gave themselves a fighting chance by beating Derek Coopers men in the final gameweek of the group stage, winning 1-0 at the San Siro, but it was a hollow victory with Basel securing their runner up spot by virtue of their slightly better goal difference. Bayern had crumbled under the pressure of a competitive group and finished bottom with AC Milan landing safe passage through to the latter stages of the Europa League.

Three days later and off the back of their early December defeat in Milan Liverpool travelled thirty or so miles east to take on Manchester City, a side Cooper as yet had failed to beat. The Reds former manager Salomon Rondon was still in charge at the Etihad and it would be great for the fans if Liverpool could claim all three points. Unfortunately The Citizens were once again too strong and remained in control throughout, dominating possession and limiting the visitors' efforts on goal. Two early first half goals from City were enough to see them coast to an easy 2-0 win in front of their home fans. It was a particularly spiky end to the game with Liverpool picking up three yellow cards late on as their frustrations boiled over.

Back to back defeats meant Liverpool approached the busy Christmas period in poor form looking to chase down both Manchester clubs in the Premier League and progress in the FA Cup when the historic cup got underway for the top flight clubs. They got off to a good start, beating West Ham at home (3-1), before suffering a minor setback at the hands of QPR who were surprising football fans up and down the country with their form in the 2038/39 season. It was a solitary goal from Henk Theuns, a Dutch striker who had played under Cooper at Juventus, which got the 1-0 victory for QPR who were chasing a European slot.

Liverpool returned to winning ways on Boxing Day, delighting the home fans with a 2-0 win despite left back Alexander Frank seeing red early on in the second half with the game at 0-0. Frank was clearly after a winter break of his own and his needless red card had rendered him unavailable for the next three fixtures. Cooper took a dim view of the Germans behaviour and fined him two weeks wages by way of a punishment. Victory away to Stoke (4-1) followed two days later without the suspended Frank ahead of further wins against

Sheffield Wednesday (3-1) on New Years Day, Brighton (3-1) and Watford (1-0) before beating Championship side Leeds (3-0) in the third round of the FA Cup.

The January transfer window was now open, but Cooper had decided against making any big signings. He was interested in a number of potential targets, including Igor Obradovic who was currently on loan from Real Madrid, but the prices being quoted for all players were simply ludicrous. A number of promising youngsters joined the club for relatively small fees as Derek once again looked to establish a conveyor belt culture at the club, developing and either playing or selling on talent from across Europe and beyond. All players signed by Cooper in January arrived at Melwood as the window opened on the first of the month and it was highly unlikely that Cooper would be delving back into the market in early 2039 preferring to wait it out until the summer.

There were also no outgoings of note as Cooper looked to keep his squad intact and push on through the end of January and into the remainder of the season. There were a number of loan deals as promising players such as Durval, Aya Diouf and Idris Tas were allowed to leave provided their new clubs agreed to the level of playing time deemed necessary by the manager.

Derek Cooper and his Liverpool side were now on a six game winning streak that had taken them up to the 22nd of January and a home match against top six side Chelsea. Liverpool and both Manchester clubs had established themselves as the only real contenders for the league title and there was a big gap opening up between themselves and the rest of the Premier League. Victory against The Blues would further widen that gap and a solitary goal from Brazilian Anderson Miguel was enough to secure a 1-0 win for Liverpool. However, the win came at a cost as both Angelino Kayala and Igor Rusalic picking up injuries. The fractured wrist suffered by Kayala would keep him out for at least five weeks whilst the twisted ankle of Rulasic would mean a two week lay-off.

Having successfully widened the gap over the chasing pack Liverpool's next task was ensuring they weren't left marooned behind City and United. Derek had a terrible record against his North West rivals from Manchester and sadly the trend continued at Old Trafford once more as United won 3-0 with goals from midfielders Lewis Andrews and Rodrigo Godoy as well as Bolivian winger Carlos Ceregatti.

Manchester United had joined City in extending their lead over Derek Coopers men and he now knew it would take a miracle, or at the very least a dramatic drop off from both clubs, were Liverpool to win another Premier League. Nottingham Forrest arrived at Anfield off the back of the disappointing defeat and an early penalty for the home side was converted by Gustavo Penalba. They never looked back comfortably winning 3-0 with Igor Obradovic and Mohamed Yao joining the Argentine forward on the score sheet.

That home win was perfect preparation for the FA Cup fourth round match against another Championship side as Aston Villa travelled to Anfield looking to eliminate Cooper's side. The FA Cup was a competition that Derek Cooper was very keen to win, it was a trophy that was dripping in history and he had been present at one of the greatest finals, back in 2006 as a Steven Gerrard inspired Liverpool came from behind late on to eventually beat West Ham on penalties. To win the competition as the manager of Liverpool would be the realisation of a dream that had potential roots in that final at the Millennium Stadium in Cardiff.

There was a slight distraction going into the match as German full back Alexander Frank prepared to travel to China to talk to Shanggang about a potential £15m move to the Far East. Frank played in the match, and put in a steady performance as Liverpool ran out 2-0 winners thanks to a brace from Mohamed Yao. The home fans were made to wait, but the goals in the seventy-second and seventy-ninth minutes were enough to see them into the hat for the fifth round which was drawn live on telly following the final whistle. It was another home tie as Liverpool were drawn first and followed by Derby, to complete a hat-trick of Championship opponents for Derek Cooper.

The win against Villa was to be the last time Alexander Frank wore the red of Liverpool as he agreed to join Shanggang having agreed personal terms on the £15m deal the Chinese club were offering. £15m was simply too good a price to turn down for a thirty-one year old who was reaching the twilight years of his career. Frank had been a reliable player for Cooper having signed him at both Madrid and Liverpool, so he wasn't going to stand in the way of a final pay day for the German.

Frank left the day before Cooper turned fifty-one and the day after his side travelled to the south coast and suffered a humbling defeat (3-0) at the hands of Bournemouth. Nobody played well and a particularly bad first half performance left them trailing by three and unable to mount any sort of comeback.

There was only a trip to Selhurst Park to face Crystal Palace before Liverpool returned to Champions League action and the double header against Dutch side Feyenoord. Picking up a win would be Coopers preferred preparation and his side duly delivered all three points although it wasn't without difficulty as Palace piled on the pressure late on to make the Liverpool fans and management very nervous. Goals from Miguel, Cordova and Penalba had Liverpool seemingly on easy street and Cooper looked to rest a couple of his main men, but goals in the seventy-sixth and then the ninety-third minute made for a tighter finish that it should have been.

Feyenoords De Kuip home had been a regular battleground for Derek during his time in Holland and he returned to do battle once more looking to inflict another defeat and take his side back to Liverpool with a healthy advantage. American Michael Bradley was now in charge following in the footsteps of Paolo Sousa and Gio van Bronkhorst who had managed the club for just over twenty years between them. It was a performance very similar to that of a week ago on the south coast from Liverpool and early goals from Dirk Thys and Mario Nagy had the home side up by two goals at the break. Cooper could have made eleven changes at half time and really laid into his players aggressively telling them that it wasn't good enough. The second half was only slightly better, but another Feyenoord goal arrived as Filipe Garcia made it 3-0. Liverpool managed to save a little face as left winger Lesther Cordova found the back of the net in the eighty-fourth minute to make it 3-1 on the night leaving it all to do in the return leg for Cooper and his Liverpool side.

Disappointed and downhearted his side returned to their mammoth task of trying to claw their way back into some sort of title race and progressing through to the quarter finals of the FA Cup. Frustratingly his side put in a very good performance on their return to domestic action comfortably dismissing Arsenal in front of their home fans (3-0) before beating Derby at Anfield by the same score line (3-0) to kick off the month of March and see them through to that quarter final stage. Back to back wins heading into the Merseyside derby was better form, six goals scored and none conceded, but that counted for little when facing off against their city rivals. Mounir Chafik put The Toffees ahead before Spanish central defender Jose Rodriguez was sent off for Liverpool just five minutes later to curtail their comeback and hand Everton a rare derby win (1-0).

A home win against Spurs (3-1) followed the disappointing derby defeat and came three days before the crunch second leg Champions League tie with Feyenoord. That match at Anfield was crucial with Liverpool having failed to turn in any sort of performance in Rotterdam nearly a month ago. Cooper was confident and knew his side were more than capable of winning by the two goals to nil score line that would see them through to the next round.

Liverpool were much better this time out and were largely in control during the first forty-five, although Feyenoord were a constant threat on the counter attack. It took until the forty-ninth minute for the home side to make the breakthrough and it came courtesy of right back Igor Rusalic, giving hope to the Anfield faithful. The game was slowly ebbing away and with just one more goal needed Cooper began to look to his attacking options from the bench. Gustavo Penalba, Mohamed Yao and Igor Obradovic all entered the fray hoping to nick that elusive second goal. Unfortunately for Derek Cooper Feyenoord caught the Liverpool backline out with seventy-three minutes on the clock leaving them twenty minutes to save their European season. Regista Gregory Buisson scored a second goal for Liverpool with eighty-six minutes played, but sadly that Dirk Thys goal for Feyenoord had been enough to end Coopers hopes of another Champions League win. Feyenoord progressed 4-3 on aggregate over the two legs and Cooper had to concede that they had been worthy winners, Liverpool simply hadn't been good enough.

Elimination from the Champions League meant Cooper was looking at a season without silverware unless he could guide his team through what would be a fiercely contested FA Cup. The Premier League was all but out of reach and even an unbeaten end to the season wouldn't be enough to overhaul the Manchester clubs with both sides in imperious form domestically. Liverpool put in a stellar performance on their return to Premier League action, travelling to Southampton and winning comfortably (4-1) ahead of what would be a tough FA Cup quarter final away to Chelsea at Stamford Bridge.

Chelsea's renovated home stadium now accommodated a crowd of 60,000 and they were in full voice on the 23rd of March 2039 when Derek Cooper visited with his Liverpool side looking to make the FA Cup semi finals. The first half was largely even, with Liverpool perhaps having slightly more of the play, but it ended with the sides deadlocked at 0-0. The second half started badly for Cooper and Chelsea took the lead through French winger Luca Carrere. As his side looked to find a way back into the game they were picked off again with a quick fire double from Chelsea. On sixty-three minutes Italian striker Alberto Montesi added a second before Spaniard Lolo Guttierez scored a third on sixty-eight minutes to sew up the victory for Peter Niemeyer and his Chelsea side.

Defeat at Stamford Bridge meant that Cooper would be finishing the season trophy less leaving the Community Shield he won in his first game in charge at Liverpool as his only silverware to date. The remaining seven games of the season were now all about securing Champions League qualification as soon as possible and playing themselves into form ahead of the 2039/240 season.

Ideally he was aiming for seven wins, but that was soon shot down by Norwich City who travelled to Anfield and inflicted an unlikely defeat (1-0) courtesy of a late Canaries goal. A draw away to Leicester followed (0-0) before they faced the visit of title challengers Manchester City. Cooper had yet to beat Rondon and he didn't hold out much hope this time out either, there seemed to be a mental block when it came to the Manchester clubs who he seemed unable to beat.

Luis Espinoza got Liverpool off to a flyer with a goal in the opening minute before he added two more later in the game to complete a hat-trick and help his side to an impressive 5-2 victory. Further first half goals from Lesther Cordova and Angelino Kayala saw Liverpool lead 3-1 at half time before those two from Espinoza completed the win. It was a big win for Cooper and came at a time when he was feeling frustrated at a perceived lack of progress at the club. He had felt that his side were miles off competing for the titles he so desperately craved, but this proved to him that it could be done and he was building a club that would challenge for silverware. This one win reinvigorated the manager and gave him the belief that had been waning following a disappointing season and dropped points at home to Norwich and away to Leicester.

A rejuvenated Liverpool now faced their four final fixtures and they recorded three wins and one loss, scoring twelve goals and conceding four. The side won away to West Ham (4-2), at home to Stoke (6-1) with a goal for young winger Jean Menga and a hat-trick for Angelino Kayala before they won again at Turf Moor against a spirited Burnley side (2-0). QPR travelled to Anfield on the final day of the 2038/39 season and completed an unusual double of 1-0 victories over Liverpool with both home and away victories coming courtesy of a Henk Theuns goal as he tormented his former boss, which was something Derek was keen to point out to the Dutchman at the final whistle.

Liverpool had been knocked out of the Champions League at the first knockout round stage, the FA Cup at the quarter final round and they had finished third in the Premier League on seventy-nine points behind Manchester United in second on eighty-three points and champions Manchester City on eighty-five points. Of their thirty-eight games for the 2038/39 season Liverpool won twenty-five, drew four and lost nine compared to a record of twenty-seven wins, four draws and seven losses for the champions. Aside from the extra two losses the main difference between the sides came in the goal difference columns as both Manchester clubs finished with a goal difference of sixty, compared to forty-one for Derek Coopers men. Liverpool scored seven less than United, but a whopping fifteen behind City. Coopers men also conceded the most of the top three sides, only four more than the eventual winners, but twelve more than a stingy United. Derek's end of season report read "Must do better" ahead of the next campaign.

Derek had been frustrated by the teams' performances throughout 2038/39 and he knew many of the players were capable of more. Lesther Cordova was a player with immense talent, but that didn't always translate onto the pitch and although nine goals in thirty-four appearances with an average rating of 7.10 wasn't bad for a debut season in English football, it was only a glimpse of what Derek knew he was able to contribute. Mexican Luis Espinoza had been the standout performer and claimed the clubs player of the season award with an average rating of 7.54 and eighteen goals in forty-four appearances. Igor Rusalic (7.49), Angelino Kayala (7.48) and Fresnel Kitoko (7.51) all ran Espinoza close, but the midfield general had finished as the clubs top scorer and his contributions were rightly acknowledged.

The output of the attacking players in terms of goals had been disappointing with only Anderson Miguel (12) and Angelino Kayala (15) joining Espinoza in double figures which once again had Cooper questioning his strikerless system. Was he lacking the talent he had been blessed with whilst at Real Madrid, or was the tactical set-up just not suited to the Premier League? Cooper was working on a tactical approach that would see him revert to using a lone striker, but he didn't feel quite ready to give up on his unique approach just yet despite his misgivings.

Cooper headed into the summer with a large number of potential targets, but many were considered too expensive with the club looking to sign younger talents and develop them as a more cost effective transfer policy. It was a recruitment model Cooper had worked to previously and he agreed with, so he would only be entering the market for players that he knew could grow whilst at the club. This meant that Cooper would once again be keeping faith in his current crop of senior players, although some had been angling for moves or looking for more regular first team action.

The staffing was largely kept the same, although Roberto Carlos was relieved of his duty as the clubs Director of Football with Marc Overmars coming in to fill the vacancy. Cooper had briefly worked with Overmars whilst at Ajax and had been impressed with the Dutchman's way of working. Former Arsenal man Tomas Rosicky also joined from Aston Villa to work as an U23 Coach whilst Cooper raided Real Madrid for a Goalkeeper Coach and an U23 Sports Scientist he had hired in Madrid.

Liverpool and their manager moved quickly to move on those players who had either stated an intention to leave or were no longer wanted ahead of the clubs pre-season schedule. Thirty-one year old club legend Alin Marginean had been wooed by Paris Saint-Germain and the £50m offered by the French outfit was well above his market value so Cooper reluctantly accepted their offer. English winger Peter Jarvis wanted more first team football than Cooper was inclined to offer and left for Arsenal in a £19m deal whilst central defender Drazen Musa joined their North London rivals, Spurs, for £30m. Croatian striker Ivo Vukovic was a decent player, but he was no better than the younger players coming through behind him and left for QPR in search of more game time. The £40m paid by Rangers was also considered extremely good business by Cooper, for a player who had failed to make much of an impact following his arrival at Liverpool for £1.5m back in 2033/34.

Having made a serious amount of money via player sales Cooper decided to take the plunge on a Brazilian midfielder he had been watching for some time. Celsinho was predominantly a central midfielder but he could also operate as an attacking midfielder as well as a striker and his versatility through the middle as well as impressive figures during a four year stint in Portugal with FC Porto made the twenty-five year old the perfect marquee signing. Liverpool paid Celsinho's £40m release clause and he agreed terms on a long term deal worth £150k a week.

Celsinho arrived at Melwood as the transfer window opened on the first day of July and was joined by a number of young players Derek hoped would improve whilst at Liverpool Football Club. Daniel Dams joined from Dinamo (£2.5m initially which could rise to £4.5m), Robin Birner arrived from Borussia Monchengladbach (£2.5m initially which could rise to £6.5m) and Jorge Teixeira made the move from Benfica for just £450k. There were a number of other promising youngsters signed, but those three represented the bigger outlays and harboured the most hope.

Pre-season got underway on the pitch as it usually did with a behind closed doors friendly against the U23 side before moving on to more testing matches against teams such as Zenit, AS Saint-Etienne, Red Bull Leipzig, Basaksehir and Ludogorets. It was wins across the board for Liverpool throughout pre-season with the exception of a thrilling 3-3 draw against the French club Saint-Etienne who were still very much benefitting from the tycoon takeover that happened in 2035. In fact in all eight friendly matches Liverpool never failed to score less than three goals and in some cases hit six and even nine past their opponents which gave Cooper some hope that his side would manage an improved goals total for the upcoming season.

There was also another big money arrival late on in the season's preparations. Despite Cooper feeling he would only enter the market for younger prospects at reasonable prices he decided that when the opportunity to sign twenty-one year old Turkish right winger Ahmet Yilmaz came up he would have been a fool to ignore it. Once again Liverpool had to pay the players release fee, which stood at £30m, but Benfica had made it clear that there would be no deal done unless that fee was met. The outgoing funds were offset by the sales of back up right back Marko Popovic to moneybags Saint-Etienne for £27m and ageing attacking midfielder, Miguel Ribeiro who wasn't interested in signing a new deal with Liverpool and therefore left to join Southampton for £18m.

Derek Cooper and Liverpool had a favourable start to their 2039/40 Premier League campaign and the only real early season test would be the trip to the Emirates for the third game of the season before facing Manchester United for the first time mid way through September. The United game was scheduled to take place following gameweek one of the new Champions League competition and Liverpool had once again been drawn in Group G alongside Maccabi Tel-Aviv, Cordoba and Juventus. Derek was particularly looking forward to the two matches against the Old Lady, it was always nice to face off against his old sides in competitive matches.

Liverpool travelled down to Bournemouth for their opening fixture and a relatively comfortable 2-1 victory was soured by a serious injury to Mohamed Yao who was likely to miss around four months of action with a damaged achilles tendon he picked up very early on. Goals from Lesther Cordova and Gustavo Penalba came before half time and the side managed to hold out for the win despite the home side pulling a goal back after fifty-two minutes.

A home win against Crystal Palace followed the opening day victory (3-0), with Cordova and Penalba getting the goals again, two for the Honduran winger and one for the Argentinean attacker. Then came the visit to Arsenal which brought the first disappointment of the season with former man Peter Jarvis key in the Gunners victory. Jarvis opened the scoring before Espinoza drew Liverpool level, but in a tight game it was an eighty-first minute winner from Arsenal centre back Nathan Wildig.

Liverpool bounced back in emphatic style in their next fixture putting Aston Villa to the sword(5-0) with a couple of debut goals for another new signing at the club. Twenty-one year old Italian attacker Amadou Mboup signed from Italian club Cesena for £18.5m up front, but that fee could rise as high as £32m should certain performance related bonuses be met during his time with the club. He got off to the best possible start, signing his five year contract the day before running out at a packed Anfield to score within seven minutes of his first appearance. Cooper hoped it was indicative of what was to come from the young man moving forward with Liverpool. An own goal and a Jean Menga strike as well as another first Liverpool goal for winger Ahmet Yilmaz completed the scoring on the day.

There was an international break scheduled for the two weeks following the Aston Villa victory and this allowed Cooper and Liverpool to conclude their summer transfer business. It had been a busier window than Cooper had anticipated and he had sanctioned the sale of several big names that saw an income in the region of £240m with late deals for midfielder Josip Matesan (Southampton, £18m) and Ange Kouassi (£35m, West Ham) added to the earlier sales of Marginean and Vukovic amongst others.

The late deals for Mboup and Sebastian Tello, a young Argentinean central defender from Lanus, for potentially £7.5m pushed the spending up to around £97m, but that had the potential to rise should certain clauses in some of the deals be met. The extra income was the main reason for Cooper changing his initial recruitment plans, but it also allowed Cooper to invest in other areas of the club, such as youth recruitment and training facilities, all of which he was keen to improve at any given opportunity.

As the players returned to domestic action following their international exploits Mboup continued his fine form scoring in the next two matches. A win at home to Leicester (3-0) where he kicked off the scoring and again in the first win of the 2038/39 Champions League campaign against Maccabi Tel-Aviv at Anfield (1-0). In his opening three performances in the famous red shirt of Liverpool he managed to score four goals and play a part in securing three wins. It also meant Derek had guided his side to four wins from their first five Premier League matches as they prepared to head to Old Trafford in an effort to put the Red Devils recent dominance to bed.

Didier Digard was now the main man in charge at Manchester United having replaced the retiring Unai Emery in the summer. Digard was the former manager of Paris Saint-Germain and Real Madrid having followed Derek Cooper in the Madrid hot seat back in 2037 and going on to win one La Liga title as well as the Champions League and European Super Cup in his two years there. The Frenchman was clearly a world class manager, but Cooper hoped to catch him cold as he adjusted to life in the English Premier League.

Digard hadn't made a perfect start at his new club, United had been beaten by City in the Community Shield and had dropped points in an away defeat at Southampton. They had however been victorious in the other five matches they had played so far in 2039/40. Digard obviously had his team fired up and Coopers Liverpool looked unable to cope with the intensity of their hosts, United raced into a four goal lead before Liverpool could muster a consolation goal in the seventieth minute through Angelino Kayala. The game ended in a humbling 4-1 defeat for Cooper who was once again left angered by his inability to cause Manchester United any problems in yet another North West derby.

Failure to beat United wasn't the end of the world in the grand scheme of things, there was still a lot of football to be played, this defeat wouldn't determine the outcome of their season, but Derek Cooper was becoming increasingly frustrated by his inability to beat the clubs most historic rivals. He now needed to put this defeat behind him and concentrate on the upcoming matches against Stoke, Newcastle and Cordoba.

There was a narrow victory in the EFL Cup third round tie against Stoke (3-2) before another disappointing performance in a league match. Angelino Kayala put Liverpool ahead at St. James' Park, but his goal was soon cancelled out by the home side who held on for the 1-1 draw. Angelino Kayala put in another performance in the sides next match away in Spain as they took on Cordoba in gameweek two of the Champions League. He grabbed a hat-trick and player of the match award in the comfortable victory (4-0). The home side were not helped by their Brazilian defensive midfielder Raul who was sent off in the first half with his side already trailing by two goals. Celsinho scored the other goal of the game and notched his first for Liverpool as they coasted to two wins from two in Group G.

Celsinho scored his second Liverpool goal three days later as they just about saw off the challenge of Blackburn, who were looking to capitalise on the tired legs of Coopers men. Late goals made the 4-1 score line look a little more comfortable than it might have been on another occasion. Lesther Cordova returned to scoring ways at Ewood Park notching two of the sides four goals and he found the back of the net in the following match, a home win against Chelsea (3-0). Further goals from Espinoza and Buisson in midfield helped Liverpool to their second victory in October.

The 18th of October saw Liverpool return to European action and Derek Cooper return to his former home, the Juvents Stadium, Turin. Juventus had been in good form so far and had remained unbeaten, although they had only managed to draw at home to Cordoba and away to Maccabi Tel-Aviv. The club had re-signed the Dutch striker Henk Theuns from QPR in the summer for a fee in the region of £14.25m having sold him to the London club for £11m the season before. Theuns had proved a constant thorn in his ex-managers side during his time in England and he struck again in Italy, helping himself to the match ball as he scored all three of Juve's goals in a 3-2 victory. Goals from Kayala and Yilmaz got Liverpool back on level terms in the second half before Theuns put away his third in the seventy-second minute to secure the win and move Juventus into a position to challenge Liverpool for top spot in the group.

Upon their return to England there was no respite as the Merseyside derby loomed large on the horizon. There were just three days rest for Cooper and his men before they looked to turn in a better performance than they had done last time against Everton in the 1-0 defeat of March. Mounir Chafik once again got on the score sheet, but it wasn't enough to grab an Anfield win for Everton as second half goals from attackers Yilmaz and Cordova carried Liverpool to a deserved victory (2-1).

Liverpool then had the chance to exact revenge on Arsenal for the early Premier League defeat as they travelled to Anfield to contest the EFL Cup fifth round tie. Cooper rotated slightly, but he wanted to show Arsenal what his side were really capable of so played to win the tie. His boys responded well to his will to win and delivered an emphatic 5-1 victory. Watson, Espinoza, Rodriguez, Kayala and Rusalic scored the goals that meant Liverpool were now through to the EFL quarter final, which was the furthest they had made it during Cooper's time at the club. With the Premier League proving to be a very tough nut to crack the EFL Cup represented a real chance to add some silverware which had been lacking so far during his time back in England.

Having played five games already in the month of October, the sixth, at Brighton's newly built and imaginatively named Brighton Stadium, proved a game too far for Coopers Liverpool side. A Luis Espinoza penalty just before half time wasn't enough for the Red Men to earn a share of the points and goals either side of that penalty got Brighton the win (2-1). Liverpool had been drawn against Brighton in the EFL quarter final and they now hoped for a repeat of the revenge victory his side had turned in against Arsenal in the previous round.

The Premier League defeat at the hands of Brighton was to be the last time Derek Cooper and Liverpool tasted defeat through to the middle of December, a run that stretched eleven matches across three competitions and took them right up to their visit to the new home of Manchester City - Gabriel Barbosa Arena.

Juventus came to Anfield in the game immediately after the Brighton loss and Cooper was desperate to save some face and avenge the 3-2 defeat in Turin. Stopping Henk Theuns from scoring would significantly increase Liverpool's chances of a result with the Dutchman having scored winning goals the last three times he had faced a Cooper side. Another penalty from Luis Espinoza got Liverpool off to a flyer on three minutes, but Theuns wasn't to be denied and he levelled the game at 1-1 just three minutes later. Amadou Mboup then scored the third goal of the game in the opening ten minutes as he made it 2-1 to the home side after eight minutes making it a great game for the neutrals. Liverpool then scored two more before half time to assert their dominance and stake their claim for the three points. Juventus tried to mount a comeback in the second half and a goal in the seventieth minute gave their players hope, but it was short-lived as winger Jean Menga completed the scoring in the 5-2 win.

A draw away to Spurs followed (1-1) with Liverpool unable to capitalise on the home side going down to ten men in the first half. The other four fixtures in November saw Liverpool pick up wins against Watford (3-1), Maccabi Tel-Aviv (2-0) and West Ham (3-1) before reversing the 2-1 defeat suffered to Brighton in the Premier League to progress in the EFL Cup quarter final with goals from Penalba and Kayala either side of the break enough to set up a semi final against Manchester City.

December kicked off with another win, this time away to Stoke (2-1), but the month would not prove to be as fruitful as November had been with a lucky home win against Norwich (1-0) sandwiched between bore draws at home to both Cordoba (0-0) and Southampton (0-0). There was then a win against last season's bogey team as a Henk Theun-less QPR fell to a 2-0 defeat with goals from wingers Yilmaz and Kayala.

Gabriel Barbosa Arena was opened as the new home of Manchester City in 2039, it holds 81,000 and was named in honour of the club legend that signed for the club for £85m back in 2022/23 before moving on to Espanol in 2030/31. Ironically Gabriel Barbosa was now a member of Derek Coopers backroom staff working as an Under 18's Coach at Liverpool. Cooper hoped that having the stadiums namesake on his side would prove a lucky omen and the signs were promising when Liverpool twice took the lead through midfielder Celsinho, but Manchester City kept coming back and cancelled out both strikes with goals of their own. With the game poised at two goals each it looked for all the world like the teams would share the points but disaster struck for Liverpool and goalkeeper Felipe Renan as he scored a ninety-first minute own goal to hand all three points to Manchester City. It was a bitter pill to swallow for Cooper who was still desperate to start taking points off the top two teams in the Premier League.

Liverpool marked the halfway point of the 2039/40 Premier League season with a win away to Crystal Palace (3-2) making their record nineteen games played, twelve wins, three draws and four defeats. The defeats against Manchester City and Manchester United once again left Liverpool in third place and chasing their North West rivals going into the second half of the season. There was an EFL Cup semi final coming up as well as the start of Liverpool's FA Cup campaign to look forward to, but Cooper was annoyed to have slipped behind in the title race once more.

It was a repeat of the opening day fixture against Bournemouth to kick off January's action, but there was to be no repeat of the Liverpool victory as a ninety-third minute equaliser from Swedish winger Felix Svard earned The Cherries a share of the points, much to Cooper's frustration.

Ahead of the Bournemouth fixture and with the opening of the January transfer window Liverpool and Derek Cooper saw an influx of new players. Canadian goalkeeper Mateo Neri signed on a free from Montreal Impact, Russian central midfielder Egveny Orlov signed from Dinamo Moscow for an initial £5m, but that fee could rise to £12m and in the biggest deal of the window twenty year old Dutch attacking midfielder Joeri van der Maarel signed from Groningen for £27.5m.

Whilst there were no more permanent departures plenty of Cooper's young players were sent out on loan across Europe to get some regular senior first team football. Evgeny Orlov went straight out to Hertha Berlin, Gustavo Troiani joined Cardiff, Antonio Stilinovic went to FC Lorient in France and Laurant Perrot joined Galatasaray for the remainder of the season joining the likes of Idris Tas, Aya Diouf, Sebastian Tello and Durval who were already out on loan and gaining some much needed playing time.

Liverpool had been beaten by Arsenal in the earlier Premier League fixture, but they put five past them for a second time this season this time out winning 5-0 at Anfield follwing their EFL Cup win back in October. Lesther Cordova and Ahmet Yilmaz got two goals each and Gregory Buisson added another to complete the thrashing. There was a disappointing debut injury for van der Maarel, but thankfully it wasn't serious and he was soon back in full training with the rest of the squad.

The Arsenal result was exactly what the side needed as they prepared to face off against Manchester City in the first leg of the awkward two legged EFL Cup semi final. Liverpool had been drawn away from home for the first leg and returned to Gabriel Barbosa Arena looking to take control of the tie.

Things started well for Derek and his men as Lesther Cordova opened the scoring on the thirty-first minute, but that was to be the only bright spot of what turned into a particularly abject performance from the reds. By the time the half time whistle sounded Liverpool trailed by three goals to one and had been completely blown away by a resurgent Manchester City. The Citizens continued to dominate throughout the second half and Cooper was left embarrassed and furious when the final whistle sounded to bring an end to the debacle. City had scored three more goals without reply and absolutely smashed Liverpool 6-1 to render the second leg in two weeks' time completely irrelevant.

It was now important that Derek didn't allow one terrible performance to infect upcoming matches, he needed his side to dig deep and show plenty of character for the remainder of January and beyond. Important wins followed away to Aston Villa (2-1) and Barnsley (2-0) with goals from Jean Menga in the sixth and ninety-second minutes seeing Liverpool through the FA Cup fourth round to face Arsenal for a fourth time this season. Cooper was pleased to have returned to winning ways with the visit of Manchester United to Anfield just around the corner in their next Premier League fixture.

Red Devils manager Didier Digard had returned to his former club Real Madrid to make the marquee signing of the January transfer window so far, spending and eye watering £95m on French attacking midfielder Abdul Youssouf. Youssouf was in fact a Derek Cooper signing during his time as Madrid manager with the Englishman having paid Lille £25m for his services back in 2034 and the now twenty-four year old came back to haunt the man who signed him originally as he coolly dispatched a thirty-fifth minute penalty to put United ahead. Things then went from bad to worse for Liverpool as Lesther Cordova picked up a second yellow card which was followed by the inevitable red leaving the home side with ten men and just over twenty minutes to get something from the game. Luckily for Cordova his indiscretion seemed to fire his team-mates up and Bulgarian attacking midfielder Metodi Totev made the most of rare first team action by drawing Liverpool level in the fifty-seventh minute to earn an unlikely share of the points.

There was part two of a Manchester double header to follow as City made the trip to Anfield for the second leg of the EFL Cup semi final. The tie was all but a done deal and Liverpool would only be playing for pride with them overturning the heavy 6-1 loss a virtual impossibility. Cooper told his players he would settle for nothing less than victory and they duly delivered leaving Cooper asking why they put in such a poor performance last time out. Second half goals from Ashley Fletcher and Angelino Kayala cancelled out the opening goal from City's legendary attacking midfielder Emmanuel Tagoe.

Pride partially restored it was back to Premier League action and a disappointing loss away to Leicester (2-0) and a win at home to Newcastle (3-0) either side of a fantastic FA Cup fourth round tie which Liverpool won 4-3 against a tough Arsenal side. Liverpool had been 4-0 up courtesy of a Lesther Cordova hat-trick and a rare Tony Watson goal with just ten minutes left of the game, but somehow Arsenal nearly took the game to a replay scoring three goals in just eight minutes in what would have been a disastrous collapse.

There was a birthday visit to West London up next for Cooper as he looked to celebrate with a win at Stamford Bridge. The result left Cooper in no mood for festivities and a lacklustre performance from his side was punished by an efficient Chelsea as they won 2-0. The sides lack of consistency was making challenging for silverware incredibly difficult and Cooper was beginning to become frustrated by the intermittent defeats. By not winning their matches against City and United, their closest title rivals, Liverpool could ill afford to drop precious points against the likes of Bournemouth, Leicester and Chelsea.

A return to Champions League action was just around the corner and a tough trip to Monaco and their new Ettori Stadium which had been their home since 2033. Before the trip to the wealthy principality Liverpool bounced back domestically with a tense 2-1 home win against strugglers and prime relegation candidates, Blackburn Rovers, winning courtesy of an Ahmet Yilmaz brace.

Liverpool were looking to make their mark in the Champions League having not featured in a final since 2007 and the 2-0 defeat to AC Milan in Athens that Derek Cooper had watched at home in Lowestoft as a nineteen year old. They had emerged top of the pile in Group G this time out on thirteen points ahead of Juventus in second on eight points. Juventus would now play Gelsenkirchen whilst Liverpool faced the third best team in Ligue 1. Yaya Sonogo was now in the managers seat at Monaco with the ex-Arsenal striker having taken over from Sergiy Rebrov in 2033.

Monaco were a good side and not to be underestimated, Cooper needed his players to turn in a decent performance and score what could be a vital away goal come the end of the two legs and the one hundred and twenty minutes plus of football. Coopers big players turned up when it mattered and goals from Cordova, Espinoza and Celsinho secured an emphatic away win (3-0) and grabbed three vital away goals. It also meant a clean sheet to take back to Liverpool in nearly a months' for the reverse fixture of the two legged affair.

The games came thick and fast following the sides return from their European exploits and impressive wins in the Merseyside derby against Everton (4-0) and in the FA Cup fifth round against Huddersfield (4-0) followed their return to England. Kayala and Celsinho scored goals in both victories and Celsinho in particular was beginning to have a real impact on the sides performances with Cooper delighted at how the Brazilian was performing at the club. There was late drama in Liverpools next match against Brighton as Ahmet Yilmaz scored a ninety-first minute winner to spare the blushes of both Kayala and Penalba who had both missed penalties in the match. It was now four wins on the bounce, twelve goals scored and none conceded, just the sort of form Cooper knew his players were capable of, but had so far failed to produce as often as was required of them to win trophies.

The final domestic fixture before the arrival of Monaco saw Watford hold Liverpool to a 1-1 draw at Vicarage Road to put a dampener on the recent run of victories and clean sheets. Monaco had a three goal deficit to overturn and that lead should have been extended by the home side in the fifteenth minute, but unfortunately Angelino Kayala failed from the spot for the second time in three matches. Three eventually became four in the thirty-eighth minute when Kayala atoned for the earlier miss to make it 1-0 on the night and 4-0 to Liverpool on aggregate. Sanogo clearly got into his side at half time and they came flying out of the blocks in the second half scoring a quick fire double in the first six minutes of play to really put the pressure on Coopers men. One more goal for the French side would put the cat amongst the pigeons and two more without reply would see them eliminate Cooper and his side. Thankfully Liverpool woke up and rallied together to keep Monaco at bay for the remainder of the game losing 2-1 on the night but progressing through to the quarter finals 4-2 on aggregate.

There was no rest for Liverpool as they returned to domestic action just three days later, beating Tottenham (3-1) before winning an FA Cup quarter final at home to Fulham (4-1) having had three more days in which to prepare. By now Cooper was aware that he would face off against Sporting Lisbon in the Champions League quarter final and Manchester United in the FA Cup semi final. In the final Premier League match before heading out to Portugal Liverpool laboured to a 1-1 draw against a resilient West Ham side that were helped by a wasteful Liverpool and a Fresnel Kitoko own goal which cancelled out the Luis Espinoza strike.

Sporting had been league champions in Portugal for four of the last five seasons and they would be a hard nut to crack for Cooper and his Liverpool side. They had seen off Real Sociedad in the previous round, but it had been a narrow victory and they had conceded three goals in the tie. Liverpool had been in good form in front of goal and the manager and fans alike hoped to see it continue in Lisbon. The home side obviously had their own game plan and they implemented it brilliantly in the opening stages, keeping Liverpool at bay and taking the lead themselves through Brazilian striker Adriano Guerreiro in the twenty-third minute. Now it was all about how Liverpool responded and Cooper was confident in his sides ability to recover. Anderson Miguel picked the perfect time to socre his first goal since pre-season as he levelled the game at 1-1 just after the thirty minute mark before Metodi Totev scored another important goal for Cooper in the eighty-fourth minute having replaced Ahmet Yilmaz. Liverpool had snatched a narrow victory, but it was a win that came with two very important away goals to take back to Anfield.

There were now just five Premier League matches remaining and Liverpool needed to win them all to have any chance of winning that elusive league title. Manchester City were still leading the way and looking likely to retain their title, but Manchester United were still catchable in second. The first of those remaining domestic fixtures came in the middle of both Sporting matches and saw a rotated side run out easy winners (3-0), but take casualties in the process as both Jean Menga (sprained ankle) and Joeri van der Maarel (back strain) suffer injuries that would keep them out of contention for around a month each.

Just like that it was back to European action and a Champions League quarter final for Derek Cooper and his Liverpool side. They were 2-1 up and had a fantastic chance of making the semi finals, a stage Cooper had not reached in the competition since his time in Madrid. Adriano Guerreiro once again opened the scoring mimicking events of the first leg, but yet again Cooper had faith in his men, it was 2-2 on aggregate and Liverpool would progress via the away goals rule. They could sit back and hope to prevent another Sporting goal, but that wasn't how Cooper did things and his side remained on the front foot looking to win the match. His bravery was rewarded in the sixty-ninth minute by Angelino Kayala and then again in the eightieth minute by Gregory Buisson as Liverpool won by the same 2-1 score line as they had done in Portugal to progress 4-2 on aggregate and reach the Champions League semi finals. Liverpool fans were beginning to dream of European glory once again.

Liverpool were joined in the draw for the semi final by Manchester City, Real Madrid and Paris Saint-Germain, there was no easy option and Cooper knew he would have to beat one of the very best in Europe if he was to make the final in Marseille come May. As luck would have it Liverpool would be drawn against Real Madrid, Cooper's former club and fourteen time winners of the European Cup.

An unimpressive performance at Carrow Road, home of Norwich City and closest professional club to Derek's home town of Lowestoft, saw two goals from Mohamed Yao at either end of the game snatch a win (2-1). Yao opened the scoring in the second minute before concluding it again in the ninety-second to spare Liverpool blushes against a Norwich side who were actually doing better than many had predicted.

From the humble surroundings of Carrow Road it was off to one of footballs great pantheons and an arena that Cooper had enjoyed the great pleasure of calling his home for just shy of five years. The Santiago Bernabeu stadium was a daunting prospect for many footballers, but Cooper believed in his group of players, they had made it further than many football fans had predicted, united a fan base and brought back chants of "Allez, allez, allez" to the terraces. Liverpool were the underdogs and they hoped to spring a surprise on the big boys of Madrid.

The entire starting eleven for Real Madrid had played for Derek Cooper whilst he had been in charge there with ten of that eleven having been signed by him. The only exception was Mohamed Oudghiri who had come through the clubs youth set up prior to his arrival. As the game got underway Liverpool settled into their rhythm well and actually took the lead through an ex-Madrid player as Mohamed Yao found the net on eight minutes. Things were going well for Liverpool, but Madrid were slowly playing their way into the game and in a disastrous five minutes before the break they grabbed two goals through Bartosz Korzeniewski and their world class attacking midfielder Enzo Moreira. Liverpool emerged from the changing rooms for the second half looking to keep things tight whilst hoping to add some more goals of their own. Unfortunately the occasion seemed to get to the young squad and experience shone in the Madrid squad which boasted footballing royalty amongst their ranks. Moriera added a second before substitute Yann Doucet added a fourth in the final minutes. The final whistle confirmed the 4-1 defeat for Liverpool and in all likelihood ended their hopes of reaching the Champions League final.

Southampton were up next in the Premier League for Liverpool. They had three games left; Southampton included and were still in the hunt for a runners up spot although the title was all but guaranteed to be heading back to Manchester City. Cooper wanted three points down at St.Marys, but he also wanted to come through the match with no injuries. Just ten minutes had been played when influential midfielder Celsinho pulled up with what looked like a hamstring injury, not ideal given it would be at least a two week lay-off and he would miss the crunch Real Madrid game as well as the FA Cup semi final against Manchester United. Thankfully Derek was spared the pain of a defeat as well as the injury and goals from Cordova, Yao and Yilmaz secured a routine win (3-0).

Liverpool headed into the home leg of their Champions League semi final with Real Madrid as even bigger underdogs than they had been a week or so ago in the Bernabeu. They had been largely written off by fans and pundits alike and that was fuelling Derek Cooper. He knew the enormity of the task, overturning a 4-1first leg defeat against a European powerhouse such as Real Madrid was as tough an ask as he had faced in his career, but the doubt was the basis of his team talk. He told his players that no-one expected them to get a result and they could go out and play without any pressure. No-one saw Liverpool making that final in Marseille.

Despite the odds being stacked against their side the Liverpool fans turned out in force and threw the weight of Anfield behind the team. The players responded and got the unlikely comeback off to the best possible start when Brazilian Anderson Miguel found the back of the net for only the second time this season, the other coming in the Champions League match against Sporting. Eight minutes played and 1-0 to Liverpool, 4-2 on aggregate and game on. Liverpool continued to pile on the pressure and familiar faces who had stood so firm in Madrid began to crumble at Anfield. Guillaume looked shaky between the sticks and Liverpool were peppering the goal of the Belgian who had already been beaten once. One became two after thirty-three minutes with veteran midfielder Ashley Fletcher finding the back of the Madrid net. Real Madrid needed half time, they had to regroup and stop the flow of a Liverpool side who really meant business.

Cooper used the half time break to once again tell his players that the pressure was off, adding that he knew they were capable of better, which was quite a statement given that they were beating Real Madrid. One more goal would be enough to see them through on the away goals rule, but the way things were going Cooper couldn't help but think his players were capable of getting more. The second half continued in the same vein as the first forty-five. Real Madrid looked off the pace and Liverpool looked like they smelled blood. Ahmet Yilmaz scored the third goal for Derek Cooper's side on fifty-seven minutes and handed them control of the tie. Now it became a game of stick or twist for Derek, did he look to consolidate what they had and ride out the remaining half an hour or so. He decided to stick and kept his side and the set up exactly the same waiting until the ninetieth minute to make any changes, bringing on Jose Rodriguez and Branislav Djuricic in an attempt to break up play and waste some valuable seconds. It was agony for the staff, players and fans as the clock slowly ticked away the two minutes of added time, but when that final whistle finally blew the roof came off Anfield. Liverpool had completed yet another unlikely European comeback, one that would go down in the clubs history and it had come under the watchful eye of Derek Cooper. Liverpool would be in Marseille and they would be playing in the 2039/2040 UEFA Champions League final.

Historic European comeback complete the side returned to domestic action against recent bogey team Queens Park Rangers. Although they had beaten the London side earlier in the season without their talismanic striker Henk Theuns, the void had been filled and it was another former player of Derek Cooper. Two goals from Ivo Vukovic who joined his new side for £40m in the summer, came back to haunt his old club and manager as he twice put QPR ahead. Fortunately goals from Fletcher and Penalba were enough to rescue the draw (2-2). That left Liverpool with just one Premier League game left to play, at home to champions Manchester City who had also been confirmed as the other Champions League finalist. In a weird twist they would play each other twice in the final two weeks of the season and although the Premier League was out of Derek's reach, the Champions League was very much up for grabs in the all English final.

Before those season defining games there was another important fixture for the club as they travelled down to Wembley to take on Manchester United in the FA Cup semi final. It was The Red Devils' last chance of silverware and it showed in a one sided match in which Liverpool looked to have one eye on the upcoming European showpiece. Derek's side never got going, played within themselves and were duly put to the sword. Davis, Walker and Ortega scored the United goals in a convincing 3-0 win. There was a further blow for Liverpool as impressive Honduran winger Lesther Cordova pulled up with a hamstring injury and would now face a race to be fit for Marseille.

A draw and a defeat wasn't ideal form heading into a match that meant a whole lot more now than many though it would have done. Both sides now wanted to win for the psychological advantage it would hand them going into the Champions League final. Liverpool could still catch United in second, but it was unlikely with them boasting a much better goal difference and facing an easier final day fixture at home to West Ham. There was an element of cat and mouse with the rotated sides fielded by both managers, neither wanted to give away their plans for two weeks time. Central defender Assis, who had finally qualified for a work permit following loan spells at Valencia and PSV, made a rare start whilst right back Djuricic and holding midfielder Parmentier also came into the side.

In truth it was a poor game at Anfield. Liverpool were disrupted and distracted whilst Manchester City had the aura that came with being crowned Premier League champions for the second season running. Goals from Mohamed Sobhy and Luis Fernandez came either side of an Ashley Fletcher strike for Liverpool and the game ended in a 2-1 win for The Citizens. It was advantage Manchester City according to the footballing world, but Liverpool had been underdogs before and it hadn't hindered them then, Cooper hoped it would suit them once more.

Cooper took his squad over to France a couple of days ahead of the final looking to acclimatise and familiarise themselves with their new surroundings. They had prepared thoroughly leaving no stone unturned in their quest for unlikely European glory. Manchester City were the overwhelming favourites, especially given their win over Liverpool just thirteen days ago on the final day of the Premier League season.

Celsinho and Lesther Cordova had made sufficient recoveries from injury to be involved in the match day squad, but were deemed only fit enough for a spot on the bench. Derek Cooper started with Felipe Renan in goal. A back four of Fresnel Kitoko, Tony Watson, Frank Seddon and Branislav Djuricic. Twenty-one year old Frenchman Gregory Buisson anchored the midfield with Ashley Fletcher and Luis Espinoza in front of him and an attacking three of Angleina Kayala, Mohamed Yao and Anderson Miguel ahead of those. Cooper had stuck to his strikerless tactic throughout the season so far and it had got them this far, now he hoped it could take them all the way to European success.

Without doubt Manchester City started as the brighter side. Liverpool were shading possession, but City looked far more dangerous with their use of the ball. It was a surprise then when Liverpool took the lead after a mistake from Manchester City's goalkeeper, David Hatfield, resulted in him being credited with an unwanted own goal in the thirty-sixth minute. It was an error that sparked City into life and Emmanuel Tagoe ensured

Liverpool's lead was short-lived, levelling the game up at 1-1 just three minutes later. Half time arrived and Cooper reminded his side that there was no pressure on them; they were still very much the outsider's choice in this match.

The sides took to the pitch at the Stade Orange Velodrome with forty five minutes between them and Champions League success. Liverpool once again took the lead and this time it came from one of their own as Mexican Luis Espinoza scored in the fiftieth minute. Once again they were unable to hold onto their lead and in the fifty-second minute Henrik Hain pegged them back once more. The game then began to spiral out of control for Derek Cooper and Liverpool as Mohamed Yao was shown his second yellow card in the seventy first minute leaving Liverpool with just ten men. Cooper had already used two of his allotted three changes with Yilmaz coming on to replace Miguel just after half time and Lesther Cordova making his return in the sixty-third minute at the expense of Kayala, but Yao had been the focal point of the team and he needed to fill that gap so Cooper used his third and final change to introduce Celsinho. With just ten men on the pitch things became immeasurably difficult and Cooper hoped his side could nick a goal or at least hold out until the full time whistle.

Things then went from bad to worse for Liverpool and Derek Cooper as he faced yet another setback in the match. In the seventy-ninth minute, not even ten minutes after Liverpool had been reduced to ten men and Cooper had used his last substitution Ahmet Yilmaz was clattered in a challenge which left him unable to continue. Yilmaz had entered the match as a forty-seventh minute substitute, but he was leaving just twenty-two minutes later with what looked like a broken foot forcing Liverpool down to nine men in a Champions League final.

Amazingly Liverpool kept Manchester City out for the remainder of the ninety minutes, but there was to be no reprieve and they now faced the prospect of defending for another thirty minutes with making it all the way to penalties now their most likely route to victory. Cooper needed his side to knuckle down and defend for their lives and if they could make it to penalties it was then up for grabs. Manchester City were now in complete control and enjoying almost total domination over Liverpool, but Cooper's men defended stubbornly as the minutes slowly ticked away. Despite all their attacking talent, and the fact their opponents were down to nine men, Manchester City were unable to find a winner and the game would head to a penalty shootout.

Everything that could go wrong for Derek Cooper had gone wrong in the final, but his side had made it as far as penalties and they were due their slice of luck. Cooper chose his takers, with many having scored from the spot throughout the season, although there had been some misses along the way too. Cooper was unable to look as Espinoza ran up to take the first penalty of the shootout and felt the sag in the shoulders of his assistant manager as Hatfield made the save. Henrik Hain then slotted City's first penalty home to hand them the advantage. Branislav Djuricic made the long and lonely walk to take his spot kick which he duly dispatched much to the relief of all in red. There was no mistake from Tagoe as he put City back in front at 2-1 with two kicks each. Cordova was up next for Liverpool and Cooper began to get the sense this just wasn't his night as Hatfield made yet another save. It was now vital that Renan made a save for Liverpool, the shootout was getting away from them and they needed something to get them back in contention. Christian Herrera stepped up for City and a poor penalty was pushed away by Felipe Renan to give Liverpool just what they needed. Three kicks apiece and it was still 2-1 to Manchester City. Renan had given Liverpool a lifeline, but Celsinho now needed to put his kick away to put the pressure on City's next taker. The Brazilian midfielder fluffed his lines, just as Espinoza and Cordova had and Hatfield made his third save of the shootout. It was now down to English centre back Simon Hancock with the Manchester City player one kick of a football away from winning his side the Champions League. Felipe Renan was powerless in the Liverpool goal and Hancock converted his penalty to win the 2039/2040 Champions League final for Manchester City and devastate all those of the Liverpool persuasion.

Derek Cooper congratulated Benoit Proust, who had taken over from Salomon Rondon when the Venezuelan left to join Borussia Dortmund, fulfilled his media commitments and then retired to the dressing room to commiserate his players and lament what could have been on another night. He stayed up into the small hours chatting with his coaching staff as they looked to improve heading into 2040/41 and start winning some trophies for the club. Liverpool had a young squad, but they were getting stronger season after season and Cooper hoped they would learn and grow collectively following the immense disappointment they had just experienced together.

Once back at Melwood Derek was able to take a proper look at the performance of his players throughout the season. Luis Espinoza and Lesther Cordova shared the player of the season award as they both achieved an average rating of 7.40. Espinoza made fifty-four appearances and was a virtual ever present, scoring fifteen goals, whilst Cordova made forty-four appearances scoring sixteen goals. The spread of the goals during 2039/40 was pleasing for Derek Cooper given the sides' relatively low tallies in previous seasons. Fletcher (10), Celsinho (10), Penalba (10) and Yilmaz (15) joined Espinoza and Cordova in double figures as Angelino Kayala top scored for the side with twenty-one goals. Amadou Mboup was close to the double figures club as he made an impressive start to life on Merseyside scoring nine in his twenty-four appearances. Jose Rodriguez had made a decent start to his time with the club too and was now more than capable of stepping into the shoes of ageing central defender Tony Watson.

It was a second consecutive season third place finish for Liverpool as they once again failed in their effort to overhaul the Manchester clubs in the Premier League. Liverpool actually finished the 2039/40 season on seventy-seven points, two points less than their tally of the year before. They were just three points behind Manchester United on eighty, three points less than their total of 2038/39 and ten points off eventual winners Manchester City on eighty-seven which was two more than their winning total of last season. Liverpool won twenty-three times, drew eight and lost the other seven, scoring seventy-nine and conceding thirty-seven. They scored exactly the same as 2038/39, conceded one fewer, lost four more games and drew two fewer. Cooper knew there was more lurking within his side, he had seen them grow this season and compete with the likes of Real Madrid and Juventus. With the right additions and further player development they could mount a serious title challenge and try to win a major trophy or two.

Derek Cooper's time with Liverpool so far had yielded just one trophy, a lone Community Shield back in 2037. Since then they had been runners up in the Premier League 2037/38 and losing finalists of the Champions League in 20239/40. The next step had to see Cooper begin to win trophies with the side he had assembled. Off the pitch Cooper had made progress improving the depth of players at the squad and had worked tirelessly to build an impressive network of youth recruitment utilising the clubs excellent academy facilities. The club was in a much better position financially and they were close to being able to compete with the Manchester clubs in what was available to them in terms of transfer budgets. The only problem Cooper had was that he was reluctant to bring in an established player that would command wages well in excess of £200k a week when he was able to pay less inflated fees, sign players on long contracts with the option for extensions and develop them at the club. It was his modus operandi and he didn't foresee that changing anytime soon. In fact, the signing of Marc Albrighton back in 2017/18 was still the clubs record transfer, then manager Marcelino paid Leicester £42m for the wingers services, a deal that Cooper had been unable to believe as a fan and still struggled to understand as an elite manager.

As always pre-season was when Cooper was at his busiest on and off the pitch. There was a pre-season tour of China scheduled alongside other friendly fixtures, whilst there were many new players coming into the set-up and many familiar faces leaving for pastures new. The standout arrival was Brazilian midfielder Alanzinho who arrived for a fee of £15m rising to £19m from Santos in Brazil. Santos had produced players such as Pele and Neymar and Cooper saw a bright future for the twenty-three year old that had recently been making the

Selecao squad on a consistent basis. Evandro, another Brazilian arrived from Vit. Guimaraes with Cooper paying his £7.5m release clause to add depth down the right hand side of the attack.

Joining Alanzinho and Evandro was twenty-four year old goalkeeper Eugenio Ojeda as Cooper activated his £6m release clause and twenty-one year old Greek left back Leonidas Leoutsakos from Panithanikos for £12m. Whilst both players were unlikely to dethrone either Felipe Renan or Fresnel Kitoko, they were available at a very reasonable price and offered very good competition in a squad in which young players were given the opportunity to thrive. If they weren't an ideal fit for Cooper and the club, both players were assets that were only going to appreciate as they hit their prime years.

As good as Derek Cooper was at finding value in the transfer market he was equally as adept at offloading his deadwood for overly inflated prices boosting the club coffers by squeezing every penny out of the buying clubs. Fringe players Gwenael Catherine (£10.75m, Fulham) and Ivan Krumov (£9.25m, Aston Villa) brought in a combined total of £20m for the club having signed for just £1.5m. Veteran defender Tony Watson had reached an age that meant a decline was inevitable and when Juventus showed an interest in taking the Englishman Cooper accepted a deal worth £15m for the club. Aya Diouf had failed to make a substantial impact at Liverpool and he was moved on returning to France to play for Marseille after an £11m deal was agreed returning a small profit on his £8m original fee. Full back Pedro Jainero had arrived at Liverpool for a paltry £16k back in 2038/39 and he left in search of first team football joining Premier League club Newcastle and securing the club a healthy profit with the £4.5m fee.

There was one deal agreed that Cooper originally had no plan to make with Angelino Kayala having finished as the sides top scorer last season, but there was interest from a number of clubs which had unsettled both manager and player. Kayala was thirty-one years old and in a similar vein to Tony Watson, was not getting any younger. Cooper got the impression it was either recoup some money now before the decline set in and he either lost the player on a free or had clubs coming in with low ball offers. Juventus showed a serious interest and agreed to stump up £17m, which Cooper figured was about as good as he was going to get. Kayala had been an excellent player for Cooper during his time at Liverpool and he was reluctant to see him leave, but Cordova was beginning to shine in his own right and it felt like the right time for both parties to say their goodbyes.

Several of Cooper's young starlets also flew the Liverpool nest, but only temporarily as they sought first team football that would prepare them for life in the Premier League. Russian Egveny Orlov joined Real Betis, Sebastian Tello agreed to join Oviedo, Durval was at Sporting, Brazilian winger Ademar was at Elche and Antonio Stillinovic was playing in Italy with Atalanta. Whilst Cooper and Liverpool benefitted from their young players going out and getting first team football Derek also maximised his income by charging the loaning clubs for the pleasure. Fee's ranged from £60k per month up to £250k per month and it proved to be a lucrative way for Cooper to further enhance the clubs income with some of the loan fees covering the transfer fee Cooper had paid to bring the players to Liverpool in the first place.

Out on the pitch pre-season had been going well and players were once again getting going through training and friendly fixtures in preparation for the new season which would begin at home to Chelsea on the 17th of August 2040. Pre-season included wins against Monaco (6-3), FC Hiroshima (2-1) and Gimnasia (2-0) as well as three victories on a pre-arranged tour of China. The tour to China was draining for everyone involved, but Cooper still felt tapping into the Asian market would allow the club to benefit financially.

Soon it was time for yet another season to get underway and the 2040/41 season would represent Derek Coopers twenty-fifth as a football manager. He was hoping he would be able to mark his quarter century with a trophy, getting the campaign under way with a win at home to Chelsea (3-1). Metodi Totev had really impressed over the summer and had made the most of a starting spot scoring two with the third coming courtesy of Anderson Miguel. Cooper started the season with a couple of new faces which included Armin

Elsebrock in goal for the injured Felipe Renan and Argentinean central defender Juan Jose Sosa in at centre back. Sosa was developing into a very good central defender and Cooper was delighted to have him available following loan spells at Vitesse and Red Bull Leipzig to qualify for the required work permit.

Opening day victory secured it was then on to Brighton and a disappointing goalless draw which saw a man sent off for the home side, but it was too late in the game for Liverpool to take advantage. The side then bounced back with victory at home to Arsenal (3-0) with Totev helping himself to another brace and Celsinho grabbing the other. It was then onto the first international break of the season and the closing of the summer transfer window.

Cooper had made a couple of late signings and the arrival of Jair Ninco for £5.5m represented the biggest outlay. The nineteen year old attacking midfielder joined from San Lorenzo in Argentina and looked to have all the talent required to go far in the game. Cooper snapped him up early and tied him down to a long term contract hoping to nurture him into the first team in the coming years. Ninco was immediately sent out on loan tom Basel in Switzerland to get some first time football under his belt and work towards the required work permit.

Recently signed Eugenio Ogenda left the club on loan as he headed to Bayern Munich. The German club were paying £100k a month for his services as well as paying his full monthly wage for the duration. It was a good deal for both the player and the club. There was one permanent departure agreed as Cooper somehow managed to convince West Ham to part with £25m for Portuguese full back Laurent Perrot. Perrot had been signed by Derek for £300k in his first season with Liverpool, but he failed to make a single appearance and joined the hammers off the back of loan deals at Cardiff, Braga and Galatasaray. It was an almost unbelievable deal for the club.

Players returned following their globetrotting whilst on international duty and it was straight back into the thick of it with the return of Champions League and EFL Cup alongside the Premier League. September was a busy month with five fixtures across the three competitions. They started with back to back wins against Swansea (4-0) and Dinamo Bucharest (2-1) in Group D of the Champions League. A win at home to former bogey side QPR (3-0) followed in their return to Premier League action before a vastly rotated Liverpool side comfortably beat West Ham (3-1) in the third round of the EFL Cup with a hat-trick from Amadou Mboup who was keen to make a claim for a more regular starting spot. Watford away was the final game in September and Liverpool were left frustrated as they turned in a below par performance which was punished by a Watford side who had finished fifteenth last season. The 1-0 defeat was the first loss of the season and ended Cooper's unbeaten start.

October went one better than September as there were six fixtures scheduled across the same three competitions. Included in those six fixtures were Real Madrid in the Champions League and Everton in the EFL Cup fourth round in an all Mersey affair. The month kicked off with the visit of Madrid and a Sebastien Marie opener for the visitors was cancelled out by Gregory Buisson in the second half to give each side a share of the points in the 1-1 draw. Luis Espinoza was on hand late on in their next match at home to Burnley. The visitors had once again taken the lead at Anflied and they very nearly held on for all three points as it took Liverpool until the ninety-second minute to pull level. The October draws continued as Crystal Palace held firm at Selhurst Park (0-0) with both sides unable to break the deadlock.

Three games down and three to go it hadn't been an overly successful month for the club. They were unbeaten, but they were also winless and Liverpool hoped to change that as they travelled to Dynamo Kyiv for gameweek three of Group D. Liverpool afforded their Ukranian hosts a two goal lead before they clicked into gear and raced back to what proved to be a comfortable victory (5-2). Ahmet Yilmaz and Gustavo Penalba both scored their first goals of the season away in Kyiv and they both added to their tallies three days later as Liverpool beat Stoke at Anfield (3-0). Cooper once again employed heavy rotation for the EFL Cup match, it was the ideal opportunity for him to do so and it had worked well in the previous round against Premier League opposition. Liverpool didn't fare so well this time out and in a competitive Merseyside derby left Goodison Park empty handed having lost 1-0 to their city rivals.

Into November and Liverpool travelled back across Stanley Park to take on Everton at Goodison, this time in the Premier League. English winger and academy graduate Tim Keen was handed a start and made the most of his opportunity scoring what looked to be the winner in the seventy-ninth minute. It would have been a dream debut for the young man, but sadly a mistake from Juan Jose Sosa resulted in an own goal just two minutes later to rob him of his big moment and nick a point for Everton (1-1). Another draw wasn't ideal and Liverpool had now dropped six vital Premier League points in their last three league games. It wasn't title winning form and Cooper knew he couldn't afford to give any ground away to either Manchester club who were likely to be the main title rivals yet again.

Liverpool were unable to shake the draws in their next fixture, although luckily it was in Europe rather than the Premier League. Dynamo Kyiv made the long trip to Anfield and were a lot better defensively than they had been a month ago. The 0-0 draw left little for the fans to get excited by and Cooper was beginning to become frustrated with the sides lack of a cutting edge. Upon their return to domestic action against Southampton Liverpool raced into a three goal first half lead before conspiring to try and throw it all away in the second forty-five. Luckily the goals from Penalba (2) and Keen again were enough to see off the Saints comeback and secure a valuable return to winning ways (3-2).

Two more victories followed and Aston Villa succumbed to a Brazilian inspired Liverpool with goals from Evandro and Celsinho enough for the narrow away win (2-1). There was then a glut of goals at home to Dinamo Bucharest in gameweek five of Group D as Celsinho (2), Penalba, Menga and Totev all found the back of the net in the win (5-0). Totev had been missing through injury and Cooper wondered whether the Bulgarians absence had been detrimental to the sides form.

December started with two tough games against teams of the highest pedigree. Manchester United visited Anfield on the first of the month before Liverpool travelled to the Bernabeu on the fourth of the month. Cooper had a woeful record against both Manchester clubs, but most notably against the red half of the city. Failure to secure positive results against United had been a constant source of disappointment for him during his time on Merseyside. He was desperate to put it right this time out and give the fans something to cheer and laud over the travelling support. Cooper would have settled for a narrow victory, but his players were dominant throughout the game and an early goal from Yilmaz in the eighth minute set Liverpool on their way to an important and well overdue win against Manchester United (4-0). Ahmet Yilmaz added a second as well as further goals from Celsinho and Jean Menga to complete the scoring.

Confidence was high following the United win and Cooper in particular was delighted to have that monkey off his back. Real Madrid represented another very tough challenge and this final match in Group D was likely to determine who finished as winners and runners up in the group. Liverpool went into the match knowing that only a victory could topple Madrid and stop them from progressing as group winner. The game followed a familiar pattern of that in gameweek one as Real took the lead through Belgian international Sebastien Marie before Liverpool pegged them back, this time through Celsinho. Unfortunately the game wouldn't end in a draw this time out and a late goal from Nuno Conceicao was enough for the home side to snatch all three points. As a result Madrid topped the group on sixteen points ahead of Cooper's Liverpool on eleven.

December closed out with a flurry of Premier League fixtures over the congested festive period. It started with a draw against Bournemouth (1-1) before wins followed against West Ham (4-0) and Norwich (2-0). Leicester then halted the momentum with Liverpool succumbing to yet another draw (1-1) despite the early promise of an early opening goal from Penalba in the third minute. The month culminated in a match against current Premier League and Champions League champions Manchester City. Cooper had a slightly better record against the Citizens and the recent result against the other Manchester club gave him hope that his side were now capable of competing consistently with the league heavyweights. The Liverpool fans were given a late Christmas present by the players as they played out of their skins on the way to a statement victory (5-0). City hadn't been as impressive during the 2040/41 season as they had been in the previous two campaigns, but to beat them so convincingly was still unexpected. Ahmet Yilmaz was the standout performer on the day scoring a memorable hat-trick alongside goals from Menga and Penalba. A miserable day for City was complete when former Liverpool defender Tomas Sliny was sent off in the second half on his return to his old stomping ground.

It was now onto January, the opening of the winter transfer window and the New Years Day trip to a chilly Stadium of Light. Sunderland were back in the top division following a four year stint in the Championship and looking likely to be heading straight back down this season. Liverpool arrived and completed a professional job with goals from Penalba and Alanzinho enough for the win (2-0). The win up north signalled the halfway point of the season and Liverpool had won twelve, drawn six and lost just one of those nineteen matches. Manchester United were in the driving seat, but Manchester City had looked off the pace and Liverpool had taken advantage to move up to second place with a view to taking on the leaders in the second half of the campaign.

Back to back one goal wins got the second half underway as both Brighton (1-0) and Chelsea (1-0) were dispatched before there was a goal fest against Arsenal at the Emirates. Liverpool travelled to North London looking to keep their winning run going and they were on the right end of an emphatic score line (5-2) with Yilmaz continuing his fine form in front of goal and adding two more to his tally.

Winning Premier League games was the main objective, but Cooper would love a run in the FA Cup, a historic tournament he hoped to win sooner rather than later. His record throughout his career in domestic cups wasn't great and that theme continued in this season's third round tie away to Hull. A rotated Liverpool side should still have had enough about them to see off their Championship opposition, but it wasn't to be and a solitary goal from the home side was enough to grab the win and secure them safe passage into the fourth round. Elimination from the FA Cup left Liverpool with just the Champions League and the Premier League to compete for. Realistically Cooper knew he was unlikely to make back to back European finals so it was vital that they continued to pick up points in the league and apply pressure to Manchester United.

A win at home to Swansea duly followed (2-1) with goals from Menga and Yilmaz again. The Swansea match was the last game before the winter transfer window closed and signalled the end to Coopers transfer dealings for the current season. A number of younger players had arrived at the club with Portugal and South America continuing to provide the majority of Cooper's signings. The two main deals saw promising goalkeeper Edgardo Reynoso sign from San Lorenzo for £5.5m and central defender Hernan Sanchez from Gimnasia for an initial £2.5m. Cooper had agreed a deal which could rise to £6.5m for Sanchez after the young defender impressed in the pre-season friendly between the two clubs. Scouts had tracked the lad ever since and he had done enough to convince them of his potential and secure a permanent move to England.

Cooper once again used the winter window to cash in on some of the fringe players who were unlikely to break into the first team picture moving forward. Goalkeeper Andres Costa left for Blackburn (£4.8m) and fellow shot stopper Matteo Neri joined Newcastle (£1.5m). Frank Cheyne departed for Germany and Hertha (£14m) and club veteran Ashley Fletcher was allowed to leave for £7m as he joined Ajax in search of first team action having fallen down the pecking order in recent months. All in all, with permanent sales and the loans that included substantial fees Cooper raked in an impressive £149m for the club over the two windows, not bad considering he spent just £55m on reinforcements.

January madness over for another year it was back to matters on the pitch and February got underway in the worst possible manner as the QPR hoodoo returned courtesy of former Liverpool man Ivo Vukovic who scored three of Rangers' four goals on their way to victory (4-1). The team turned it around on the gaffers' birthday with a much improved performance for a comfortable win at home to Watford (4-0). The high point of the Watford game was a goal and a return to action for Honduran winger Lesther Cordova who had been out for five months with a broken leg he sustained during pre-season training in an unfortunate collision with a teammate.

Liverpool then managed to put a run of form together that saw them win four games on the bounce keeping four clean sheets in the process. It was always pleasing to shut the opponents out and Cooper didn't think Liverpool had done it enough under his management. Following on from the Watford win Liverpool beat Burnley (1-0), Crystal Palace (4-0) and Red Bull Leipzig (1-0) at Anfield in the first leg of the Champions League first knockout round. RBL were a good side who had been challenging for Bundesliga titles in recent years, winning it back in 2036/37 and the 1-0 win was not a bad result, although Cooper felt his side would need to score in Germany to really secure their quarter final spot.

In between RBL fixtures Liverpool contested three Premier League games, including the Merseyside derby at Anfield. A win at Stoke followed (3-1) with a goal for Russian midfielder Evgeny Orlov who had returned to the club following a successful loan spell at Betis for the first half of the season. A devastating defeat followed as Liverpool conspired to throw away the lead to hand bragging rights to Everton following their surprise win (2-1). The next game was an action packed visit to St. Mary's Stadium as both clubs had a man sent off and two goals were scored in favour of Liverpool. Miguel Ribeiro was dismissed against his former club for the hosts before Alanzinho saw red for a second yellow in the second half.

It was time for the squad to travel to Germany and take on Red Bull Leipzig at their RBL Stadium which had been built in 2025. The one goal lead was a precarious one and Cooper knew his side would need to get amongst the goals if they were to win the tie. Sitting back to defend a one goal lead would be suicide in this competition. Liverpool never got going and mustered just two shots on target in the ninety minutes of play. Leipzig were the much better side, but even they weren't particularly effective in front of goal managing to hit the target just four times. Unfortunately for Liverpool and Derek Cooper two of those four beat Felipe Renan between the sticks and eliminated Liverpool 2-1 on aggregate. Cooper knew his side had needed to score and failure to do so left them with just eight games left of their 2040/41 season and ensured there would be no return to a European final.

Eight Premier League games left, starting with Aston Villa before a trip to Old Trafford. Visiting Manchester United so soon after Champions League elimination wasn't the ideal time, but Liverpool did have the confidence that the 4-0 humbling of their hosts earlier in the season offered them. Liverpool hoped for a confidence boosting win against The Villains, but an early goal for their opponents meant Evandro's strike was only enough for a point (1-1). It certainly wasn't the best result given that they were chasing down their next opponents and made completing an unlikely double over Manchester United as their only real chance of staying in the title race.

Luis Espinoza opened the scoring at Old Trafford with just four minutes on the clock and Derek Cooper hoped his side could press home their early advantage and dominate as they had back in December. United levelled mid way through the first half through Abdul Youssouf, but undeterred by the home sides reply Liverpool continued to play their game and were rewarded five minutes later when Ahmet Yilmaz put them back in front at 2-1. In a game that was quickly becoming stretched Liverpool once again failed to defend their lead as Alessandro Rossi and then Ronnie Walker found the back of the net in quick succession to send United in at the break winning 3-2. Liverpool were still very much in the game and they toiled throughout the second half, but further United goals from Walker and a Liverpool own goal killed the game off and effectively ended Cooper's title hopes. Whilst catching United was still mathematically possible they had been handed the advantage, an advantage they were unlikely to surrender given the quality of players available to their manager. All Cooper could do now was keep winning games and hope that it would be enough to capitalise on any Manchester United mistake. If Cooper failed to win their remaining games there was an outside chance they would be caught by City, but it was almost certain that Liverpool would improve on consecutive third place finishes and make it into the top two.

Liverpool won their next three fixtures, beating Bournemouth (3-1), West Ham (2-1) and Norwich (4-1). Egveny Orlov was staking a claim for a starting spot and the now twenty-two year old scored two in the match against Bournemouth. Following the Norwich match Liverpool travelled to Manchester City once again hoping to grab all three points. The confidence Cooper had gained from beating both clubs comfortably earlier in the season had been eroded by the recent defeat by United and he took on Manchester City feeling less than certain of getting a result. Tomas Sliny completed the unwanted double of being sent off in both league fixtures, home and away, as he was shown a straight red card just before half time. Liverpool should have taken advantage of the extra man, but instead they looked laboured and unable to break through the City resistance. The home side actually took the lead on fifty-three minutes before shutting up shop and hanging on for all three points in the 1-0 win.

Impressive home wins against both Manchester clubs had now been overshadowed by disappointing away losses. Cooper really needed to assert himself in those fixtures if he was to ever get his hands on what was proving to be an elusive Premier League title. Liverpool finished their current campaign with a win at home to Sunderland (5-0) which included a Cordova hat-trick before a poor final performance away to Leicester which ended in defeat (2-1). Cooper was particularly pleased for Cordova who had recovered well from a horrific start to his 2040/41 campaign. A broken leg was never easy to come back from, but he had been in good form towards the end of the season scoring four goals in the final two matches, in fact Cordova managed to grab nine goals in just fifteen appearances. It left Cooper wondering just how good the winger could have been had he not suffered with a bad injury.

When it came to the end of season awards it was practically a clean sweep for Turkish winger Ahmet Yilmaz as he picked up the player of the year award as well as being crowned the clubs top scorer with eighteen goals. His average rating of 7.56 over thirty-six appearances was only bettered by Lesther Cordova at 7.58 for his fifteen game cameo. Had the latter been fit for the duration of the campaign there was every chance it would have been his name on the player of the year trophy. Brazilian central defender Assis had a breakout season for the club with thirty appearances, two goals and an average rating of 7.53. Other standout performers included Mexican midfielder Luis Espinoza (7.47), French winger Jean Menga (7.47), French defensive midfielder Gregory Buisson (7.36) and Argentinean central defender Juan Jose Sosa (7.35).

Once again the goals had been shared throughout the side with no one player head and shoulders above the rest. It had been a real team effort with goals coming from all over the park. Ahmet Yilmaz top scored with eighteen but there was a fifteen goal haul for Penalba, twelve for Espinoza and nine each for Celsinho and Cordova. Liverpool had scored seventy-nine goals in the Premier League season of 2039/40 and they had managed seven more this time out with a 2040/41 total of eighty-six which was considered progress by Derek Cooper.

Liverpool finished the season in second place behind champions Manchester United. United won the league with a points total of eighty-eight, six points ahead of Liverpool in second and sixteen points ahead of Manchester City in third who had suffered a dramatic drop in form having won the last two Premier League titles. Stoke and Leicester were the surprise packages of the season as they finished in fourth and fifth respectively although they were well off the pace with sixty-four and fifty-eight points. Elsewhere Chelsea finished down in ninth, Arsenal in seventh behind Everton in sixth.

It had been a disappointing season away from the Premier League as Derek failed to add any trophy to the clubs collection. The Champions League was eventually won by AS Saint-Etienne who beat defending champions Manchester City in the final to win their second title in three years. The FA Cup was won by Chelsea who beat Brighton in the Wembley showpiece whilst the EFL Cup was claimed by Merseyside's other team, Everton, as they beat Manchester United in the final.

Derek and Liverpool were getting closer, but he knew that more was needed from both himself and his players if they were to take that final step and win some silverware together. Cooper had persisted with his strikerless philosophy since arriving in England and he had questioned the system a couple of times previously, but with the 2040/41 season behind him he began to think about reverting back to playing with a recognised striker. There was a strong spine developing in the side with the emergence of both Assis and Juan Jose Sosa in defence, Alanzinho and Evgeny Orlov in midfield, but there was no out and out goal scorer. There were players at the club who were more than capable of playing through the middle. Penalba, Cordova, Durval and Mboup were all arguably better suited to playing as a striker but up until now had been used either out wide or as the attacking midfielder operating as the centrepiece of the attacking three.

There was no obvious striker available to Liverpool as Cooper began to canvass potential summer signings for the club. He would prefer to promote from within his current crop before going out and spending a huge fee on bringing a new face to Liverpool. He was however looking at a number of potential targets that he felt would once again add further depth to the options available to him. Most were up and coming young players beginning to make their mark with their current clubs and some were relative unknowns that Cooper's extensive recruitment programme had unearthed from across the world.

Every player in Derek Cooper's squad had their price and should a club meet those demands he would reluctantly allow that player to leave Liverpool for pastures new. Over the summer of 2041 there was intense interest in a number of Derek's first team regulars. Many he managed to hold on to, the majority were on very long deals and Cooper was able to convince them to stay with the club if they voiced any interest in leaving the club. There were however, two very big deals agreed at the very beginning of pre-season. Cash rich club AS Saint-Etienne came in and paid £80m for Gustavo Penalba who expressed his desire to be allowed to speak to the French club that had recently bought their way to two European Cups. Derek accepeted the offer knowing that he had other striking options available to him and realising he was unlikely to get such an offer again. The next big offer came in from Germany and Bundesliga royalty Bayern Munich who were willing to part with £70m to get their hands on Belgian defensive midfielder Thibo Parmentier. Cooper was a little happier to accept this deal given that Parmentier had largely been kept out of the side by Gregory Buisson who was a younger and more effective option in the Regista role. Cooper had paid £37.5m for Parmentier and just £8.25m for Penalba so to sell the pair for a combined £150m was incredible business for the club and showed Coopers transfer model was in good working order.

There were a number of less emphatic departures from the club during July with Armin Elsebrock (Nottingham Forrest, £5m), Ewerton Bouvie (Valencia, £9m), Tiago Miranda (Valencia, £15m), Mohamed Yao (Wolfsburg, £22.5m) Antonio Stillinovic (Stoke, £15m) and Samet Gezer (Borussia Monchengladbach, £13m) all leaving the club for pastures new with each player leaving for more money than Derek Cooper paid for them. Yao had cost just £2.3m from Real Madrid and Tiago Miranda £350k from Portuguese club Braga.

As the players returned from summer holidays and began to put in the hours on the training pitch in preparation for the beginning of the season there were a number of new faces arriving at the club. Twenty-one year old attacking midfielder Robert Torres arrived from Real Madrid with Cooper unable to turn the opportunity to sign his former player down at just £2.9m. Belgian goalkeeper Mohamed Nasrollahjoined from Anderlecht in an incentive heavy deal which would see an initial outlay of £4m potentially rise to around £13.75m. Cooper had been following the young stopper for a while and had been consistently priced out of a deal so he was delighted to finally acquire his signature on a long term contract. Cooper doubled down on young goalkeepers in the window as another player he had been trailing became available. Cooper paid Montpellier £8.5m for their nineteen year old shot stopper Frederic Petit.

More Belgians arrived as Guy Nsangou (Eupen, £4.5m rising to £9.5m) and Lucas Chevalier (AA Gent, £21.5m) also made the trip across the North Sea to link up with Cooper and his Liverpool side. Chevalier in particular was an exciting prospect and Liverpool fans had every reason to be excited by the eighteen year olds arrival. He was already a decent central midfielder with the potential to become one of the best players at the club having already played twenty-five times for AA Gent's first team last season.

There was a nice reunion for Derek Cooper and one of his former scouts as Kangana Ndiwa once again joined Cooper's backroom staff. They had first worked together over twenty years ago when Ndiwa done some part-time scouting for Kirkley and Pakefield. Even then Derek knew he could trust his scouts' judgement and they linked up once more at Juventus. Ndiwa had been employed in Turin ever since and with Cooper expanding his recruitment team again in the summer it was time for the former Congolese international to end his thirteen year stint in Turin and return to England once more.

The summer of 2041 also saw a huge landmark moment for Liverpool Football Club as final plans were agreed and signed off for the club to leave Anfield and move into a new stadium. To compete with the likes of Manchester City and Manchester United Liverpool needed to maximise income at every possible opportunity and the limited ability to expand Anfield had begun to hold the club back. Cooper had asked the board for a new stadium a couple of times during his tenure, but the finances simply weren't in place for the club to commit to such a large investment. Thanks to Coopers transfer model and the large influx of cash generated from player sales during his time at the club the board had decided to green light the build and all being well Liverpool would be in their new home come the end of June 2043. The board had also announced that Liverpool's new stadium would hold a capacity of 72,592 and it would be named Dalglish Park in honour of club icon Sir Kenny Dalglish.

Liverpool embarked on a brief mini tour of America to kick off their pre-season with victories against New York Cosmos (2-1) and New York Red Bulls (3-0). Similarly to with the Asian Market, Cooper hoped to raise the clubs presence in the United States and showpiece games like these would help in that process. Having returned from their trip stateside the club were straight into the remaining friendly matches which included games both home and away against sides such as Juventus, Roma, Real Madrid and AC Milan. Cooper consciously picked tougher opposition with a European pedigree in an attempt to get his squad up to speed with the new tactical set up as soon as possible. The only blot on Liverpool's pre-season fixtures was a 2-2 draw with Real Madrid, every other match resulted in a win for Derek Coopers side and whilst there may have been no points up for grabs he hoped to garner some positive momentum into the opening Premier League fixtures against Hull and Aston Villa.

Before those Premier League openers Cooper once again weaved his transfer magic offloading Danny Barker to Watford for £6m, Robin Birner to Foirentina for £8m, Anderson Miguel to Marseille for £28.5m and twenty-seven year old English defender Frank Seddon to Real Madrid for a whopping £48m. Seddon had been displaced by Rodriguez, Sosa and Assis and was unlikely to win his place back anytime soon so the money put up by Madrid was welcomed by both manager and player. With the latest flurry of outgoings Cooper had seen the transfer income for 2041 hit the £323m mark which was a huge sum of money that would further enhance the clubs financial status.

Liverpool wanted to win a trophy this season, primarily the Premier League, but they would settle for any sort of competition win. Starting the season well was of paramount importance, especially given that the Manchester clubs performed at such a consistently high level between them. In fact the Premier League title had gone to one side of Manchester for twelve of the last thirteen years with United winning four to the eight of City. Hull were up first and goals from Ahmet Yilmaz and Jean Menga secured a routine win (2-0) to get the season underway. Durval started through the middle for Liverpool in the returning striker role and was largely underwhelming, but it was early days and Cooper was determined to give all options a fair shot.

Another win followed against Aston Villa (2-0) as Liverpool won by the same score line keeping a second consecutive clean sheet. This time the goals came courtesy of Metodi Totev and Swedish striker Filip Nilsson who had waited since his arrival in 2038/39 to make his debut for the club. He replaced the lacklustre Durval up top and made the most of his opportunity scoring five minutes after his arrival on the hour mark. Next came the first meeting of Liverpool and Queens Park Rangers who had become kryptonite to Cooper's side. It was no different this time out and Ivo Vukovic once again came back to haunt his former manager scoring the second in a 2-1 win for QPR.

Manchester City at home was the final game of August for Liverpool and the defeat to QPR placed added importance as Cooper didn't feel his side could afford to lose any more ground to a title rival so early in the season. Obviously there was still a very long way to go, but losing to Manchester City at this stage could well crush the sides confidence and leave them unable to recover from the blow. City's impressive Brazilian striker Pedrinho opened the scoring in the thirty-third minute and Derek feared a collapse could be on the cards, but his team fought back superbly and were rewarded with parity when Jean Menga found the back of the net in the seventy-third minute. The game ended 1-1 and in truth it was a fair result with neither side having done enough to take all three points. Cooper felt that by not losing the match they had gotten over a very early hurdle that could have stopped Liverpool in their tracks before a title challenge had begun.

With the transfer window closing and having brought a decent amount of money into the clubs kitty Derek Cooper splashed out on some new blood. The recruitment team had highlighted an impressive Belgian right back who was playing for Standard over in his homeland and Derek took the plunge, investing an initial £12.5m in the eighteen year old. Malory Thys had only made a handful of appearances for the club, but had surprisingly been on loan at Wolfsburg in the Bundesliga for a short spell. The way the deal had been structured meant that Thys could end up costing the club £24.5m, but it was a fee Cooper was confident spending on the young man. Denny Napolitano also joined the club in a similar deal from Italian side Torino. Napolitano was a central midfielder that had spent the previous season out on loan at Entella where he made thirty-six senior appearances. Liverpool paid £12m up front with a further £8m to be paid if certain targets were met and once again Cooper felt it was a reasonable price for the eighteen year old.

Liverpool returned to action in mid September following an international break by visiting Stamford Bridge to take on Chelsea. Another strike for Jean Menga was only enough for a point, although this time Liverpool had taken the lead in the match rather than coming from behind in their second consecutive 1-1 draw. It had been a poor start to the Premier League for Liverpool and Derek Cooper was less than happy with two wins, two draws and one loss. He was almost thankful for the distraction of a return to Champions League action.

Liverpool had been drawn in Group E this time alongside Zenit, PSG and Swiss champions Basel and they kicked off their campaign by travelleing to Russian side Zenit. Amadou Mboup came in to play the striker role to replace the disappointing Durval and the ineffective Totev and he looked to have blown his chance as the side were heading for defeat at 2-0 down with just under an hour played. It took until the hour mark and a goal for the Italian striker to jumpstart a very poor performance. Mboup scored his first goal on sixty minutes and two more followed in the seventy-first and the seventy-second minutes to complete his hat-trick and the Liverpool comeback. Central defender Assis then added a fourth for good measure wrapping up the win (4-2) and getting the Champions League campaign off to the best possible start.

The goals continued to flow on the sides return to England and domestic action. Big wins against Nottingham Forrest (4-0) in the Premier League and Huddersfield (5-0) in the EFL Cup third round helped the sides' confidence to grow moving towards the end of September. Sadly there was another return to the Jean Menga 1-1 draws as he once again scored the only goal in a Premier League stalemate, this time against Swansea at the Liberty Stadium. Liverpool had already dropped nine points from their opening seven fixtures which hardly constituted title winning form. Derek Cooper was frustrated and he told his team as much in a team meeting informing them that he knew they were capable of much more than they had been showing.

Another tough game was around the corner, but it was a test Liverpool passed with flying colours. PSG came to Anfield looking to state their intentions to top Group E, but they were sent packing by the home side with their tail well and truly between their legs. Durval scored his second and third goals of the season whilst Espinoza, Yilmaz and Buisson also got in on the act completing the impressive win (5-2). Former Juventus players Bill Sarachan and Prince Nsiala-Ekunde played for Paris Saint-Germain with Sarachan now their club captain following his £47.5m move to the club in 2036/37.

Statement win in Europe complete Liverpool then worked hard to carry on their unbeaten run, adding a further five games to take it to twelve games without losing. A win at Arsenal (3-1) came four days after the PSG result and further wins followed against Southampton (1-0) and Basel (1-0). There was then another poor draw at home to Leicester, although this time there would be no goal for Jean Menga and the game would end in a very dull 0-0. The twelfth game was the EFL fourth round tie away to Ipswich and Liverpool were lucky to remain unbeaten as Nilsson scored a ninety-first minute equaliser in time added on to take the match to extra time and penalties. All five Liverpool takers held their nerve and secured a 5-4 penalty win for Derek Cooper to take Liverpool into a quarter final tie with Manchester City.

The twelve games unbeaten then ended courtesy of Morten Rasmussen and his Crystal Palace side. A lone goal from French attacking midfielder Sebastien Clerc was enough to secure the Eagles an unlikely win (1-0) in early November. Once again both Manchester clubs were the early pace setters, but Liverpool were still clinging onto their coattails and would be looking to reel them in over the coming weeks. A confidence boosting win in gameweek four of the Champions League against Basel (4-1) helped the side when they returned to domestic action as they won against Bournemouth (2-0) and smashed Everton in the Merseyside derby (5-1) with a derby day hat-trick for Ahmet Yilmaz to write himself into the clubs folklore and make him a hit with the fans no matter what.

Durval had begun to find the back of the net a bit more often and he followed up his two goals in the Bournemouth win with another against Everton and whilst he didn't find the back of the net in a disappointing draw with Zenit at Anfield (1-1), he did find the back of the net a further two times in the next match, a 4-1 victory at home to Watford. Liverpool were already 4-1 up when frustration got the better of Arthur Lambert and he was sent off to really hamper any hopes the Hornets had of getting themselves back into the game.

The 3rd of December saw Cooper take his side to The Gabriel Barbosa Arena for their EFL Cup quarter final tie against Manchester City. Derek took the opportunity to rotate his side and rest several key players. There were starts for Petit in goal, Leoutsakos at left back, Hrvoje Miletic as the defensive midfielder and Robert Torres in midfield. The EFL Cup gave managers the perfect platform for fringe players to get some game time and Manchester City had the same idea choosing to rest some of their more established players. Menga gave Liverpool the lead early on before Ian Spooner equalised just before half time and in truth that was the only action of note in what was a very poor ninety minutes. Extra time loomed and the game suddenly came alive with a flurry of goals that saw Menga complete a hat-trick and somehow end up on the losing side. City raced into a 3-1 lead before Menga's two extra time goals pulled Liverpool level and looked to have sent the game to a penalty shootout, but just as Cooper was beginning to select his penalty takers Uruguayan midfielder Matias Correa popped up in added time to nick a 4-3 win for City.

Luckily it was back to winning ways in the Premier League fixture at London Stadium against West Ham (2-1) and although not convincing in victory Cooper was pleased with the three points nonetheless. The final Group E game followed as Liverpool travelled to Paris in gameweek six. The Reds were already confirmed to top the group irrespective of the result at PSG's De Bruyne Stadium, but they were at risk of being caught should they fail to win and Zenit manage to win in Switzerland against Basel. As it turned out the various permutations were irrelevant and both Liverpool and PSG would progress from the group into the knockout stages after a 2-1 win for Paris Saint-Germain with former Liverpool striker and £95m man Andre Santos scoring the winner against his former club.

Champions League was now done and dusted until the knockout rounds resumed in February so it was back to domestic action and the games were virtually non-stop as they entered the notorious festive period. Three days after the PSG defeat there was a very late Tim Keen goal to nick a win at home to Spurs (1-0) who had returned to the top flight having won the 2040/41 Championship season. Manchester United were then the next visitors to Anfield and it was a tempestuous affair which saw both sides reduced to ten men. Carl Bishop saw red for Liverpool before Russian full back Kirill Mogulkin was dismissed for the visitors. Abdul Yousouff scored his now customary goal against his former manager to put United ahead, but Liverpool fought back to level the match through Alanzinho immediately after half time. The red cards disrupted the second half and neither side managed to find a winner meaning Liverpool recorded their fourth 1-1 draw of the Premier League season. Cooper would ideally be taking points off his title rivals at home, but he could accept the draws he had managed against the Manchester clubs this season as it was better than getting beaten.

Liverpool were now approaching the halfway point of the 2041/42 season and to celebrate they completed a league double over Hull with another victory (2-0) before they recorded the clubs biggest ever Premier League victory at home to Stoke City (7-0). There were four goals from Mboup as well as strikes from Cordova, Assis and Orlov. The 7-0 win came on Boxing Day and was the perfect gift for the Liverpool fans that turned out on a bitterly cold afternoon to support their team. However their joy was short-lived and a late Alanzinho equaliser away to Brighton was all for nothing when in the final minute of normal time the home side nicked a win (2-1) in the next fixture.

Liverpool had now played twenty of their thirty-eight Premier League matches winning twelve, drawing five and losing three which Cooper doubted would be enough to win the title if they repeated those numbers in the second half of the season. In order to have a real shot at the title Liverpool needed to consistently be putting runs of wins together, including the matches against the Manchester clubs.

Liverpool were still in both the FA Cup and the Champions league and Cooper felt that his side had a decent chance in either competition. They had made the Champions League final not long ago and a repeat wasn't out of the question. Liverpool had been drawn against Juventus in the first knockout round which was a tie Cooper was looking forward to. During his time in England so far Cooper had failed to make his mark on the FA Cup, he had never made the final, just the one semi final, and that was something that he really wanted to put right. A team such as Liverpool should be regularly competing for the premier domestic cup in England.

Liverpool's next Premier League encounter was against Aston Villa at Villa Park on New Years Day and it was the late, late show for Derek Cooper as he was made to wait until the eighty-sixth and ninety-first minutes for his sides' goals. Evgeny Orolov continued his impressive rise to prominence with the first goal and Swedish striker Filip Nilsson added to his tally in injury time. The Villa game coincided with the opening of the January transfer window and a number of new player arrived as Cooper continued to reinvest the £323m made in player sales during the summer.

Most of the deals Cooper now agreed with potential selling clubs were for a reduced initial fee, but were heavily loaded with add ons and future incentives. He avoided sell on clauses where possible and instead added fees for certain amounts of club and international appearances knowing that some players would be sold on for a profit before hitting those targets. Seventeen year old midfielder Mohamed Fofana signed from AS Monaco for £3m potentially rising to £11.25m whilst his club mate and defensive midfielder Marco Binetti signed for £3.2m up front and a possible £10.5m with add ons. The biggest deal was agreed for Italian central midfielder Leanardo Grieco who Roma were willing to let go for £7m now and a further £16m in incentivised add ons. At seventeen Grieco still had plenty of room to develop and Cooper had no doubt he could be a potential first team player in the coming years.

It was time to get the FA Cup campaign underway for Liverpool and they had been drawn away to long time Championship club Derby who had recently hired former Newcastle defender Chancel Mbemba as their new manager. Derby had in fact spent two seasons in League One between 2024 and 2026, but since then had recovered to be a solid mid table club in the second tier of English football. Liverpool were coming off the back of a gruelling run of fixtures and Cooper took the decision to rotate his squad and give some of the less regular players some game time. Petit started in goal with Belgian right back Malory Thys getting a run out alongside Evandro, Leoutsakos and Robert Torres who were all in need of some minutes.

The rotation hampered the fluency of Liverpools performance and held them back in terms of securing a positive result. They were much the better team, but lacked the killer instinct that comes with familiar faces playing together. Liverpool managed to deny the home side a single shot on target, which was nice, but it wasn't going to win the game when they failed to find the back of the net themselves. As such the game petered out to a very uninteresting 0-0 that would not feature very highly on the running order of the evenings highlights show.

Liverpool would get another shot at Derby in a week's time back at Anfield, but before then they faced a QPR team who had been consistently taking points off Derek Cooper's sides for the last couple of seasons. Liverpool restored the more regular starters to the side and goals from Filip Nilsson and Lesther Cordova wrapped up what was usually a trick fixture with minimal fuss (2-0). Cooper now had to decide whether he was confident enough to rotate his side once more with home advantage now in their favour, or whether it was better to stick with the regulars and risk them in two games in a short space of time.

Cooper chose to rotate, too many players were close to the dreaded "red zone" already and he didn't want to risk injuries to key players with so much still to play for. Petit, Thys, Miletic, Evandro and co should have more than enough to see off a poor Derby side. Recent January signing Leonardo Grieco was also handed his debut and given a chance to impress the Anfield faithful for the first time. Liverpool were much more dominant than they had been at Pride Park and it quickly became a question of when and not if Liverpool would score.

Derby barely made it out of their own half as the game quickly became attack versus defence for large periods. It looked like the game would be heading into the break all square, but Derby handed their hosts a golden opportunity to take the lead giving away a penalty in stoppage time at the end of the first forty-five. With no regular taker on the pitch Evandro stepped up confident he could tuck the penalty away, but the confidence proved to be misplaced as the Brazilian missed the spot kick. The half time whistle was blown immediately and Cooper was given the chance to give his side the kick up the bum he felt they needed. The talking to worked and Amadoub Mboup had the ball in the back of the Derby net less than a minute after the restart to give Liverpool the lead. Egveny Orlov then picked up an injury that was likely to keep him out of action for around a month which was frustrating for both the player and the manager. Back on the pitch Liverpool were in control without really making it out of second gear and a 1-0 win was confirmed by the referees whistle to signal full time. Derby had improved on their home showing as they managed to get one shot on target this time out, but in truth they were never really in the game and Liverpool were comfortably through to the fourth round, albeit having had to play an inconvenient replay.

The goal and performance of Mboup meant he kept his place in the side for the trip to face Manchester City four days later. Orlov missed out through the sprained ankle he picked up and there were recalls for Espinoza, Celsinho and Renan in goal amongst others. It was a role reversal for the Manchester clubs this season and whereas City had been slightly off the pace last season they were setting the pace for this campaign. Liverpool had drawn and lost to City already this season so Derek was desperate to complete the set and inflict defeat on them infront of their own fans. It was a fairly even game in the first half until Liverpool asserted themselves just before half time to score two goals and hand them the advantage going into the break. Amadou Mboup repaid Cooper's faith with a forty-second minute goal which was swiftly followed by Cordova and a goal in the forty-fourth minute. Manchester City tried to mount a comeback in the second half, but they weren't able to break through the Liverpool backline of Renan, Rulasic, Kitoko, Assis and Sosa. It remained 2-0 for the duration of the second half and Liverpool claimed a victory that cut City's lead at the top of the Premier League.

The win at Manchester City kick-started a run of form that saw Liverpool win their next five Premier League matches as well as progress in the FA Cup, although that required another replay following another disappointing draw on their first attempt. The League wins came at home to Chelsea (4-0), away to Nottingham Forrest (4-1), at home to Swansea (3-0), away to Arsenal (2-0) and at home to Southampton (3-1). The FA Cup fourth round draw with Tottenham (2-2) came between the wins against Swansea and Arsenal and Cooper once again chose to rotate, although less so than he had in the previous round. Even with a more established starting eleven Liverpool required a replay to progress and that win came at Anfield (4-1) before the League win against Southampton.

That run of six wins and one draw took Liverpool past the end of the January transfer window, beyond the managers fifty-fourth birthday and up to the first leg of the Champions League first knockout round match against Juventus. There had been no player's leave the club on permanent deals in January as Cooper fended off any interest in the hopes of keeping his talented squad together. There were some players leaving on loans, most notably midfielder Marlon Estevao as he signed for Betis with them paying £250k per month to take him on and forward Isidore Noel who joined Club Brugge for £100k per month. The early January arrivals of Fofana, Binetti and Grieco were joined later in the month by striker Saul Munoz from Valencia for a flat £2.4m fee, Scottish left back John McLeod from Hearts for a fee which could reach £3.5m and Moroccan goalkeeper Omar Aarab from Rennes in France for £2.6m which could rise to £9m given the add ons inserted into the deal. Cooper was happy with the window and felt that each player would go on to either play for the club or make them a profit once they had developed.

Liverpool had been drawn away for the first leg of the Champions League tie with Juventus. Derek preferred playing away from home for the first leg and in that regard he was happy. Being back in Turin and the Juventus Stadium always brought back fond memories and this time was no different, he loved the city and the clubs fans, but there would be no favours on either side for this match. There was now only a smattering of familiar faces in a Juve squad that included Henk Theuns, Jose Cristo, Tony Watson and Angelino Kayala. Jose Cristo had actually been sold to Liverpool from Juventus before finding his way back to The Old Lady via Dortmund and West Ham. Current Juventus manager Manuel Cordeiro had chosen a very different recruitment path to that of Derek Cooper and Liverpool by signing older players that had benefitted from playing experience elsewhere. Unfortunately for Liverpool that experience showed when it came to the football and away goals from Mboup and Buisson were not enough to stop a Juventus side that hit top gear and were clinical in front of goal. Henk Theuns once again turned it on against his former boss scoring two goals alongside another Derek Cooper signing during his time at the club, Sandro Ribiero, who went one better than Theuns and grabbed a hat-trick. Ribiero had been signed by Cooper for just £100k from Portuguese club Braga back in the summer of 2031. His rise to prominence had seen him go out on loan to clubs that included Maritimo, Cesena, Valencia and Chievo amongst others before he stamped his mark with his parent club. At twenty-eight Ribiero is now worth north of £20m, is a full international for Portugal and has just scored a Champions League hat-trick in a 5-2 win against Derek Cooper and his Liverpool side.

Derek and Liverpool returned to domestic action with a league and FA Cup double header against Leicester City still cursing the potency of former strikers over in Italy. A win away to Leicester in the Premier League (1-0) courtesy of another Gregory Buisson strike softened the blow, but the following draw (0-0) in the FA Cup was another source of irritation. The draw of course meant another fixture taking the total of extra games in the competition to three in as many rounds. Cooper had once again played a slightly rotated team, but not through choice this time as his squad was being tested by competing on multiple fronts. The excellent run of Premier League form in particular had meant that there was now a real chance of competing with Manchester City for the title, but they needed to maintain their current form, a tough ask considering they had Champions League and FA Cup survival to contend with.

Another draw followed the FA Cup result with Leicester and it came in the form of a 0-0 at home to Crystal Palace. Liverpool were the better side mustering six shots on target to the one Palace registered, but it wasn't to be and the away side held firm for the duration. Liverpool once again fielded a rotated side in the FA Cup against Leicester with Cooper knowing it was a risk he had to take. The games had really mounted up, his squad was being stretched and the good form of December through to early February had started to turn leaving them winless in three of their last four fixtures. Unfortunately the Leicester replay would be a bridge too far for the likes of Petit, Bishop and Durval who were brought into the starting line up at the King Power Stadium, falling behind and never recovering to lose by two goals to one. Liverpool had once again been eliminated from the FA Cup well short of the clubs expectations whilst Cooper's domestic cup failings continued.

The FA Cup defeat then had a knock on effect that Cooper had hoped to avoid as Liverpool suffered defeat in their next Premier League fixture against an average Bournemouth side (1-0). That meant Liverpool had dropped four crucial points in their last two league games, something they could ill afford to do given that Man City were still in and around them at the top of the table. It was also less than ideal preparation for the second leg of the Champions League tie with Juventus which was now the clubs next fixture. Since the 5-2 first leg defeat in Turin Liverpool had embarked on their worst form of the season playing five, winning one, drawing two and losing two. Liverpool had home advantage and would need to make the most of the Anfield crowd as they had done two years ago against Real Madrid, another of Cooper's former clubs, in the semi final that year. Three goals without reply would see Liverpool through and Cooper knew it wasn't impossible, but he also knew it would be incredibly tough for his side to do. He applied a similar tactic as he had done two years ago telling his side to go out and play with no pressure, nobody realistically thought they could overturn the three goal deficit so they had nothing to lose in that respect.

The game started well for Liverpool, they looked bright and seemed to have put the recent poor form behind them. Amadou Mboup got the comeback underway when he rifled home after just eighteen minutes leaving plenty of time for the side to find the other two goals they needed. Juventus were trying to control possession, but they weren't looking particularly threatening and Ahmet Yilmaz got a second goal for Liverpool on thrity-two minutes as Liverpool looked to go for the jugular. Time was in favour of the home side and they were two thirds of the way through their unlikely comeback. Juventus made it to the break 2-0 down, but winning 5-4 on aggregate and they obviously regrouped coming out as a much more cohesive unit for the second forty-five. They cleverly used fouls to break up the play; committing twenty-two to Liverpool's nine come the end of the ninety minutes. Liverpool were ahead on shots and shots on target too, but the only stat that mattered, goals, remained the same. The two early goals weren't enough and try as they might Liverpool simply couldn't find the third goal they required. Juventus progressed and Cooper wished the club and their fans all the very best for the next round, he hoped they would go on to lift the famous trophy that he had failed to get his hands on during his time with the club.

Liverpool had failed to make it past the first knockout round of the Champions League for the second consecutive season with the club failing to kick on from their final appearance of 2039/40. Elimination against Juventus had also left Cooper with seven Premier League fixtures to try and save their title challenge. The defeat to Bournemouth as well as the draw to Crystal Palace meant they couldn't afford any further slip ups as for the first time under Derek Cooper they were in with a chance of pipping both Manchester clubs to the Premier League title. City were still in the Champions League having come through their first knockout round match against Bayern Munich and whilst that could be a blessing for Cooper it could also go the other way and help them gather the required momentum to put a formidable run of form together at just the right time. Derek Cooper and Liverpool fans around the world hoped it was the former.

The results of Manchester City would mean very little if Liverpool didn't play their part by winning their remaining games. They started with the Merseyside derby, a game that no Liverpool fan liked to drop points in, even more so when it involved a potential title spoiling result. Twice Liverpool were pegged back by an Everton side that were very much in the mood for spoiling any potential party. Goals from Cordova and Mboup gave Liverpool the lead, but they were negated on both occasions to give Everton a share of the points (2-2). As bad as the Everton result was, the following game away to Watford, was worse. 30,000 were inside Vicarage road to witness ex-Liverpool midfielder and academy graduate Jimmy Worrall score in the seventh minute to seal all three points for his new club. Liverpool had been handed an almost immediate way back into the game, but Durval missed the ninth minute penalty to set the tone of a turgid performance in which only the two central defenders got a match rating of over seven.

Cooper could feel the title slipping away from him. Manchester City were in imperious form going into the run in whereas his Liverpool side had choked, winning just one of their last five Premier League games. Cooper was almost resigned to the fact that the bad patch of form was going to end up costing the club come the 18th of May and the end of the season. Manchester City's drop off had come much earlier in the season and they had recovered excellently to chase Liverpool down, piling the pressure on until the younger Liverpool side began to crack.

Thankfully wins against both West Ham (2-1) and Tottenham (2-0) kicked off the final run of games with the West Ham victory coming from a ninety-third minute winner from Malory Thys after The Hammers had scored an equaliser in the eighty-ninth minute to seemingly break Derek Coopers heart. Luckily Thys pulled them out of that particular hole and they recorded back to back wins in the league for the first time since the end of February and beginning of March.

There was now just three games remaining and Cooper knew that three wins would be enough to win him the Premier League title he had been trying, yet so far failing, to add to his list of honours. It wasn't a horrendous run in, but the obvious stumbling block came in their next fixture and a trip to Old Trafford to take on Manchester United, a side Derek had consistently failed to beat. Both City and Liverpool had three games left to play each. Liverpool had Manchester United away, Brighton at home and a final day trip to Stoke. Manchester City had Crystal Palace at home, Bournemouth away and Everton at home with a Champions League semi final second leg to play between Palace and Bournemouth too. Liverpool had played thirty five games and had amassed seventy six points whereas City were one point behind them on seventy-five. It was all to play for and the title was in the hands of Derek Cooper and his young squad.

Liverpool played Manchester United on the Friday evening, the day before City were in action against Crystal Palace. A win could really put the pressure on City, but beating United away was a tall order and something Cooper had never managed as Liverpool manager. Kane Davis put United ahead on twenty-nine minutes, but Cooper's side responded magnificently and a five minute double salvo from Evgeny Orlov meant Liverpool went into the break leading 2-1. Cooper rallied the troops telling them there was more to come, but it failed to have the desired effect and Manchester United grabbed a deserved equaliser through Ronnie Walker just before the hour mark. On the balance of play a draw was absolutely a fair result and it was a hard fought point to Liverpool, but it could also represent the tipping point in the race for the title.

The following day Manchester City kicked off against Crystal Palace as the Liverpool players were put through a recovery session back at Melwood. The game was on in the background and Cooper tried and failed to occupy his mind with other things finding himself checking the score every five minutes. The breakthrough in the match came in the fifty-eighth minute and it came courtesy of a Crystal Palace forward, Richel Friedli, but unfortunately for Liverpool the ex-Real Madrid and Saint-Etienne man had put the ball past his own keeper and had given Manchester City the lead. City held on to their one goal advantage and took themselves to seventy-eight points; one ahead of Liverpool's seventy-seven. Two games remained and it was advantage City.

Liverpool had the advantage of eight days rest before their next Premier League fixture, whereas City faced both PSG and Bournemouth within a week. Liverpool needed to make the most of their extra rest and go into the game against Brighton fully focussed on securing all three points. This time Liverpool and City played at the same time and both managers would have been fully aware of goings on in the other game. Cooper had eyes on the City match, but he was also fully focussed on getting the job done.

Brazilian forward Durval got the game off to the best possible for Liverpool, settling everyone inside Anfield down with his first minute goal. With one goal under the belt Liverpool began to settle into their natural game and it was only a matter of time before more goals came. Over at Bournemouth Stadium the game remained all square until Pedrinho put the visitors ahead in the twenty-eighth minute. Cooper was made aware of the score line, but it changed nothing for him, he still needed to get the win at Anfield. Durval was putting on his best performance in a Liverpool shirt and he followed up his opener with a second goal on thirty-five minutes before completing his hat-trick from the penalty spot a minute before half time. It was effectively game over and Liverpool played out a relatively uninteresting second half to seal three important points. City also held on to their narrow advantage down on the south coast with the solitary goal enough to get the win and fend off Liverpool. The gap was still one point and there was just one game left to play.

Sunday the 18th of May 2042 was the final day of the 2041/42 Premier League season and Liverpool travelled to face Stoke at their Bet365 Stadium, a side they had put seven past in the reverse fixture at Anfield earlier in the campaign. Fans across Liverpool were left in an uncomfortable position as they found themselves cheering on their Merseyside rivals as they played their final game of the season against Manchester City. Stoke proved to be much more resilient on their home patch and Liverpool spent the first forty-five trying and failing to break them down. It was still goalless at Gabriel Barbosa Arena too, so there was still just one point separating the two teams at the top with forty-five minutes of football left to be played.

The game at the Bet365 stadium resumed and Liverpool knew that failure to grab all three points would see the title head to Manchester yet again. Liverpool continued to draw a blank in Stoke whilst the game between Everton and City sprang into life. City took the lead in the fifty-sixth minute, but it was short lived as they conspired to shoot themselves in the foot. First they conceded an Everton equaliser before Spanish winger Mikel Gonzalez was dismissed for a second yellow card in the sixty-eighth minute. There was now twenty minutes left to play and all Liverpool needed was one goal. Provided Everton continued to do them a favour and hold off against the ten men of Manchester City. The clock slowly ticked down and Cooper threw on Mboup, Menga and Torres in a desperate attempt to shake his team into life, the game was drifting away from Liverpool and if anything, Stoke looked the more likely to score in the game. Cooper went all in and pushed everyone forward, changing to all out attack, the game was still level in Manchester and the title was tantalisingly close. Liverpool simply couldn't find the goal they required and with the only action of note in the other game a red card for Everton in the ninety-second minute, it was a massive opportunity missed for the club. They had once put seven past Stoke, but had failed to muster just one when it had really mattered. Manchester City were crowned Premier League champions and Derek Cooper felt totally crushed by the weight of disappointment.

It was a long and despondent journey back to Liverpool for the players and staff, Derek Cooper felt as low as he could remember. When he started out on this journey he could only dream of managing Liverpool and winning a Premier League title and he had been so damn close. Of their thirty-eight games Liverpool won twenty-four, drew nine and lost five, City in contrast had won the same number, drawn ten and lost four. They won the league on eighty-two points and Liverpool were just one point behind on eighty-one, ahead of United in third with seventy-seven points after a disappointing season for them. It had come down to such fine margins and Cooper replayed games the side should have won over in his mind wondering if there was something he could have done differently. In truth he was immensely proud of his players and the club was now beginning to bear the fruits of their transfer policy with a number of players approaching their peak years, they were only going to get better.

Cooper had lost Champions League finals, one at The Bernabeu, home to Real Madrid who he was manager of at the time, but the draw away to Stoke was the most painful result of his career. The fans felt it too, they had been so close to another Premier League title and they had been few and far between for a club the size of Liverpool. There was a small consolation for the Liverpudlians of a red persuasion, and that was the fact that Everton finished bottom of the league and were relegated to the Championship for the third time in recent history.

On the pitch the switch of tactic, back to operating with a striker had seen the club move up to second place, but Derek Cooper felt he was still lacking a real potent front man. The system had improved the side, but the options available to him in Durval, Mboup and Nilsson had been too inconsistent and none of them made it to twenty goals in the season. Mboup top scored with sixteen, Durval managed fourteen and Nilsson grabbed eleven. Their average ratings of 7.08, 7.02 and 7.38 backed up the fact they there was a lot more to come from a player in that position. Nilsson's 7.38 was slightly better than the other two, but only by virtue of having played less games, almost half the others in fact.

Luckily goals still came from the other members of the side and Yilmaz contributed fifteen off the right wing, Menga managed eleven which was over double his tally of the season before and Cordova added nine. Espinoza's goals had dropped off slightly this time out and he failed to hit double figures for the first time since joining the club as he scored seven in thirty-five appearances. Celsinho's output was also down, just four from him in twenty-six games. Both Espinoza and Celsinho had played fewer games this campaign thanks to the emergence of both Evgeny Orlov and Alanzinho. Orlov in particular was making his case to become the main man in the middle of the pitch at just twenty-three. He scored eight goals in thirty eight appearances and achieved an average rating of 7.27, but Cooper felt the sky was the limit for the young Russian and his ability.

Player of the year could have gone to either central defender with both Assis and Juan Jose Sosa shining in their starting roles. Sosa played more often, but Assis was more lethal in front of goal and with an average rating of 7.53 and four goals to his name the Brazilian defender was handed the award as voted for by the fans. At twenty-two and twenty-three years of age the pair still had many years ahead of them and Cooper was sure the best was yet to come as they accumulated the experiences they needed to be considered world class defenders.

Ahmet Yilmaz was another player who was approaching the peak of his powers. He scored fifteen goals and played forty-six times, a figure only beaten by the forty-seven appearances that season of club captain Fresnel Kitoko at left back. Yilmaz was now twenty-four and was considered by many as a world class winger, a description backed up by his thirty-eight Premier League goals in three seasons.

Six foot five monster Fresnel Kitoko had gone from strength to strength since joining the club and his average rating of 7.38 over forty-seven appearances was testament to why Cooper had picked him as the club captain. He was now twenty-four and was another member of the squad who was making it towards his best years. In fact, as Cooper sat back and assessed his squad he quickly realised that all his players had their best years ahead of them. Felipe Renan was considered a veteran of the side at just twenty-six years old. Cordova, Rodriguez, Kitoko and Alanzinho were all twenty-five whilst Yilmaz, Mboup and Durval were twenty-four. Age was no barrier for Cooper and Buisson had been at the club since he was seventeen. He was now twenty-three and was an established member of the starting eleven making that Regista role his own and valued upwards of £30m.

Cooper quickly realised that although the 2041/42 season had ended in disappointment there was still a huge amount for him to be excited about. The club were in a great place financially with money to spend and no pressure to sell, they were on the verge of moving into a new stadium and they had a young and talented squad that were coming into their prime together hungry for success. There was a case for the argument that 2042/43 could be the best season Derek Cooper and Liverpool Football Club would ever have.

Preparation started in earnest with Derek Cooper actively seeking a proven goal scorer to help take his team to the next level. He considered going back in for the Polish striker Rafael Szalek who he was aware of from his time in Madrid. Szalek was about as potent a front man as you were likely to find and had scored twenty plus for the last seven seasons, but AS Saint-Etienne wanted monopoly money for their star man and it was a deal that looked increasingly unlikely to happen. There was another option Cooper was keen to explore and that was the availability of Igor Obradovic.

Cooper had signed him permanently as a young player whilst at Madrid and had taken him on loan during his first season in Liverpool, but a permanent deal had been out of the question at the time and Liverpool moved on to other targets. In the intervening period Obradovic had completed a season long loan at AC Milan before moving to Arsenal for £7m and then onto Red Bull Leipzig for £23.5m. The move to the Emirates hadn't worked out for the Serbian striker although he did manage twelve Premier League goals in just twenty-three appearances. He had fared better in the Bundesliga and had an impressive debut season in Germany with fifteen league goals in twenty-three appearances with an average rating of 7.33. Tentative enquiries made by Liverpool suggested that Leipzig would be open to a deal, but that it would mean Liverpool breaking their transfer record.

Cooper worked hard in the period before the transfer window re-opened to make sure the club had the finances in place to agree some potentially huge transfers for the club. As with previous seasons Liverpool utilised the loan market with monthly fees inserted into the deals to bring in some lucrative revenue. Players such as Rusalic, Tello, Ninco and Candela brought in £300k per month whilst the likes of Ademar, Tas, Agathymo and Napolitano made around £250k each month for the club. Some Liverpool fans were surprised by the number of players Cooper was allowing to leave the club, especially players such as Rusalic who had a number of first team appearances under his belt, but it was all part of Coopers plan for the coming season. He wanted to streamline the squad and add some real quality to complement the existing core players. It was a ruthless way of working, but Liverpool had been so close last time out that the manager felt he needed to do something drastic to drag them over that final hurdle.

Derek had taken the decision to have his squad return to training a week earlier than usual as he felt the extra time with the squad would help them all to bond and be extra prepared come the start of the season on the 9th of August. Liverpool would also be competing in the Community Shield this year as Manchester City completed the league and FA Cup double, meaning the league runners up would play them in the Wembley showpiece. That meant the season starting slightly earlier for Liverpool which was why Cooper had pulled everyone in off their holidays a week earlier.

The first friendly of a packed pre-season schedule against the Under 23's squad was planned for a month before that Community Shield match so it was all go behind the scenes as Cooper and his recruitment team worked on getting various deals done. There had been long and protracted negotiations between Red Bull Leipzig and Liverpool Football Club, but a deal was agreed the day before the transfer window opened and Igor Obradevic was officially unveiled by Derek Cooper on the 1st of July. Liverpool had agreed to smash their long standing transfer record paying an initial £80m to secure the Serbians signature and with add ons that fee could rise to a whopping £98m. Cooper was delighted to have his man and he really believed that Obradovic was the man to take Liverpool to the next level.

Whilst Liverpool were sending club ambassadors back and forth to Germany trying to thrash out the Obradovic deal Cooper was made aware that another Bundesliga based player could possibly be available, but again it would cost the club some serious money. The negotiations were taking a little longer than they had done with Red Bull Leipzig and at one stage Cooper was close to pulling the plug because of the sheer scale of the money being talked about to make the deal happen. He had never imagined spending £80m on a player, let alone the potential fee he was now looking at spending, but he reasoned a player was worth whatever he deemed necessary and given the money available in modern football the fee was almost irrelevant.

Having already spent £80m Cooper looked to sell fringe players where possible with Brazilian midfielder Marlon Estevao leaving to join Wolfsburg for £40m and Iranian centre back Hosain Esmaili agreeing to join Spurs for £13m. There were then further departures agreed as Liverpool progressed through their pre-season fixtures which included Filip Zmiric joining Southampton for £13m whilst Bertrand Rousseau joined Mainz for £17m. Rousseau had been another brilliant deal for the club with Cooper having paid just £20k for his services back in 2039.

Behind the scenes pre-season was proving to be a success, there was one record signing in the door with the potential for a second still a possibility. Performances on the pitch had also been pleasing and Cooper saw his side win all their matches. All eight wins were very comfortable and came against some tough opposition. They beat the Under 23's (6-3), AC Milan (5-0), Bristol City (5-0), Juventus (5-1), Barnsley (4-0), Balikesirspor (5-1), Kasimpasa (6-0) and Torino (7-0). The Torino victory was not only notable for the seven goals scored, but also because it saw the clubs newest recruit in action for the first time since his arrival two days prior to the game.

Baba Diarra was a twenty-one year old German left winger who was capable of operating down the right hand side as well. He had been playing in Dortmund for the last two seasons having signed for £32m from Bundesliga rivals Mainz. In those two seasons with Borussia Dortmund he had made sixty six appearances and achieved average ratings of 8.10 and 8.21 announcing himself as a world class talent. In fact his impressive performances last season had seen him pick up the Balon D'or for 2041, winning the prestigious prize at just twenty years old. His emergence on the world stage had alerted not only Cooper, but a host of elite managers looking to add him to their club. The fee's being talked about were astronomical and there was a long back and forth between the clubs before a deal could be agreed. The fee Liverpool were willing to pay Borussia Dortmund would not only smash their recently set transfer record, but it would see Baba Diarra installed as the most expensive footballer ever. Liverpool agreed to pay an initial £145m to sign Diarra with a further £20m if and when certain targets were hit. £165m was an astronomical fee for a footballer and Cooper had never imagined he would be signing off on such a ridiculous transfer when he started out as a manager.

Derek Cooper had decided to splash the cash on Baba Diarra because players of his calibre very rarely became available at any price. He rationalised it as simply too good an opportunity to pass up for the club. Liverpool had hopefully added firepower with the arrival of Igor Obradovic and Cooper hoped the addition of Diarra could see Liverpool really get the best out of their new striker with added creativity. Diarra had made fifteen assists in thirty-three Bundesliga outings last campaign and his eye for a pass would hopefully blossom further under Derek's tutelage. The fact both Diarra and Obradovic were signed before the competitive fixtures got underway was a massive boost to everyone at the club and it was now all eyes on the trip to Wembley to take on the all conquering Manchester City who not only won the Premier League and FA Cup, but also the Champions League of 2041/42 as well.

City had added players in the summer too as Italian international James Izuchukwu joined from INTER for £66m and Senegalese striker Tidiane Diop arrived in a £42m deal from Montpellier. Derek was happy that his transfer business was exactly what the club had needed, but only time would tell if they had done enough to usurp the current champions. The Community Shield would be an early litmus test for Liverpool and a game Cooper was eager to win having not added to his victory back in 2037.

Cooper got the 2042/43 season underway by debuting a brave new tactic he had been working on behind the scenes all summer. It was best described as an asymmetric 2-3-1-3-1 with two central defenders, two wingbacks pushed up in line with a central defensive midfielder. There was then just one central midfielder offset to the left hand side operating between the two lines of three. Ahead of the central midfielder were two wingers with an attacking midfielder offset to the right hand side playing behind the lone striker who would play centrally, as with the defensive midfielder. The tactic had performed well in pre-season tests and Cooper felt by moving one of the two central midfielders into an attacking midfield role there would be more options in an attacking phase of play, hopefully creating more chances for the clubs new striker.

The team selection for the match against Manchester City was just as brave and both Obradovic and Diarra were set to make their full debuts for their new club. Cooper selected Felipe Renan in goal, Juan Jose Sosa and Jose Rodriguez in central defence with Fresnel Kitoko and Malory Thys in the new wingback roles. Gregory Buisson reprieved his Regista role as the defensive midfielder with Evgeny Orlov operating as the left central midfielder. Debutant Baba Diarra started out on the left wing with Ahmet Yilmaz on the right hand side. Durval operated as the new right of centre attacking midfielder behind the clubs new number nine Igor Obradovic. It was a side that excited Cooper and he couldn't wait to see what they could do against a side as strong as Manchester City.

The first half was a fairly uninteresting forty-five minutes of football as both sides felt their way back into competitive action. Liverpool had settled into the match well and were showing signs that they were more than capable of matching the treble winners. Cooper told his players that there was much more to come from them in the second half, adding that he had faith in each of his players. Liverpool began to dominate the ball early in the second half slowly asserting themselves before Russian midfielder Orlov continued his rise to a prominent member of the first team by putting Liverpool ahead on the hour mark. One nil up and in the ascendancy Manchester City were struggling to breach the Liverpool backline whilst The Reds continued to threaten with their new look tactic. On eighty-three minutes there was a debut goal for £80m man Igor Obradovic to secure a reasonably comfortable 2-0 victory for Liverpool and win the 2042 Community Shield. Club captain Fresnel Kitoko joined Derek Cooper in following the rest of the team up the steps at Wembley before they were handed what fans of the club hoped would be the first trophy of many in 2042/43.

As well as the goal for Obradovic there had been a first assist of the season for Baba Diarra as the two new men linked up nicely for the second goal. Liverpool had been the much more creative side in the final with sixteen shots and eight of those on target compared to eight shots and four on target from Manchester City. The match was seen as a glorified friendly by some members of the football community, but Cooper saw it as the first step on their path to success. Overcoming Man City so early meant that they now knew it could be done and they were capable of pushing them all the way. There was now a week before they got the Premier League campaign underway at home to Watford and Derek needed to make sure they got off to the best possible start.

Liverpool had been handed a kind start to the new campaign with games at home to Watford, away to Arsenal and home to Bournemouth ahead of the end of August and the closing of the summer transfer window. Before Liverpool hosted Watford there was one final piece of incoming transfer business completed as Cooper agreed to pay an initial £30m for Dietmar Burmeister. Burmeister was a twenty-two year old German international who had been plying his trade in the Bundesliga with Stuttgart for the last seven years and the attacking midfielder could be the final piece of the Liverpool jigsaw and Cooper was excited by what he could bring to the side. The arrival of a new attacking midfielder facilitated the departure of Joeri van der Maarel who joined Real Madrid for £28m having failed to make an impact since arriving from FC Groningen. Eugenio Ojenda's time at the club also came to an end in early August with Cooper looking to balance the books as Cordoba agreed to pay £13m for the Argentinean goalkeeper.

Anfield was expectant as Cooper made one change to his Wembley starting eleven with new man Burmeister coming in for Durval who dropped to the bench for the game against Watford. Liverpool were completely in control throughout the season opener and the winning margin could have been a lot greater than the 5-0 win recorded at Anfield. Watford failed to register a shot on goal in the ninety minutes of play whereas Liverpool managed an impressive seventeen. Yilmaz got the scoring started in the eleventh minute, added a second before half time and secured his hat-trick from the spot on fifty-six minutes. Baba Diarra then grabbed his first Liverpool goal before a Kitoko really rubbed salt in Watford wounds by adding a fifth and his first Premier League goal in three seasons.

Liverpool needed to continue the good start they had made, but they faltered away to Arsenal who caught them off guard with two early goals. Derek's side were unable to recover and suffered an early season defeat (2-0) that they really could have done without. Cooper had really wanted to start in the best possible way and the early defeat was a set back in his grand plans. The new trio of Obradovic, Burmeister and Diarra all had off days and there were signs that they had more work to do on the training ground to perfect Cooper's tactical plan and their on field chemistry.

Cooper replaced Burmeister with Durval in the starting eleven for the Bournemouth match whilst Obradovic and Diarra were fortunate to hold on to their starting spots. It was a decision that paid dividends as the pair linked up to score Liverpool's third and final goal in another comfortable Anfield win (3-0). Buisson gave Cooper's side the lead on eighteen minutes before Juan Jose Sosa scored the second of the game before half time. It would take until just after the hour mark for the new boys to link up but it secured the first Premier League goal of the season for Obradovic.

Following the Bournemouth game players headed off to represent a multitude of nations for the first international break of the season whilst there was some unexpected deadline day drama at the club. Cooper had completed his summer recruitment and he was more than happy with the squad, but when Southampton came knocking with a £25m offer for Mexican midfielder Luis Espinoza Cooper had a decision to make. Espinoza had yet to feature in a match day squad so far this season and had fallen behind exciting Belgian Lucas Chevalier in the pecking order. His lack of game time hadn't gone unnoticed by the player and he was keen on a move away from the club, but he was an experienced member of the squad and at twenty-eight was still capable of performing in the Premier League. In the end Cooper decided to accept the offer and allow Espinoza to leave in search of the first team football he desired. The Espinoza deal was completed with just a couple of hours of the window remaining to conclude Liverpool's summer of spending. Although they had spent big Cooper had sold cleverly to be able to recoup around £168m in player departures along with a substantial fee garnered from the loan deals.

Players returned to the club ahead of Liverpool's next Premier League fixture away to Brighton. The game against Brighton was another early season away day disaster for Cooper as his side failed to find their rhythm again. They weren't helped by the departure of Gregory Buisson who saw red in the second half with Brighton already winning 2-0. They added a third goal through Nikola Srdanovic to complete a miserable day on the South Coast for Derek. Liverpool were denied another away victory and Cooper needed to look at the vulnerability of his new tactic away from Anfield.

There was another away fixture on the horizon as Liverpool headed to Portugal for their first game of the Champions League campaign. They had been drawn in Group D along with Porto, Real Madrid and Basel which was a tough group, but one Derek still hoped to progress from. Porto were up first and Cooper decided against making major adjustments to the tactic instead preferring to tweak some of the player roles and team mentalities. It produced a much better away performance from Liverpool, but they were unable to hold on to an early goal from Obradovic and allowed Porto back into the game with a twentieth minute leveller. Liverpool shaded the game in terms of stats but were unable to find the second goal they needed to secure their first away win of the season.

Liverpool had won just two of their opening five fixtures of 2042/43, not including the Community Shield victory, and that was hardly the sort of form that won you trophies. Derek Cooper hoped a strong end to September would lift the team and propel them forward into October and November with fixtures against Chelsea, Real Madrid and the two Manchester clubs. Cooper needed to refine the sides approach to away fixtures to pick up more points on the road whilst continuing to dominate games at Anfield.

West Ham were up next in the Premier League as they visited Anfield hoping to catch Liverpool on a rare off day at home. Baba Diarra had Liverpool one goal in front after nine minutes and fellow new man, Burmeister, added a second on twenty-one minutes. Two then became three before half time as Egveny Orlov scored on twenty-seven minutes to all but seal another comfortable home victory. Cooper took the chance to rest an Igor Obradovic who wasn't having his best game and he was replaced by fellow Serbian striker Dejan Dimitric to make his first appearance for Liverpool having been at the club since 2039. Dimitric had a debut to remember as he scored the fourth and final goal of the game in front of The Kop.

The win against West Ham was followed by the third round of the EFL Cup as Derek Cooper took his side down to The Valley to play Championship side Charlton. Liverpool made nine changes to the starting eleven and just Juan Jose Sosa and Hrvoje Miletic held onto their places. A second minute goal from the home side was soon cancelled out and Liverpool asserted themselves in the second half to win the game (3-1) and progress into the fourth round. An own goal and Filip Nilsson joined Miletic on the score sheet for the victory.

Liverpool were yo-yoing between cup and league action for the next few fixtures and there was a Premier League fixture against Chelsea to come three days following the Charlton match. Liverpool returned to the capital looking for three points and that was exactly what they got. Baba Diarra was in inspired form and showed exactly why Liverpool had paid all that money to bring him to the club. He scored a brace to put Liverpool two goals ahead before Argentinean striker Hector Muslera pulled one back before the break to make it 2-1. There was very little else of note in the game as Liverpool consolidated and Chelsea failed to break them down or find a way back into the game. Gregory Buisson was forced off following a clash of heads and the twenty-three year old Frenchman looked to be suffering from concussion as he left the pitch meaning he was likely to miss the upcoming game against Real Madrid.

Three consecutive victories was the perfect preparation for the visit of Tobias Sippel and his Real Madrid side for gameweek two of the Champions League. Madrid had beaten Basel in the opening round of fixtures whilst Liverpool had only managed a draw against Porto. If Liverpool wanted to win the group they would need a positive result here to put themselves back in contention. Amadou Mboup was given a start ahead of an out of form Obradovic who had failed to score in the last three matches and he made the most of his chance by putting the home side 1-0 up on twenty-three minutes. Baba Diarra then continued his fine goal scoring form adding his third in two games on thirty-one minutes. The half time whistle sounded with Liverpool 2-0 up and coasting their way to three points. Dietmar Burmeister then made it 3-0 to Liverpool slotting home a sixty-fourth minute penalty before Real Madrid and Pierre Millet fluffed their lines from twelve yards just minutes later. Had Millet scored it may have made for a nervy finish, but he missed and Liverpool saw the game out at 3-0 to top Group D after two matches.

Amadou Mboup retained his place for the league game at home to Crystal Palace, but Obradovic made his claim for a return to the starting line up with a goal from the bench in a 3-0 win. Burmeister got Liverpool off to a flying start scoring his first goal of the game with less than a minute on the clock and his second just seven minutes later. The early double demoralised Palace and they never really troubled Liverpool who were comfortable in victory. Another Premier League win followed away to Nottingham Forrest (1-0) courtesy of an Ahmet Yilmaz first half goal. The wins against Palace and Forrest meant Liverpool had won their last four league fixtures and their last six in all competitions. Cooper hoped to keep the run of wins going starting with three more points in the Champions League away to Basel.

For long periods of the game against Basel Cooper felt his side were destined to drop points. The home side were 2-0 up at half time and they were faced with a very angry manager at the break. Cooper laid into his side telling them that they had fallen well below the standards they had set for themselves and he expected of them. Yilmaz scored his second in two games just before the hour mark, but Liverpool were made to wait for their comeback as first Sosa and then Orlov managed to find the back of the net in the final ten minutes of play. Liverpool snatched a win (3-2) when really Basel deserved something out of the game for their spirited display. Seven points from three matches meant Liverpool topped Group D at the halfway point and were well on course for qualification into the knockout stage.

Cooper then hoped to make it eight consecutive wins for Liverpool as Aston Villa travelled to Anfield on the 25th of October 2042, but two games in four days had taken its toll and they could only manage a draw (1-1). Gregory Buisson scored in the ninth minute to cancel out a fifth minute opener from Villa and Liverpool were unable to push on and convert their dominance into goals. A wasteful Liverpool managed sixteen shots in the game, but only six of those found their target and just the one beat the Aston Villa goalkeeper. The Villains had put and end to the Liverpool winning run although they remained unbeaten in nine.

Liverpool had looked to have put the patchy form of the early season behind them, but their next match, a tough EFL Cup fourth round tie against Chelsea, would put that to the test. It was important they got back to winning ways and started their next winning streak. Cooper once again chose to rotate his squad given that it was a long season and he had good depth within the squad. Dejan Dimitric was one of those players brought into the starting line up and the Serbian rewarded Cooper with an impressive brace to win the game for Liverpool (2-0). Dimitric scored either side of half time at Anfield to push Liverpool through to the EFL Cup quarter final where they would play Manchester United.

A wet Saturday afternoon in Stoke, three days after the victory against Chelsea, saw a poor Liverpool performance which wasn't helped by an injury to Baba Diarra on thirty minutes. Derek lost his main creative force to a sprained ankle and the side struggled to a really disappointing 0-0 draw. Once again Liverpool had been very poor in the final third, failing to stick away any of their twenty-four shots on goal. Yohan Pele was the much happier manager with a point earning him a stay of execution whilst Derek was left frustrated by four dropped points in their last two Premier League matches.

With a drop off in Premier League form it was a welcome return to Champions League and the gameweek four visit of Basel to Anfield. Games against Manchester City and Manchester United were up next in the league for Derek Cooper and he hoped the change of competition would reset the clubs current form. Against Basel Liverpool were unrecognisable from the team that had played at Stoke three days earlier and there was an emphatic 7-1 win for Cooper's men. Burmeister in particular was outstanding and was named player of the match for his first half hat-trick. Lesther Cordova helped himself to two goals whilst Obradovic and Sosa got one each too. Martin Frei scored a worthless consolation for Basel in added time at the end of the first half with Liverpool having already put six of their seven away.

The win against Basel was exactly the sort of result Cooper had hoped for heading into the games at home to Manchester City and away to Manchester United. Once again, as with every other season during his time in England, the two Manchester clubs represented his main title rivals. As of yet he had been unable to find a way to beat both clubs in one season having finished as runners up to Manchester United and then City in the last two campaigns. Reigning champions City were up first and twenty-one year old English striker Ian Spooner had them ahead inside ten minutes, but Liverpool came back superbly with goals from Cordova in the forty-first minute and Igor Obradovic in the forty-seventh minute to win the game (2-1). Beating City at home was only part of the job, and the tougher test was to come at Old Trafford after the November international break.

Players returned from national duties and Cooper worked hard to get his side ready for another big Premier League fixture. On the 21st of November 2042 Liverpool made the short trip to Manchester to play title rivals United. Bartosz Korzeniewski was now very much the main man at United and the man Cooper signed for Madrid for just £2m was valued in excess of £50m. The twenty-four year old Polish winger showed his quality against his former boss scoring two goals as United ran out 3-1 winners. Korzeniewski opened the scoring from the spot on thirty minutes before a Felipe Renan own goal extended that lead on fifty-four minutes. Obradovic pulled one back on the hour mark before Korzeniewski added his second in the ninetieth minute to seal Liverpool's fate.

The win against City had been good, but the defeat to United had been a real disappointment for Cooper and the Liverpool fans. Too many times Liverpool had been on the wrong end of the score line against their historic rivals and it was still a real source of frustration for Derek. His Premier League irritations were put to one side following the defeat as Porto visited Anfield in gameweek five of the Champions League campaign. Once again Liverpool benefitted from the change of scenery and two goals from Orlov secured an easy win (2-0). Orlov also missed an eighty-ninth minute penalty to deny himself a hat-trick for the first time in his career. Liverpool were completely dominant in the tie and Porto failed to register a shot on target in the ninety minutes of play. The win meant Liverpool were likely to qualify as group winners and whilst it was still mathematically possible for Real Madrid to catch them, it would require a huge win for them when Liverpool visited the Bernabeu in the final gameweek.

The final game of November came in the form of a Premier League fixture away to West Brom. Both Durval and Alanzinho made the most of starts in the game as they scored three goals between them in the Liverpool victory (3-0). Durval grabbed a brace playing in the attacking midfielder role whilst Alanzinho deputised for the rested Orlov following his midweek exploits against Porto.

December kicked off with a return to EFL Cup action and the chance to avenge the Premier League defeat to Manchester United. Derek Cooper fielded a rotated side, but kept a handful of regulars in to balance the side out. Diarra started on the left hand side and regular centre back pairing Sosa and Rodriguez also started the match. Cooper really didn't want to lose to United again and the EFL Cup represented a real chance of silverware for the club should they eliminate another of the top sides. Manchester United had also put out a strong eleven that included Korzeniewski, Youssouf and Kane Davis as they too obviously wanted to win the quarter final tie.

Liverpool had home advantage and after forty minutes they had a goal advantage too courtesy of Lucas Chevalier from the middle of the park. Cooper told his side to keep up the good work in the second half, but United found a way back through Eric Ambronn in the sixty-eighth minute to level the game at 1-1. Filip Nilsson then put the home side back in front five minutes later and Cooper hoped his side had enough resilience to see out the remainder of the game. It looked like they had done enough, but then in the final minute of the ninety Ronnie Walker slotted home to deny them the win and the game headed into extra time.

Cooper and his Liverpool players could have done without the extra thirty minutes of play they faced, but failure to win the game in ninety minutes meant it could not be avoided. Filip Nilsson had been sent on by Cooper for Dimitric in the sixty-first minute and he scored twelve minutes after coming on. His legs were fresher than the defenders he was now facing and it began to show in the first half of extra time. Nilsson grabbed his second goal of the game in the ninety-fourth minute before adding his third and fourth goals further into the match. United were unable to cope with the energy and Baba Diarra also got himself amongst the goals. Liverpool had blown Manchster United away in extra time to win the game 6-2. Nilsson had four goals to his name come the end of the tie and Ahmet Yilmaz had put in an excellent performance on the right hand side creating four of the sides' six goals.

Cooper and Liverpool were through to the semi final of the EFL Cup, but victory had come at a cost with thirty minutes extra football on top of an already busy upcoming winter fixture list. The 6-2 win was just the first of eight matches planned for December alone with another seven now scheduled for January. It was all hands to the pump for Liverpool and they followed the EFL Cup win with a mixed bag of results. A win against Hull followed (4-1) before a defeat at the Bernabeu in the final game of Group D (2-1). The loss to Real Madrid had no bearing on the final standings of the group and both Real Madrid and Liverpool progressed with the English club topping the group.

Liverpool returned from Madrid with the bit between their teeth and got stuck into Fulham at Craven Cottage thumping them for five with a hat-trick for Durval alongside goals for Buisson and Obradovic (5-0). A draw at home to QPR followed (1-1) with Obradovic finding the back of the net to rescue a point. The Serbian striker failed to make it three in three as the side played Swansea away from home, but luckily Orlov, Nilsson and

Diarra scored in the win in Wales (3-1). Leicester were the visitors to Anfield on Boxing Day and Liverpool threw away a seemingly comfortable home win. Orlov and Diarra both scored again to have Liverpool 2-0 up as the clock ticked into the ninetieth minute, but Liverpool lost their focus and threw away their lead. Leicester scored in the ninetieth and the ninety-second minute to leave Derek Cooper raging in the home dressing room. The eighth and final game of the month came away to Norwich at Carrow Road and Cooper demanded a reaction from his team. The duly obliged and closed out the month as they had started it with a decent win (4-1).

The pattern of winning a league game and then following it up with a draw had cost Liverpool four vital points and the Leicester game in particular left Cooper incredibly frustrated. December gave way to January and just three days after the Norwich win Liverpool were throwing away yet more vital points in another draw, this time away to Watford (1-1). Liverpool had opened their season at home to Watford and the trip to Vicarage road represented the beginning of the second round of fixtures. So far Cooper's men had picked up twelve wins, five draws and three losses. They were in and around the clubs at the top of the league with the Manchester clubs and surprise package Brighton who were defying pundits and flying high. Liverpool needed to turn some of their draws into wins and maybe they would be able to sustain a serious title challenge.

It was now three wins and three draws in their last six Premier League matches and thankfully there was a break from league action to get the FA Cup underway for the club. Liverpool had been drawn against a fellow Premier League side in Bournemouth and travelled to the South Coast looking to make it through to the fourth round of the competition. An early opener for the home side was quickly cancelled out by the goals of Keen, Cordova and Obradovic to seal the victory Cooper desired (3-1) and earn Liverpool a spot in the fourth round.

Premier League action followed against Arsenal before the first leg of the two legged EFL Cup semi final with Leicester. Arsenal had beaten Liverpool earlier in the season, but there was no repeat performance at Anfield as the home side came from behind thanks to goals from Obradovic to win (2-1). It was then eight days before their next league fixture where Liverpool wanted to end the recent win followed by draw routine. Between league games the side travelled to the King Power Stadium looking to take the initiative in the semi final. Liverpool once again fell behind to an early goal, but came back into the match with goals from Diarra, Keen and Mboup winning them a rather comfortable first leg tie. It was then back to Bournemouth for the second time in eleven days for a Premier League fixture that Cooper hoped would yield the same result as the FA Cup tie, a Liverpool victory. The visiting side asked all the questions, but it was the home side who found the answer with former Liverpool man Peter Eccles coming back to haunt his former club and the manager who sold him with the winning goal late on. The win, draw pattern had been broken, but not in the way Cooper had hoped and it was now over a month since the side had registered back to back wins in the Premier League.

Next up and the penultimate game of January was against surprise package Brighton who were right up there in terms of the Premier League. Losing to them now would certainly open the door for The Seagulls to gain more ground on The Liver birds. Thankfully Liverpool put the upstarts in their place and goals from Diarra, Obradovic and Buisson secured an important three points (3-0). The final game of the month saw Leicester return to Anfield, the scene of their late comeback on Boxing Day, hoping they could overturn the 3-1 defeat of the first leg. There was another late goal in the game, but this time it was the only goal of the game and it came thanks to Ahmet Yilmaz from the penalty spot. The eighty-eighth minute spot kick saw Liverpool through 4-1 on aggregate and secured their spot in the EFL Cup final to be contested at Wembley on the 1st of March 2043. Liverpool would play Swansea in the final with the Welsh club having beaten Championship side Colchester in the other semi final.

Throughout January Cooper had kept a close eye on the transfer market although there were no huge transfers planned given the enormous spend by the club over the summer. There were a couple of arrivals however with young Brazilian winger Ronny Reinaldo arriving for £5m and French defensive midfielder Alain Vigouroux joining for £3m. Both players arrived from French club Lyon and could see the fees rise to a combined £28.5m if they developed as hoped with the club. Two former first team regulars were allowed to leave the club in search of more first team opportunities as Clesinho left for AC Milan with the fee set at £16m and Metodi Totev was allowed to join Arsenal when they agreed to meet the £40m asking price. Remarkably when all the winter business had been concluded Cooper had once again managed to bring in more money than he had spent. Quite a feat for the club considering they had spent £265m on new recruits. With the combination of player sales and the loan fee's garnered Liverpool had made £272m across the two windows, turning a small profit for the club.

December and January had been two of the toughest months Cooper had faced as a manager and to still be competing across all four competitions was a minor miracle and testament to the strength of the squad he had put together. Fifteen games in two months was a gruelling schedule and Cooper hoped his side could really kick on now they were through the worst of it and had more knockout football to look forward to.

Goals came thick and fast in the next two fixtures as both West Ham (5-2) and Chelsea (7-0) were put to the sword in impressive fashion. Obradovic got himself three goals across the two victories as did the returning Dietmer Burmeister who had been out of the team having suffered a loss of form over the festive period. Thankfully for Liverpool they had done all the hard work in the Chelsea match by half time which was just aswell given that Hvroje Miletic was sent off ten minutes into the second half. They were already 6-0 up by that point, but his ill discipline could have proved costly on another occasion. The wins continued and the day before Cooper celebrated his fifty-fifth year his side beat Cardiff (3-1) to reach the fifth round of the FA Cup.

February proved to be a prolific month for Liverpool as they continued to find the back of the net on a regular basis. There were four goal hauls in back to back Premier League games against Crystal Palace (4-1) and Nottingham Forrest (4-0) before they returned to European action and continued to score at will. Liverpool had been drawn against Italian club INTER for the first knockout round of the Champions League and would travel to Milan to contest the first leg. Having already scored twenty-three goals this month confidence was high and it showed in yet another clinical performance. Liverpool dominated possession and found the back of the INTER net four times through Obradovic, Diarra and a double from Ahmet Yilmaz to take a comfortable lead back to Anfield (4-0).

The unstoppable winning run had come at the perfect time for Derek Cooper and his men. They had scored four goals in each of their last three fixtures and had kept two clean sheets in their last two matches. Their next match was the EFL Cup final and it represented a well overdue chance for Liverpool to get their hands on some silverware. Cooper had just two Community Shields to his name and had lost the only other final he had made it to, losing to Manchester City in the Champions League final of 2039/40. Throughout his career Cooper had struggled to win domestic cups and he was desperate to win Liverpool their first EFL Cup since 2036/37.

Cooper had beaten Swansea 3-1 back in December and he hoped for a similar outcome at Wembley. He picked a strong side to start the game, but was true to a number of players who had got them this far. Petit started in goal as he had done in every other round whilst the back four consisted of Thys, Rodriguez, Assis and Leoutsakos. Buisson anchored the midfield with Orlov operating in the left central midfield role. Ahead of him was Diarra, Durval and Yilmaz with Obradovic playing as the lone striker. Swansea lined up with a defensive looking 4-4-1-1 hoping to absorb the Liverpool pressure and score a breakaway goal to win the match.

Liverpool had prepared correctly and it showed in their strong start as first Obradovic and then Yilmaz got themselves on the score sheet. Obradovic put Liverpool ahead inside a minute and the second came with less than twenty minutes having been played. Liverpool were in complete control and Cooper was able to enjoy the occasion. Standing pitch side in his club suit whilst winning a Wembley cup final was something he never expected to experience and with his side now two goals ahead he was determined to not let it slip. He warned his side against complacency and a sixty-fifth minute goal from Swansea threatened to rain on the Liverpool parade before Burmeister restored the two goal cushion five minutes later to settle everyone down again. As the final whistle sounded Cooper was as relieved as he was happy, it was his first proper trophy as Liverpool manager and he hoped it wouldn't be his last, there was still so much to play for.

Club captain Fresnel Kitoko had been rested for the duration of the EFL Cup campaign and he deferred to vice Captain Jose Rodriguez to lead the players up the steps at Wembley to collect their prize. Lesser men would have changed from club suit to a full kit and taken the limelight for themselves, but Kitoko was more than happy to share the victory and watch his teammates lift the trophy from the sidelines. Cooper assured the big man that his time would come promising him it would be worth the wait.

Despite not scoring in the final substitute Filip Nilsson picked up an award for most goals in the competition with four of his six coming in the extra time win against Manchester United in the quarter final. Yilmaz was also announced as the top provider with his four assists in that very same match enough to earn him that award. All in all it had been a successful EFL Cup campaign, but it was the smallest of the trophies available to Cooper and he was now hungry for more having had his appetite whetted at Wembley.

The staff and players had a small party to celebrate, but with three games coming in the next nine days there was no time for the squad to take their eye off the ball. A day's rest was all Cooper could afford his players and they were back in training before travelling to Aston Villa in the Premier League three days after the Wembley final. The days rest didn't have the desired effect and Liverpool dropped points on their return to league action drawing 0-0. There was then another three day turnaround before the visit of Stoke and Cooper demanded a better performance from his players. They duly obliged and goals from Obradovic and Burmeister delivered the win he had asked of them (3-0). The three day cycle continued with the clubs FA Cup fifth round tie away to Fulham. Liverpool missed a golden opportunity to win the cup tie when Filip Nilsson missed a second half penalty. Thankfully they would get another bite of the cherry in two weeks time with a replay of the fifth round tie as it finished 0-0 at Craven Cottage.

The games continued at a relentless pace and there was barely time to recover before the next game was upon them. Liverpool made the journey to face Manchester City in a game against one of their title rivals, although in truth Manchester City had not hit the heights of their previous campaign and were lagging slightly behind the others. Derek wanted to continue his own sides' title push with a win. Despite two goals from Obradovic and an eighty-seventh minute equaliser from the left boot of Baba Diarra Liverpool were unable to hold on to the 3-3 and conceded in time added on to lose 4-3. Liverpool had been 3-0 down before they had turned up and got themselves back into the game so the late defeat was particularly galling for Cooper and his players. They now needed to pick themselves up off the floor with games against INTER and Manchester United in the next week.

Liverpool had done all the hard work in the first leg of their Champions League tie with INTER winning 4-0 away from home. All they needed to do was avoid a humiliating defeat, but Cooper was confident that they could push on and send a message to the other sides left in the competition. INTER were once again unable to cope with the attacking threat of Liverpool and goals from Obradovic and Carl Bishop, who was making a rare start, sealed a 3-0 win on the night and a 7-0 aggregate victory over the two legs. Liverpool meant business.

The win against INTER and progression into the Champions League quarter final meant the side were in confident mood ahead of the visit of Manchester United. United had emerged as Liverpool's closest title challengers although Brighton were continuing to push both clubs hard and were refusing to give up their unlikely challenge. As confident as Cooper and his players had been pre-match they were completely blown away by their visitors in the opening twenty minutes. Goals from Ronnie Walker and Kane Davis had the home side three goals behind and in danger of being thumped. Thankfully the players got their act together and began to drag themselves back into the match. Obradovic pulled one back on twenty-three minutes, but that was the extent of the sides' comeback in the first half. Cooper let his players have it at half time, he didn't lose his cool very often, but this was unacceptable and he let his players know in no uncertain terms.

Durval was then introduced early on in the second half and the twenty-five year old Brazilian had an almost immediate impact scoring Liverpool's second goal ten minutes after his introduction. Liverpool were now the side in the ascendancy and Durval grabbed his second and Liverpool's third on seventy-five minutes scoring from the spot with United defender Yan having received a second yellow card for his foul in the box. From leading the game by three goals United were hanging on at 3-3 with ten men defending for their lives. Liverpool were unable to find the fourth goal they needed to complete the comeback and had to settle for a share of the points which wasn't actually the worst result in the world for the home side. United had been unable to close the gap and Liverpool maintained their advantage.

The draw at home to Manchester United was the sides' third meeting of the season, but it wasn't to be their last as the two clubs were drawn together in the Champions League quarter finals. Liverpool would travel to Old Trafford first, on the 14th of April, ahead of the second leg at Anfield on the 22nd of the same month. Before the European ties at United there was a potential FA Cup double header for the club as a consequence of fixture congestion. The fifth round replay against Fulham came ahead of a potential quarter final away to Newcastle should they navigate their way past The Cottagers.

Liverpool were the much better side this time out against Fulham and goals from Obradovic and Jose Rodriguez were more than enough to see Derek Cooper and Liverpool through to the FA Cup quarter final (3-0). Newcastle away awaited Liverpool in the next round. There was eight days break between the ties and it allowed Liverpool vital time to recharge their batteries with many players allowed a break from training by the manager. The rest did just the trick and the players rewarded their manager's kindness with an away win (2-0) and progression into the semi finals. Durval was on form at St. James' Park scoring both the sides goals and earning himself a player of the match award in the process. The Brazilian thanked his manager for the much needed rest in his post match interview stating it was a contributing factor to his impressive performance.

FA Cup duties fulfilled and extended it was onto Premier League action and games at home to West Brom and away to Hull. Both games yielded three points and four goals for Derek Cooper's men, but they were helped in both matches by early red cards for their opponents. West Brom were reduced to ten men after five minutes and were punished by Orlov, Thys and Obradovic (4-0). Hull faired no better and they had a man sent off after six minutes with the four Liverpool goals coming through Buisson, Grieco and Menga, who was back from an earlier loan spell and looking to force his way into Cooper's plans (4-0). A run of four games and four victories was the perfect form to be hitting at this point of the season as the club looked to be competitive across three competitions.

The back to back 4-0 wins in the league brought the club up to the first leg of their European tie with Manchester United. Cooper never liked playing league rivals in Europe, it somehow changed the dynamic for him and just didn't feel right, but he had to play the hand he had been dealt and that meant taking the short trip to Manchester on a Tuesday evening. Liverpool had been in good form, buoyed by the goal scoring prowess of Igor Obradovic who had eight goals in his last seven matches and was becoming a real threat to opposition defences now he was fully integrated at the club. Were Liverpool to make it through another round in Europe the Serbians goals may well prove vital.

Cooper picked a starting eleven of Renan, Thys, Assis, Sosa, Kitoko, Buisson, Orlov, Diarra, Durval, Menga and Obradovic and having been suitably inspired pre-match by Cooper Kitoko led them down the Old Trafford tunnel and into battle once more. European games were often more cagey as managers employed a more long term approach, knowing there would be a return leg needed to settle the outcome of the tie. Because of that the first half passed without incident and the score remained at 0-0. Cooper told his men there was more to come and they needed to find it in the second forty-five, especially when United took the lead through Youssouf who scored the opening goal of the tie on fifty-seven minutes. Liverpool weren't stunned by the blow and they continued to plug away in the game. Diarra and Durval were withdrawn for Yilmaz and Burmeister and the substitutions had the desired effect as Ahmet Yilmaz laid on a seventy eighth minute equaliser for

Obradovic. The game remained at 1-1 and Liverpool had the coveted away goal to take back to Anfield. The draw was probably a fair result on the night with very little between either of the sides. Liverpool had done well to come from behind, but Cooper knew they would need to be better in the home leg if they were to make the semi final.

Elsewhere in the Champions League the other English clubs weren't fairing too well. Brighton were trailing Real Madrid 3-1 and had to visit the Bernabeu for the second leg and Manchester City were down 4-3 after losing at home to PSG. In the other, all French, quarter final Saint-Etienne looked almost certain to make the semis having won 3-0 at home to AS Monaco. It was still all to play for as Liverpool and United prepared for the second leg that would determine which side took that next step in the competition.

Fulham were the visitors to Anfield in between Manchester United ties and the London club took advantage of a distracted Liverpool to snatch a 2-1 victory. Obradovic found the back of the net once more, but his ninety-second minute goal did nothing to alter the outcome and Fulham took an unlikely three points with them as they departed Anfield. Liverpool had been much the better side and their failure to find the back of the net was a consequence of their wastefulness in front of goal.

They could not afford to be wasteful in their next Anfield encounter as Manchester United were welcomed for the second leg of the Champions League quarter final. European nights at Anfield were special and Cooper called for fans to turn out in full voice for the occasion. The United team bus was welcomed in typical boisterous fashion with flares accompanying the usual chants and songs of the home faithful. Derek Cooper and his players were treated to a carnival approach to the ground as the fans turned out in their thousands to spur the side on in the match that was to come.

It was much the same team that had started at Old Trafford although Branislav Djuricic came in at right back for Malory Thys and Ahmet Yilmaz came in on the right wing for Jean Menga. Both Thys and Menga took their spot on the Liverpool bench alongside the likes of Rodriguez, Burmeister, Nilsson, Miletic and Petit. Cooper rarely named a substitute goalkeeper, but had gone against the norm on this occasion for fear of losing Felipe Renan costing them a semi final spot. The game began with the score poised at one goal each and both sides wanting to secure a win over their bitter rivals. Durval got Liverpool off to the best possible start by scoring the opening goal on the night after twenty-two minutes. It was advantage Liverpool and that one goal lead became two eleven minutes later when Baba Diarra found a way past Alain Olivier in the United goal. The Reds were 2-0 up on the night and leading 3-1 on aggregate as the half time whistle sounded. Cooper rushed back to the dressing room keen to get his point across to his side. Telling them to concentrate had backfired in the past so he decided on a different course of action and explained that although they were doing ok he knew they were capable of more. The hope was that the players would be keen to show the manager that they did indeed have more in the tank and cruise to a comfortable victory.

The Liverpool players responded well to Cooper's words and two more goals followed in quick succession from an unlikely source. Jose Sosa scored his first goal of the game on fifty-five minutes and added his second five minutes later. Liverpool were 4-0 on the night and 5-1 ahead on aggregate. With just half an hour left to play Cooper was quietly confident that his side had the victory in the bag, but he wasn't one to show those sorts of feelings. A United goal on seventy minutes from Ronnie Walker momentarily shook Cooper's belief, but his side were more than capable of seeing out the remainder of the tie and they claimed an impressive win at Anfield to see them into the semi final (5-2 on agg).

As expected Real Madrid, PSG and Saint-Etienne had also made it through their quarter final matches and it would be one of the French outfits up next for Cooper as he avoided his old club. Liverpool would host Saint-Etienne in the first leg of their semi final on the 5th of May before travelling to France on the 13th of May. Saint-Etienne should have cruised through following a 3-0 first leg victory at home to Monaco, but they ended up scraping through on the away goals rule following a 5-2 defeat in the second leg. The away goals of front men Szalek and Penalba had been just enough to see them through and Cooper hoped he had seen a weakness in them that he would be able to exploit when they met in May.

Liverpool and Cooper really were now into the business end of the season where every game could see ramifications in terms of silverware for the club. There were four Premier League fixtures remaining with twelve vital points up for grabs, a trip to Wembley for an FA Cup semi final against Burnley before a potential final and Champions League matches home and away to Saint-Etienne. Should Liverpool do the unthinkable and beat both Burnley and Saint-Etienne Liverpool would have nine fixtures left to play of the 2042/43 season.

Premier League bogey side QPR were up next following European victory and even a brace for ex-Liverpool striker Ivo Vukovic wasn't enough to stop the invigorated Liverpool side as goals from Obradovic and Menga secured a nervy win (3-2). QPR had been 2-0 up at the break but Liverpool responded brilliantly knowing that failure to secure the win would give United and Brighton the chance to reel them in at the top of the league. Attention turned to Wembley following the win at Stan Bowles Stadium and Liverpool had been drawn against Championship opposition in the form of Burnley. It was a favourable draw for Liverpool and meant they avoided Manchester City who were playing Premier League opposition in Nottingham Forrest, although it was still a match many felt City would have little trouble in winning.

Cooper didn't like the FA Cup semi finals being contested at Wembley, in his mind it undermined the occasion of the final and he would gladly see the return of neutral venues such as Villa Park being used. However the Football Association were unlikely to change their ways and he was resigned to taking his side down to London and the countries national stadium. Cooper was serious about winning the competition and picked a suitably strong starting eleven. That eleven completely blew their opponents out of the water in a match that was one of the most one sided semi finals ever contested. Baba Diarra started the scoring in the third minute and Dejan Dimitric finished it off in the seventy-fifth minute with Liverpool's seventh goal. In between were two for Durval, one each for Menga and Yilmaz and another for Dimitric who was on as a substitute. Durval missed the chance of a Wembley hat-trick on the day missing from twelve yards to bring a loud and sarcastic cheer from the forlorn Burnley fans. They did manage a consolation goal on the stroke of half time to make it 3-1 at the break, but Liverpool never gave them a chance in the second half and the 7-1 final score line could have been more.

The FA Cup semi final was the final game of April and May kicked off with yet another semi final for the club, this time at Anfield as they played host to Saint-Etienne, managed by Robbert Schilder who had played in Holland before managing Huddersfield, Swansea, Ajax, Holland and Red Bull Leipzig to name but a few. His side was chock full of familiar faces and included former Derek Cooper players in Eddy Landre, Alassane Diop, Christian Olsson and Gustavo Penabla. Penalba was the only ex-Liverpool player of those having left the club for £80m in 2041.

Cooper selected a starting eleven of Renan, Djuricic, Rodriguez, Sosa, Kitoko, Buisson, Orlov, Diarra, Durval, Yilmaz and Obradovic which was virtually his best eleven on paper. Saint-Etienne represented a major challenge and many pundits had been unable to call the outcome of the two legged tie. Liverpool started the game brightly and were the much better side, but they failed to assert themselves on the game despite dominating the ball for long periods. Too many players were having average games and as the second half got underway Cooper began to think about making some changes. He had told the lads he was unhappy with them at half time, they had been so good recently and now it looked like their killer instinct had all but deserted them. Durval, Yilmaz and Obradovic were all sacrificed in an effort to shake up the sides' performance with Burmeister, Cordova and Nilsson introduced in their place. The game looked to be heading to a disappointing 0-0 for Derek Cooper and the Liverpool fans, but in the eighty-second minute substitute Filip Nilsson stole a march on his marker to fire home the winner. It was a deserved victory for Liverpool, but Cooper was annoyed that his side had failed to score more than one goal from their twenty-nine shots in the match. His side would need to be more clinical in the second leg if they were to make it to the Champions League final.

Liverpool faced Norwich in between Champions League legs and it was a chance for Cooper to return to familiar surroundings in Norfolk as he faced his biggest month in football management. Cooper had secured one trophy already, but within the next four weeks he could get his hands on another three. That would make it the most successful season of his career to date and would create history with Liverpool Football Club. Derek Cooper was desperate to see that happen, but he had to take it one game at a time and Norwich at Carrow Road were next on his agenda. Lucas Chevalier came in for Egveny Orlov and there were also starts for Militec, Cordova and Fillip Nilsson who kept his place up top following his late winner midweek. Nilsson had soon repaid his manager with a brace inside the opening ten minutes to start Liverpool off on their way to an easy 4-0 win. All four goals were scored by lads brought into the side by Cooper with Cordova and Militec joining Nilsson amongst the goals.

And just like that it was back to Champions League action and knockout football. Liverpool had ninety minutes to book their place in the Seville final. Saint-Etienne had won the competition as recently as 2040/41 and had been beaten finalists last season so they knew what it took to go all the way. Cooper had of course taken Liverpool to a final once before, back in 2039/40, and he felt he had a much stronger squad this time out. The hosts were trailing 1-0 and had left Liverpool without an away goal, but that didn't mean they were out of the tie and when Rafa Szalek put them ahead in the thirty-second minute they were very much in with a shout of making the final. Thankfully Liverpool responded well and a goal from Jean Menga just before half time was exactly what they needed, it was a great time to score. 1-1 at half time and 2-1 to Liverpool on aggregate with the bonus of an away goal made it advantage Liverpool. Saint-Etienne would need to come out and attack hopefully leaving some space for the away side to catch them out and put the tie to bed. Cooper told his side that they were doing well, but that there was more to come from them in the second half. When Juan Jose Sosa headed in a second for Liverpool on seventy-nine minutes it all but sealed their place in the final, but that place was put beyond doubt with Menga's second goal of the game on eighty-seven minutes. Cooper was delighted and come the final whistle shook hands with his opposite number and exploded onto the pitch to celebrate with his side. The dream of a rare quadruple was now becoming a real possibility. There were now four games remaining; Premier League matches against Leicester and Swansea, an FA Cup final against Manchester City and a UEFA Champions League final in Seville against Real Madrid.

Liverpool hadn't been beaten in nearly a month, since they had lost to Fulham in the league and the incredible run of form had come at just the right time for the club. Morale was high and the games couldn't come quick enough. They had won six games on the spin with three of those being semi finals and another a quarter final, so they had been important matches making the run even more impressive. The squad was being used and everyone was pulling their weight. When one of the regular starting eleven needed a rest there was always someone ready and waiting to take advantage and stake a claim for a spot of their own. Nilsson had come in and done well and Menga had been amongst the goals on more than one occasion.

With the Premier League still not a done deal Cooper played a full strength side away to Leicester despite having the FA Cup final just four days later. Cooper was desperate to win the league and with Brighton and United still chasing his side down he couldn't afford a slip up now. He feared the worst when Leicester took the lead in the twelfth minute, but he needn't have worried and his big summer signings really came through when it mattered to win the game (2-1). Obradovic scored his first goal in four games to pull Liverpool level before Baba Diarra scored the winner on the hour to secure all three points. The win left Liverpool on seventy-nine points with one game to play and Brighton on seventy-seven points with one game remaining too. It was all to play for on the final day of the season as the Premier League title still needed to be won.

Liverpool and Derek Cooper now had three games of the 2042/43 season remaining and each one amounted to a cup final for the club. Two of them actually were cup finals, but the Premier League game against Swansea could also see them win or lose the league title. Manchester City in the FA Cup final was up first and Liverpool returned to the national stadium for the third time this season knowing that a win would secure the clubs second trophy of the season. Cooper decided against replicating the famous white Armani suits of the Spice Boys, but there were specially designed club suits to be worn by all players an staff to commemorate the occassion.

It was unusual for the FA Cup final to come before the end of the Premier League season, but that was exactly what was happening this time out. Although Cooper was desperate to win the league title, he also knew that the chance to win the FA Cup was not something to be taken lightly and he picked a strong squad to face Manchester City. Renan would start in goal with the other ten starters coming in the shape of Djuricic, Rodriguez, Sosa, Kitoko, Militec, Orlov, Diarra, Durval, Menga and Obradovic. There were places on the bench for Assis, Thys, Buisson, Burmeister, Yilmaz, Grieco and Petit. Manchester City had been poor in a season that fell well below their usual high standards and the FA Cup represented their only hope of winning silverware in the 2042/43 season. Their fans were hoping they had enough in the tank to see Liverpool off at Wembley.

Liverpool had been announced as slight favourites pre-match and the early exchanges looked to confirm those predictions. Liverpool had more of the ball and were looking the more dangerous side in terms of chances created. However stats counted for little if you failed to put the ball in the back of the net and just before half time Manchester City managed to do exactly that. Ian Spooner put The Citizens ahead with forty-two minutes played and it was a lead that lasted until the half time interval. Cooper used the break to tell his players that what he had seen from them in the first half was not good enough. Their first half display had been slightly disrupted by an ankle injury to Durval, but Burmeister was a more than competent replacement and it was no excuse for the lack of cutting edge from his side. The manager urged them to do more in the second half, the cup final was at risk of getting away from them and he didn't want his players leaving the Wembley pitch with any regrets.

Liverpool once again started the half as the better side and this time they were able to convert their superiority into a goal as Igor Obradovic found the back of the net in the fifty-eighth minute. The goal not only pulled them level, but filled the players with the belief that they could go on and get more goals. They didn't have to wait long and it was that man Obradovic as he once again netted on the big stage just after the hour mark. Cooper had plenty of options on the bench, he could introduce Buisson to sure things up or he could add another central defender in the form of Assis. For once though Cooper decided against making any substitutions, his side were on top and in control. Making unnecessary changes could stop that momentum so despite the narrow 2-1 score line Cooper held off making any subs. The clock slowly ticked away and at no point did Cooper feel unnerved by the Manchester City attack. His defence were doing their jobs perfectly and although Manchester City had the players capable of threatening they simply weren't being allowed to do so. Cooper was experiencing an overwhelming sense of calm and as the referee blew the full time whistle he allowed a solitary fist pump to illustrate his delight. Liverpool had performed when required and the 2042/43 FA Cup was now theirs to collect from the Royal contingent at the top of the steps.

Cooper and his players had secured their second major trophy of the season, third if you included the Community Shield, but they still had two games left with two more trophies up for grabs. The two remaining trophies were arguably the biggest two and represented the chance for Cooper and his men to make history and cap off a truly historic season in style. The only negative to have come out of the cup final was the injury to Durval which meant the Brazilian would not get the chance to write himself into the history books as he had been ruled out of the final two matches with a sprained ankle.

Having a Premier League round of fixtures left to play following the FA Cup final was unusual and it required a quick turnaround. With just four days before they took on Swansea Cooper was forced to curb any potential celebrations. They would have to wait until after the conclusion of both the Premier League and the Champions League. Brighton were still more than capable of catching Liverpool and pipping them to the title, but they had a slightly tougher match away to Nottingham Forrest. Cooper would need to be kept up to date with the score from the City Ground as a Brighton win would mean Liverpool needing to avoid defeat to secure the title.

The game at Anfield got off to the worst possible start for the home side as Swansea found themselves 1-0 up inside a minute. Not the start Cooper had envisaged for his side and it instantly put his side on the back foot. Liverpool were up against it though thankfully it was still 0-0 in Nottingham and Liverpool would be crowned Champions if everything stayed as it was. There was then a double blow that threatened to end Cooper's Premier League dream, firstly Daniel Price found the back of the Liverpool net for a second time to put Swansea 2-0 ahead and that was followed by the news that Alberto Paz had fired Brighton ahead putting them top of the league.

It was all coming undone at the vital moment for Cooper, he was staring the possibility of watching the Premier League title slip from his grasp. Good news followed from Nottingham and not only had Forrest got themselves level, but they had gone in front to restore Liverpool at the top of the table. As half time whistles blew up and down the country Liverpool were 2-0 down, but more importantly Brighton were also losing 2-1 to Nottingham Forrest. Liverpool were the masters of their own destiny, but right now that involved overturning a two goal deficit. Cooper tore into his side at half time telling them that they didn't look like a side that wanted to win. They needed to show something else in the second half. Yilmaz was introduced for Menga at the break, but Liverpool once again began to labour as the play resumed.

Their comeback hopes were then dealt another blow as Miletic was shown a second yellow card on sixty-two minutes. Not an ideal situation when you're two goals behind and a league title is up for grabs. Swansea charitably got a man of their own sent off nine minutes later, but Liverpool still couldn't find a way through. There was no news from Nottingham which meant Liverpool were still in pole position should the games end now. It was the eighty-sixth minute before anything else of note happened and it came in the Forrest versus Brighton game. A Brighton player had found the back of the net, but mercifully Giorgio Romanelli had put the ball past his own keeper and made it 3-1 to the home side. Cooper could begin to relax, his side had been awful, but it was looking like they had done just enough throughout the season to be crowned champions of the Premier League 2042/43. The full time whistle signalled the end of the season and was the cue for an Anfield pitch invasion that saw Cooper and his players lofted high onto the shoulders of those fans that had supported the club through thick and thin. The invaders were cleared back to the stands and the Premier League trophy was produced, kissed and hoisted high into the air by Fresnel Kitoko. Of all Cooper's trophy victories this one had been the hardest to attain and it tasted all the sweeter for it. Liverpool had won every competition they had competed for so far this season and there was just one more game left to play for club and manager to complete a historic trophy haul.

Liverpool actually finished 2042/43 with their lowest points tally since 2038/39 when Cooper had led them to a third place finish behind both Manchester clubs, but seventy-nine points from thirty-eight games had been enough to win them the title and Cooper wasn't about to complain about that. The drop off in Manchester United and Manchester City had no doubt helped Liverpool, but the emergence of Brighton as a top club had run them close. It was important to remember that in all previous campaigns Derek Cooper had largely failed to make his side competitive on more than one front, whereas this time out they had taken on all comers in all competitions and were now one game away from a five trophy season. People were beginning to write that it was written in the stars for Liverpool, that no-one could stop their march to glory and whilst it did feel that way to a certain degree Cooper and his players were taking nothing for granted. They were holding off celebrating what had been the biggest season of their careers in the hopes of adding one more reason to celebrate. The squad were off to Spain and a Champions League showdown with Real Madrid.

Real Madrid were on course to secure their fourth consecutive La Liga title, Felice Mair was the new club captain, Enzo Moreira was vice captain and Belgian international Sebastien Marie was now widely considered their key player. They were a club well known to Derek Cooper and he had signed many of the players that made up their likely starting eleven for the final. That meant however, that Real Madrid also knew a lot about Derek Cooper. Madrid had won fourteen Champions League's in their history, compared to the five of Liverpool. They were a club with European pedigree and they represented very tough opposition. Durval had been ruled out of the final and had failed in his bid to make himself available for a spot in the match day squad, but other than that Cooper had a full squad at his disposal for the game.

Derek Cooper named an eighteen man match day squad for the final which saw Renan, Djuricic, Sosa, Rodriguez, Kitoko, Miletic, Orlov, Diarra, Burmeister, Menga and Obradovic in the starting eleven whilst Assis, Thys, Buisson, Cordova, Yilmaz, Nilsson and Alanzinho had to settle for spots on the bench. Cooper had bravely decided against naming a substitute goalkeeper preferring to load his bench with options to change the game if required to do so. Real Madrid lined up with Guillaume, Gasmi, Dum, Bruyninckx, Alonso, Millet, Vinicius, Eduardo, Van der Maarel, Doucet and Marie in a classic 4-2-3-1 formation that was preferred by current manager Tobias Sippel. Former Liverpool players Jair Ninco and Frank Seddon took their places amongst the Real Madrid substitutes for the evening.

Derek Cooper didn't fear Real Madrid and he told his team that although they should show their opponents the respect they deserve they too should not fear them. They were there to be beaten and that is exactly what Cooper planned to do. His side had been in fine form, Swansea at home aside, and the game plan was to take Real Madrid on with an exciting brand of football that would wow the fans and bring home the European Cup. Liverpool's match got off to the best possible start when Egveny Orlov slotted home after just two minutes of play. Liverpool were 1-0 up and had no intention of relinquishing their early grip on the game.

Real Madrid had been stunned by the early goal, but recovered well to stop Liverpool taking further advantage of their fast start. Despite being the better side for large portions Liverpool had been kept at bay and it remained just 1-0 at the break. Cooper chose to praise his players telling them that they were doing well and he was pleased with their efforts. He wanted to encourage them to kick on in the second half and put the game to bed. Once again Liverpool looked the better side, but they picked up a couple of yellow cards and both Burmeister and Miletic were withdrawn and replaced with Buisson and Alanzinho to avoid picking up a second caution. Yilmaz had also been introduced for the largely ineffective Menga and the changes seemed to have a positive impact as Jose Rodriguez put Liverpool 2-0 up on seventy-five minutes, just after Cooper had made his final change.

All Liverpool needed to do now was maintain concentration and the trophy would be theirs. They looked to keep things tight for the next ten minutes feeling that by doing that they would knock the wind out of Real Madrid and demoralise their players. Not only did Liverpool manage to keep Madrid out, but they added a third when Igor Obradovic scored in the eighty-first minute to make it 3-0. There was no coming back from that for Madrid, everyone involved with them looked resigned to defeat and inwardly Cooper was almost certain he had them beat. Victory was confirmed as the referee blew the final whistle and Liverpool Football Club were finally able to celebrate what had been a truly unbelievable season. Fans, players and staff were all able to release the feelings of joy that had been building since they claimed the FA Cup seventeen days ago and added the Premier League title along the way.

Derek Cooper joined Fresnel Kitoko in lifting the final trophy of the season high into the Seville night air to the delight of all involved with the club. Winning trophies with Liverpool had been a tough nut to crack, but Cooper had finally done it and boy had he done it in style. Celebrations on the pitch lasted well into the night and after countless laps of honour, a crazy number of photographs and a rousing on field speech Cooper was finally back in the dressing room sipping beer from the bottle and soaking up the joy emanating from the squad that he had built. Not one of the players involved in the final with Real Madrid had been at the club when Cooper arrived, it was a squad built entirely in his image and he couldn't be more proud of them all if he tried. Even Durval seemed to have made a miraculous recovery, aided by alcohol, to join in some samba dancing with fellow Brazilians Felipe Renan and Alanzinho to mark the victory.

The final three games of 2042/43 had arguably been the three biggest games of Cooper's managerial career with each one a final. His side had failed to beat Swansea, but their name still made it onto the Premier League trophy, and they came through the matches against both Manchester City and Real Madrid with victories intact. This was undoubtedly the best end to a season that Cooper could ever have imagined. He was beginning to think he was destined to win just the Community Shield at Liverpool, but in one unbelievable season he had added an EFL Cup, an FA Cup, a Premier League title and a second Champions League of his career.

As the squad and staff returned to John Lennon airport the following afternoon they were greeted by fans that had turned out in their thousands to welcome them. An open top bus tour had been pre-arranged and all five trophies were proudly shown off throughout the afternoon and into the evening as Derek Cooper and his squad of players once again celebrated their historic achievement. The City of Liverpool had never seen scenes like it, there were people on top of traffic lights and hanging out of windows as the bus completed its route around the City. The huge crowd chanted each player's name as they were presented outside City hall on a big stage that had been erected for the occassion, but the biggest cheer of all was saved for the man of the hour as Derek Cooper lifted the Premier League trophy above his head. The sense of pride he felt at finally securing Liverpool some meaningful silverware was indescribable and he nearly lost his composure multiple times during his emotional speech to the assembled crowd. Thankfully the players were on hand with a champagne shower before the waterworks made an appearance.

Once the Euphoria began to subside and the alcohol haze began to clear Cooper was able to reflect what on what had been a truly momentous season. Liverpool had backed the manager in the transfer market throughout his time with the club, but no more so than in the summer just gone where they broke their transfer record twice. Igor Obradovic and Baba Diarra had both come in and made instant impacts. Obradovic managed thirty-four goals in all competitions and Diarra chipped in with twenty-six assists for the year. Fourteen of Diarra's assists came in the Premier League and made him the leagues top contributor for the season. The Germans performances for club and country had won him successive World Player of the Year awards as well as the Liverpool player of the year award for 2042/43. He made fifty-six appearances in his debut season scoring nineteen goals as well as the twenty-six assists to obtain the sides' highest average rating of 7.70.

There were a number of other players posting average ratings of well over seven, which was remarkable given the sheer number of games the players had taken part in. Seven members of the squad had made over fifty appearances for the side whilst a further three recorded over forty. Obradovic top scored for the club with thirty-four goals, but there were double figure tallies for Diarra (19), Burmeister (17), Yilmaz (15), Durval (14) and Orlov (14). Orlov was another player that had really stood out throughout 2042/43 hitting double figures from midfield and achieving an average rating of 7.41 from his fifty appearances. Central defender Juan Jose Sosa was another shining light and his performances were deserving of the 7.50 average rating he managed from fifty-one appearances.

As Cooper sat and poured over the data he realised that every single player had performed out of their skin for him and Liverpool Football Club. They had matured from perennial bottlers to champions of multiple competitions and Cooper couldn't have been more proud of the empire he had built. He had identified players such as Durval, Orlov, Sosa, Assis and Yilmaz during his time at the club and he had nurtured their talent allowing them to progress into world class players.

The squad was now off enjoying some rest and recuperation enjoying time with their families after a long and tough season. Cooper would soon join them and he had big decisions to make. For the first time in his managerial career his hunger for success had been abated by the trophies he had won with his players. Cooper had enjoyed a long and successful career, but the last few years with Liverpool had been the toughest and they had taken their toll on him. He had poured everything he had into his time with the club and it had left him physically and mentally drained. Cooper was unsure if he had enough left in the tank after such a long season to do it all again. He would only stay on if he was able to fully commit himself to the Liverpool cause once more; he was an all or nothing manager who presided over every little detail. He had spoken to his assistant manager, Edwin van den Berg, who had recently replaced the retiring Aitor Olmo and informed him of his inner turmoil. Berg urged Cooper to go on holiday and recharge his batteries before making a hasty decision on his managerial future.

Cooper knew he could never manage another club following his time at Liverpool, to manage there had been a boyhood dream and to fulfil that had completed him. He wasn't sure international management was for him and throughout his career he had turned down opportunities to manage a plethora of different countries, England included. Having turned down the Three Lions in the past it was unlikely that the opportunity would arise again, but if it did it was certainly something for Derek Cooper to consider. His options were limited, his career had given him so much that he had almost been spoiled and Derek was very conscious of knowing the right time to take a step back. The more he thought about his future the more he felt the time may well be upon him. He had given so much of his life to football and it had given him plenty in return.

Derek had been fortunate enough to be given the chance to manage eight different clubs in six different countries across twenty-six seasons. He had won fifteen league titles and twenty-one cups earning two promotions along the way. He had seen his teams score a whopping 3,066 goals in the 1,425 matches he had managed whilst conceding just 1,271 - less than a goal a game. Of those 1,425 matches he had won 927, drawn 242 and lost 256 giving him a career win percentage of 65%. Derek Cooper had signed 599 players during his career to date at a cost of £1.97Billion whilst he sold 297 for a combined £2.58Billion.

With numbers like those it was tough to argue that his career had been anything other than a success. He had achieved more than he had dreamed possible on his first day as a manager at Kirkley and Pakefield Football Club. As he looked back through what had been an impressive and eclectic career he began to appreciate the enormity of what he had accomplished. Derek Cooper had never been sacked during his career and that was the one standout fact that he was most proud of, not many managers could say they had started from the bottom and made it all the way to the top without being dismissed once or twice along the way.

Should Cooper choose to finish his managerial journey in the coming weeks he would find himself in illustrious company in the Hall of Fame. Derek Cooper was now ranked as the top English manager; his thirty-five trophies dwarfed the fourteen won by Bob Paisley in second place and Brian Clough's ten in third. In terms of the all time list Cooper had made it into the top ten alongside the likes of Mourinho, Ferguson, Ancelotti, Guardiola and Conte. Former Spurs and Watford goalkeeper Heurelho Gomes was number five on that impressive list of names having won an unbelievable forty-seven trophies as the manager of Flamengo in his native Brazil.

Derek Cooper would not be making a hasty decision and as he boarded his first class flight to Dubai with his family he was still very much undecided on what the future held beyond some sun, sea and a few cold beers.

DEREK COOPER MANAGERIAL CAREER - A BREAKDOWN:

CLUB:
Kirkley & Pakefield.
Eastern Counties Premier League.
Semi-professional.
England.

MANAGED:
01/07/2016 TO 25/07/2018 (2 years, 24 days).

COMPETITIONS:
Eastern Counties Premier Division Winners 2016/17.

HONOURS:

HONOURABLE MENTIONS:
Narrowly missed out on back to back promotions; finishing 3rd and losing in the playoffs semi-final in 2017/18 season.

Played: 99
Won: 50
Drew: 20
Lost: 26
Win Percentage: 53%

CLUB:
Maidenhead United.
Vanarama National League South.
Semi-professional.
England.

MANAGED:
25/07/2018 TO 12/07/2020 (1 year, 353 days).

COMPETITIONS:
Vanarama National League South Winners 2018/19.

HONOURS:
Vanarama National League South Manager of the Year 2018/19.
Vanarama National Manager of the Month Once 2019/20.

HONOURABLE MENTIONS:
Narrowly avoided relegation in the Vanarama National League against the odds.

Played: 97
Won: 39
Drew: 21
Lost: 37
Win Percentage: 40%

CLUB:
T.N.S (The New Saints).
Dafabet Welsh Premier League.
Professional.
Wales.

MANAGED:
12/07/2020 TO 21/04/2022 (1 year, 283 days).

COMPETITIONS:
Nathaniel MG Cup Winners 2020/21.
Dafabet Welsh Premier League Winners Twice. 2020/21 and 2021/22.

HONOURS:
Dafabet Welsh Premier League Manager of the Month Three Times 2020/21.
Dafabet Welsh Premier League Manager of the Month Three Times 2021/22.

HONOURABLE MENTIONS:
Narrowly missed out on UCL Group Stages, losing in the final playoff against AEK in 2021/22.
Playing in the Europa League Group Stages in 2021/22.
Acquired the National C coaching licence in 2020.
Acquired the National B coaching licence in 2021.

Played: 93
Won: 57
Drew: 17
Lost: 19
Win Percentage: 61%

CLUB:
Ross County.
Ladbrokes Scottish Premier League.
Professional.
Scotland.

MANAGED:
21/04/2022 TO 31/01/2024 (1 year, 285 days).

COMPETITIONS:

HONOURS:
Ladbrokes Scottish Premier League Manager of the Month Three Times 2022/23.
Ladbrokes Scottish Premier League Manager of the Year 2022/23.
Ladbrokes Scottish Premier League Manager of the Month Once 2023/24.

HONOURABLE MENTIONS:
Left the club top of the Ladbrokes Scottish Premier League, which they would go on to win in the 2023/24 season.
Acquired the National A coaching licence in 2022.
Acquired the Continental C and B coaching licences in 2023.

Played: 87
Won: 50
Drew: 20
Lost: 17
Win Percentage: 57%

CLUB:
Ajax.
Eredivisie.
Professional.
Holland.

MANAGED:
31/01/2024 TO 10/01/2028 (3 years, 344 days).

COMPETITIONS:
Eredivisie Winners Three Times. 2024/25, 2025/26 and 2026/27.
Europa League Winners 2024/25.
Dutch Super Cup Winners Three Times. 2025, 2026 and 2027.

HONOURS:
Eredivisie Manager of the Year 2024/25.

HONOURABLE MENTIONS:
Investment in youth saw the U19's win 4 consecutive league titles & the U19's UCL in 2026/27.
Acquired the Continental A coaching licence in 2024. Finished my coaching qualifications; obtaining the Continental Pro Licence in 2025.

Played: 189
Won: 139
Drew: 24
Lost: 26
Win Percentage: 73%

CLUB:
Juventus.
Serie A.
Professional.
Italy.

MANAGED:
10/01/2028 TO 25/06/2032 (4 years, 167 days).

COMPETITIONS:
Serie A Winners Three Times. 2029/30, 2030/31 and 2031/32.
Italian Super Cup Winners 2031.

HONOURS:
Serie A Managers' Manager of the Year Twice. 2029/30 and 2030/31.

HONOURABLE MENTIONS:
Runners up in the Europa League 2028/29.
U20's side were U19's UCL winners 2029/30 as well as back to back league champions from 2028/29 to 2031/32.
Frederico Antunes named as European Golden Boy 2028.

Played: 225
Won: 157
Drew: 29
Lost: 39
Win Percentage: 69%

CLUB:
Real Madrid.
La Liga.
Professional.
Spain.

MANAGED:
25/06/2032 TO 25/05/2037 (4 years, 334 days).

COMPETITIONS:
Spanish Super Cup Winners five times. 2032, 2033, 2034, 2035 and 2036.
La Liga Winners four times. 2032/33, 2033/34, 2034/35 and 2036/37
Spanish Cup Winners three times. 2032/33, 3034/35 and 2036/37
UEFA Champions League Winners. 2035/36.
European Super Cup Winners. 2036.

HONOURS:
La Liga Manager of the Year Four Times. 2032/33, 2033/34, 2034/35 and 2036/37.

HONOURABLE MENTIONS:
UCL Runners up 2034/35. Losing 1-0 to Manchester United.
U19's winning three consecutive U19 UCL titles.

Played: 304
Won: 219
Drew: 55
Lost: 30
Win Percentage: 72%

CLUB:
Liverpool.
English Premier League.
Professional.
England.

MANAGED:
26/06/2037 TO PRESENT. (5 years, 355 days)

COMPETITIONS:
English Community Shield Winners twice 2037 and 2042.
EFL Cup Winners 2042/43.
FA Cup Winners 2042/43.
English Premier League Winners 2042/43.
UEFA Champions League Winners 2042/43.

HONOURS:
Premier League Manager of the Month ten times 2038-2043.
Premier League Manager of the Year 2042/43.

HONOURABLE MENTIONS:
UCL Runners up 2039/40 losing on penalties to Manchester City.
Baba Diarra won the 2042 World Golden Ball award as well as the European Golden Boy award for the same year.
Jean Menga was named European Golden Boy for 2040.

Played: 331
Won: 213
Drew: 56
Lost: 62
Win Percentage: 64%

CAREER TOTALS. (UP TO 19/06/2043)

CLUBS MANAGED: **8.**
SEASONS COMPLETED: **26.**
MILES TRAVELLED: **5,578.**
PROMOTIONS: **2.**
LEAGUE TITLES: **15.**
TOP LEAGUE TITLES: **13.**
DOMESTIC CUP WINS: **17.**
EUROPEAN CUP WINS: **4.**
PERSONAL AWARDS: **35.**
SACKINGS: **0.**

GAMES PLAYED: **1,425**
GAMES WON: **927.**
GAMES DRAWN: **242.**
GAMES LOST: **256.**
GOALS FOR: **3,066.**
GOALS AGAINST: **1,271.**
GOAL DIFFERENCE: **1,795.**
WIN PERCENTAGE: **65%.**

PLAYERS BOUGHT: **599.**
VALUE BOUGHT: **£1.97B.**
PLAYERS SOLD: **297.**
VALUE SOLD: **£2.58B**
PLAYERS RELEASED: **45.**
HIGHEST FEE SPENT: **£145m for Baba Diarra from Borussia Dortmund 03/08/2042.**
HIGHEST FEE RECEIVED: **£95M for Andre Santos to PSG 13/07/2037.**

TROPHIES WON:

Eastern Counties Premier Division.
Vanarama National League South.
Dafabet Welsh Premier League X 2.
Dutch Eredivisie X 3.
Italian Serie A X 3.
Spanish La Liga X 4.
English Premier League.
Natahaniel MG Cup.
Dutch Super Cup X 3.
Italian Super Cup.
Spanish Super Cup X 5.
Spanish Cup X 3.
English Community Shield X 2.
EFL CUP.
English FA Cup.
UEFA Europa League.
UEFA Champions League X 2.
UEFA Super Cup.

A SNAPSHOT OF THE WIDER FOOTBALL MANAGER 2017 WORLD:

Away from the life and career of Derek Cooper the wider footballing world was a strange and intriguing place. The English public were still waiting for football to come home and the years of hurt had now made it to seventy-seven. Tottenham Hotspur and Everton had been amongst the teams relegated from the Premier League whilst Brighton and Stoke had qualified for the Champions League. Barnet had made it as high as the Championship whilst Northampton and Blackpool had found themselves down in the Vanarama National League.

There had been some strange managerial careers and appointments which is best illustrated by Romelu Lukaku. Following his retirement from playing Lukaku began his coaching career as manager of Mansfield before moving onto Leyton Orient, Derby, Brentford and then Gillingham in League One. Paul Pogba had a stint as the French national team boss between 2040 and 2042. Pep Guardiola was sacked after a year in charge at Stoke and Fernando Torres took the Swansea job in 2041. Christian Benteke had been manager of Arsenal since 2042 following a spell in charge of the Belgian national side. Charlie Adam was in his eleventh year as manager of Scotland and Antoine Griezmann had been in charge of Newcastle for a period between 2037 and 2040. Perhaps the most surprising managerial reign in the world was that of Jose Mourinho at Manchester United as he stayed in the job for sixteen years and two days winning eight league titles and twenty-eight cups for them. In the year 2043 England were managed by a former colleague of Derek Cooper as his former assistant from both Maidenhead and Ross County, Daniel Brown, had left his role with Norwich to take the prestigious job.

In 2042 Derek Cooper smashed the transfer record when he spent a huge £145m on Baba Diarra from Dortmund. It proved to be a great piece of business for the club and Diarra more than repaid Cooper's faith in him. Large transfer fees were nothing new and Manchester United had parted with a cool £103m back in the January of 2021 to sign Harry Kane from Spurs. Kane too repaid the faith shown in him by then manager Jose Mourinho as he went on to score 118 goals in 212 appearances for the club. There were many other big deals around that time as Martin Odegaard joined Chelsea from PSG for £101m in 2022. Saul left boyhood club Atletico to sign for PSG as well for a costly £91m in 2021. Marko Pjaca was another to join the big spending PSG leaving Manchester City for £89m in 2022 whilst Gabriel Barbosa became a City legend following his £85m move from Paris in 2022. Both Manchester clubs had consistently spent big and of the fifteen highest transfers come 2043 ten had been completed by either City or United.

England and their fans were still waiting for an end to the years of hurt. They had failed to add to the World Cup win of 1966 although they had made it to two finals in 2026 and 2034. Harry Kane was now the all time leading goal scorer for his country with sixty-eight goals which included the 2026 Golden boot for his six goals in Mexico. Nathan Wildig was the record appearance maker having represented the Three Lions no fewer than 148 times. Wildig had come through the ranks at Wolves before moving to West Ham and then Arsenal, finishing his career with Norwich City. Gareth Southgate enjoyed a four year spell at the helm before he stepped aside to usher in the Eddie Howe era. Howe spent an impressive eleven years in the role and although he failed to win any silverware he did take them to their first World Cup final since 1966, losing 2-1 to Belgium in Mexico City. Frank de Boer was the next man in the England hot seat and he remained in charge for nearly four years, taking England to their next World Cup final where they were beaten 3-2 in extra time by Germany in Japan. Paulo Sosa was then chosen by the FA and he lasted a further three years with no real success to his name before retiring from management and paving the way for Cooper's old assistant Daniel Brown to take the job. Browns one victory to date came in the European International League where his side exacted some form of revenge on Belgium by beating them 1-0 in the 2043 final.

England's failure to win a World Cup had continued and it was now often reported that Mexico had won more World Cups than the Three Lions. Mexico had won the competition in both 2022 and 2042 and now boasted two gold stars on the famous green jersey. There was even an unlikely victory for the Czech Republic as they were crowned World champions in 2030 having beaten Portugal 5-2 at the San Siro in Italy. Portugal had been the standout European side having completed a hat-trick of European Championship victories in 2016, 2020 and 2024. There was still no tournament victory for England despite hosting the competition in 2028 when Spain beat Germany in the Wembley final. Ukraine were the surprise winners of the tournament in 2036 as they beat the German hosts 2-1 in the final.

Life in the Premier League was tough for anyone who wasn't Manchester City or Manchester United. They had established themselves as the dominant forces within the league and even Derek Cooper had a tough job reeling them in with his Liverpool side. Since Leicester had shocked everyone and won the title in 2015/16 Manchester United or Manchester City had won the league for twenty-one of the next twenty-seven years. Arsenal had managed three league victories whilst Liverpool had managed two and Chelsea just the one. It was lean pickings for anyone outside of Manchester as Mourinho picked up eight titles for United during his time there whilst Pep only managed one title in nine years at City. The majority of their league wins came courtesy of Emery (3) and Allegri (2) as well as Simeone (1) and Rondon (1). There was a unique record for Salomon Rondon as he won the Golden Boot as a player in 2019/20 with twenty-three goals for West Brom before he won the Premier League title as a manager with Liverpool in 2036/37 seventeen years later.

The Champions League was not immune to the Manchester effect and both sides enjoyed success in Europe's elite club competition. Cooper had been a losing finalist to both Manchester United and Manchester City with Real Madrid and Liverpool respectively. In the last twenty-seven years either club had won the competition twelve times. There was a seven year spell from 2028 to 2035 where United won it three times whilst City won it four times back to back. In other years there were wins for Roma, Napoli, Arsenal, PSG and Bayern Munich before the money of AS Saint-Etienne bought them a couple of titles in 2039 and 2041. Real Madrid remained the club with the most Champions League victories at fourteen, but United were hunting them down and had made it to nine wins. City meanwhile were now up to six Champions League wins and were level with league rivals Liverpool.

Sevilla still held the record for the most Europa League victories with five and the tournament had won by a variety of sides over the last twenty plus years. Cooper had won it once with Ajax back in 2024/25. Liverpool had won it as recently as 2032/33 whilst other Premier League sides Leicester, Chelsea and Arsenal had all had their names engraved on the trophy. Other clubs to have won the tournament included Stuttgart, Juventus, Dortmund, Marseille, Porto, Benfica, Lyon and Wolfsburg to name but a few. Whilst it didn't hold the magic or prestige of its bigger brother the Europa League still threw up some great clubs as its champion.

Lionel Messi and Cristiano Ronaldo continued to dominate the world of football at both Barcelona and Real Madrid. Ronaldo retired at the age of thirty-eight having made 429 appearances for the club and scoring 354 goals. Following his retirement his first venture into the world of management came at Birmingham City where he was appointed in March 2026. Between November 2026 and February 2036 Ronaldo had brief spells at Milwall, Ipswich, Nottingham Forrest, West Ham, West Brom, Middlesbrough and Santa Clara. His final managerial role was at Gil Vicente before he retired from the game at the age of fifty-six.

Messi ended his playing career at Barcelona at the age of thirty-six with 418 goals from 592 appearances between 2004 and 2023. His first non-playing role was as coach of Eibar's Under19's, a position he held until April 2029 when he took up the position as coach of West Ham U23's. In March 2030 he was handed his first managerial job with Notts County. His time in England didn't go to plan and a twenty month sabbatical followed his departure from the oldest club in England. His next role came in March 2032 when he was appointed as coach at Spanish side Heracles. Messi then took the opportunity to become a manager again in 2036 when he was appointed at Czech First Division side Brno, a role he still held come the end of the 2042/43 season despite having won no silverware. In terms of their post playing career's neither was particularly successful, but Cristiano probably edged out his long term rival.

FROM THE AUTHOR:

This save was without doubt the feather in my Football Manager cap. I have never invested so much time into a save despite clocking up countless hours on other versions; FM17 will forever have a special place inside my heart. I have stayed true to the save throughout this account of Cooper's career and have painstakingly gone back through the save countless times fact checking and making sure I have all the correct information.

I really hope the enjoyment I had in playing the save comes across throughout the account of his story. Going back through everything to write this was such fun and it really brought the save back to life. There were times where I couldn't wait to get the words down on the page and then there were other times when I knew a tough defeat was just around the corner and I relived the disappointment.

Shortly after leaving school I really got into reading and decided that I wanted to write a book of my own, the only problem came with finding the subject matter for such a thing. Football Manager seemed the obvious choice for me. I lacked the knowledge to write a complicated novel, but I possessed a deep understanding and love for the Football Manager series and my save on FM2017 was the perfect story. It allowed me to immortalise the career of Derek Cooper and provide me the opportunity to share the save with likeminded individuals. I have never been able to look back through previous saves so to have this story to look back on and enjoy for years to come is something I am incredibly proud of.

Special thanks must go to my great friend Sam who was with me every step of the way whether it be reading through what I had written or helping me with some photo ideas for a potential front cover. He was always on the end of the phone despite travelling the world with work and I will always be grateful for that.

Thank you for taking the time to read the story of Derek Cooper and I hope it wasn't as dull as "a biographical account of a fictional football mangers career" suggests it should be. If you have indeed enjoyed the book then why not let me know on Twitter (@DJTacon17) or by sending me an email (dan_tacon@live.co.uk) as I would love to hear from you.

Printed in Great Britain
by Amazon